RANDOM
HOUSE
LARGE
PRINT

ATOMIC LOVE

JENNIE FIELDS

ATOMIC LOVE

RANDOM HOUSE
LARGE PRINT

Copyright © 2020 by Jennie Fields

Published in the United States of America by Random House Large Print in association with G. P. Putnam's Sons, an imprint of Penguin Random House LLC.

Cover design: Sandra Chiu
Cover images: (woman) Rekha Garton / Arcangel; (background) Conrado Dela Cruz / EyeEm / Getty Images; (formulas) Triff / Shutterstock

The Library of Congress has established a Cataloging-in-Publication record for this title.

ISBN: 978-0-593-29549-6

www.penguinrandomhouse.com/large-print-format-books

FIRST LARGE PRINT EDITION

Printed in the United States of America

10 9 8 7 6 5 4 3 2 1

This Large Print edition published in accord with the standards of the N.A.V.H.

For my beloved Aunt Rosalind
who reveled in the beauty, majesty,
and power of words

ATOMIC LOVE

CHICAGO, 1950

CHAPTER ONE

The hot touch of the city still on her, Rosalind unfastens her stockings and drops them in the bathroom sink with a handful of washing soda. A habit from the war years. She made it through 1942 to 1944 with two stalwart pairs because she treated them like rare orchids. Jesus. She knew girls who had to draw lines up the backs of their legs because they'd torn their last pair and couldn't buy new. Lines that by two P.M. were smeared like lipstick after a desperate kiss.

One didn't lose the feel of the war, the rationing, the terror of opening the newspaper each morning and seeing the worst. Rosalind would never forget the sting in her throat watching the man next door weep as he changed the blue star on his Sons in Service flag to gold. There were no sons in her family, but she and Louisa did their bit. For a while Louisa polished torpedoes in a defense plant. And what Rosalind did one might say ended the war altogether. But she knows it will haunt her until she dies.

◆ ◆ ◆

These days she stands behind the Used and Antique Jewelry counter at Marshall Field's department store, sorting and selling. There are lives entwined in the artifacts she peddles: tucked behind an oval of glass on the back of a Victorian brooch, a perfectly braided plait of silver hair from someone's mother. A ring glittering with a row of gems—a ruby, emerald, garnet, amethyst, another ruby, and a diamond—the first letters of each spelling "regard." Georgian men gave these rings to women they loved but couldn't marry. Rosalind can't help wondering about a woman who'd wear evidence of love she could never fully possess.

Rosalind is a scientist. After the war, returning GIs took the important jobs back from women. **You can go now. We've returned.** Chances are she'd have lost her spot even if things hadn't gone wrong with Weaver. It doesn't mean she doesn't miss her days in the lab.

On her way home, stepping out of Field's tonight, tired and sad, she passed an extraordinarily tall man leaning against the **Summer Frolic!** window. He was openly staring at her with remarkable blue eyes. At Wabash, she glimpsed him again. When she crossed Erie, there he was, his fedora pulled low over his brow, hurrying to catch the light. Broad shouldered. Powerful-looking, with a purposeful stride. That's when Rosalind noticed he was pressing his left wrist against his ribs—like a woman holding a purse to keep it from being stolen. A war injury, maybe? He must have trailed her onto Lake Shore Drive, for when she turned down the street to her entrance, she caught a flash of blue eyes watching from across the street.

Frank, her doorman, ushered her in. "Miss Porter. Best time of year, isn't it?"

Maybe that fellow was just going her way, a coincidence. All through the war, men flirted with her until they found out what she did. Braininess always blunted her appeal. Now that she's thirty years old and still unmarried, people have begun to call her "handsome." She hates the damn word. It would bolster her self-esteem to have a stranger find her attractive. Her biggest fear is that she will become **that** woman— the one who lives alone, whom no one notices when she walks down the street. A woman who's become invisible, negligible. **Poor Miss Porter. She never had much of a life.**

⑊ ⑊ ⑊

Cranking all the living room windows open, she invites the lake breeze into the room. No matter where she's gone to follow work (and Weaver, God help her)—Tennessee, Washington, the deserts of New Mexico—she always ached to return to this glittering lakefront, its sailboats and towering buildings.

Shucking her blouse, removing her brassiere, she lets the breeze chill her perspiring skin. Living on the nineteenth floor, facing the water, no one can see her. She does this every hot night, a ritual that lets her momentarily wear the cool breath of the lake. Her nipples harden in the draft. Her hair lifts off her shoulders. Once, she was a sensual woman, a woman who'd learned to seek pleasure. It was her secret. And the desire for pleasure hasn't stopped, just the means to satisfy it. Between her naked breasts dangles the chain Weaver gave her long ago, a tiny gold-and-platinum box swinging from it. She's rejected all that pertained to Weaver except this, an antique he brought back from England. The miniature box has a lid that can be opened. A shredding piece of parchment hides within, the word "Patience" written on it in faded brown ink. She should give the necklace up. She should forget about Weaver forever. Wearing this trinket is hardly better than a woman cherishing a regard ring. But what she **should** do and what she is capable of doing are often two sides to an unsolvable equation.

Having lost her job with the project, she can now barely scrape together enough money for the Lake Shore Drive apartment she rented with such ambitious dreams. She'd broken into the top echelons of science. Nobelist Enrico Fermi mentored her, believed in her, counted on her. He'd turned his prized student into an asset. And for a time she got to swim in the warm waters of elemental discovery, all while earning more money than most women could ever expect. The apartment's dazzling view, the neat kitchen with its modern pullout range, the doorman, and the in-house commissary remind her that once she was no ordinary girl. Now she feels less than ordinary. But at least her present job won't end up killing more than 150,000 people.

In the midst of supper, her telephone rings. Having gone to the trouble of baking a pork chop, as thin and sad as it is, she's not going to answer the damn phone. Later, after the dishes are washed and she's taken her bath, the phone rings again. She knows who it is. Louisa never calls past nine. Her girlfriends are too exhausted by their children to ring at this hour. Her best pal, Zeke, is out of town. She feels her jaw tighten. She could decide not to answer. But the curious scientist in her can't tolerate unanswered questions or telephones.

"Hello?"

"Rosalind."

She takes the gut punch of the mellifluous voice, the crisp British accent. He's called three times this week.

"Roz. Are you there?"

"What do you want?" she asks.

"You." She feels sick. He is everything she abhors. And everything she craves.

"Weaver, leave me alone. I mean it."

"Listen. I need you to hear me."

He's just begun calling again. After four years of silence. After he stole the years when she might have found a husband. After he robbed her of her career.

She hears him take a deep breath. "Roz, we were as close as two people can be. I was better with you. I know you were better with me. Please tell me you'll see me."

"No."

"Just once. So I can explain—"

"What could you possibly explain?"

"What happened."

"It doesn't matter anymore." But of course, it does. "You told me to never speak to you again. I assumed you meant it."

"No. No! I'm going to explain all of that. Listen, here's my number. When I was off in Los Alamos, I turned off my phone and lost my old number. Please write the new one down. Do you have a pen?"

She doesn't and has no intention of finding one.

"Hyde Park 3-5806. Got it? Hyde Park 3-5806." He repeats the numbers deliberately, hypnotically. "I'm saying it one more time. I know how your memory works. Hyde Park 3-5806. Call me." Later, as she lies in bed, the prefix and digits play in her brain—a poisoned refrain.

⽇ ⽇ ⽇

The men in the lab called one another by their last names. So she took to calling him Weaver. Hazel eyes of constantly changing color, impressive brown hair, a dimpled Cary Grant chin. He was the cartoon of a good-looking man. He knew it, and this was the thing she disliked most about him. His swagger. His certainty. She was aware from the start the man was a flirt, and not just with her. His tony accent would have thrilled any girl. Weaver was recruited from Cambridge University to join the Manhattan Project in New York. Fermi brought him to Chicago a year after Rosalind began in the lab.

When she asked Weaver if he liked the city, he said, "It doesn't matter where I am as long as I'm working on something important." She wanted him to cherish Chicago, to see its brawny wonder, to note the architecture and the lakefront. She told him it was the ultimate American city. The heart of the country. Weaver did appreciate food and art. "There are ripping good steaks here. I'll give you that." But he was a man who lived in the hills and valleys of his equations and theories, lived for proving himself right.

Science always gave them something to talk about. She and Weaver loved to argue about neutron sources. Had Fermi walked away from powdered beryllium too soon? She thought so. He didn't. And what about this secret new element, plutonium, produced by bombarding uranium-238?

"There's our future," she said.

"It's too hard to produce."

"That's what we'll create at the Hanford Site. I'll bet you a thousand dollars."

"I'd rather it was a thousand dinners together." He reached out his hand to seal the deal and then drew her hand to his lips. He still owes her years of dinners.

Rosalind had her own vision of what she wanted out of the project. She knew that piercing a single uranium atom could create more than three million times the energy of fossil fuel. If harnessed, channeled, it could be put to constructive use, heating cities and running machines in a clean, endlessly available way. But when she shared the idea with Weaver, he smirked.

"Duchess, the Nazis are working on an atomic weapon. Right this minute in their little lairs, twirling their mustaches. No one is thinking about anything but the war right now. We're dedicated to self-defense, pure and simple."

She was annoyed but not surprised. She watched the men around her and was disturbed at how much they enjoyed the war, seemed stirred to life by the conflict. Marking trees, proving themselves right, defeating others. The ability to draw power from an atom: Could it ever be safe in male hands?

CHAPTER TWO

In a restaurant like the Berghoff, pulsing with families, couples, tables of six, a lone diner is bound to stand out, especially one as tall as Szydlo. Which is why he's asked for a spot by the left wall: far enough away from Rosalind Porter's table for four, close enough to observe her. As Rosalind leans toward her niece, her golden earrings glimmer against the ebony of her hair.

Szydlo's been watching her for two weeks now, could draw her with his eyes closed: the shiny black hair barely contained by tortoise combs, skin as pale as milk, wise arched brows. She could be Hedy Lamarr's sister. Once, he passed close to her on the street, just to be near, not forty paces behind. And what he picked up wasn't perfume. Instead, the scent of warm honey. He thinks of it when he's restless in bed: the pure, round aroma of her. And it arouses him despite himself.

Watching Miss Porter speak to her brother-in-law and shake her head at her sister, he realizes that up till now, he's seen her as a lone figure. So it's fascinating to note, even in this moment with other people around her, there's a side flick of her eyes, a glance down at her hands, that says even among family, she feels apart.

This is what he's learned about Rosalind Porter: She shops at the A&P and buys simple, cheap things as though she's on a budget—fruit from the bruised bin and the cuts of meat on sale. She walks with an abstract look as though her mind is awhirl with facts and figures. He's watched her at the bank pointing out an error in her account. The manager came by to apologize, so she must have been right.

She's organized, habitual, leaves the apartment at the same hour each day and arrives home at the same time. She rarely sees her friends because they live in the suburbs. When she talks to them on the phone—he experiences a shameful delight listening in—they rattle on about themselves, their children, and their husbands, and she encourages them. They only ask how she's doing at the end of the call, then hurriedly ring off. The exception is someone named Zeke. Zeke asks her innumerable personal questions. He has all the sway and female flirtatiousness that Miss Porter lacks. He's clearly an old friend. When they go out to dinner together, she hooks her hand into Zeke's elbow. When she speaks to him, she looks up into the sky and laughs.

There's love there. Just not the kind most people understand.

Miss Porter has no obvious religious affiliation, rarely wears a hat, often dons sandals to walk to work. Once, on Lake Shore Drive, she stopped to look out at the lake for more than five minutes. Szydlo had to stand in the shadows of one of those big stone houses to watch her, hoping no one would come out and tell him to get off their lawn. He was transfixed by her full skirt puffing taut as a sail in the lake breeze. Her black curls flared into a luxurious corona. When she turned, she looked as though she didn't know where she was. What had she discovered in the dark wink of the lake?

As she talks to her niece now, he notes she suddenly seems blissful and intimate. The tender way she pets the girl's hair, the way she leans toward her, it's obvious how much she cherishes her mirror image, this ten-year-old girl who looks astonishingly like her. If Rosalind Porter is a lone, icy figure, her love for her niece melts her.

〰 〰 〰

"Should I order the Wiener schnitzel or the sauerbraten?" Ava whispers to Rosalind. Ava's been a regular at the Berghoff since she was two. No kids' menu for her.

"Do you feel in need of a hug or a giggle?" Roz asks.

"Which is which?"

"The hug is the sauerbraten. The Wiener schnitzel is more fun."

"Why haven't I had it? Wiener schnitzel. **Wiener schnitzel!** You say it."

Rosalind does until they're both laughing. Dinners with Louisa, Henry, and Ava are Rosalind's true north. Louisa is twenty years older than her, the only mother Rosalind remembers, and she feels closer to Henry than she ever did to her father. After Louisa was born, their mother was unable to have another child. And then in her forty-second year, she was astonished to find herself pregnant. Six months after baby Rosalind arrived, she was dead from ovarian cancer. Was it the cancer that had made her fertile at last? Or was it the pregnancy that set the cancer on its fatal course? The result, in any case, was a motherless child.

For years, Rosalind was regaled with the tale of her upbringing at every one of her birthdays, a tradition like "The Star-Spangled Banner" being sung at a baseball game. How many times has she listened to how, having lost his wife, Dr. Porter employed a housekeeper to care for his daughter? How he came home one winter afternoon to hear the baby wailing all the way from the sidewalk and discovered Rosalind lying on the floor naked except for a dirty diaper. When he lifted her, her skin was icy. He'd autopsied dead bodies with lips less blue. And where was the housekeeper? In the dining room passed out beneath the dining room table, her skirt rucked up to display a pair of pink garters with a pouch for a flask, which was empty, as was the flask in her hand. **And that's how Louisa came to take care of you.**

This was the story Rosalind heard long before she understood its meaning. (**Why was the housekeeper on the floor? What's a flask?**) When she was old enough to discover more, she questioned Louisa, her father, and Henry. Each had his or her own way of telling the rest.

From her father she learned that after the housekeeper was sent away, the doctor's neighbor, Estelle, "lent" them her maid while she was in Michigan for the summer. But a full-time babysitter needed to be found, and fast. The doctor rejected one candidate after another. He was fifty-six years old and an important man: he'd given up his private practice to become Coroner's Physician for Cook County. Organized crime was on the upswing. Hardly a week passed that "Dr. Joe" wasn't pictured in the **Tribune** standing by a blowfish-swollen cadaver raised from the depths of the Chicago River. Dr. Joe was a city treasure! Front-page headlines read, DR. JOE

TESTIFIES O'FLAHERTY WAS SHOT FROM THE OPEN WINDOW WITH A TOMMY GUN!

"I was an important man. How could I care for a baby, and a girl at that?" her father explained. "I had come to think some nice family who'd had trouble conceiving could give you a better life."

"You wanted to give me away?"

"Well, it was for your own good—and mine, of course." She doesn't think she's ever gotten over that sentence.

Louisa says she told their father, "If you give the baby away, Mother will roll in her grave."

"Then, what am I to do?" he asked. "Estelle's housekeeper walks around with a Theosophical Mysticism pamphlet in her apron pocket. Raised by the hired help, your sister will grow up feral, or worse, a Democrat! I'm not meant to take on the responsibility of a baby. I'm a **man**!"

A man. Men did important work. Women were scaffolding. That's what their mother had taught Louisa. Which meant her excellent high school grades signified she'd be good at making the grocery money come out even at the end of the month. She might, in her free moments, read a book for pleasure. College was never even considered.

At twenty-one Louisa had achieved what her mother had once deemed a woman's greatest success: acquiring a good husband. She and Henry lived a few blocks from her father in a brand-new bungalow. They were looking forward to some unencumbered months of romance and breakfast in bed before a family came along. It was the end of 1920. The war was over. Women could vote, were showing off their ankles. She and Henry planned a bicycle trip in Wisconsin. They even talked about taking the train to New York City and then a steamship to Paris. "We were in love. We wanted to be a couple first. Not a family. I wanted to be a pretty girl with a man on my arm," Louisa told Rosalind years later, still bitter, it seemed.

But rather than leave her baby sister to the Theosophists, Louisa and Henry brought home Rosalind's crib and high chair and prepared themselves for sleepless nights. Like all abandoned babies, Rosalind was needy. "You dug your fingers into my arm whenever I tried to put you down. Like a baby monkey," Louisa told her.

This description still makes Rosalind cringe.

Henry's point of view has always been kinder. "You were something! What a gift! You spoke at nine months. Counted to one hundred by the time you were a year and a half. And your first word was 'why.' 'Why take my spoon away?' 'Why must I go to sleep now?' 'Why?' At two and a half, when milk spilled and dripped off the tray of your high chair onto the floor one day, you asked, 'Why circle?'"

She loved hearing Henry's stories about her, but this one especially. Henry told her that he stood up from the breakfast table to look where she was pointing and saw that each drop made a perfect radiating ring in the already pooled milk.

"Good question," he told her. "Well, I'd say that each drop of milk is round. So when it hits the already spilled milk it makes a round impression. A circle."

Henry went on to explain what he knew about surface tension. About how molecules clung together from all directions to make each drop a sphere. He even drew her a diagram.

"This is asinine. She can't possibly comprehend," Louisa complained.

But later, he's often told Rosalind, after he tucked her into her crib, he was pulling down the window shade when she pointed to the full moon. "Why moon a circle? Moon is molecules?"

"The moon?" he asked. "Yes."

"All-together molecules? In all dee-rections?" She moved her hands to demonstrate. He looked up at the orb in the sky with a smile. "And that was the moment, kid, I knew you'd be a scientist."

⫼ ⫼ ⫼

"I've been thinking of trying to find a science job again," Rosalind ventures quietly now, looking at everyone at the table, but mostly addressing Henry. This is a fearful thing: her love of science, which has betrayed her.

"Good for you," Henry says. "Good for you."

"I miss it," she says.

"I've wondered."

"I try to go to lectures. I still get the **Journal of Applied Physics** and the **American Journal of Physics.** I try to read what I can."

Louisa's nostrils flare. "With all the GIs back, do you really think a science position would be open to a woman?"

Rosalind opens her mouth, then closes it.

"You're special," Henry says. "You can do it just like you did before."

"You **can,** Rozzie!" Ava says. But Rosalind realizes Louisa's right: Who will hire her, especially after Weaver's report?

Henry reaches across the table and squeezes her hand. "This is what you're meant to do. You just need to believe it again."

While Ava eats her Wiener schnitzel with enthusiasm and Louisa rants about their horrible new neighbors and her fear of creeping Communism, Rosalind frowns, shakes her head, then glances about, wishing to distract herself from the sick feeling that roils inside—the feeling that she'll never be happy again. The Berghoff is jammed with families. Lovers. Everyone else seems to be having a fine time. Except, at a table by the wall near the bar, Roz spots a man. Even seated, he's taller than everyone around him. She takes in his flattop haircut, his even features, the fact that his table is set for one. Why is this handsome man dining out alone? And then, even with the bar half blocking her view, she notes the way he presses his wrist against his ribs. Her mouth goes dry. **It's him.** She's sure of it. The man who followed her home yesterday. He glances up and their eyes lock. She can tell his are blue from halfway across the room. The most extraordinary, electric blue. She loses the thread of her sister's conversation. What is he? An admirer or a madman? She experiences a chill.

"Have you gone deaf, Roz?" Louisa asks. "I just asked which suburb did Jane Ann move to?"

"Oh . . . sorry . . . Glenview."

"Right. Glenview. That's the one I want to check out for us."

"We are **not** moving to the suburbs," Henry says. "You okay, Roz? You've gone all pale."

"No. It's nothing. Sorry. My mind wandered." Lots of men were injured during the war. It's probably not the same one at all. Still, her heart is slamming. She slips her arm around Ava's shoulders.

"So how much fun was that Wiener schnitzel?"

she asks, pushing the words through the tight-
ness in her throat.

"So fun! It's my favorite now." Rosalind
glances up and watches the man's azure eyes
leave her face with the suddenness of fingers
being snatched from a burning stove.

CHAPTER THREE

The following week, Rosalind spots him running in the rain to catch her bus at the next stop. Dripping wet, he steps onto the vehicle without acknowledging her gaze. Later, she feels him watching her and it makes her prickle. What does he want? She notices him two days later at Janice's perfume display, just when the store's about to close. He pushes bottles from side to side as though evaluating them. But when Janice asks if she can help, he shakes his head and leaves. Rosalind feels increasingly scared. Why is this man always there, a flicker in the corner of her eye? She considers calling the police, but he hasn't done anything wrong. If he comes near her on the street, she imagines that she will scream. A siren in the din of human movement.

Zeke, the one friend who loves her no matter what she reveals about herself, has begun calling him "Shadowman." Inseparable since adolescence, she and Zeke are each other's cheering section and speak often. The fact that he can never love her as a man loves a woman is a sad truth that somehow binds them closer. "I want a painfully accurate description of this fellow, Bunny. Every. Single. Detail," Zeke says.

"Well, he's attractive in a brooding sort of way. Weirdly tall. Intense blue eyes. His hair is short, blond. He moves like an athlete. Why would he follow me?"

"You know I love riddles." He clears his throat. "Okay, two possibilities: He finds you attractive, or you're on his hit list."

"Would a man follow a woman so assiduously if he just **liked** her?" she asks.

"You're a pretty girl," Zeke says.

"He can't be following me for a good reason."

"Maybe the poor fellow's found love and is too shy to approach. Even handsome men can be shy."

She sighs. "I'd say there's a twelve percent chance of that, and an eighty-eight percent chance there's something nefarious going on. Thanks for trying to make me feel better, though."

Later, alone, thinking of the man, she starts to shake and has to pour herself a slug of Chianti from a half-drunk bottle Zeke brought her more than a year ago. After she lost her job in '47, she started drinking a little, then a lot, trying to combat the loneliness, the pain of not knowing where her life was going. It wasn't just the loss of Weaver; it was losing herself as a scientist that wounded most. One minute she and her fellow physicists were crossing a virgin space together. **No one** had ever reached the other side, and they could **see** it, practically touch it. **Her** ideas were making it easier for them to reach the infinite. Then nothing. She was barred from the party. Shunned. No Weaver. No science. The oblivion of alcohol seemed a necessary recourse.

But oblivion is a wounding place. She was waking up groggy. Her memory—which Fermi once called photographic—was compromised. She could no longer multiply complex numbers in her head or recall the thousand details of ordinary moments as she usually did. Once, she woke up on the floor. Just like her father's infamous flask-toting housekeeper.

So she employed science. She calculated how long it would take to completely excrete the alcohol. She studied how alcohol is metabolized, its effect on the liver. Its long-term effects. The mathematics of sobriety, she told herself. She stopped cold turkey. Each night she tried to multiply larger and larger numbers in her head. She glanced at photographs and tested how many objects she could remember. She calculated. She kept charts. And she held on to Zeke's bottle of Chianti to remind herself she had power over her own desire to hide from pain. She should have thrown it out, she thinks now. It's been a long while since she's drunk a sip of alcohol. And this wine has surely turned. Black residue sinks to the bottom of her glass. But envisioning the tall man with the blue eyes, his interest in her suddenly overwhelming, she swallows it down, sediment and all.

◦ ◦ ◦

Friday, as she's stepping out of the dentist's office building, she spots her pursuer at the bus stop across the street, reading a newspaper with a frown. It's time to put a stop to this. Her heart dancing against her throat, her hands clenched tight, she approaches. He looks up with a start.

"Why are you following me?" she asks. There are hundreds of people around. Still, her heart's slamming.

Sun lines splay around his brilliant cornflower eyes. Long blond lashes and the sudden rosiness of his cheeks lend him a certain vulnerability. She tries to focus on that.

"Look. Miss Porter, can I buy you a cup of coffee?" **Dear God. He knows her name.**

"I need to get back to work."

"If you'd had your tooth pulled, you'd have been delayed." He points to the building from where she's just come. "Your supervisor won't guess."

"How do you know where I was? Who **are** you?"

"Over coffee." He's glancing at the neon sign across the street. WINDY CITY DONUTS. There are plenty of people inside, despite the off-hour.

"What makes you think I'd have coffee with you? I want you to stop following me. Do I have to call the police?"

He takes a breath and, with a pained smile, reaches into his jacket. Pulling out a worn wallet, he reveals a brass badge and an ID.

"My name is Charles Szydlo." His voice is soft and careful. "FBI."

She's so surprised, it takes her a moment to say, "You're joking."

He shakes his head.

"What could you possibly want with **me**?"

"Come sit for a few minutes," he says, glancing again across the street. "I'll explain."

She takes a deep breath, hesitates, and then nods. An FBI agent. The improbability of it hits her. As they cross at the corner, she tries to get a sense of him. Erect, isolated. A soldier once, for certain. Before the war, she imagines he was a different man. The spray of lines around his eyes tells her that at one time he smiled a great deal. Now he doesn't smile at all. He points through the bakery window to a pan of crullers with chocolate glaze. "I'm getting one of those. You?"

She shrugs. "Sure."

Inside, he approaches the counter and pays for their treats, managing his wallet and pulling out the bills with one hand. His fingers are long and graceful. His other hand, Rosalind observes, is withered, covered in a spiderweb of scars and thickened skin. She can't help feeling sorry for his injury. She has an urge to reach out and explore the raised welts.

The hostess shows them to a table near the front window.

"Miss Porter." He gestures to the opposite banquette, suggesting she sit first. It chills her, hearing her name again. Is he here to accuse her of something? She's aware of her own breathing and the ticking of her heart in her ears.

Sliding into the booth across from her, he removes his hat, sets it beside him. "So you're waiting for an explanation . . ."

A waitress comes before he can say more, plunks down two thick white mugs, and starts pouring a cup for Rosalind.

"No coffee for me," she says.

"Surely you want something to drink?" he asks. "Tea maybe?"

She nods.

"Please bring the lady tea."

"You want the joe I poured?" the waitress asks him.

He silently slides the mug toward himself. He unrolls the bag of doughnuts with one hand, then plucks a paper napkin from the silver holder and sets a cruller in front of Rosalind.

"I'm actually not much of a coffee drinker myself. Just thought it might be good with doughnuts." He takes a bite of his cruller. "These are good. You should try yours." She can see the man is making an effort to be friendly, nonchalant.

"Why am I here?" she asks.

He leans forward, stares at her for a moment before he speaks. "You worked with Fermi on the Manhattan Project, didn't you?"

For years she was instructed **never** to reveal a thing about her work. To say only that she had a job at the Metallurgical Laboratory. As for the trips to Oak Ridge and Hanford and Los Alamos, oh God, those endless desert nights in bed with Weaver—she told her family they were pleasure trips with girlfriends. Sitting with Mr. FBI now, she doesn't say a word. She observes how he so carefully hides his hand. No matter how long it's been since she lost her job, she still protects the project in the same way.

He stares at her with those water-hued eyes.

"Tell me about your relationship with Thomas Weaver," he says.

"Weaver?" she asks. "Why?"

"He interests us."

"Well, he doesn't interest me anymore. I want nothing to do with him. I certainly don't want to discuss our 'relationship,' as you call it."

Szydlo merely sits back and shakes his head.

"You're a pistol," he says.

"I'm glad I amuse you."

He takes a sip from his mug. "I bet you intimidate a lot of guys. A nuclear physicist."

"Not anymore." She frowns at him. "I sell jewelry." Even after three and a half years, speaking the words aloud sends a ripple of irony through her.

"Were you surprised when Weaver started calling you again?"

"How . . . how do you know he's been calling?"

"I know you've said no. You haven't seen him anyway?"

"I don't want anything to do with him. I told him to leave me alone."

"Actually, you told him . . ." He pulls a little notebook out of his breast pocket. "'Stay out of my life.'" He glances up meaningfully.

"I . . . How . . . ?"

"We've been tapping your telephone."

It takes a moment for her to swallow this indigestible pit. The day before yesterday, she'd complained to her friend Marie about her monthly cramps. Heat crawls up the back of her neck.

"I'm sorry we had to compromise your privacy," he says. "Of course, we had a court order."

"I haven't done anything wrong."

"It's not you we're after."

"But it's me you're following. You're not very good at it. I've spotted you more times than I can count."

"What did your friend call me? Shadowman? Like a radio character. It's hard to tail someone when you're six foot seven."

Remembering that she'd told Zeke that Shadowman was menacing but attractive, Rosalind experiences a chill that makes her scalp tingle. **She'd described him in detail. Those eyes!**

"I just had to make sure you weren't one of Weaver's contacts before I approached you."

"Contacts? What does that mean?"

"I know you told Mr. Weaver you don't want to see him. We—the FBI—would like you to change your mind."

"Wait. I'm confused."

The waitress brings her hot water at last.

"Almost forgot, darlin'," she says, yanking a tea bag out of her pocket, tearing off the wrapper, and plopping the tea into her cup before shuffling off.

"We want you to call that number he gave you. To start seeing him again."

"Why?"

"Because he wants you back in his life. And

we need to know what he's up to. Do you recall the number he gave you?"

"Hyde Park 3-5806."

"He said you'd remember." He looks at her admiringly.

"What does the FBI want with Weaver anyway?"

"We think he's involved with some ugly stuff. You've already seen how terrible I am at tailing people. Help me out here and I'll tell you more." He flashes her a crooked grin. **So he** can **smile.** He's especially attractive when his face lights, even if it's only a flicker, then gone. "You were close once," he offers.

"That's exactly what I've been trying to avoid."

He nods knowingly. "I know it ended badly."

She pretends to worry more out of the tea bag, dipping it in and out of the water. Ended badly? Weaver separated her from all that mattered in her life.

"What is it you think he's done?"

"And may yet do," he says.

"Something so bad you'd go to all this trouble?"

He nods, his eyes saying she doesn't know the half of it.

"Couldn't you just arrest him or hang him by his toes or whatever it is you people do?"

"We don't want to arrest Weaver yet. We want him to reveal his contacts, then catch him in the act."

"In the act of what?"

She looks up to see Szydlo blinking at her, weighing her trustworthiness.

"Do you still have an allegiance to him?"

"I hate the man."

"Then maybe we could persuade you to help us out?"

"What is it you think he's done? I deserve to know."

His eyes catch hers and he looks at her for quite a while without a word.

"Catch him in the act of what?" she asks again.

"This isn't a petty crime."

"What isn't?"

"Treason."

CHAPTER FOUR

Ten thirty P.M. and the FBI halls are silent. Even the Polish cleaning ladies—who regularly offer up novenas that Charlie will marry one of their daughters—have stashed away their vacuum cleaners and headed home. The newly installed air conditioner has clicked off, and without its circulation, Charlie can smell the perfume of the last telephone operator. He yanks off the apparatus, walks over to the bank of windows, and shoves them open, one after another. Enjoying the damp breeze on his face, he takes in the dazzle of city lights, extends his hand beyond the sill to catch the needles of rain. The radio this morning warned that the temperature would drop tonight. It's already colder.

He's sat through phone surveillance more times than he can count, usually helped along by a good book, daydreams. Tonight, Hemingway's **Across the River and into the Trees** hasn't done the trick. The **Tribune** crossword puzzle went too fast. And all that's left of the pork sandwich from Keeley's are a few crusts smashed inside a ball of white paper. He's growing irritated and jittery. Why hasn't Miss Porter called Weaver? As they'd parted, he'd said, "Call him tonight, Miss Porter. Do it for your country." She even smiled when he said that. Women. Jesus Christ. He doesn't know how to make them do a damn thing.

After he returned from Mitsushima, when Linda—whom he'd counted on to be waiting— tore him in two, he joined the FBI to avoid women. Like the army, the FBI was a male bastion of facts and information. And a chance to do some good in a world that felt overwhelmingly evil. After the war, they took injured men if they could prove themselves at Quantico. That, too, was part of the appeal. To be better than the others, outperform expectations. Being athletic, naturally diligent, detail oriented, he's good at what he does, and here, he barely has to confront a woman except for an occasional secretary.

They assigned him at first to Peoria. He didn't know a job could be so boring. But he was still recovering from his years at Mitsushima, and the anonymity of Peoria suited him. No one knew him well enough to ask why he looked so gaunt, so exhausted. In Chicago, he'd blocked the pain from the war by staying busy: first by finishing law school in record time, then by training for the FBI. The sleepy silence of Peoria, however, invited pain. Those weeks of boredom gave him time to sweat his war experience out of every pore, to mourn a life of trust and innocence.

When he got the call that he was being transferred back to Chicago, he was surprised and relieved. He returned to the basement apartment at his sister Peggy's house—the one he lived in during law school—and still, somehow, hasn't left.

The transfer to Chicago came for one reason: because he spoke Polish. Most agents never return to their home offices. There's something almost cruel about the way the Bureau assigns people to places they'd rather not go. But in Chicago, there are Polish gangsters to nab, Polish citizens who need protection, and they told Charlie his ability to translate would be invaluable. Then, after a mere two weeks of chasing Jimmy "Bananas" Banasiak, he was transferred to the newly beefed-up espionage squad, where he's never once used his Polish. Now his only job is to catch Russian spies.

The FBI is at the forefront of the new Cold War, and Charlie's on the front lines. For the last six months, Wisconsin Senator McCarthy has been proclaiming that even the State Department itself is infested with spies. The average citizen has started to expect Soviet spies to pop out of storm drains. Half the country's beginning to glance sideways at the other parents at PTA meetings, questioning old friends' loose talk over cocktails. There's no one who hates Communists more than FBI Director J. Edgar Hoover, but office rumor has it that even he is annoyed with the senator. "Lies and overstatements undermine the whole Bureau," he's said. It's true: The new Red Scare is leading to a lot of dead ends.

But what Charlie's working on—routing out the people who shared bomb-building information with the Russians—well, **that** is both real and urgent. When the Russians tested their version of the A-bomb last year—so much sooner than anyone expected—it shook the world. And now they've caught Klaus Fuchs, a German-born scientist who worked at Los Alamos. He's been spilling what he knows, although the Russians made sure he was never told the names of other scientists who aided them. Fuchs reported, most alarmingly, that he heard another scientist has promised to pass information on the still hypothetical hydrogen bomb.

Charlie focused on Weaver for a number of reasons (timing, access, proof of early Communist sympathies), and last month, he felt certain enough to approach Binder with his plan to recruit Miss Porter. He planned to appoint someone else to tail and sweet-talk the lady scientist, someone like Dick Hazelmill. Dick always has a woman on his arm, albeit a flashy one who can't put two sentences together. Binder scoffed and blew an enormous cloud of smoke right into Charlie's eyes.

"A physicist? She's too sharp for Hazelmill. You're the brainy, sensitive type, Szydlo. A smart woman's more likely to warm up to you."

"I hardly think that's me, sir. Besides, I'm too tall to tail anyone."

"You're the one. Get on it." Before the war, his sister used to say girls were drawn to him like moths to a porch light. He played center on his high school basketball team, graduated top of his class, received a scholarship to Champaign. At the age of thirty-one, Charlie thinks he's the last one who should be assigned to handle a woman. He's come to believe women exist to disappoint men. Besides, what girl would want a guy with a mutilated hand who glances away whenever a woman's eyes meet his with interest?

Tonight, Rosalind Porter is living up to her sex's penchant to disillusion. **Calm down,** he tells himself. **It's just a setback. So what if she hasn't called Weaver yet?** He's angry at himself for feeling so disheartened.

After what he went through in the war, he should know better. He's alive. He's not in pain. He has a raincoat to pull on, shoes that aren't torn and wrapped in burlap. For too long he

didn't have either. He's eaten a good dinner—
that sandwich from Keeley's was delicious. In
captivity, he ate nothing but tainted rice, an occasional morsel of fish old enough to stink. With
so little in his belly, suffering from beriberi, after
hours on a raised wood slab with only a rice-husk
mat beneath him, he wasn't sure that he'd wake
any given morning.

**He'll never be warm again, doubts he'll live
until spring. It's so cold, the flesh beneath
his fingernails aches. His toes are blue. His
skin, a dead lavender. Huddled beneath the
blanket, knees to chest, one foot folded beneath the other. Damn blanket's thin as a
cobweb. As cold as he is, his muscles burn.
All day he hoisted fifty-kilo sacks of cement
from a freight train to a warehouse. The prisoners are building a dam for Nagoya. When
he drops the sacks on the pile, the cement
bags expel ghostly clouds of lung-irritating
dust. He coughs them out now, moves closer
to Harris. All the men share their pallets. It's
the only way to stay alive. They don't care if
their bed partners smell rank. If the bones
of their bedmates press through their skin.
Heat. Humanity. He coughs again.**

**"Can it, Szydlo," Harris says. "I need my
sleep."**

"Sorry."

"I tell ya, when I get home, I'm going to sleep under that fat quilt my granny made in my own damn soft bed without you, pal."

"Likewise."

"And I'm going to turn up the radiators until everyone in the house wakes sweating and swearing. I don't care what my ma says about the bill."

"Yeah. Oh yeah."

Charlie thinks of his own soft bed in his room at home, the pillowcases his mother embroidered with bluebirds, the crisp, ironed sheets, the warm eiderdown. What's the likelihood he'll ever see any of it again? Or his parents?

A few hours later, he wakes. Thin, blue mountain light is scratching through the small, high window. The guard they hate the most, whom they call Gargle for all his throat clearing, has opened the door. He'll beat any man who doesn't jump from his bed. Charlie's shivering more than usual. Has the temperature dropped precipitously? Is he sick? He shoves Harris's shoulder. "Bud, get up. Gargle's here. Move it."

Nothing.

Raising his head, he glances over. Harris lies there looking more comfortable than he has in months.

"Harris?"

The knowledge creeps up Charlie's spine: He touches his bunkmate's hand. It's stone-cold.

Later, two other inmates carry the body away, no one supporting Harris's head, so it flops from his neck like a fish on a line. Charlie wants to call out, Take me too! He's sobered to realize that the idea of death gives him more hope than living.

⦀ ⦀ ⦀

Startled out of his thoughts when the light on the switchboard begins to flash—Miss Porter's getting a call—Charlie grabs the headset and yanks it on. He shivers. The memory has left him with the same old question: Why has he lived when so many others died?

"Hello," Rosalind answers. She sounds distracted, tired.

"Hello, Roz."

That plummy British newsreel enunciation could only be Weaver. "It's late. I'm sorry. I didn't wake you, love, did I?"

"I was just . . . just getting ready for bed."

"I know I've been a bore, calling too often," Weaver says. "But I need to see you. If you'll give me a single chance. That's all I'm asking."

"No."

"But you don't know what's at stake for me." Weaver sounds choked up.

"All right. What's at stake for you, Weaver? Tell me."

"My life's been broken since I left you."

"And mine hasn't?"

"Listen. I know you're angry. You have every right. But hear me out. See me one time. Let me tell you what really happened."

Silence. Then: "Why should I trust you?"

"Because I have things to say that might change your mind. If you only knew the truth . . . you'd understand." And then, lowering his voice into a covert whisper, he says, "I can't say any of this over the phone." Charlie sits forward. Does Weaver suspect the line is tapped?

"It's late," Miss Porter says. "I'm going to bed."

Oh Christ! Say yes to him!

"Tomorrow night. I'm begging you."

Miss Porter takes a breath loud enough for Charlie to hear. Maybe she's too tired to resist. Maybe Weaver's worn her down. Maybe she's doing it because she believed Charlie when he told her that the world's safety rests on her shoulders. For whatever reason, she says, "Fine, Weaver. Forget dinner, though. Forget wooing me. If you want to see me, come at eight P.M. tomorrow. Don't stay more than an hour. And don't expect me to feed you."

"Thank God and thank you," Weaver says. "Sleep well, Duchess."

She hangs up without a good-bye. Charlie yanks off the earphones and laughs out loud.

⯐ ⯐ ⯐

Rosalind sits in the dark in her living room. On the ceiling, the lights from Lake Shore Drive dance and spin. She needs to go to bed. She needs to forget the phone call. How will she fall asleep with Weaver's voice in her head? Weaver once was her drug—one that gave her pleasure, then left her desperate. Well, she's clean now. With Weaver still living in Hyde Park, and Rosalind no longer traveling to the South Side for work, she's managed not to run into him a single time. The last thing she wants is to be drawn back into her addiction. When she sees him, she'll say to his face, **Stop calling. Give it up. It's over. I'll never let you back into my life.**

If Special Agent Szydlo was listening, how smug he must feel that she said yes. He even briefly suggested that seeing Weaver again gave her a shot at revenge. She's never seen herself as a vengeful person. But she is curious. Could Weaver truly be the brute who's put their entire world on edge?

As much as she once loved Thomas Weaver,

there was always a wall of mystery around him. A silence, a darkness, the suggestion of secrets. Why has he been calling out of the blue? Why must he see her suddenly? What if, for just one night, she could tear down that wall, expose his secrets, and then, joyfully, set them aflame?

⫿ ⫿ ⫿

When Charlie gets off the L at Damen, the streets have puddled; the wind is merciless. Thank God he brought a raincoat this morning. In the first two blocks, he passes two drunks, a fellow in a waiter's uniform, and a shivering young prostitute in a flimsy yellow dress. She asks, "**Hej, chcesz się zabawić?**" wondering if he's looking for fun.

"**Przepraszam, nie,**" he says.

She's clearly hungry and cold. There's nothing about her that looks fun. There are so many Displaced Persons from the war now, souls battered by change and loss. Since the Jerries invaded, they say more Poles live in Chicago than any city outside of Warsaw. He's ready to hand her the five-dollar bill in his wallet. But before he reaches her, a car sidles up and she gets in. He can't help aching for her young life.

Walking down the side streets, all he hears are his own footsteps and the howl of an alley cat. Polish people go to bed early, get up early, work hard. His sister's house is an 1893 worker's cottage with a peaked roof, small and modest. Its location in Wicker Park is its asset. Her husband, Mack, often bends an elbow at the corner bar, Szczęście. The kids go to Burr School. Peggy can walk to St. Mary of the Angels near where their parents once lived in twenty minutes. She doesn't miss a morning. She used to say, "Come with me, Charlie. You know. Say a few prayers." But as one of the guys struggling to survive with him in Mitsushima used to say, "God and me ain't pals no more."

The house looks dark now; they must have all gone to bed. Charlie's apartment is Peggy's converted cellar, with its own door to the outside. Stone outer walls. A curtain separates his bed from the so-called living room. A makeshift john raised up a step and a shower with a drain in the floor. No kitchen. If he got home in time, he'd eat upstairs with Peggy and her family. He can't remember the last time that happened. The first of every month, he stuffs twenty dollars into the jar on her kitchen counter, his share of the cost of food he never eats.

After changing into chinos and a sweatshirt, he climbs the steps to the kitchen hoping to grab a Hamm's from Peg's icebox. He always feels exhausted these days but still finds it hard to sleep. Sometimes beer helps. Sometimes nothing helps.

He's startled to find Peggy sitting at the kitchen table.

"Oh, sorry," he says. "Didn't know you were up."

"It's your kitchen too." She points to a bowl of fruit. "Want a peach?" She's already bitten into one and is wiping the juice from her chin. He notes her golden brown hair is yanked tightly around prickly, netted curlers. Why do girls do painful things like sleep on rollers? Peggy's hair is always perfect. Her clothes are immaculately ironed, her shoes polished.

"What I really need is a beer."

"I wish you'd eat something."

"What'd you make for dinner?"

"Stuffed cabbage. It was good."

"I bet it was."

He opens the icebox, filled with glass bowls of leftovers. He sees the stuffed cabbages, fat babies snuggled in a row. A single cabbage roll per man might have helped protect him and his friends from beriberi during the war. Now it's just one choice among many. The rolls will be eaten the day after tomorrow. Peggy runs a neat, frugal household. She learned it all from their mother, who never wasted a grape in her life. He finds a Hamm's and pops off its top on the bottle capper attached to the wall. Charlie pulls out a chair and sits across from Peggy.

He closes his eyes when he drinks down that

first cold slug—the best he's felt all day. It's as though his soul has been balled up and the beer loosens it at the edges. He sighs, with pleasure more than anything. He's home. He's safe. His sister prays for him, even if he won't pray for himself.

"You okay, kid?" she asks.

"Sure. Why wouldn't I be okay?"

"I don't know. You work like a madman. Can't remember the last time I saw you smile."

He shrugs. "Yeah? When was the last time you even saw me?"

She laughs. "Stevie asked me the other day, 'Does Uncle Charlie still live here?' I said, 'Last I heard.'"

"Sorry."

"Even on Sundays, we come back from church and you're gone. Where do you go?"

"I don't know. Square dancing? Toastmasters? Knitting circle?"

She shakes her head at him. "When did you become a comedian? Is work good? You still hunting Commies?"

"Best I can."

"Is it true what that Senator McCarthy says, that there's a whole list of spies in the State Department?"

He shakes his head. "No. He's a kook. There may be one. Even two. We have no proof."

"I'm relieved. I'd look lousy in a babushka."

He laughs. "You'd make it stylish."

Her face turns serious. "I can't help worrying. Imagine raising kids in a Communist world. Whispering the truth while the government yells lies. Not enough food. Sharing our house with two other families . . ."

"It's not going to happen, Peg. Not here. Not now."

"It happened in Poland."

"It won't happen here. I promise."

She leans over and kisses his cheek. "Thanks to guys like you. I'm proud of you, kid. Listen." She grabs his shoulder, abruptly changing tone. "I've been thinking about setting you up with Sherry Nowak. She's Laura Mlynarski's little sister. Very pretty girl. Blond and petite . . . and a perfect nose. An absolutely perfect nose."

"I'm not interested in Sherry Nowak's nose."

"How about the rest of her?"

"Not right now."

She squints her eyes, presses her lips together with annoyance.

"You know Linda doesn't deserve your loyalty," Peg says. "Never did."

"It's not about Linda."

"I wonder," Peg says, shaking her head in a worried, scolding way. The curlers bob. "You've been back almost four years, Charlie."

"I know how long I've been back."

"So what are you waiting for? Ma would have

been pushing you to find someone if she were alive."

"Well, Ma isn't here."

"Yeah. More's the pity." When Charlie looks at Peggy these days, he sees their mother when she was young. Confident. Kind. The same blue eyes. There wasn't a person in the neighborhood who didn't count on Lidia Szydlo, didn't come to her for advice. She knew the right herb to soothe your cough, the right prayer to ease your heart, the right thing to say when no one else understood.

She died of pneumonia in April of '45, just months before the end of the war and Charlie's release. Peggy said St. Mary's was so crowded for her funeral that people were standing in the vestibule. His father, who passed away a year after Charlie got home, told his son it broke his mother's heart that she was the one who'd insisted he sign up early for the army, before the draft. She considered it her fault that Charlie ended up in the Philippines and might never come home.

"It killed her. Plain and simple."

"You're saying she died because of me?" he asked his father, not sure he could bear the weight and pain of another lost life. His own mother.

"I'm going to bed," he tells Peggy now, setting his bottle in the empties bin for return to the store.

Peggy gets up and reaches out for him.

"Come here, kid," she says.

He comes over with a shrug and she throws her arms around his waist, which is as high as she can reach. He hears the clock ticking above the door, crickets out on the grass. The gunk she squirts on her curlers smells like maple syrup.

"I love you, you know that, right?" she asks.

"Sure," he says. "I know, Peg."

"I just want you to be happy, that's all."

"I am happy," he says.

She shakes her head. "Never lie to your sister. It's bad policy."

"Okay, boss." He kisses her once on each cheek, then trudges down the stairs, lightened by the beer, darkened by his sister's disappointment in him. Maybe she's right: He can't help feeling bleak as he looks around at the concrete floor, the low ceiling. When he came back from the war, he often thought of suicide. He could taste the poisonous tang of the gun oil, feel the cool metal of his service revolver slipped between his lips. Now he's thirty-one years old and living in a basement. A different kind of suicide. Not one piece of furniture down here hasn't been hard used and discarded—just like him. Stripping off his clothes, he lies in his bed, stiff, uneasy, and alone.

CHAPTER FIVE

Rosalind scouts the closet for a dress, curls her lashes, reapplies her lipstick. Watching herself primp for Weaver makes her feel ashamed. But it's been four years since they've seen each other, and she wants him to find her irresistible. She wants him to explain and apologize until he bleeds. And then she plans to detonate his heart as he did hers.

By the time the buzzer sounds, it's twenty past eight. Arrogant people are always late. She lifts the intercom receiver. Frank, the doorman, his voice high and uncomfortable, says, "It's . . . Mr. Weaver. You . . . uh . . . Miss Porter, you want I should let him up?" Frank's been guarding this building as long as she's lived here. He used to see Weaver come home with her nearly every night. Frank and Weaver had roaring discussions about the Cubs and the White Sox—Weaver's new-found American passion. "You marry him soon, you hear?" Frank said. "A girl like you should be married." And then the bombs were dropped on Japan.

She knew she was supposed to hate the Japanese. She'd heard their soldiers were cruel. And that the country was ruthless and power hungry. Still, the Manhattan Project's darling vaporized nursing mothers, little girls cradling dolls, old women pouring tea, men too ancient to fight. It sucked their houses into winds of flame, shattered their hospitals and schools. It dropped an entire town into the sun and the Americans laughed while it burned. And then they chose another town and did the same. More than one hundred thousand dreams burned in a conflagration too hot to yield smoke. Fifty thousand died later of injuries. That's when, consumed with guilt, she shut Weaver out.

"This will pass," he told her when she flinched at his touch.

"Will it?"

"I'm here. And I plan to wait until you feel better." His words touched her. And in time, she did feel herself healing, easing closer to him, rediscovering their passion. Then, one evening after work, on the sidewalk outside Eckhart Hall, Weaver told her that he was breaking it off. It was over. There was someone else. No lead-up. No explanation. Frank had to help her up to her apartment that night after she'd sleepwalked to a bar and come home too drunk to walk straight.

"The man's a rat," Frank told her. "You're better off without him. But drinking won't make it better, Miss Porter." She doesn't remember much about that night. But she does remember Frank taking her up in the elevator, settling her on the sofa, filling a glass with water, and instructing her, "Drink the whole thing down or you'll have a screeching headache in the morning."

Now the doorman asks again in a whisper, "You sure you want to see him, miss?"

"Let him up, Frank."

"Okay . . ." She can almost hear him shrugging.

Peering into the mirror by the door, she worries how Weaver will view her. But when she opens the door, she's the one who's moved. The man standing in front of her has aged radically. Nine years older than she is, he's thinner and his hair is turning silver about the ears. It gives him a wolflike quality. In the past, he exuded calm. Now there's a surprising nervous energy. Yet, in his presence, God help her, she feels twice as alive.

"Hi, Duchess."

"Weaver."

"You look beautiful. I mean, **extraordinarily** beautiful. You've no idea how happy I am to see you." He's never been this effusive before. He always acted so reticent . . . so British.

"I bought the corniest one I could find," he

says, presenting her with a box of chocolates spiked all around with gold paper lace, the words "I Love You" impressed on top in red foil.

"Well, well," she says dryly. Where did he find these four months after Valentine's Day?

"I made sure there were maple creams." Weaver is particularly wild about maple, something he'd never encountered until he reached America. She introduced him to maple syrup, maple sugar candy, maple creams . . . "Oh, and in here"—he holds up a brown bag—"cherries. I know you buy them every June."

"I don't want gifts," she says.

Setting the cherries on the hall table, he comes to her. "Don't push me away. You've no idea how I've missed you." He reaches out to embrace her, but she ducks.

"Let me get you a drink," she says. "Scotch and soda neat?"

"You remember."

"There are a lot of things I remember." She doesn't say this in a friendly way.

Relieved to have a task, she wills herself not to look at him. Lifting the bottle of Scotch out of the bar cabinet, she realizes how precious it is: bottled prewar, dust coating its shoulders. Ancient history. While he was gone, Scotch reminded her too much of what she'd lost. She hasn't tasted it since their last night together.

"I always liked this place," he says. "In the

morning especially when we'd wake to the sun coming up over the lake . . ."

His words make her throat ache, remind her of all those years they were so intimate they may as well have been married. They broke every rule she was raised by, and it never felt wrong. Sharing the sunrise, spending every day together in the lab, sitting across from each other at dinner, eating takeout. Sometimes they stopped just to hold hands. They made love on the bed, the floor, the sofa, in the bathtub, against the wall in the kitchen. After he left, she wondered again and again whether it was deeper than desire. It had been for her. But how could he have left so heedlessly? She pours a glass of Scotch for herself and forgoes the soda. God knows she needs it to face him. She takes two deep swigs before she comes to join him on the sofa.

⦙⦙ ⦙⦙ ⦙⦙

She'd just turned twenty-two when she met Weaver and was utterly innocent. You could blame it on her father. While Rosalind was growing up, he joined them for dinner at Louisa's every Sunday. It was the only time she saw him. A lively discussion of Chicago politics or women voters over the entrée inevitably led to a lecture on the dangers of the male population by dessert. Dr. Joe had seen terrible things in his job as Coroner's Physician. Women who'd chosen violent men, had tried to end unwelcome pregnancies and inadvertently ended themselves, or had fallen into lives of prostitution and met the wrong customer. In each case the moral of the story was death. Rosalind heard these warnings so often she conflated love with danger. She grew up fearful of the opposite sex while longing to embrace the threat they radiated. Dr. Joe was none too pleased when Henry announced that Professor Fermi had recruited Rosalind to work on a top secret project. "Working with all those men, Roz," Father said. "It can't end well."

But Rosalind wasn't going to let anyone keep her from what she considered her best chance to make a difference. People laughed when she said that fossil fuels would run out someday, leaving mankind stranded. She believed if they could harness nuclear energy, it would prove itself an endless source to power the world. And because Fermi applauded her involvement, there was nothing she wouldn't do to make him proud. She trekked by bus to a lumberyard to secure and negotiate a price for the endless amounts of wood they needed to build the pile. She talked long-distance to the Goodyear Tire and Rubber Company about the dimensions and shape and security of the seams of the square balloon needed to house the reaction.

The thing she did that made Fermi most

proud was designing a boron trifluoride counter that worked like a Geiger counter, ticking
off neutrons to help gauge the burgeoning reaction. Others had attempted to make just such
a tool, but Rosalind spent days experimenting
until she learned to enrich the boron to 96 percent boron-10 in order to create consistency.
The giddiness she felt when she succeeded was a
sensation not unlike falling in love. The day she
unveiled it, Fermi, Anderson, and she went swimming off the breakwater rocks at the Fifty-Fifth
Street promontory. It had become something of
a ritual after work in the summertime. But that
day, Fermi unrolled his towel to reveal a bottle
of champagne. How had he acquired such a precious commodity during wartime? "A gift from
an admirer," he said, presenting it like a trophy.
"And now I use it to admire you, Rosalinda." He
popped the cork. They passed the bottle around
laughing, sipping from its cold glass lips. She'd
never drunk champagne before and was shocked
and pleased by its sour effervescence. Nothing
had ever felt as decadent as the three of them sitting on those rocks, their feet in the cool water,
celebrating her success.

Despite the tasks she excelled at, she tried
hard not to be the team's mascot. Fifty men
and Rosalind. Other than Fermi, her colleagues
treated her like a little sister. They teased. They
played tricks. Tucking a fake mouse under her

purse. Dropping red dye into her Coca-Cola so that she had a circle of red on her lips for two days. It was hard to believe such brilliant men could amuse themselves with idiotic jokes. "Thanks, fellas. My tube of Victory Red is almost gone. And now I don't need it!"

But when Fermi wasn't there and a serious issue arose, they rarely included Rosalind in the discussions. If she overheard, she moved closer, spoke anyway. Men, she discovered, often overlooked the obvious. Or worked too hard to come up with a new idea that would reflect well on them rather than turning to the past for answers. Her ideas usually surprised them.

She quickly learned that speaking in a woman's octave rendered her thoughts inaudible. If she wanted to be heeded, she had to lower the pitch of her voice. And she discovered that speaking more slowly, with air between her phrases, made the men stop and listen. Within a year, people were including Rosalind more. They were turning to her. But because she didn't want to stand out, she took pains to credit everyone. She always tried to make the men think her ideas had been inspired by theirs.

Then Thomas Weaver swaggered in from New York. He had sailed over from Cambridge to Columbia to work on fission before the war, and it took a letter from FDR to keep him from being sent back to England to fight. In his early thirties, single, lightning smart, he wasn't afraid to stand out. In fact, he demanded it.

She heard a few of her fellow scientists muttering, "Who the hell does he think he is?"

On his third day at the lab, he approached her. "We haven't really met," he said, holding out a hand. "I'd say Fermi knew what he was doing when he put you in a lab coat. You're not just some girl." He looked at her admiringly. "I've met your counter. Pure genius."

"Thank you."

"In fact, I take off my hat to you." He removed an imaginary hat and swept down into a ridiculous bow. She laughed. Rosalind was one of the first people in the Met Lab to get past Weaver's bravado and learn to like him.

Not long after, in December, on a below-zero day, all the Met Lab scientists stood around shivering in scarves and knit caps on the viewing platform above the bitterly cold underground squash court where they'd built the pile, watching their first attempt at a sustained reaction. It was her neutron counter's beating that let them know the reaction was live. It clicked and clacked until all they heard was a roar. A heart in danger of bursting.

When her counter could no longer handle the speed and intensity, it was switched off and the chart recorder switched on. All went silent—a suspended breath that throbbed in their ears. There wasn't a scientist on that cold balcony who wasn't leaning forward. Weaver, standing beside her, reached for her gloved hand and squeezed it. In that charged atmosphere, Fermi, like the greatest of conductors, raised his arm, a salute to the universe and its magic.

"The pile has gone critical," he declared. And then everyone held their breath as Fermi allowed the pile to run. The minutes ticked off, one, two, three, four! Far longer than anyone expected. If the rate went unchecked, the entire city of Chicago would blow up, Rosalind's own atoms spinning among the wreckage. No, she told herself. The zip rod could be lowered. The control rods pushed in. Still, not a person in that room could be certain if humans were fast enough to halt a disaster. As a backup, three men stood nervously, one foot forward, one foot back, clutching buckets of cadmium sulfate to toss into the pile if necessary. By the time Fermi at last motioned for the zip rod to be lowered, there was a collective release of breath. The men set down the buckets. Fermi shook his head in wonder and smiled. Like a great navigator, he'd guided them safely through the hurricane.

⚗ ⚗ ⚗

That night, there was a party at the Fermis'. It had been planned for weeks, long before anyone knew the project would move fast enough to make this evening the perfect time to celebrate. Rosalind sipped ginger ale. Weaver sat next to her on the sofa, nursing a Scotch. She tasted his—having never tasted whiskey before—and told him she could see where the word "butterscotch" might have derived from. That made him laugh. "Butterscotch? Dear girl, you astonish me." He began to question her about why she'd been drawn to science. He asked about her family, about growing up without a mother, about being the only girl in her classes, in her major, in her field.

"It's like being the first foreigner in an isolated country," she told him. "My power is that I know the language. I find pleasure in shocking the natives by speaking fluently."

He looked at her admiringly. "You speak it more fluently than the rest of us." The heat she felt silenced her for a moment. But soon they were in a lively discussion about why actinide isotopes need odd neutron numbers to be fissile. She noted Laura Fermi watching the two of them with an approving smile. As soon as Weaver left her to refresh their drinks, Laura moved in. "He **is** a handsome fellow, is he not?"

"Yes."

"If I were younger, I would make him sweet eyes. He likes you. A blind man could see." Rosalind felt herself blushing.

"I'm only getting to know him."

"Like all men, he's too sure. That is what women are for, yes? To put men back in their little presents?" Laura's English was far better than her husband's, though sometimes her colloquial expressions became hilariously jumbled. "But you could do that, Rosalind. You have the smartness. And he would be a surprise."

"A surprise?"

"A prize, I mean. A prize."

Rosalind smiled. "Yes, a prize."

"Now, tell me," Laura said, moving closer. "You're the only one I **can** ask: Why is everyone congratulating Enrico tonight? What's happened?"

Heat rose up Rosalind's neck. "You don't know?" she whispered. "He didn't tell you?"

"I ask Enrico and he says, go take care of the guests!"

If Fermi hadn't told Laura, how could Roz break the silence, the youngest member of the team, the only woman?

"If you tell me, I won't say I know. It is a big thing, this?"

"Yes . . . very big."

"A big thing such as . . ." Laura gazed at her with chocolate eyes.

"Laura . . . please."

"Tell me anything. The very tiniest thing is more than I have."

"Well." Rosalind ground the toe of her shoe

into the carpet, searching for words. "It's as important as . . . as if he'd sunk a Japanese admiral."

Laura squinted with disbelief. Everyone knew the situation in the Pacific was dire. The American fleet was virtually wiped out and there was fear that Hawaii would soon be captured.

"You are joking at me, yes?" Laura asked.

"I'm not saying he actually sunk an admiral. I just meant it's a big thing. A very big thing."

"I trust you to tell me, Rosalind. I need to know what has happened."

"Mrs. Fermi," Weaver interrupted, passing Rosalind a glass of Scotch. "Butterscotch for you, Duchess," he said, then turned to Laura and set his hand on her shoulder. "We don't want to make our Rosalind spill the beans, do we? Signor Fermi will send her right to the doghouse."

"Spill beans? Doghouse?"

"Both are charming American expressions," said Weaver, flashing all his teeth. "Spill the beans means telling what you shouldn't. And being sent to the doghouse is what happens when you do something very, **very** bad. Like a naughty dog. Fermi will never forgive her."

Laura's lower lip pushed out into a pout and she turned to Rosalind once more. "But it is a very, very big thing, yes?"

"Yes. You would be proud," Rosalind said. "Maybe when we've all left tonight, he'll tell you. He's the one who must tell you." Fermi was watching them from the corner of the room. He lifted his glass in a toast. His eyes flashed like stars in a night sky.

⁂

At the time Rosalind was living with five other girls, mostly university secretaries, not far from campus. When the party was winding down past midnight, Weaver established that his apartment wasn't far from hers and insisted on walking her home. He hadn't come by car because they'd begun to ration gas.

"You'd be afraid of my driving anyway," he said as they stepped outside. "I learned to drive on the other side, and I keep thinking it's the lot of you who are driving like maniacs." His voice echoed in the night air. Snow squeaked beneath their feet. It was so cold, her nostrils stuck together. She could barely smell the scent of wood smoke that rose from someone's chimney. The majority of houses were dark, the streetlights too far apart. Again, he reached for her hand.

"Be careful," he said. "There lies treachery." He pointed to ice that was hiding on the walkway between white patches, black and ominous.

Despite their gloves, his touch sent an effervescence through her veins. The extent of her "experience" with men was kissing two different soldiers at the same USO dance. They ended up getting into a fistfight with each other. Now handsome Thomas Weaver was clutching her hand. She had no idea what to make of it. Why on earth would he choose her?

All her life, she'd been the "smart" girl. That line "Men seldom make passes at girls who wear glasses" wasn't about spectacles. What man wanted to be with a bookish girl? Louisa tried to intervene. When Rosalind entered high school, Louisa insisted she get a haircut, spent time teaching her how to pluck her eyebrows. She bought her new clothes. A girl, Louisa explained, needed to look attractive and please men in order to fulfill her primary job in life: to find a mate, procreate, and make a home. "It's the natural order," she explained. Maybe it was the hollowness in her voice that made Rosalind bristle. If it was the natural order, why was Lou always so miserable? And why did she often sound like she was reading from a script? Still, after Louisa gussied her up, Roz did feel more special. And boys did seem to notice.

Then, when the Superintendent of Schools, basing his insistence on test scores and teacher raves, plucked her from Hyde Park High to begin at the University of Chicago at the age of sixteen, it didn't endear her to the boys. Adeptness at math and science didn't win her a university lothario either. Her friend Zeke warned her that she simply had to make an effort to hide that she knew more than every man she met. This moment with Weaver was utterly new: a man who seemed to appreciate her **for** her brains. She felt totally off-balance.

"I think Rosalind is a splendid name," he said.

She shook her head. "It's too old-fashioned. I don't know what my parents were thinking."

"It's Shakespearean. Don't argue."

She laughed.

"Truth is . . ." His voice faltered. He turned and smiled nervously. "Do you notice at the lab that I'm always staring at you?"

She had no idea what to say. She had never presumed this handsome man could be romantically interested in her. They were colleagues who argued about the merits of powdered beryllium.

"Listen, I . . . I've tried not to feel anything for you, but I can't make a go of it . . . I know I should." His mouth was trembling. Realizing that under the thunder of his swagger was something defenseless, her heart fishtailed, swishing between desire and fear.

He brushed his gloved thumb over her lips.

"If I kiss these lips, I won't want to stop," he said. "Roz, come home with me," he whispered. "Please . . . My apartment isn't far."

Her father had taught her that men were predators, and he'd just spoken the very words the evil ones spoke to lead innocents down the path of no return. A light snapped off inside her.

"I need to get home," she insisted.

"Please?" he whispered again.

"I'm not the girl you think I am. Good night, Weaver." She started walking toward her house. Brisk enough to escape him. Not brisk enough to slip and kill herself. He easily caught up.

"I'll walk you home, then, shall I?" he asked, all British gallantry.

"Yes," she said. "I'd appreciate that." He reached for her hand and tucked it into his elbow, the protective squire now.

"I do think you are quite beautiful," he said. "I also think you don't know it."

⚕ ⚕ ⚕

After that, he courted her with flowers, dinners, long walks. Winter grew into a wet spring. It felt like the sun would never shine. After days of no sun, she found it hard to get out of bed. But Weaver seemed even more affected. His ever-changing eyes dulled to a sad, faded blue. He smoked insistently, as though he were trying to draw any tidbit of happiness he could find out of each cigarette.

One late afternoon, as he walked her home from campus, their umbrellas clashing, he said, "I have to tell you something."

"Okay."

"In England, I was married."

Her stomach dropped as it had once on a giant roller coaster. "Married?"

"It didn't end well," he said.

That could mean any number of things, and so Rosalind said nothing, hoping he'd say more. But for a long time he just smoked in that forehead-wrinkling way that was his alone.

"You're not going to tell me what happened?" she asked.

He flicked his cigarette onto the ground and it sizzled as it hit a puddle. He tugged on the brim of his hat. "She died in an air raid."

"Oh . . . oh God. I'm sorry. In London or . . ."

"We lived in Cambridge but she took the train in to sign some papers. She had a friend who had a little house in Forest Hill. The woman's husband was a soldier, off fighting, and she was all alone in her house, lonely, so my wife spent the night. It was during the Blitz. During a war, one tries to act as normally as possible. To live a regular life. I didn't stop her from going into the city. I should have. I don't know why she and her friend didn't head for the shelter. The sirens went off as usual. Maybe they were laughing and drinking and thought, **What the hell. Leave it to fate.**"

"How long ago . . . when?"

"The end of October 1940." His face was impassive as he told the story. He might have been conveying a piece of history from a book. He wouldn't look at Rosalind at all. The muscles in his cheek twitched and worked. It meant he was either nervous, unhappy, or angry.

"What was her name?" Rosalind asked. He'd had a wife. She was dead. His joking, full-of-himself quality had never betrayed any of this.

"Her name was Victoire."

"Victoire?" Rosalind said.

"She was from the South of France, from Marseille, and older than me. Quite a bit older . . . Look, Roz, it wasn't a happy marriage. I guess I need to say that. I don't want your sympathy. We were struggling. Maybe I wanted her to go off to London . . . There were days I couldn't bear the sight of her."

"Don't say that, Weaver."

He shrugged. As she thought about it, it seemed to her that his honesty boded well. He wasn't looking for undue sympathy or playing up his loss. Maybe he didn't even love his wife. A young man's bad choice. "You came to America to get away from the sadness?" Rosalind asked.

"I got out of England running. There was so much pressure for Britons to join up, even though I was doing important war work that most couldn't. Healthy men were supposed to don uniforms and beat the Nazis. I'd have made a lousy soldier. I'd be dead by now. When I joined the Manhattan Project, it was an opportunity to lose myself in something important. To be somewhere safer. To breathe again. I didn't much like New York, but I felt safe. Then I moved to Chicago and found you. I'm sorry I didn't tell you about Victoire. I haven't said anything to anyone." He wasn't crying or filled with misery, but at that moment she felt deeply moved. The rain beat on their umbrellas as she brought her hand to his face, caressing his cheek with her thumb, her fingers aroused by the prickle of his beard.

"Weaver," she said. "I think . . . I'd like you to take me home. Your home . . ."

His lips parted with surprise. "Are you sure?" he asked, breathless.

She merely smiled.

That night, they became lovers. Damn her father's warnings. This was what she wanted more than anything: to feel close to another human, heart, breath, and mind. To give. To get. To feel alive in a way she'd never known possible. She soon discovered she wasn't the dull, brainy woman she'd pegged herself to be, but a body alive and sensual, moving like seaweed in a rising tide. Insatiable. Unshameable.

〰 〰 〰

Yet amid the joy, there was always something closed off in Weaver. Even when they slept together side by side and ate toast across the table from each other, she could still never get through the murkiness to discover the black heart of his misery. Was it a moment in his past that quietly tortured him? A dirty secret he couldn't share? Or Victoire, whom he proclaimed he never really loved? Maybe he'd lied about that. It made itself known as a silence in the middle of a conversation, a dull distance in his eyes. A certainty that he would never be entirely Rosalind's. There were even times he went out and wouldn't tell her where he'd been. "A man has to keep some things to himself," he'd say. And then, after a trip to England, he brought her the little necklace with the word "Patience" stuck inside.

How unsettling it all was. Why couldn't people be equations? Mathematics and hard science were based on certainty. Weaver was right. There was none when it came to humans. On those rare occasions when she found the courage to ask what troubled him, he changed the subject. Even on their best days, at any time a cloud could slip soundlessly over their sun.

Later, she reflected, perhaps this was part of his appeal. She might have been a scientist, but she'd read what most girls read. She'd encountered Heathcliff. Mr. Rochester. Mr. Darcy. Max de Winter. Wasn't landing a dark, secretive man the ultimate goal in romance? And after all, he'd chosen **her,** an unsophisticated, science-minded girl. Not the sort men usually loved, as Louisa so often pointed out.

⁕ ⁕ ⁕

And then in late February of '46, more than three years after their love affair began, he dropped her. From the top of the Palmolive Building to the concrete. It was after work. He met her as she was coming out of the building. He wasn't around as much in those days. Traveling off to Los Alamos. Oak Ridge. Washington, DC. She'd been deeply depressed since Hiroshima and Nagasaki, pushing him away, angry at everyone. Her job had changed, too, and not in a satisfying way: She was teaching Fermi's classes while he was away.

"Listen, we've got to talk," he said.

"I've got a headache," she said. "Never had a bite of lunch. Sorry. If it's something important, let me at least go grab a cup of tea and a sandwich at Hartwick's."

"No. Look, I can't . . . I can't see you anymore."

"What?"

"It wasn't meant to be—you and me." He spoke so quickly, so distractedly, she wasn't sure she understood.

"What are you telling me?" she asked.

"I'm sorry. We've got to end this."

"End what?"

"End this . . . this romance." His hands were balled into fists. His face was white.

Romance? Even through her depression over the bombs, even despite distraction and distances, she saw their love as flexible enough to absorb disappointment, anger, truth.

"What have I done?" she asked. "Was it being sad all the time? I know I've been hard on you since the bomb, but I'll do better. I swear it." It had to be her fault, to have made him draw away so inexplicably. "I know it's been lousy to be with me."

"No. It just wasn't meant to be. It's not worth discussing."

"Not worth **discussing**!" She said it too loudly. Colleagues flowed out of the building all around them. He hadn't even had the courtesy to take her somewhere private, to try to explain.

"I can't talk about it anymore," he said. And he turned to leave. She felt she might be sick. Or faint. The sidewalk moved beneath her and the sky wavered overhead.

"Don't go. You've got to explain this to me. I love you, Weaver. No matter what I've done. You know I love you."

He turned back, his eyes nearly black. He hissed, "There's someone else. That's all you need to know." Then he walked away.

She opened her mouth to call him, but nothing came out. As though wading through water, she groped her way to a bench under a tree, facing away from the street. There was a paper coffee cup on it, which she slapped aside. It bounced on the ground; then the wind picked it up and rolled it noisily down the block. It was cold, not the sort of weather when anyone should sit outside. Still, she sat, huddled into her coat, too dumbfounded to weep. She didn't move for so long, she could barely feel her feet when she finally stood and headed for a bar, where no amount of drink made the pain go away.

॥ ॥ ॥

With a Scotch in hand, Weaver seems right at home now in her apartment. He asks her about her life, then looks alarmed when she says she's selling jewelry at Field's.

"Dear God, couldn't you teach physics or something?"

She takes in his newly lean face and notes the concern pressing down on the edges of his eyes.

"Science and I have parted company," she says.

"I don't believe it. Why?"

"You know why."

Weaver peers into his glass. "But you love science," he says softly. "You once said . . . you lived for its mystery and . . . what was it?"

She sighs. "Reliability."

The first time she said that, he told her she should write it on a blackboard for students to memorize.

"Yes, reliability. Exactly so. Surely your feelings haven't changed."

"I loved that everything seemed solvable and measurable with time. But the destruction we created, Weaver . . . how do we measure that?"

He looks up at her, frowning. "We had a war to win."

"Can you defend it so easily?"

"I have to."

"Well, I can't. Who was it that said the world breaks everyone? Well, we broke the world. You and me and Anderson and Zinn and Fermi. Every single day, the earth teeters on the edge because of us."

"Darling." He lays his hand on hers.

"Don't touch me." She hisses the words and notes how his mouth quivers.

"Rosalind . . . I have to touch you. All I think about is touching you."

"I hate you, Weaver." She was so intent on staying calm, neutral, cold, but her voice is full of venom.

"You have every reason to hate me," he says. "Don't think I don't know it." He shakes his head. He looks distressed. "But I will do whatever it takes to make it up to you. We're here.

We're together. We're going to talk this out."
His lips are pale. Time seems to have eroded the
certainty he once exuded. Perhaps certainty is
something only young people possess. "As for the
bomb, it's not that I don't recognize the power of
what we wrought. But it's done. Behind us."

"It's in front of us all. And now that the
Russians have the bomb"—does she see him
wince?—"the end can't be far away."

"No, you're overstating it. And you know it."
He slugs down more Scotch. "They're working
on using nuclear power in positive ways now.
That was your passion. You need to be part of
that."

"Even if I were able to forgive science for what
we created—after that report you wrote, who'd
hire me?"

Weaver rubs his forehead, doesn't look at her.
"You have no idea how sorry I am," he says.

"It **was** you." No one in the lab would admit
it, but she'd been sure Weaver had instigated her
firing. Fermi was out of town, but after a damning report was written about her instability, even
Fermi couldn't have saved her. Weaver reaches
out and touches her hair tenderly, fondly. He
tucks a strand behind her ear.

"I told you not to touch me."

"You have no idea what I feel for you . . ."

His words are washed away by her ire. "You

wrote that report. Who else knew what I was going through?" She remembers it far too well, the tumbling blocks of her life: First she lost her father; then she lost Weaver; for a while she lost her mind; and then her job. It all crashed down. And her love for science, already battered by the bomb, collapsed in on itself.

"You're a born physicist, Roz. You can start again . . ." She expects she's going to laugh sarcastically, but instead, she hears herself make an ugly sobbing sound. A wet intake of breath and a hiccup. It rises uncontrollably, like a wave of nausea. Damn. Why did she agree to see him? Why did she listen to Szydlo?

"I'd do anything to make it right," he says, his usually round voice a rough whisper. "I can make it up to you if you'll let me."

She stares at him. Could this man really be sharing secrets with the Soviets? The Soviets who seem to have little respect for liberty or even life itself. The Soviets who have tucked their people behind an Iron Curtain of lies.

"Why have you come back now?"

He blinks. "There are reasons I can't explain quite yet. But if you can't forgive me, I don't know what I'm going to do." He laces his fingers into hers, and for a moment she lets him. His touch sings on her skin. She's had just enough Scotch by now to welcome the gorgeous familiarity of it. He leans forward and kisses her, gently at first. His lips are hot. Not warm, but flaming, as though he has a fever. My God, the taste of his kisses, the feel of him as he pulls her toward him. Desire engulfs her and she lets out a stricken moan as he kisses her deeply. **Weaver!** Then, setting both hands on his shoulders, she shoves him away with more force than she knew she possessed.

"Roz . . ."

"Go!"

"I know you love me as much as I love you," he says. With his left hand, he gently, purposely caresses her neck before hooking her necklace around his finger. When he lifts it, the little platinum-and-gold box swings free. "You still wear it."

But even with the Scotch in her, even though his touch still thrills her, she tugs the pendant from his hand and stands.

"Please. Please go."

"Roz . . . I love you. We're meant to be together." How easy would it be to let the overwhelming swirl of desire suck her down past reluctance. But she's aware he's both the siren and the unforgiving undertow. And she's no longer a girl willing to drown.

She moves to the shelf in the entrance and picks up his fedora. "Go," she says again. "And don't expect me to ever see you again." With a wounded look in his eyes, he takes the hat. At the door he turns. "I'll keep coming back," he says. "I won't let this go."

"And I'll keep saying no."

"Then I'll die trying."

CHAPTER SIX

In school, Rosalind learned the word "atom" comes from the Greek, meaning "indivisible." Once, the atom was the smallest particle known to man, and therefore it was thought impossible to divide. Her adult life has been defined by splitting an atom. But if she ever falls in love again, she wants her love to be like the ancient Greeks believed an atom to be: unbreakable. It would take a special sort of man, perhaps one that doesn't exist. The alternative is to be alone the rest of her life.

She's mired in this dark thought when Charles Szydlo steps up to her counter the next morning. Removing his hat, he holds it to his chest as though saying the Pledge of Allegiance.

"Can I help you?" she asks without looking up.

"How did it go with Weaver?"

"Not here," she says. She hardly slept all night. Her sheets might as well have been studded with broken glass. Too large a part of her mourns the loss of who she once was. Weaver's visit brought it all back: her love of science, her lapsed membership in a rarified boys' club. It wasn't until Weaver left that she recalled she'd invited him over in the first place because he said he had something he had to tell her. Something that couldn't be spoken on a telephone. Something she imagined Szydlo would want to know. She, with the perfect memory, had forgotten. She, who was going to expose all his secrets and then put him out with the garbage, didn't ask a single question of him.

Instead, he'd evoked an almost uncontrollable wave of desire in her, which now leaves her shamed. It's the agent's damn fault. She would never have been curious enough to see Weaver if not for Szydlo's urging.

Pulling out a tray of rings, she turns them one at a time until they sit just right.

"You saw him last night," he says.

"I said not here."

"No one can hear us."

"Not here." She glances up just long enough to see Szydlo's insistent blue eyes. Pulling out another tray—this one of necklaces—she straightens the chains on the black velvet, recalling how Weaver caressed her neck as he lifted the chain to prove she still loved him. Szydlo sets his hat on the counter and reaches out with his good hand to still her wrist.

"I think you'd better tell me what's going on. Look at me, Miss Porter."

His touch seems presumptuous. What makes him think he has the right to lay his hand on her?

"I don't want to do this," she says.

"Do what? Talk to me?"

"I don't want to see Weaver again. I don't want to spy on him. I don't want to report in to you. And I never agreed I would . . ." She feels an angry pressure behind her eyes. "I'm **not** going to see him again."

"Did Weaver hurt you? Please tell me what's going on." He's still confining her wrist. At the same time, he looks worried.

Her supervisor, Adele, walks by and says, "Can I help you, sir?"

He yanks his hand away. Adele must think he's some beau and they're having a lovers' spat.

"She's helping me find a gift for my sister," he says.

Adele stands there, unconvinced, guarding her employee. Agent Szydlo stares silently at the tray of necklaces and Rosalind squirms. How will she end this discussion?

"I think she'd like that one," Charlie says, pointing to a golden locket etched with a swallow, studded with seed pearls. Rosalind lifts the locket and drops it into his large hand.

She takes a deep breath. "It's beautiful," she says, trying to steady her voice. "I've always loved this one."

"It **is** beautiful." He deftly turns the piece over with his fingers and actually seems interested in it. "It's the bird that caught my eye . . . My mother used to embroider bluebirds on everything," he says. "It reminded her of the old country." His mouth softens with the memory.

Rosalind feels Adele's eyes watching.

"What country was she from?"

"Poland."

Trying to keep her voice true, she says, "In Victorian jewelry, a swallow represents the hope that someone will return, as swallows do."

"That would have been so appropriate," he says. "Although, my mother didn't live to see me return from the war." His voice is soft and sad.

"I'm sorry . . ."

"Is it expensive?"

She turns the tag over. "It's thirty-five dollars. A lovely gift for your sister."

He looks up at her, smiles nervously. If Adele weren't nearby, she'd give him an out and say, **I know it's a lot. Don't worry about it.**

"I'll take it."

She raises her eyebrows as if to say, **You sure?**

He nods. Adele turns and looks suspiciously at the two of them, then turns away again.

"If you can wait, I'll gift box it for you," Rosalind says.

"That would be helpful. I'm not much at wrapping . . ." No, of course, with one useful hand, he wouldn't be. Turning her back, Rosalind finds the appropriate-size green velvet box fitted with a card. She slides the chain into two cuts at the top of the card, presses it into the jewel box, then slips the velvet box into a Field's cardboard box and finishes with the signature gold ribbon.

He takes out that badly worn wallet of his, the corners squashed and polished and round. She spots the gleaming slice of badge in the middle. He sets the wallet on the counter so he can thumb out the bills with his good hand, spreading them like a hand of cards.

"Please take what you need," he says.

"I know your sister will love it," Rosalind says. She counts out the money, softened somehow by the fact that he needs help to pay.

"There you go." She drops three coins into his hand. He pockets them, puts away the wallet, lifts the box, and tries once again to catch her eye.

"Thank you," he says.

Adele, who's been behind the counter pretending to straighten the display on the wall, turns to watch him go.

"Tell your boyfriend we don't allow any fraternizing during business hours. And certainly no quarreling. And just because he bought something—"

"He's not my boyfriend," she says. "I have no idea who he is."

※ ※ ※

Charlie frets. What on earth has set Rosalind Porter off? Is it because Weaver was injurious or because he was loving? He doesn't consider himself very good at reading women. Once he actually believed he was one of the few men who understood the opposite sex. Back before the war, when he loved Linda Dubicki, everything he did got the reaction he longed for. How cocky he was then. Other girls were openly interested in him. But just being in the same room as Linda made him quiver. A round blond goddess whose throaty laugh was all the music he'd ever craved. She smelled of autumn leaves and limeade and flowers all at once. When he leaned her against the brick wall outside the gym for a kiss, her body yielded and her lips opened to the press of his mouth like a rose in the heat of June.

He sighs now, recalling the thrill of it. Evenings in the Dubicki basement were a pass to wonderland. Nothing in his Catholic upbringing had intimated that life contained such pleasures. She got off work at Kaminski's Bakery early on Friday afternoons and took the train down to Champaign nearly every weekend while he was in college. Because she stayed with her prim cousin, they made love in empty classrooms, in dark cornfields. He came home from their night of cornfield love with a cricket in his underwear and mosquito bites all over his backside.

Birth control was frowned upon in their Catholic neighborhood, though condoms were quietly hidden behind counters for those who didn't believe. Nevertheless, when he was home in the summers, Charlie went blocks beyond the neighborhood to buy the forbidden necessities because he knew if he'd picked them up at Lisowski's or Jagoda's, his mother would have heard all about it by the end of the day. She declared Linda flighty, silly, not good enough for her son. It was the one time he openly ignored her. He loved Linda and was certain that they would be devoted to each other forever. When he returned from the war, he discovered the truth. His years as a POW had constructed a house of scar tissue around his heart. And as soon as Linda took one look at his hand, she nailed shut its only door.

⊫ ⊫ ⊫

After closing hours, Rosalind spots Agent Szydlo waiting outside of Field's like he was the first day she noticed him. He steps in beside her and she wonders how to shake him off.

"You're not expecting **him,** are you?" he asks softly.

"No."

"Mind if I join you?"

"I'm walking to Lincoln Park."

"All that way?"

"The bus costs money."

"Not that much."

"More than I can toss away."

"What's in Lincoln Park?"

"A lecture." This lecture series is one of the few frail threads connecting Rosalind to science. All week, she's been looking forward to tonight's talk. She wishes she wasn't so tired.

She feels him staring at her. "What's the lecture?"

"Gravitational Time Dilation."

He shakes his head. "You're making that up, right?"

"Einstein made it up. I didn't have to."

"Time can dilate?"

"It runs slower where gravity is the strongest."

"Gee, seriously?"

"It's not a joke. The lecture's about how they're structuring the latest experiment to prove it."

"So science **does** still matter to you?"

She glances at his long, thoughtful face and frowns. "Why did you think it didn't?"

"Because you don't seem to want to work as a physicist anymore."

"Oh." The words sting.

"Passion for something's a gift," Szydlo says. "A person shouldn't throw it away."

She opens her mouth, falters. "I didn't think I was going to get a lecture on the way to my lecture. Why do you even care what I do?"

She watches as he draws his injured hand even closer to his ribs.

"I read Fermi's evaluations of you up until you lost your job. I can't imagine a more positive acknowledgment of someone's brilliance."

"Oh . . ." She's sorry she spoke to him harshly.

"Why is a girl like you selling jewelry?"

"I have bills to pay."

"Couldn't you get another job at a university or lab somewhere? With your background . . ."

"After Weaver's report?"

"Have you tried?"

It's a question she asks herself nearly every night. Why doesn't she at least try? What's stopping her?

She shrugs.

"That was a dirty trick," he says. "Weaver reporting you as mentally unstable, getting you fired."

Szydlo must be trying to stir her up—to make her say yes. It's not hard. Her anger at Weaver is right on the surface.

"He was a rat."

"But why let him win?"

His question is so apt it knocks the air out of her. She's pondered it so many times: What's keeping her from science? Part of it is the horror of what all their elegant theories wrought, where it's put the world. The rest is so much more complicated . . . so much more personal. She knows she needs to understand it, hack her way through what's impeding her.

"Tell me what you love about physics. I know nothing about it." She turns to see his eyes are patient, curious.

"Well, I love that it's utterly reliable. That you can actually trust that the laws of the universe won't fail you."

"Unlike people?"

She looks over at him, surprised. "Exactly."

"I should have been a physicist," he says. That makes her smile. "Go on. Tell me more," he says.

"With the laws of the universe, if something surprises you, it's because there's a hidden law at play, one that begs you to discover it," she says. "My faith in physics is probably as close as I come to having a religion."

Has she ever said it out loud? Physics is the opposite of her father, the opposite of Weaver. People lie, turn their backs, break your heart. Even before Weaver hurt her, she knew she trusted physics more than she trusted him.

"Listen, Rosalind," he says. "May I call you Rosalind?"

"I guess."

"You can call me Charlie. I'd like you to."

She glances at him and then quickly looks away. "Okay."

"Listen, when I came by Field's today, you seemed upset. Did Weaver hurt you last night?"

"It depends what you mean by hurt . . ."

"You tell me. I'm not savvy about these things."

"What things?"

"Men and women . . ." She notes the concern in his eyes. "Did he hurt you?" he asks again.

"Not the way you mean."

Hearing their feet marking out a rhythm on the pavement together, she can tell he's taking shorter steps to match hers. "Then, in what way?"

She shakes her head, can't think how to explain it. "It was hard to be with him."

"Because you hate him so much?"

She hears her own voice come out small and bewildered. "Because I love him too much."

"Oh." Does Charlie sound disappointed? Or is she disappointed in herself? Despite how much she hates what Weaver's done to her, how much she should loathe him, after she pushed him out the door last night, she felt gut punched, left with an ineffable longing. She loathes that he still has power over her.

"How did he seem to you?" he asks.

"Like himself. Only older. Thinner. Maybe more nervous."

"Nervous about what?"

She shrugs.

"He said he had something to tell you . . . something he couldn't say on the phone."

"We had a drink. He didn't tell me anything. He was just trying to . . . soften me up, you know?"

Szydlo says in a pointed voice, "And did he succeed?"

She expels a sound that's somewhere between a laugh and a huff.

"What?" he asks.

"In the movies, a girl would slap a fellow for the way you asked that question."

"Sorry. It **did** seem like he wanted to tell you something."

"Well, he didn't." She hears how terse and angry she sounds. But his questions aren't wrong. Why didn't she find out what Weaver wanted to tell her? Why did she lose her bearings the moment Weaver stepped into her apartment?

"Look, Rosalind." Szydlo's voice is kind. "I'm sure it will take time for the man to open up. He'll tell you more when he thinks you're close again, back together."

"Back together? I haven't told you I'll do this. I haven't agreed to anything."

"No." His voice is even, patient. "You're right.

You haven't agreed. I still hope you will, though, as hard as it might be—"

"You have no idea how hard that would be."

"You're right. I don't."

They don't speak for a while, but he lingers beside her. She can almost hear him thinking about what she's said. She wonders if he's planning to walk her all the way up to Lincoln Park.

"Did you tell him you don't want to see him anymore?" he asks after a while.

"Yes."

"Did he take you at your word?"

She pauses, then shakes her head.

"Good," he says.

"It's **not** good."

"Look. I know you still care for the guy despite yourself. And you're not a disloyal person, are you?"

"No."

"So I propose you take a little time to see what happens. And don't think about me. Or the FBI. Or what we want to know. Okay? You'll decide if you want to see him again. You'll decide if you want to learn more from him."

They walk for a while, Rosalind pondering what he said. Though she never asked for this assignment—spying on Weaver—the man still intrigues her as much as he repels her. Is it possible he's done awful things, is capable of future choices that could affect all the people passing them on the street? Everyone on this planet? She shivers.

"I don't want intimate details, you know," Charlie says. "What goes on between you and Weaver isn't my business. But you're the only one who can get answers. The only one he'll talk to. If you could just play it out, get him to open up . . . and see if he tells you anything important. Won't you try?"

She doesn't answer.

"Think about it. See how you feel when he calls again, because my bet is that he will."

He pulls a cream-colored card out of his breast pocket. "Call me day or night," he says. "On the front's my office number. If you hold the card, sorry, I'll write down my night number on the back." She takes the card and holds it in her palm so he can write on it with his one good hand. "When he says something meaningful— and I think he will—you'll want to reach me. Keep it with you, okay?"

"But even if I agree to see him again, if he really is involved in . . ." She stops at the word. "**Treason,** as you said, wouldn't my reporting to you be like sending him to the electric chair?" Even as she says it, she thinks if he's done what the FBI is suggesting, he deserves nothing less.

"If he cooperates, gives us other useful names,

he could get off easy. Have you heard about Klaus Fuchs, the man they arrested for passing atomic secrets?"

"Yes, of course." She's been reading all she can about the atom bomb and the Soviets, though every word hurts. The whole world is on edge because of something she helped create. It seems only right that she should monitor it.

"You probably know: Fuchs admitted his guilt. Gave us names. He's in jail. But because he's co-operating, he'll get off in a few years. Rosalind, you're a person who sees the difference between right and wrong. I also sense you're a woman who has the courage to stop a wrong. You know Weaver and his pals are working on a hydrogen bomb hundreds of times more powerful than the A-bomb."

"I don't have clearance anymore," she says.

"C'mon. You know it. We all know. The **Chicago Tribune** knows it. Maybe you can't stop the Russians from having the A-bomb. But what if you could stop Weaver from sharing H-bomb secrets?"

"Didn't Fuchs say someone's already passed those secrets?"

"No. He heard secondhand someone was in place to share those secrets. What if that person is Weaver? What if you could stop him?"

Rosalind turns to look at Agent Szydlo. She finds her own breath shallow. Her heart jangling.

"If the Russians succeed first, it could be the end of the line. Chicago . . . poof," Charlie says. He makes a gesture with his hand clenched, then popped wide. "Weaver's someone who knows things. Someone who could give the Soviets the final clues to their puzzle. Would you want to be the woman who could have stopped millions of deaths but didn't **for personal reasons?**"

His words make her scalp prickle.

"Look," he says. "I don't blame you for not wanting to be part of this. I get that you're afraid to get involved with Weaver again. It will take courage on your part. But let me put it this way: What you decide today could actually change the fate of the world. How many times is a person given that sort of choice?"

CHAPTER SEVEN

Saturday, Weaver calls, asking if Rosalind would like to take the bus down to Grant Park.

"I know you don't want to see me. But there are things I need to tell you."

"Not today."

"See me one more time. After that, I've said my piece."

"I can't."

"Rosalind, I'm not giving up."

"Sorry. I can't today." Her instincts are to tell Weaver to never come within ten feet of her again. If it were just about her own needs or safety, she would. Especially after what happened last night at the lecture. She had chosen a seat in the last row, praying she wouldn't run into anyone from the project, and her heart sank when Sam Stone chose the same row two seats down. She tried to be invisible, to shrink back in her chair. She hadn't seen him for three years, hoped he wouldn't recognize her. But halfway through the lecture, she felt him glancing over. Afterward, he grabbed her arm. "Oh, my dear Rosalind, so incredibly good to see you," he said with overly sympathetic eyes. "We still miss you. And talk about you. Worry about you, frankly—me and Hilberry and Agnew." Three years have passed and they're still worried. As though they expect to hear she's just been released from a mental institution. How foolish would she be to let Weaver back into her life after what he's done to her? Still, she was moved by what Agent Szydlo said, and concerned enough about what's going on behind the Iron Curtain to never want them to have another shred of information. She helped to make this horrible bomb. Isn't it her duty to stop the spread of something worse?

But her niece, Ava, is coming to spend the weekend. And it allows her, if just for a moment, to put Weaver off. Ava's visits are what Rosalind looks forward to most. Everyone sees Ava as the family miracle. After Louisa took Rosalind into their home, she expected to have a child or two of her own. She and Henry tried. But just like their mother, Louisa saw year after year pass with no pregnancy. She called her infertility the family curse. Her situation was even more unfair: At least their mother had had the pleasure of giving birth to Louisa before she faced a sea of barren years.

When Rosalind moved to a dorm in her senior year of college (it was very much Roz's choice to escape her sister), Louisa began to experience nausea, exhaustion. She was certain she had the same ovarian cancer that killed their mother. Even before she visited the doctor, she met with their lawyer and made up a will. Instead, the dyspepsia and fatigue turned out to be Ava making herself known. In six more months, an angel was born.

A few months after the birth, and having had three glasses of wine one night, Louisa told Rosalind, "After you moved in, I couldn't have a child of my own. Like a curse. Then you leave, and pop goes Ava. And the irony is she's a carbon copy of you! The Grimm Brothers couldn't have created a more twisted tale!"

Later Louisa demurred. "You knew I was joking, right?" If it **was** a joke, it certainly wasn't funny. But Rosalind couldn't help herself: She fell in love with baby Ava the minute she saw her. In these last few years, Ava's started staying with Roz often, mostly to give her mother a break. When they're together, alone, Ava complains about Louisa. "Mama's mad one minute. All lovey-dovey the next," she's reported. "What is **wrong** with her?" It's something that Rosalind has long wondered.

Happily, Rosalind and her niece are a love

match. Ordinary things, done together, feel lyrical: fixing grilled cheese sandwiches. Spending hours on Oak Street Beach erecting sand palaces, strolling the lakefront at dusk, counting sailboats. They paint each other's toenails birthday-cake pink. And do acrobatics. Roz lies on her back in the living room with her legs raised and bent, and Ava climbs up and flies like an airplane, so long-legged and free. So unmarked yet by wrong choices. Ava is the one thing in Roz's life she never questions, never regrets.

The buzzer sounds from the lobby and Roz's heart lifts.

"Send her up," she tells Moses, the weekend doorman.

"Your sister's coming too," Moses reports.

When she opens the door, Ava marches right in with her round patent leather suitcase.

"Hey, kiddo, drop it in the bedroom."

"I always do."

"Lou, this is a surprise!" Then Roz notes her sister's face. "What's the matter?"

"Henry and I just had the fight of the century. Never had anything like it before . . ." Her voice is shaky and reduced.

Henry can be grumpy, but he's always given Louisa a pass on things no one else would stomach. She's the wasp and he's the sleeping bear. She stings him and he rolls over with a grunt and goes back to sleep without even swatting a paw. Rosalind can't help wondering what's pushed him too far.

"Do you want to talk about it?"

"If we ever have some privacy."

"How 'bout you stay with us? Spend the day. We'll go to the beach or walk down Michigan Avenue. It will get your mind off things." All these years, she's longed to break the barrier between her and her sister but has never had a clue how.

Louisa shakes her head. "No. I just wanted to tell you."

Ava comes out of the bedroom wearing Roz's newest sprigged straw cap. A small fault in the straw, and Laura in Hats had given it to her for a steal. "Aren't I beautiful?" Ava asks.

"Glamorous beyond words," Rosalind says. Ava goes up to the hall mirror to view her new look, but Rosalind sees she's glancing at her mother while tilting the little hat back and forth.

"I've got to go," Louisa says. "Thanks for taking her."

"Call or join us. Anytime all weekend, okay?"

Louisa just shakes her head.

"Have fun," she tells Ava, her voice flat.

Ava stares at the door after she's gone.

"They're fighting." She lets out a deep breath. "Good thing I can spend the weekend with you, huh? Want to play Monopoly?"

"Go get the board." Rosalind keeps three of Ava's favorite board games under her bed. "And while you're there, put my hat back where you found it."

"But I'm so glamorous in it!" Ava says, blowing a kiss.

✳ ✳ ✳

Almost an hour into a scorching game, there's a knock at the door. Only other residents from the building knock without being announced by the doorman. Rosalind gets up from the floor and peeks through the keyhole, astonished to find Weaver. Her first instinct is to pretend she isn't there, press herself against the wall and wait until he's left, but she knows she can't do that in front of Ava.

He smiles nervously when she opens the door. "You'll have to forgive me," he says. "I had to come."

"How did you avoid the doorman?"

"He was helping someone get a cab. I marched right in." Of course. Feeling entitled gives a person power. He's wearing a crisp seersucker jacket, khaki pants, tan bucks, juggling an armful of carnations and lilies. He squeezes her arm as he steps by her into the apartment, though it wasn't her intention to let him in. How handsome he looks; how vulnerable she feels. Why does she **still** feel equal measures of furor and attraction for the man?

"Well, it's Ava, isn't it?" he asks, spotting the game in progress on the living room floor.

"Do I know you?" Ava asks.

"I'm Tom Weaver. The last time I saw you, you were in diapers."

"No. The last time you saw her, she was already reading," Roz says. "Do you remember Mr. Weaver?" she asks Ava. She is trying to keep her voice steady. She is trying not to show her upset to Ava.

Weaver shifts the flowers into his other arm, crouches down, and holds out his hand to the girl who remains cross-legged by the game board.

"Hello again, Miss Ava," he says.

She takes his hand and glances at her aunt with a confused frown.

He straightens and heads for the kitchen as though it's the most natural thing a visitor might do. "You still have that blue glass vase in the first cupboard?" It comes back to her how he pronounces "vase" to rhyme with "Roz." And how he always takes over. She hears him puttering in the kitchen, cutting and snipping and adding water. Ava continues to shoot her questioning glances. Feeling her cheeks coloring, she wonders how she can explain to her niece why Weaver's here when she isn't even sure herself.

Emerging with a charming arrangement, he

looks pleased and sets it on the coffee table in the living room. In the old days, he often bought her flowers and arranged them. That was the thing about Weaver: He was highly capable in all sorts of unexpected ways.

"How would you girls like to go down to Grant Park and maybe the Art Institute?" he asks. **I propose you take a little time to see what happens,** Charlie told her. **And don't think about me. Or the FBI. Or what we want to know.** Is she strong enough to let Weaver back into her life without allowing him to trample her?

"I love the Art Institute," Ava says. "And Grant Park."

"It's warm," Weaver says, "but there's a great breeze."

"Can we go, Rozzie?"

"What about Monopoly?"

"We can get back to it later. Right?"

Rosalind looks from one to the other. Both of them have their eyebrows raised. What will Lou say if Ava tells her the hated Weaver, of all people, took them on a pleasure trip down to Grant Park? On the other hand, she imagines Charlie Szydlo nodding with encouragement.

"Please," Weaver says, coming up to her. "It would mean more to me than you know. Just this once?"

"Just this once," she repeats. At least Ava will

be there as a buffer. But why has Weaver ambushed her? This man who may or may not be selling secrets to the Russians. What's so critical?

As they head for the door, she notes him eyeing her. His handsome features are frayed; he looks diminished somehow. Yet, he's smiling and still far too attractive.

"Let's go, ladies!" he says.

⚖ ⚖ ⚖

Grant Park is full of families enjoying the cooling trees and the breeze off the lake. At Buckingham Fountain, Ava asks for three pennies and makes three separate wishes, which she refuses to reveal. Then Weaver takes a half dollar out of his pocket.

"A penny won't do the trick for this wish," he pointedly tells her. He turns his back to the fountain and, closing his eyes, tosses the coin over his shoulder. It lands with a loud splash. "Had to be the left shoulder or it wouldn't come true," he says.

"What?" Ava gasps. "You didn't tell me **that**!" Her pennies are gone.

"I think that rule only applies to me. But just in case . . ." He fishes out three more pennies and drops them into her hand. She flings them over her left shoulder one at a time, each with a great sense of import.

"C'mon, Rozzie, aren't you going to make a wish?"

Rosalind used to wish something bad would happen to Weaver. Now that she has the power to make it come true, she shakes her head, darkened by his closeness, his humanness.

When they pass an ill-dressed, unwashed man rattling a can of pennies, Weaver pulls a five-dollar bill out of his pocket.

"How you doin', buddy?" he asks.

"Lots better now," the man says, astonished by the bill, which he folds into his pocket.

"Here's to good luck," Weaver says.

"Why'd you give him so much money?" Ava asks when they're far enough away that the man can't hear. "My mother says bums should get jobs."

"The way I see it," Weaver says, "with rotten luck, any of us could be that man. Sometimes a fellow can't find a job. Sometimes he's sick."

"You gave him five dollars. Are you rich?"

He stops and smiles. Rosalind can see Ava surprises, maybe even charms him.

"I'm richer being with you and your aunt Roz today. The richest I've been in a long, long while," he says.

He buys them Popsicles from a man with a cart. Both Weaver and Ava choose turquoise.

"What flavor do you think this **really** is?" she asks him.

"Blueberry?" he suggests.

"I think it tastes like the sky."

They sit on a bench side by side, Ava between them, kicking her long legs. Rosalind notices her observing Weaver, smiling. Apparently, he charms her, too. Rosalind, on the other hand, keeps wondering how she ended up in Grant Park with the one man she least wants to see. He's always gotten what he wanted. But she can't help being surprised at his new kindness. And how he makes Ava smile.

∿ ∿ ∿

The Art Institute is surprisingly quiet for a Saturday. A few grandmotherly types in potato-sack dresses. One large family. Perhaps it's too beautiful a day to be inside. Instead of climbing the grand staircase to the skylit rooms of Impressionist paintings, Weaver leads them down to the lower level first.

"What's down here?" Ava asks Weaver.

"Ever seen the Thorne Rooms?"

"I don't know."

"You have," Rosalind says. "The dollhouse-size rooms?"

"Oh, those!"

Roz took Ava to see the rooms three or four years ago. Now her niece's patience and interest will surely have grown. Roz has always loved these perfectly scaled miniatures of rooms throughout history. They're not just dollhouse cute, but breathtakingly exact tableaux of other eras, with glimpses out doors and windows to gardens and streets beyond. So intricate, so authentic. Lit as though real sun is shimmering through glass windows. Rosalind feels she could step into each scene, sit on the perfectly upholstered sofa beneath a crystal chandelier, drink from the teacup waiting on the table, gaze at the intricate decorative plaster ceiling, and rest her feet on an Aubusson rug.

"They're so dreamy," Ava squeals.

The English hall from the Tudor era. The chic California breezeway from 1935. Roz loves them all.

"It's like going on a trip, don't you think?" Roz asks Ava.

"Even better."

"Come here, Ava," Weaver says. He holds out his hand to help her niece up onto the riser built so children can have a better view. "Who do you think takes a bath in this grand room?" The placard reads, FRENCH BATHROOM AND BOUDOIR OF THE REVOLUTIONARY PERIOD, 1793–1804. An oval stone bathtub is sunken into the floor of the room, decorated with lions' heads and brass chains. The room is lit with candle sconces. A stone fireplace is there to warm a bather.

"A princess," she posits.

"A French princess," he tells her.

"Her name is Ermine Gina," she declares grandly.

"What a perfect name for a princess."

"She's so beautiful, men faint when they see her," Ava whispers. "One right after another." Weaver beams at Rosalind. Rosalind can't help but think that soon poor Ermine Gina will surely meet the guillotine.

◉ ◉ ◉

By the time they've investigated every Thorne Room, seen the Impressionists, and stepped out of the museum, the sky has deepened to gray flannel. At the edge of the horizon Rosalind observes flickering lights, and a moment later comes the distant gurgle of thunder.

"Hungry?" Weaver asks.

"I am!" Ava says. Roz has been moved by his interest in Ava. She's begun to think he really is a different man than she once knew. Is it possible he's truly sorry for betraying her? That something seismic has magically changed him or led him to regret his choices? It would have to be magic, because she doubts people are capable of real change. **If I let him in, I've got to remember it's only for the FBI. Only to do the right thing.**

"See there down the street?" he says. "Tin

Sing. They have wonderful egg rolls. And egg foo yong. Do you like Chinese, Ava?"

"Is Chinese food all made of eggs? I never tried any," she says.

He laughs. "I don't even think there are eggs in egg rolls. Not sure why they call it that."

Fat yellow taxis glide up and down Michigan Avenue. A breeze has picked up off the lake. It will rain for certain, which will hopefully dispel the heat. In front of them, a little girl is licking an ice cream cone. She's leaving sticky chocolate dots all along the sidewalk. Roz is doing her best not to step in them. In her heels, she stumbles into Weaver.

"Steady there, girl," he says taking her arm.

"Steady theah, gel," Ava repeats in his English accent, giggling. She grabs Rosalind's other arm. Together they cross the street.

A complex red Chinese cornice announces the entrance to Tin Sing. The neon sign in the window blinks: BEST CHOW MEIN. It's just five, but patrons are already dining. The hostess seats them at a table near the window, just behind the neon sign.

"What a pretty family," she says as she hands them their menus, bowing.

"Thank you," Ava says, trying not to laugh.

Weaver looks at them both warmly. "I agree. We are a lovely family."

Ava says, "Thank you, **Father**!" and then turns

to Rosalind to whisper, "Do you know where the ladies' room is, **Mother**?"

Rosalind points to a sign in the back, which spells out the word "Restroom" in faux Chinese letters.

"You want me to come?"

"No!"

Roz watches her walk away, poised and self-certain.

"She's wonderful," Weaver says.

"I think so."

"In her, I see you as a little girl."

"I was never so full of life."

"You won't persuade me of that."

He takes her hand and kisses it. She doesn't draw away. She can smell his shaving soap, his warm, masculine aroma she once knew so well.

"Give me a chance," he whispers, pressing her hand to his cheek. "That's all I'm asking. I love you so. Just being with you again is everything to me."

Her heart hurts as though it's filling with too much blood, too much life, after being asleep for years. Did he ever tell her he loved her like this in the past? Can she even for a moment trust it?

"Can you say what you need to tell me?" she asks.

He shakes his head. "Not now," he says. "We need time alone for that."

"Can't you just give me an idea of what it is?"

He shakes his head. "I promise. Next time we're alone." Next time. Each time he sees her, he assumes there's a next time.

The waiter brings a pot of tea. The sky flickers. The thunder draws nearer. Ava comes back and sits with a contented sigh. Just then, rain begins to pelt the window. It's a glorious sound. They're inside, together. The hot tea is grassy and calming. Weaver starts telling a story of a dog he had when he was a boy, imitating his father's Yorkshire accent. By the time the meal comes, he's imitating the dog's facial expressions. Ava is laughing so hard she can hardly eat. Roz feels Weaver's leg pressing against hers. She could move away from him but doesn't. **He is a drug.** Still, the joy of Ava's hilarity, the tenderness when his eyes rest momentarily on her face, are richer and more rewarding than anything she's felt in a long, long time.

When Weaver drops them at her front door (with Frank now on duty, glowering at him), he kisses Ava's hand and tells her it's been a pleasure spending time with her. He kisses Rosalind's lips and whispers, "Thank you, my love."

Ava has a tired, happy expression on her face as they ride the elevator up to the apartment.

"Mr. Weaver is so nice. Isn't he your old boyfriend? The one my mommy doesn't like?"

Rosalind nods. "She doesn't trust him because once, he broke my heart."

She unlocks the door, cranks open the windows. The rain has cleared. The breeze is soft.

"In the movies people are always breaking each other's hearts, then making up and living happily ever after," Ava says. "Maybe you and Weaver could too . . ."

"We've had a long day, dolly. Time for your bath."

"Someday, I'd like to find a man just like Weaver. We'll eat sky-blue Popsicles. And maybe by then . . . by then, we can live together on the moon. You could visit us. You could even live with us."

"You're sweet," Rosalind says. "And I appreciate the invitation. But grown people need lives of their own."

"You should marry Mr. Weaver, and you can both come live with us—in a **separate** moon house," Ava says, looking like she's solved an impenetrable mystery. "I can be your bridesmaid. I'm very good at holding bouquets." She smiles a perfect, puckish smile.

"Darling, if I'm planning to marry Weaver, you'll be the first to know."

CHAPTER EIGHT

Sunday, in his good suit and tie, Charlie walks to mass with Peggy and her family. Peggy couldn't be happier if he'd handed her a gallon bottle of Chanel No. 5.

"I've been praying for this," she tells him, kissing his cheek. She's a picture. Freckled and coiffed, her caramel-colored hair tucked under a navy hat. The golden locket he bought her at Field's gleaming. As they near St. Mary's, there's a parade of people on the sidewalk heading toward the church. When the rest of the family is ahead of them, Mack slaps Charlie on the back.

"Old man, you **were** my hero. How'd you let Peg whip you back into being an altar boy? You're breaking my heart."

"You think I'm making a mistake coming to church?"

"I think if you get hit by a bus tomorrow, you may get a free pass to heaven. But that's not where the fun girls are."

Charlie considered two options this morning after a night of no sleep: heading to the gun range in Bridgeport, which, surprisingly, is open on Sundays, or going to church. Church is closer and opens earlier, and it's probably unwise for a man with no sleep to handle a firearm. He's hoping he'll find a moment of peace beneath the vast arches of St. Mary's, in the liturgical music, in the old rituals of childhood, if not with Jesus or God. He's still on the outs with them.

It's just that ever since Friday evening he can't shake a feeling of unease about Rosalind Porter. He feels guilty for what he's pushing her into. He can tell Weaver represents a real threat to her. But is that really what's haunting him?

His tie feels too tight—Peggy ties all his ties. They wait in his closet, hanging like a row of nooses. Once he has one around his neck, he wiggles the knot up with his good hand. The system works except when he slides the knot too high. He's never been able to loosen his tie without ruining the knot. He runs his finger around his collar because, damn, it's warm today.

In front of him, his niece and nephew are dressed like miniature adults. Stevie in a suit with long pants, Cindy with white gloves, white anklets. Both in hats. By the time they reach the church, Stevie doffs his, revealing that his mop of red hair has darkened with perspiration. Cindy hands hers to Peg.

The church is huge but already filling. Thank heavens the cavernous ceiling is keeping the room cool. Charlie picks out old classmates across the aisle. And Peggy's friends, too. A few look startled to see him. Some wave. Three of his old teachers, all nuns, are in attendance together. They nod as they see him, with serious, cautioning lips pressed. They look the same as they did fifteen, twenty years ago. Childlike and sexless. And then coming up the aisle he spots Linda Dubicki, a baby on her shoulder, a toddler trailing behind her. Linda. He should have known she'd be here. She's pregnant. Her face is so painted she doesn't look like the same girl. He takes a deep breath, closes his eyes for a moment. And when he opens them, he sees her husband, his old classmate, Stash Majewski, scuttling up the aisle, trying to control the toddler who keeps veering off one way or another. Stash has grown a beer belly and hasn't had time to shave. His suit no longer fits. The seams along the arms are threatening to pop their stitches. He looks exhausted.

"Oh, for heaven's sake, Stash. Hurry up," Linda snarls from the pew. "If it weren't for you, we wouldn't be late to begin with."

Maybe Charlie should believe in God. Because

there but for the grace of his grotesque hand goes he.

※ ※ ※

Father Janowski hasn't changed since Charlie saw him four years ago. His hollow face and skeletal fingers terrify children. Ichabod Crane with a high, chirping voice. Peg made Charlie go see him when he got back from the war. Father spent a lot of time worrying over Charlie's crisis of faith, yet never once asked him what happened during his captivity, nor what happened to his hand. One time when Charlie tried to tell him about how people around him were beaten or beheaded for the most minimal infractions, and how his hand was destroyed, Father Janowski was so uncomfortable, he jumped up and said another parishioner was waiting to see him.

The mass begins in its droning way. Lack of sleep and Latin are a potent brew. Twice, Mack has to elbow Charlie in the ribs. Charlie once read if you can't stay awake, you should bite your tongue. He bites too hard, releasing the dirty-penny tang of blood. His biggest fear is that if he falls asleep, he'll wake with a nightmare, shout out, embarrass his family. It's cruel how a man who's been to war has to relive the suffering long after the actual torment has stopped.

To keep himself awake, he glances over at

Linda. He has more than once characterized losing her as an amputation. The pain of what she did to him after the war burns like his hand when he tries to sleep at night, yet when he actually touches the injured skin, he experiences no sensation. Similarly, when he glances at Linda now, pregnant, her lipstick a bright pomegranate red, he feels nothing whatsoever.

⫴ ⫴ ⫴

Linda was worried but supportive when Charlie's mother insisted he enlist. Everyone knew the draft was coming and America would join the war by the end of the year. Poland needed defending. "You're a smart boy, Charlie," his mother said. "You could save Polish lives."

"A guy has to think about his duty to the world, doesn't he?" Linda whispered to him later. "I guess it's part of being a man." Charlie was flattered that she thought of him as a man. Her soft smile told him she'd be proud of him in a uniform, proud that he'd go bravely forward to defend the old country that held a place in their hearts. He looks back now, remembering his naivete with bitterness.

The letters Linda sent him while he was in training could have made a stone blush. It was a wonder the censors didn't pocket her confessions. But the letters that stick with him now are the tamer, sweeter ones. They sketched out dreams that Charlie and Linda shared: a brick suburban house with a glider on the back porch and a garage for a family-size Chevrolet. Two children: a tall, sincere boy like him; a girl as blond and pretty as her.

"You go overseas, my love. Our children are waiting . . . ," she wrote.

Then, instead of being sent to Europe to defend Poland, he was shipped to Corregidor, a Philippine island at the entrance of Manila Bay. Hot, disease-ridden. Lined up like target practice, every airplane in the Philippines was blown to bits the day Pearl Harbor was bombed. The few tanks that were available were so new, no one really knew how to operate them. And not enough food had arrived to keep the troops in full rations. Underfed, badly armed, sick with dysentery, Americans and Filipinos were soon forced to surrender to the enemy. In the Japanese culture, surrender is the ultimate shame. Death is preferable.

Beaten, starved, humiliated at every turn, the captives were sent to a hellhole called Camp O'Donnell. Charlie was lucky he'd been stationed on Corregidor. Those stationed on the Bataan Peninsula arrived after a nine-day march with no food or water. Thousands fell along the way. Of those who survived, many died in their first few hours at O'Donnell.

Charlie lived. But each day made him wonder why. After months in the Philippines, he and a few hundred more were loaded onto a rickety ship to Japan. Surely, they thought, the camps in Japan would be better.

As soon as they arrived, they were stripped naked, their filthy khakis and shoes thrown into a burning pile. Creatures in white suits, hoods, and masks sprayed them with noxious fumes to kill the lice. They were handed pajama-like gray prisoner clothing made for five-foot-six men. The pants came to just below Charlie's knees. The shirt could hardly be buttoned. The strange black canvas shoes had an insert between the big toe and the next and were closed in the back with two eyelets. Charlie had to tear the fronts open entirely to force them onto his size fourteen feet. "Giant. Freak!" one Japanese guard spat at him in surprisingly good English. Since there were no soles under the front half of his feet, he wrapped his toes in layer after layer of burlap torn from the bags that had held the shoes. In their new uniforms, the prisoners were loaded onto a train headed to a town high in the mountains.

It's raining when the train stops. Ice-cold rain spatters from matte skies the color of nickels, stinging their skin, running into their eyes. Herded with bamboo sticks, they're force-marched down a mile-long slope so muddy, it

sucks the canvas shoes from their feet. Charlie loses the burlap that covered his toes, turns around, and grabs it before it's trampled. It's nearly dusk by the time they arrive at the river where the camp is located. The buildings are so new, they ooze pine tar. There's bark on the wood and spaces between the slats. Forced to stand in the yard, Charlie tries to keep his body from shaking by conjuring images of hot showers, hot cocoa, Linda's arms. His toes throb in the biting air. Even the oppressive heat of the Philippines would be preferable to this bitter cold. The commander steps up to a jerry-built podium looking cozy in his heavy wool coat, a fur-adorned hat. He barks, "Japan win. We eternal sun. You, American light bulb. You die. We laugh. You die. We laugh!" One of the guards is moving down the row of men, randomly striking out with a bamboo stick. Charlie's height and his exposed legs must call to him. The bamboo lashes into one unprotected calf, then sears the other.

"You die!" the guard yells up at Charlie's face. "You die! We laugh!" Charlie feels a rivulet of blood coursing down his right ankle. More blood down his left. I'm okay, he thinks. Just cuts. And then as the long bamboo bludgeon cracks down on his neck beneath his left ear, a sensation flares: a shot of flame, a jolt

of electricity. Crumpling to his knees, he sees black, then red, then gold.

"You die," the guard says. "We laugh." Can he have come all this way on a tin boat, vomiting and praying, only to die his first few hours in Japan? He covers his head, waiting for the next blow.

⊯ ⊯ ⊯

Charlie blinks and glances around the church, tries to settle his racing heart. Has he made a noise? Called attention to himself? Something, for Peg grabs his hand, looks at him with a worried expression. Jesus. But no one else is staring. Thank God. Only she heard. His lungs hurt. Sometimes when he detours down these dark corridors, he forgets to breathe. Now he sucks in air like a parched man guzzling water. Peggy squeezes his hand. **I'm alive,** he thinks. Father Janowski is beginning his homily. It won't be long until they can go home. Thank God.

The homily is about the third commandment, "Remember the Sabbath day, to keep it holy." Janowski starts quietly, about how they are all here to celebrate the Sabbath, here in the benevolent arms of St. Mary's. Charlie's relaxing. He feels better. St. Mary's, the church where he sat between his mother and father every single Sunday. Beautiful St. Mary's. Where he felt safe and part of a community. "But what happens if you don't come regularly?" Father Janowski squeaks. "What happens if you think there are better things to do on a Sunday? What happens when you turn your back on the Lord week after week after **week**?" As Janowski's voice grows shrill, Charlie realizes Father is staring at **him.** When he looks around—is it madness?—the whole congregation has turned its gaze his way. Including Linda, whose bright red lips are smiling sympathetically, but Charlie looks away.

"Sin is fed by laxity!" Father says. "We are meant to worship God with a special effort on Sunday. When we don't, we lose our way. We die inside. Our hearts grow empty and we have little to give. Maybe **nothing** to give!" Charlie has nothing to give. All he wants to do is leave and never come back.

When the service is at last over, longing for air, for escape, he hurriedly follows Peg and Mack down the aisle. But before he can reach the door, he's accosted by Linda Dubicki. She's once again holding her little boy. The kid's nose is snotty; he's drooling and rubbing it on the shoulder of her pink dress. Her face is swollen, probably from the heat and her pregnancy, her neck and chest flushed. Where is the girl he once loved under all that makeup?

"I can't believe you're here, Charlie," she says.

He takes a breath. "Neither can I." Each word costs him.

"How's saving the world going?" she asks.

He shrugs.

"How's motherhood?" he asks. He wants to leave. He never wants to see her again.

"Well, take a look," she says. One child is pulling on her; the little one is playing with the mucus he's smeared on her dress. "It's no picnic."

"Gotta go catch up with Peg," he says, walking away.

"Please, Charlie, wait," she calls after him. He has no choice but to answer her.

"Yeah?"

She runs up to him. "I can't stop thinking of when we were together," she whispers. He keeps moving, but she follows urgently, child in her arms, toddler attached to her skirt. She leans uncomfortably close. He can smell her talcum powder, or is it the baby's? "The way you touched me, Charlie. I think of that . . . all the time."

"Yeah. Those days when I had both hands, Linda. Those were **great** days." The bitterness in his voice embarrasses him. She blinks uncomfortably, shifts the baby to her other shoulder. He would never have said it if he hadn't been overtired.

"I wish things were different," she says. "If only I hadn't . . . I should never have said what I did."

"Yeah? You got that right."

He can't believe she's telling him this in church, people all around. He heads for the door.

"Charlie!" she calls.

What the hell does she want? This time, he ignores her. His mother would have boxed his ears for being rude, even to Linda, whom she abhorred. Still, it's a relief to put space between them. Why on earth did he come?

Later, Mack asks as they walk home, "What did Dubicki want? The way she was eyeing you all through the service, it looked like she wanted to screw you on the floor of the church."

"Yeah, something like that."

"Imagine how excited Father Janowski would have been," Mack says. He imitates Janowski's shrill voice perfectly. "Lord on high, come down and smite these two sinners!"

◆ ◆ ◆

Charlie knows Peg's going to start making lunch. She's tying on her apron. He should help. Set the table or something. But he's too tired. Feels almost sick. He goes down to his apartment. His head hurts and he can't get Linda Dubicki's face out of his mind. Or the thoughts of Mitsushima that came to him in church. He touches his neck, tracing the scar with his finger, and sits for a moment, reminding himself he's okay. He's alive.

He gets out of his church clothes—what a fool he was to go—and finds chinos and a T-shirt. Picking up the new **Charlie Parker with Strings** album, he sets it on the record player. Lying on the bed, he feels as empty as a beggar's purse, letting the sweet buzz of Parker's sax wash over him. Images of Rosalind Porter come to his tired brain. Sure, since Friday, he's worried about what he's gotten her into. But a man shouldn't lie to himself. Something about Rosalind Porter gets to him. Her rare brew of brilliance and veiled vulnerability and, yes, even the anger.

She's the first woman he's been drawn to since Linda. Of all people, the one person he shouldn't be interested in. He lets out a puff of air, closes his eyes. He whispers her name to the strains of Charlie Parker's sax. "Rosalind."

Peg calls down the basement stairs.

"We have company for lunch, Charlie. Come see who it is!"

Oh man. He'll be forced to talk, put on a smile. He sighs and gets up with a curse, shoves his feet into his shoes, turns off the jazz. He dutifully climbs the steps because Peg doesn't ask much of him. In the kitchen stands Peg's high school friend Sondra Becker. She waved at him in church, twittering her gloved hand in a child-like way. A widow since the war, she's a secretary for a lawyer. Peg's always trying to set Sondra up with some fellow or another. The woman's not unattractive. But Peg has been puzzled why no one seems to ask her out a second time.

"Charlie." Sondra holds out her hand in a formal way. She's neatly dressed, her pale hair curled, a barrette with a bow holding it behind one ear. "I was delighted to see you in church today."

Sheesh. He nods. Peg glances at him with exasperation.

"I asked Sondra to join us. She and I never get a chance to chat."

He's not astonished that Peg's trying to shove them together but that she's never tried before. Or maybe she's been protecting Sondra from what Peg calls his "sullenness."

"Glad you could join us, Sondra," he says. There. His mother would be pleased.

The lunch goes fine until Peggy says, "That was my favorite homily of the year. An excellent idea for Father to remind us why we need to go to church every Sunday. The perfect homily for a certain person in this room," she says, eyeing Charlie.

But Sondra surprises him. "C'mon, Pegs, leave your brother alone. After Ted died in the war, I couldn't step into the church for over two years."

"I don't recall. Is that true?"

"I was sure that my prayers would keep him safe. Instead, he died alone, far from me, screaming in pain. I cursed God . . ." Her face clouds with the thought, and there's a vacuum of silence at the table. The children sit wide-eyed, staring at each other. Charlie wonders who told her he died in pain. Most officers would tell widows their husbands died instantly.

"That's when you need church the most, though, isn't it?" Peg asks.

"You might think so. But you can't know how hard it is to find faith again. You can't know if you've never been tested. Mack came back safe and sound."

Charlie nods a sort of thank-you at Sondra. She smiles back shyly.

"But you **did** come back to church, Sondra," Peggy says.

"I came back when I was ready," she says. "I still find it hard to locate my faith some days." Peggy winces. How is it that his sister has never discussed this with her friend? Would Peggy have spent so much time trying to find her a new man if she'd known?

After lunch, when Sondra's put on her hat and white gloves and said good-bye to everyone, even kissing Stevie, who wipes her kiss away as soon as she turns her back, Charlie surprises himself by following her out the door.

"Sondra," he says. "I just wondered if you'd . . . if you'd like to go out to dinner sometime."

She looks up at him sweetly. "Look. Don't feel like you have to ask me just because Peg's pushing me at you. I don't know why she feels like she needs to play Cupid."

"I especially **wouldn't** ask because Peg's pushing you at me," he says. "I'm asking because maybe . . . maybe we have something in common. I think we could be friends."

"Oh . . ." Her cheeks color. She smiles nervously. "Well then, I'd be honored to have dinner with you, Charlie."

"I'll call," he says.

"Terrific." She smiles warmly.

It would get his sister off his back, he thinks. And she seems nice enough. She wouldn't expect it to be a love match, just a friendship. He feels he made that clear. And maybe they do have something in common. Maybe he could learn something from her.

CHAPTER NINE

Sunday night, Zeke calls Rosalind.

"Where have you been?" she asks. "You don't know how many times I've called!"

"I got home from New York late Wednesday. Then Thursday, Little Mommy fell and broke her hip. She says she tripped on her mules. But I'm sure she tripped on too much bourbon. She's in Wesley Memorial."

"Why didn't you tell me?"

"Too exhausted by the time I came home every night, Bunny. Too mad at her to even discuss it."

"Aw, jeez. I know how she can be."

"You have no idea how good it is to talk to you."

There are few people in one's life that fit like an adjacent puzzle piece. Zeke and Rosalind have been locked together since they were eleven. As smart as he was when they first met, he was a lousy student. He'd sit in science class drawing elegant ladies in intricate dresses, looking up only now and then as if from a dream. Skinny, small-boned, with light red hair, he'd already begun to dress eccentrically, wearing a tricorn hat every day for a while, then an entire cowboy outfit with a metal belt buckle so heavy it almost pulled his trousers down, then yellow dungarees the color of yield signs. The other boys wanted nothing to do with him. They called him a "fruit" and a "fairy." Rosalind didn't even understand those epithets.

But it was clear that she and Zeke were both outcasts, both derided for what made them unique, and both unlikely to change. And they were happy to spend time together. At lunch hour, after they ate their sandwiches and emptied their tiny milk cartons, Zeke would draw dresses just for her. "This is what would look good on you, Bunny, a bow at the neckline to soften your long neck," he'd tell her. She liked that he had a nickname for her. She liked that he drew her with womanish curves, though she barely had any yet.

One afternoon in eighth grade, alone in the back of the library, Zeke whispered he had a terrible secret. And if he didn't reveal it to someone, he'd get sick. His voice vibrated like a guitar string, "I'm . . . I'm drawn . . . to boys."

"Drawn to them?" she asked. "I don't get it." She imagined two magnets in science class, flying toward each other and meeting with a **whomp!**

"When I dream of, you know, of **what adults do,** you know, **sex**"—she was shocked to hear the word; even Louisa called it "marital relations"— "it's boys . . . it's boys I imagine."

"You want to have . . . sex with boys?" Rosalind had just learned about sex and it was hard to believe. Her mother and father had done **that**? Henry and Louisa did **that**?

"You hate me now. I knew you would. I knew it!" He'd never looked so vulnerable.

"I could never hate you." But she was curious: What could boys possibly do with each other? What little she knew about sex, she was fairly clear that two boys weren't built for such things. Like two buttons and no buttonholes.

"You won't tell anyone, will you? You won't say I'm a **deviant**?"

"Your secret is my secret," she said. "Forever."

She'd been reading about atoms, and it struck her that Zeke railing against his desires was like an electron in a decaying orbital. Struggling would only radiate away his energy. Weaken him. Until, like that electron, he'd be drawn inexorably nearer and nearer to the atom's nucleus and be captured. She prayed that unlike that poor electron, his craving for boys wouldn't obliterate him.

Things have turned out far better than she feared. Today, Zeke is a photographer for the **Tribune**, covering street scenes and fashion shows. He's good at it and appreciated by his peers. He's managed to make a success of his uniqueness and she's proud of him. There are men in his life, but it's a secret world. He tells her but she never lets on to another soul.

"Is your mother going to be all right?" she asks.

"You know Little Mommy. The nurses will need a vacation by the time she leaves." Little Mommy is Lona Adams. A concert pianist for about six months in her twenties. Now in her late sixties, a widow, she chain-smokes Marlboros while playing "Rhapsody in Blue" on her full-size Steinway grand. Thank heavens Zeke avoided the draft because of asthma. His mother would have packed herself along for basic training.

Lona has more than once suggested that Zeke should marry Roz. "Why not, Ezekiel?" she's asked, expelling a mushroom cloud of smoke. "You love each other more than any two people in the world. Who's to know it's not **that** kind of love. It means you wouldn't each have to be"—she looks meaningfully into their eyes—"alone for the rest of your lives." Every time she says it, Roz feels suicidal.

"But here I am rattling on and on. What about you?" Zeke asks.

"You're not rattling on. You had important news."

"I'm sick of my news. Little Mommy doesn't deserve one more second of our time. What's yours?"

"Oh . . . well, there is **some** news for a change," she says.

"Spill."

"It might shake you up."

"Good. I'm starved for something juicy."

Rosalind's been so eager to tell Zeke about meeting the real Shadowman, but Charlie warned her to only say she's seeing Weaver again. "You never met me," he warned in the doughnut shop that day. "You can't tell him about the FBI." Still, she's thought about blue-eyed Charlie Szydlo a lot since the day he walked her up to Lincoln Park. She would love to discuss him with Zeke. About how she liked his questions about science and the way he matched his long stride to hers. A sad and complicated man who's asking her to do something more dangerous than he could possibly understand.

"Weaver's come back," she says. "I saw him once and told him I didn't want to see him again. Then yesterday, he just showed up at the door." She details Saturday's jaunt to Grant Park, the Art Institute, Weaver giving the beggar five dollars, the Chinese restaurant, the steaming tea, the words of love.

Zeke surprises her by saying, "Bunny, listen, this is the best thing that could possibly happen to you."

"What? You don't really think that!" Doesn't her best friend want to protect her from the man who smashed her life in two?

"Anyone can see," he says. His voice is patient and intimate. "You've been stalled for these last four years. Like an unhitched caboose left behind on the tracks."

"That's charming."

"Accurate. From what you said, he wants to make amends. Let him grovel. It will be excellent for your soul. But, listen, whatever you do, don't give yourself up to him entirely, okay? You have to be more self-protective. You're lousy at that. You realize it, right? You always have been."

∿ ∿ ∿

Zeke should know. Back when Weaver left Rosalind, the shock that he no longer loved her settled in her bones like lead. After that ridiculous night of drinking, instead of the hangover Frank predicted, she simply couldn't get out of bed. Her father's death in June had left her raw. After the bombings in Hiroshima and Nagasaki in August, she'd experienced a deep, scalding sadness. Now with the loss of Weaver, she was paralyzed.

Maybe it wouldn't have happened if all three things hadn't occurred within a year. There was plenty of warning that Dr. Joe had been failing. He'd started making no sense, couldn't end sentences. Admitted that he "lost time" sometimes. "I don't know what I did today," he told them at dinner one night.

"You mean you didn't do much?" Louisa asked.

"No, I mean I can't . . ." His face looked pinched, grew gray. "I simply can't tell you what I did." He actually cried then. Their father, who detested tears, wept in front of them.

Her father's physician said Dr. Joe had "hardening of the arteries." Rosalind imagined a snarl of sharp, impassable bramble in his brain, a briar patch of vessels where thoughts could no longer flow. Though he complained and argued about it, Louisa moved him into her house, to the room that had once been Rosalind's. The walls were still papered with pink ballerinas. Dr. Joe muttered, "Too many damn dancers." It was one of the more cogent things he uttered in those last few weeks before a final stroke felled him.

One morning, Louisa looked in on him and he'd turned a peaceful gray-blue. "Like the color of the sky before a rain," she told Rosalind. Rosalind could see that her sister was relieved. She'd been overwhelmed by the futility of nursing a dying man while trying to keep up with a five-year-old. "He never liked crying," Louisa said at his funeral. "So I have no intention of spoiling his funeral with unnecessary tears."

Rosalind, on the other hand, was taken aback to find herself devastated. Though Dr. Joe was her biological father, he'd been hardly more than a distant, critical grandfather. And like Louisa, he seemed uncomfortable with the idea of his daughter breaking down the walls of a woman's place. "Your mother would have stopped you had she been alive. You can bet on that," he once declared. But it was because their relationship hadn't been as close as she wished it could be that his death made her feel surprisingly cheated and sad. He'd consciously chosen to stay out of her life—her own father—and it made her feel unlovable. She once heard that the bereaved mourn more for people with whom things were left unsettled. And Rosalind saw it was true.

Two months later, when the bombs dropped on Hiroshima and Nagasaki, she was still feeling tender and in mourning. Now there were 150,000 more souls to grieve for. The way she saw it, she'd murdered at least a hundred thousand people in seconds. And sent fifty thousand more to their deaths via injury. At first, she wept and railed. All those years working on the Manhattan Project, she and many of the scientists she worked with had foolishly convinced themselves that the bombs they created were only going to be used as a threat, as leverage. Instead, their invention laid waste to lands and life—life for which she would be forever responsible.

So losing Weaver just six months after that should have been the least of her woes. And yet, his leaving—so abrupt and hateful—was loss on top of loss. The pain for her was physical: volts of electricity boring through her brain, acid burning through every artery. Zeke called again and again. She lay in bed, in the dark, not able to answer. The morning after the drinking, she'd called him to say Weaver had broken it off. But after that, she forgot about work, about eating. About bathing. About life.

She opened her eyes and Zeke was standing over her bed, his crew cut an orange corona in the lights seeping up from Lake Shore Drive.

"Bunny girl," he whispered. "Are you alive?" His eyes glistened with worry. Zeke was the one who had her key, who watered her plants when she was away and had promised to burn Weaver's letters if she should be hit by a bus.

She tried to speak. No words came out. Stroking her face cautiously, he whispered, "Are you paralyzed or something? Did you take pills? You wouldn't do that, would you?" She managed to shake her head just enough for him to see. Her mind was roiling with pain, hatred, despair.

"I swear to God, I'm going to kill that man," he said. He stood with his legs spread, his fists balled, like a gun-toting cowboy ready for a showdown. "Do you have the key to Weaver's apartment? I'm going to knife him in his sleep."

"No," she managed to utter. "It's not his fault."

"Not his fault? How do you figure? How dare he do this to you!"

"It was me," she said.

"What did **you** do?"

"I loved him too much."

"Oh Jesus. So he leaves you?"

"I didn't deserve him."

"Stop it. You need to be angry. You need to want to squash him, maim him, **eviscerate** him!"

His cheering for her anger hurt. She squeezed her eyes shut. What feelings might rise in her if she let them?

"When was the last time you got out of bed?"

"I don't know."

"Or eaten?"

"No food."

"Do you plan to die in this bed?"

"I hope so."

He telephoned her sister.

Louisa and Henry came over and packed a bag of her clothes, then, with some effort—she wouldn't dress, so they had to wrap a blanket around her to get her out the door—took her to their house, back to her childhood room, where Dr. Joe had died. "I'm in the exit room," she whispered to herself. "Soon I'll disappear too." Her sister telephoned Rosalind's office, now called the Institute for Nuclear Studies, and told them Rosalind had been diagnosed with pneumonia and was in the hospital. Zeke came at least every other night to visit. Sometimes he lay down in bed with Rosalind and held her in his arms. "I love you so," he told her. "Little Mommy's right. I'm afraid I'll never love a man as much as I love you."

But she no longer loved herself. Her father hadn't wanted her. Her passion for science had led her to take part in creating the ultimate destruction. Her lover had left her for someone surely better. Every time she stumbled into the bathroom—the only time she got up—she saw no one in the mirror.

Louisa persuaded their regular doctor, Dr. Stiegel, an old friend of their father's, to come over and talk to her. Stiegel was concerned. He contacted a well-known psychiatrist named Knaumann, who agreed to see her.

Rosalind fought Louisa when she made her dress for the appointment.

"I don't want to see anyone," she cried. Louisa buttoned her buttons, pulled a brush through her hair.

"You can't stay in bed the rest of your life," she said. "This man will help."

Rosalind remembers that Knaumann's office was coldly beautiful, very modern, and smelled richly of pipe smoke. He offered her fruit candies and a glass of water. He talked to her for an hour.

"And are you angry that your mother died?" he asked her. "Do you dream of suckling on her breast?"

"Of what?" She deemed the man seriously mad.

He asked intrusive questions about her sex life with Weaver.

"Do you feel shame for having given yourself to a man before marriage?" he asked.

"Do **you** feel shame for pretending to be a psychiatrist?" Roz countered. He didn't seem to know how to answer that.

"I think you're an unusually angry young lady," he declared.

"I'm angry at myself," she said.

"And yet you take it out on me." Knaumann wrote furiously on his yellow pad.

He recommended Louisa commit Rosalind to a sanatorium for a few months or even longer. But to Louisa, a sanatorium was a place of no return. She feared her sister would be warehoused and never get better. So she persuaded him to prescribe a gentle sedative and took Roz home.

Ever since she was in high school, Rosalind and Louisa had been at all-out war. Not only had Rosalind turned her back on the domestic training Louisa had been trying to force down her throat for years—she was hilariously bad at ironing and cooking and womanly chores—but when Rosalind began winning every academic prize, when she was encouraged to graduate high school two years early and start at the University of Chicago as the youngest girl to ever attend, Louisa was not encouraging.

Henry cheered her on. Zeke said he was proud to know such an egghead. But Louisa said, "Don't get all puffed up, missy. In the end, you'll be alone."

"I'm pursuing what interests me. I'm trying to be the best I can be."

"Maybe in college you'll find a husband," Louisa offered.

"That's not what I want!" Roz cried.

Henry instructed Roz to ignore it.

"That's not why I'm going to college," she insisted.

"Of course it's not," Henry agreed. "But you won't get anywhere arguing with Louisa." She and her sister became more estranged than ever. And after Ava was born and Louisa told Roz that she was the curse, there'd been little love lost.

But when Weaver left and Roz collapsed, tectonic plates shifted. Despite the fact that Louisa had a six-year-old at home, she took in her heartbroken sister and focused on her in a way she hadn't for years. With kindness, with sympathy. "It's time for Louisa's rest cure," she whispered.

Louisa drenched her little sister in a sweetness that Roz desperately craved, hugging her ten times a day, making all her favorite dishes, and spending hours talking to her not just about happy things, which most people would have done, but about sad things too. She asked about the horror Roz felt when the bombs dropped on Japan. She asked about what Weaver's betrayal meant to her. They talked about their father, both of them scoffing about how he hadn't really been loving or interested. Everything had to be focused on **him, his** career, **his** fame. These conversations were incredibly healing. Rosalind realizes now with some shame that never once during that time did she ask about Louisa. Or wonder about **her** needs. She could blame it on her raw, desperate state. But now, years later, she wishes she'd reciprocated, at least a little, at that very moment, when they were the closest.

In any case, Louisa could not have been a more intuitive healer. There were days she encouraged Roz's baser, angrier emotions. "Let's both curse at Father and the bomb and Weaver," she said one afternoon. They screamed. They called names. It was ludicrous. It was wonderful. Her sister understood her. Her sister **loved** her. She had never been sure. Miraculously, in time, Rosalind's grief began to lift.

Away from work for more than five weeks, Roz came back still shaky, alarmed at continuing to work on the dark side of atomic power, terrified of having to see Weaver. But she came back.

And it was all thanks to Louisa. Louisa loved her after all. Even if a quiet seed was planted: **Louisa loves me best when I've failed.**

∦ ∦ ∦

Still, she wasn't as sturdy as she needed to be. One afternoon in the hall, Roz ran into Weaver. He stopped in his tracks and his breath hitched. His lips paled visibly. "Roz," he whispered, giving off a cloud of unexpected despair. **He still loves me!** she thought. **He regrets leaving me!** She was certain. No one else was around and she stepped toward him.

"Weaver," she whispered. And then, in a way that sent ice through her veins, he turned away from her.

"Please," he said. "Don't speak to me. Don't ever speak to me again." He went back the way he'd come, sending her into a torrent of weeping in the ladies' room. And that wasn't even the worst moment. There was the day she encountered the woman he left her for.

∦ ∦ ∦

It was an afternoon a few weeks later. She was stepping out to catch her bus when she glimpsed Weaver by the side of the building, standing with a striking lady. High-heeled and statuesque, the woman was urbane and exotic. Her dark hair was parted in the middle and pulled back to either side. Her eyes were as black and impenetrable as obsidian—birds' eyes. She was an olive-skinned, glamorous Wallis Simpson, the woman whom King Edward VIII had abdicated his crown for. (How many times had movies in her teen years begun with newsreels of the American woman for whom the king had given up his crown?) This woman, too, was icy and imperious. She was also older than Roz had expected. In her midforties. Maybe even fifty. Her lids were lined like an Egyptian's and she smoked a cigarette in a long green holder. This was the woman he'd chosen over her. How pale a bookish little scientist must have seemed in comparison.

The deflation was dizzying. Rosalind spun like a pricked balloon. She let the bus go without her, hid herself behind the edge of the building, close enough to register every detail of her elegant rival. The pearl button earrings, the tripled gold chain around the sinewy neck, which disappeared into her shirt in a louche, inviting way. The woman grabbed Weaver's arm with bloodred fingernails. "We must go, Thomas," she said in an accent. A French accent. He'd fallen for a woman who must have reminded him of his late wife. Weaver went off like a man on a leash. Rosalind had never had that sort of purchase over him. Later, a colleague told her they'd married. Her name was

Clemence. A name as smooth as cream sherry on one's tongue.

⬥ ⬥ ⬥

In a few weeks, Rosalind's job was gone. A report had been written that suggested she was emotionally unstable. An unbalanced person should **not** have top secret clearance, should not be working with nuclear materials, it stated, or know anything about the government's intentions or resources. They didn't say who wrote the report, but Weaver was the only person at the lab who was aware she was undone by her involvement with the bomb and suffered from bouts of darkness. He was the only one who could have guessed why she "got sick" the day after he broke her heart. Fermi had taken his family to Los Alamos and was no longer there to speak up for his student. All in a matter of weeks, she lost not only the man she loved, but her career too.

⬥ ⬥ ⬥

How she should despise Weaver. Yet, since Saturday, she's incessantly replayed that moment in the Chinese restaurant with rain streaking the window, tea steaming in her cup, Weaver animated and joking, and Ava laughing. That moment of crystalline joy has hooked itself into her heart. Tuesday night, she's agreed to meet him at the Bon Ton on State Street, their favorite restaurant during the war. He's promised this time he'll tell her something that will change her mind.

I'm doing this for the FBI, she reminds herself again and again as she walks to the Bon Ton. Still, when Weaver arrives and smiles at her across the room, she is racked by a jolt of feeling. Sitting across the table from each other, they're quiet. He takes her hand, looks at her as though trying to find meaning in her face. How nervous she feels. Her stomach tight, a light ache moving up the sides of her forehead. She's relieved when he orders them both a Scotch.

After a few sips, she says, "Did you see the headlines today—Korea?"

He nods and pulls the **Tribune** from the outside pocket of his briefcase. Together they stare at the oxymoronic words.

Yanks to Raid North Korea. Truman: We're Not at War.

"The most absurd part is here." Rosalind points to a note at the bottom of the page. "Full-Page **War** Map of Korea in Color."

He laughs. "Yes, it should read, 'Full-Page **Not-at-War** Map.'"

"I can't bear another war," she says.

"Who can?"

"They won't drop our bomb, will they?"

"I hope not, love. I hope they never drop that damn bomb again." It's the first time he's ever said anything like this to her. "Besides," he says, "the Russians have their own bomb now. Maybe because of that, no A-bombs will drop. Perhaps it's best, this balance." Is it because of Weaver that "this balance" exists? The concept makes her shiver.

"I keep asking myself, how did they learn to build their bomb?" She watches him.

"I don't know," he says. "They have good scientists." He doesn't look uncomfortable. Yet his eyes grow imperceptibly distant.

"It had to be one of us who shared the information, though, don't you think?"

He shakes his head, takes a swig of his Scotch. Is it studied nonchalance she notes? "Impossible to know." He shrugs. "But if so, it could have been anyone. Fermi or Zinn, or the janitor who cleaned up after us in Los Alamos." He scratches his ear. "Still, is it really a bad thing?"

"Of **course** it is!"

"You think that because you read propaganda against the Russians."

"It's because they're heartless. Venal!"

"Are they? Maybe so. But once, they fought

Hitler just like we did. And not so long ago. I recall sitting right here talking about the Russians as our hope on the eastern front."

Looking around, she remembers the meals she and Weaver shared at the Bon Ton during the war. The old Hungarian violinist with a violent green kerchief around his neck who played mournful tunes. The debates, the longing. Chicken paprikash, Hungarian pastry even when food was being rationed. Life during the war felt fragile, and love was its only antidote. It hardly feels less tenuous now.

"I don't think I ever told you this, but I was a Communist once," Weaver says softly now. "Back at Cambridge. It's funny, but when the Brits were vetting me, it never came up . . ."

She glances up sharply. "You were a Communist?"

"A lot of us were. I was young and idealistic and believed that wealth should be shared."

"But to never own anything of your own. Even your job is controlled by the state. People lack freedom."

He laughs. "More propaganda."

"I hear the Russian people are scrambling to find decent food. And if you disagree with the government, you might be killed. What about freedom?"

"How free are Americans who have no jobs and no money?" he asks. "How free are Negroes who do the same work but aren't paid as well and aren't allowed to sit in restaurants in the South or use the same facilities? How free are the prostitutes who work the steel mills in Gary? I bet they don't feel free."

"Are there no prostitutes in the Soviet Union? Or does the government pay them?" she asks.

"I wouldn't know," he says. "Still, I choose to live here. I want to live here and die here. With you." His voice trails off. **With her?**

"I'm ready to hear what you promised you'd tell me." Even if Weaver reveals something, will she pass it on to Charlie? The thought almost stops her, but she needs to know for herself. What can Weaver tell her that could possibly absolve him of what he did to her? "The carrot-and-stick thing is getting old," she whispers.

"I know." He blows out a puff of air, shuts his eyes for a moment. "Listen . . . back in '46, when I broke it off with you, it wasn't my choice, Roz."

"I'm sorry?"

"I had to; that's what I wanted to say. I was **made** to leave you."

She sits there blinking.

"Even after the bomb, when you were so miserable, we loved each other, didn't we? I was committed to you. I would never have left unless I had to. You must have known it didn't feel right."

She thinks of the days she couldn't get out

of bed, the morning she was fired at the Institute and sent away with a guard humiliating her as he escorted her out the door. And he's claiming he didn't **choose** to leave her?

"But you married another woman," she says.

"I know that's how it **appeared.**"

"It didn't just look that way. You married her."

"Nothing you think you know about that is true," he insists.

It hurts to breathe as deeply as she needs to.

"Then explain it." Her voice is trembling with compressed ire.

"I was forced to be with her."

"Oh, for God's sake. How is that possible? Who forced you?" Her anger is a horse that won't respond to a sharp tug of the reins. She slugs down more Scotch and immediately chokes.

"You okay?" he asks. "Raise your hands. It gives your lungs more room to spasm."

"Shut up," she says, coughing, sputtering.

He looks upset. She tries to swallow some water but it doesn't help. The coughing is making her cry and she scrabbles in her purse for a hankie to wipe her tears.

"Roz, listen," he says after a while, when the gasping finally subsides. He leans forward, cups her cheek in his hand. "I got involved in something years ago like a fool, and I'm trying to free myself. It dictated everything I did for too many years. Including leaving you. But it won't go on much longer. I can't let it."

"This 'thing' you got involved in—does it have to do with the Russians?" There. She's said it aloud.

"I can't tell you anything more. Right now, it's dangerous for you to know even this much."

"Come on."

"I'm not joking. I will tell you. Just not until I'm freer . . . and then I'll tell you everything."

Charlie told her not to push Weaver. To give him time to open up. Can she believe a word he's said? If he is involved with the Russians, he insists he's trying to extricate himself. He wants no more. Can she have faith that any of it is true? She hates how much she longs to believe him. She hates how much she cares. Love can be so tenacious.

As they walk to her building after dinner, he gently takes her hand. Then grips it. She's with a man who may have sold atomic secrets to the Russians, who may have betrayed her country. The fact that he **says** he wants out—is that enough?

When they open the door to her apartment, she reaches for the light switch, but he stops her. "It's cooler in the dark," he says.

"Yes. And prettier."

Lake Shore Drive and the glow of the city are

wavering in the last of the day's heat like a mirage in the desert. The season has been a cornucopia of torrid days and shivery cold—a typical Chicago summer. Rosalind steps to the windows to open them farther. But as she cranks out the casements, Weaver comes up behind her, presses himself to her.

"God, I love you, you know." He models her body with his hands, his lips near her ear. His breath torn and desirous. "All I've ever wanted is you."

"Maybe you should leave and come back when you can tell me everything."

"No. There isn't time." His voice breaks.

"What? What are you saying?"

"Shhhh." Weaver nuzzles his face into her shoulder. His lips are dry and burning. Kissing her from her neck to her ear and back again, despite her clenched fists, her initial coolness, he sets off a sensation that sings from her lips to the nexus between her legs and sets loose a slippery, reckless desire.

"Let me in," he whispers. "Please, let's be together again."

It's been so long since she felt anything. The sudden craving is painful and gorgeous, a drug she's ravenous for. **Why not take this pleasure? Why can't a woman be the hungry one and use a man to satisfy her own needs?** She's surprised to find herself turning, kissing him. As he gently unbuttons her clothes, she reaches for the fastening of his trousers. Her entire body feels electrified. She wants this. She needs this.

"My Rosalind," he says. He pulls her close. His skin pressed to hers, the breadth of his chest against her naked breasts, his hands on her buttocks, all make her gasp. Nothing has felt this right for a long time. Pulling her down to the floor, he caresses her where she hasn't been touched by anyone but herself in years. She is consumed by the swirling pleasure and mad with longing as he stops to draw a condom packet from his discarded trousers. When he enters her, they both cry out. It doesn't take long for them to reach a crescendo: raucous, mutual, explosive. Afterward, his full weight pinning her to the carpet, she reflects on how Zeke warned her not to give herself away, and she smiles in the dark. **I did it for me. All for me.**

⚜ ⚜ ⚜

As a child Rosalind had little sense of herself as a physical being. They say children imitate the physicality of their mothers toward them and, by mirroring, learn to understand their own physical impact. While she is sure Louisa loved her, her sister far too often withheld love for even the smallest infraction. Roz recalls running to her sister for a hug and being pushed away, and then trying hard to remember what she'd done wrong. There were days Louisa hugged Rosalind and told her what a good girl she was. Then weeks where she was cool and distant.

So Rosalind soothed herself by living almost entirely in her own head. She liked blocks and numbers and puzzles. Solving was her savior, the best way to quietly soothe herself. In school, Rosalind was forced to play games and attend gym class. But she couldn't wait until these physical interludes were over and she could get back to **thinking,** at which she felt more adept.

In fifth grade, her young gym teacher, Miss Mann, took her aside.

"Rosalind, you're perfectly capable of hitting a baseball or doing the dance steps, but you won't try. You're graceful. You're strong. But you have your head in the clouds. What's stopping you?" Miss Mann asked.

The science teacher, Mr. Roberts, was waiting for Rosalind in the lab. She'd been looking forward to it all week. The faster Rosalind answered, the sooner she'd be able to don safety goggles, grab the Bunsen burner, and watch a ribbon of magnesium shoot blue-white flames.

"I just don't see how those things will make my life better," she said.

Miss Mann smiled.

"In fact, they'll do something for you that your math and science and essays will never do."

"What?" Roz asked. **How absurd,** she thought.

"I'm going to let you figure it out. It's an experiment. You have until two weeks from Friday to tell me your findings. Until then, every time you're in gym class, or doing anything physical, I want you to think about what it's giving you. I look forward to your discovery."

Because Miss Mann set it up as an experiment, Rosalind readily took on the challenge. She kept notes, paid attention, treated it like real research. She observed the rush of energy that flowed through her muscles after dance class, how swimming left her both exhausted and calmer. How she was even good at volleyball when she paid attention. Really good. It was a revelation.

On the indicated Friday, Miss Mann pulled her aside again. "Are you ready to tell me what you've discovered about exercise?"

"I found out lots of good things," she said and enumerated them. And then before she left the echoing gym, she asked, "Do I have to stop the experiment?"

That made the gym teacher laugh. Rosalind was one of Miss Mann's favorite students after that.

But it wasn't until Rosalind first made love to Weaver that she knew the exquisite extent to which her body could offer pleasure. Weaver woke her up to a physical incandescence she didn't know was possible, and it was a great part of what made losing him so unbearable. Now, lying beneath him on the living room floor, she is washed in the sweet exhaustion of her release. She's both wildly happy and terrified.

⁂

After a while Weaver gets up.

"I need a smoke," he says. Rosalind yanks the afghan off the sofa and covers her nakedness, pulls one of the sofa pillows down to raise her head. He lights and puffs on his cigarette for a moment. But even in the dusky light, she notices his hands are shaking. His mouth looks odd.

"You okay?" she asks.

"I should go," he says. "I would really like to stay, but I have a meeting in the morning. I'm sorry. This isn't me wanting to escape you, darling. Not at all."

She sits up and, wrapping the afghan tighter, watches him dress. Ducking into the bathroom, he comes back looking slick and handsome. The comb has drawn furrows into his dampened hair. His tie is perfect.

"Listen," he says. Settling down on the sofa near her, he straightens her bangs with his fingertips. "I know it's forward of me, but I stuck some condoms in the bedside drawer for future use. Are you offended?"

"No." Now that she's tasted from the well, she craves more. He must know it.

"Also, there's something I need to give you." He reaches into the breast pocket of his jacket and sets in her hand a small sealed manila envelope. In the half dark, she can just read *Rosalind Porter* penned across it in his perfect handwriting.

Her fingers identify something hard and odd-shaped beneath the manila skin.

"What is it?"

"A key."

"To your apartment?"

He shakes his head.

"To a safe-deposit box. Put it away. Somewhere you won't forget. If something happens to me, then you can open it. But not unless something happens. Promise."

"If something happens? What sort of something?"

"Just put it away and don't think about it, please."

"You ask a lot." She stares down at the tiny envelope. All that stands between her and something she wants to know is a wisp of golden paper and perhaps a ride on the bus to his bank. "Is this a test? To see if I can follow instructions?"

"I'll know if you open it. I always know when you're feeling guilty."

It used to be true. But he hasn't guessed anything about Szydlo. Maybe he doesn't have that power over her anymore.

"Where **is** your safe-deposit box anyway?"

"The information is inside. Put it somewhere you won't be thinking about it. Your own bank. Set up your own safe-deposit box."

"And when I finally open **yours,** what will I find?"

"A note from me to you. Not to be read unless I'm gone. And things I needed to put on paper. Things that need to be told. It will tell you what to do with the information."

"That's cryptic. Are you planning on leaving the country?"

"I'm not planning anything like that."

"But why all this spy stuff? Why not just hand me your precious note? Why put it in the bank?"

"Because if I make it hard enough, you'll actually wait until something happens to me. And no one should read this until then."

"Is something going to happen to you?"

"Look. Don't let anyone have this key. No one. Not unless it's time. My life depends on it."

He means it. Utterly. His eyes in the wisp of the Lake Shore Drive lights are the color of an oak barrel. And terrified.

"Jesus. Okay . . ."

"Swear it."

"I don't want to swear it."

"Swear it," he says, snatching the envelope from her hand.

She looks at his face. It's mapped with secrets.

"If you ever loved me, you'll keep this promise. This is not a joke. It's life and death."

"Okay," she says. "Give the envelope back."

"Do you swear it?"

"I swear it." He hands the envelope to her and she folds her fingers around it. It seems so small. So potent. A little bomb that practically pulses beneath her fingertips.

CHAPTER TEN

Charlie stands in the yard shivering. Snow is falling in flakes as fat as coat buttons. They whirl and land, then teeter and are picked up by the wind again. It's his third winter in Japan and the coldest yet. A daily desperation prickles and pains him, grows more undeniable with each dawn. Every day is an insult. But today will hurt more than usual. This afternoon, the men stand staring at Dr. Firth, the only camp doctor, his hands tied behind his back, bound to the flagpole. Firth is a kind man. A gentle man. And the camp's only source of medical care. Working without medications, without even bandages or real tools, he has done all he can to treat the injuries the Japanese inflict on the GIs every day. Men have been made to carry boxes with iconic red crosses emblazoned on them and the words "medical supplies" into the warehouse up by the train station. No one has ever seen those supplies again.

So, using torn rags, Firth's stanched their blood. With a cadged sewing needle, he's stitched their facial cuts. He's even cut off gangrenous toes as hygienically as he could in such unhygienic conditions, with boiled kitchen knives (and a guard watching, taking them away immediately), and managed to save lives.

Now Firth's eyes cannot hide a desperate gleam. There will be no one to stitch the doctor up. The rumor is that when one of the higher-ranked Japanese soldiers entered the infirmary this morning, Chin Scar, Old Glass Eye's assistant, was sitting in a chair. He had the good doctor on his knees in front of him, and Chin Scar's penis was in Dr. Firth's mouth. Everyone knows Chin Scar likes men because he feels free to touch the GIs in an intimate way and loves to whisper lascivious-sounding Japanese into their ears. He is partial to good-looking men. Dr. Firth, even half-starved, is a particularly handsome man. A married man who speaks often of his beautiful wife, his family. If he's been caught with Chin Scar, there's no doubt Chin Scar forced himself on the doctor. And yet it's Firth who will have to pay. Charlie has a sharp, roiling pain in his stomach. What will they do to Firth? Old Glass Eye comes out in front of the men with a particularly evil expression on his face.

"You watch," he says to the men. "You eyes closed, you die too." And then he makes a gesture for the GIs to step back. What the hell? From his back pants pocket, Old Glass Eye pulls a stick of dynamite, the kind they've been using at the dam site. With perverse showmanship, he waves the stick at the men. His eyes are glittering with delight. With menace. Two other guards come to either side of the doctor to force his mouth open. The doctor struggles, whipping his head from side to side. But in time, his mouth is pried opened enough that the stick of dynamite can be thrust to the back of his throat. Old Glass Eye moves it in and out in a lurid gesture. Jesus! God! Charlie, who's given up praying, starts to pray. The doctor gags and shakes his head, attempting to shove the TNT stick out of his mouth with his tongue. It's lodged too deeply, merely waggles from the machinations of his tongue. And then Old Glass Eye pulls out a book of matches with a flourish, lights the stick, and runs like hell.

Charlie can feel the excruciating power of the explosion. The pressure on his eyeballs. The warm, wet substance as it lands on his

face and hands and in his hair. Human flesh. The soul of a good man. "Noooooo!"

✳ ✳ ✳

Hyperventilating, he leaps from his bed as though it's on fire. As though he could outrun the black depths of his memory. Christ. He's at Peggy's and his screams could wake the neighborhood. **Firth. Poor Firth!**

He has no patience with his mind, which doesn't seem strong enough to climb out of its prison, which forces him to relive the worst moments again and again. Children are sleeping upstairs with stuffed animals. Children who've never known fear and who he hopes will never know it. He tells himself he's warm, dry, safe, healthy. He has a real bed. Real clothes. No lice. No beriberi. No more horrors. The horrors are behind him. He'd love to climb beneath the sheets again. But his wrinkled bed is a dangerous sea of fear and memories. A place a man could drown.

Instead, he brushes his teeth, slides on his shoes, dresses more warmly than he needs to for the temperature. Anything to stop the shivering. This late, two A.M., the sky outside his basement door is the flat gray of the Russian bullets Binder displays in his office. The streets echo; the air doesn't move. But at least he's a free man. It's an American sky. He needs to move. He needs to breathe. He needs to escape.

On North Avenue, the light from Kaminski's Bakery spills out onto the alleyway. Through the window, he can see clouds of flour. When Linda worked here, he used to kiss her neck and breathe in the wheaty smell. Every inch of this neighborhood is familiar. The world is recovering. "Everything's okay," he tells himself. "Keep breathing. Everything is okay."

Christ. He needs a drink. At North and Bell, the bar that his brother-in-law likes so much is still open, its neon sign flashing SZCZĘŚCIE into the night. Though it means "happiness," inside, Charlie can see men hunched drearily over the bar. No women. No one looking happy. Mack calls it "the Polish Boys' Club" and goes there when he needs company or someone to complain to. One of the bartenders, Jurek, is an old friend of Charlie's. Whenever Charlie comes, he makes him sit at the bar and insists on listing their high school pals from the most successful to the least successful. To Jurek, the most successful is Joey Gwozdek. His flat feet or asthma—Charlie can't recall which—kept him out of the war. After changing his name to Joey Gordon, he started a plumbing company that employs eight men and works in Rosalind's ritzy neighborhood.

The least successful, Cal Piatek, was an A student, always on the student council, played the clarinet. He was a friend to everyone, a most-likely-to-succeed type. After a war injury, he's now addicted to morphine. Charlie's spotted him a few times downtown, his eyes like windows covered in rime. Charlie can't help thinking, **That could be me.** He always feeds Cal's tin can with too many coins, though Cal never recognizes him.

Charlie's relieved that Jurek isn't at the bar tonight. He's in no mood to judge or rate. Still, as soon as he's smacked by the bitter stench of beer, he hears his name. At a table, with a pitcher all to himself and an ashtray overflowing with butts, is Stash Majewski, Linda Dubicki's husband.

"Hey, Charlie," Stash says, motioning him over.

"Stash."

"Join me. I'm three sheets to the wind and ready to entertain any guy who sits in that seat." He points to "that seat" with the burning end of his cigarette, and Charlie sits down dutifully. "George," he calls to the bartender. "Bring my pal Charlie a glass. You like beer, right?" he asks.

"Yes, thanks."

"I'm on a marathon drinking spree and it's better not to do it alone. You hear what they say, right? **Don't drink alone!**"

"Linda will have your hide," Charlie tells him.

"She's already got it. And my balls too. I'm counting how many beers I've had with peanuts. I finish a glass, I put one here. But I'm too

drunk to count 'em now. You count 'em for me?"
Charlie looks over at the rows of peanuts.

"You drank that many?"

Stash nods. "So how many? Give me a hint."
Charlie feels for him. A house full of babies and
bossy Linda to contend with.

"It's a number between fourteen and sixteen,"
Charlie says.

Stash's eyes cloud for a moment as he figures
furiously in his addled brain.

"Fifteen! Jesus."

"How you feeling, Stash?"

"How does it look like I'm feeling? I'm fucked."

"I meant, how's life?"

He expects him to complain about the babies,
his job, his income, Linda. Instead, he says, "My
wife—'n' I love her, fat backside and all—is in
love with you, you fuckin' asshole."

"C'mon, Stash. That's not true."

"No? Go ask her. She tells me every time I
screw her these days, she squeezes her eyes shut
and pretends it's you." Stash's face is growing
red. These are not the sorts of things a guy tells
another guy unless he's so drunk he won't remember in the morning. The bartender brings
Charlie a glass, and Stash, drunk as he is, ex-
pertly pours from the pitcher, leaving room for
the foam.

Pushing the glass toward Charlie, he says, "I
should kill you. I've thought of it."

"That will not win Linda's love," Charlie warns him. "And I'm not interested in your wife, in case you wondered."

"How could you not be? She's beautiful. So damn beautiful. And she gives head like a god-damn whore. You teach her that?"

"Man, you need to go home, now. How 'bout I walk you there?"

"She hates me. Says I'm an ugly slob. I'm not 'refined' like Charlie Szydlo." He spits the name with such hatred, it sends a splash of cold water down Charlie's spine.

"C'mon. It's late. Don't you have to work to-morrow? Let me walk you home."

"You wanna walk me home like a date? So romantic."

"Yeah. Just like a date, Stash. Let's go. You owe them money?"

"Nah. I got a tab."

Charlie's surprised how easily Stash agrees to leave his half-drunk pitcher, his abacus of pea-nuts, on the table. He stands, wobbles, sits, then stands again.

"Nice o' you to walk me home. You're a nice guy. You have Linda's cherry in your pocket? Like a good-luck charm?"

"The air will do you good," Charlie tells him. He directs Stash out the door, wondering if he'll be picking him up off the street any minute. God knows the guy's too big to hoist. Fortunately, he and Linda live not so far, on North Leavitt, in a little brick house whose windows and door need painting. It was Linda's aunt's until the old lady died. Charlie and Linda used to visit Aunt Lily there. She made them pierogies and **kolaczkis.** When he's walked by it, Charlie's noticed the Majewskis haven't done anything to modernize the house. But how could they afford to, with two children and another on the way?

Stash weaves, belches.

"See, I'm good," he says. "I don't show I'm drunk."

"You're doing fine," Charlie tells him.

"Why's Linda so crazy about you? You're too tall. Like a giraffe."

"I can see why you think so," Charlie tells him.

"I might kill you. You ever kill anyone?" he asks. "Shoot anyone?"

"In the war."

"But not in the FBI?"

"No."

"I never killed anyone in the war even," Stash says regretfully.

"Where were you?"

"England. I was gonna be sent to France or Germany any day. Wanted to be. Never happened."

"You were lucky."

"Nuh-uh."

"Trust me, you were." Charlie holds up his hand.

"Yeah. You and your fucking magic injured hand . . ."

"You should be glad about my hand. It's why Linda threw me over."

"What?"

"She couldn't bear to look at it."

"No. You dumped her."

"That wasn't the way it was."

"Yes. You broke her heart!"

"C'mon. Look. We're here." Charlie helps him climb the steep front steps. Stash stumbles and Charlie has to catch him, wrenching his shoulder. Damn. "You got your key?" he asks. Stash rifles around in his pants pocket and pulls out an oversize ring of them, chooses one.

Linda hasn't left the porch light on. A message for Stash, perhaps? Stash can't get the key into the lock. Charlie takes it and quickly sees the key Stash chose is an old-fashioned room key, too large for the lock. One by one, he tries the rest of the keys. Then the porch light comes roaring on, the door swings open, and Linda Dubicki is standing there in a pink nightgown.

"Special delivery," Charlie says, helping Stash over the threshold into the house. Lurching, he stumbles past Linda.

"Hello, honeybun," Stash says, then darts into

the dark of the hall in a way that tells Charlie he's running to puke in the bathroom.

"How did you end up with him?" she asks, unruffled. She smooths her hair from her face. She's so much prettier without makeup, softer, kinder-looking. Her breasts are swollen with pregnancy, her perfectly round belly beautiful and evident under her nightgown.

"I found him at Szczęście."

"Of course you did," she says. "It was nice of you to bring him home. I hope he wasn't too much trouble."

"I'm glad he made it all the way home. I was worried. Well, good night." He turns to head down the steps.

"Charlie, don't go. I need to tell you something."

"It's two thirty in the morning, Linda. Go look after Stash."

"He can look after himself. You think he doesn't come home like this every night?"

"I'm sorry."

"Please come in."

"I've got to be somewhere in the morning. We woke you up—"

"It will take two minutes. That's all."

He steps into her hall. She leads him to the living room. The furniture is modest. A gray sofa with pink pillows. A striped armchair. But other than the fact that there's a large toy fire truck just inside the door to the hall, it's neat and tidy. The colors are pleasing. Peggy, he's sure, would call them pretty. She directs him to sit on the sofa.

He looks at her, her face gentle and girlish. For the first time in years, he can see why he was drawn to her. Under all her ferocious flirting and too much makeup, here's the girl he recognizes, the one he once loved.

"Charlie," she says, looking up at him with her still-water-gray eyes, "I've been wanting to tell you . . ." She stops and looks at her hands. "During the war, while you were gone . . ." She pauses again, doesn't look up. He thinks she might be close to tears. He can't imagine what she'll say. What could possibly be so vital that she needs to tell him at this hour of the morning?

"During the war, I prayed every day, never gave up believing that God would save you and bring you home safe. Father Janowski and I prayed together—mornings, evenings. I lit a forest of candles. You're all I thought about."

His throat grows tight. "Well, thanks for that," he says, wondering what she's getting at.

"But when God brought you back, it wasn't you anymore. You barely spoke and you jumped at any noise and your eyes looked haunted. And what did you weigh, eighty pounds?"

"More by then, I'm sure." How vulnerable he was, like a skinned rabbit, certain at any moment he'd be beaten or shot dead. So weak from the aftermath of beriberi that he still had trouble walking. He's tried to erase those awful months of doubt and misery that she added to so cruelly.

"And your hand . . . I knew it would prevent us from doing the things **we** wanted. **Together.** It made me angry, Charlie. Angry at God. Angry at the church. Angry at everything I once believed in. I felt betrayed by my faith." She takes a deep breath, as though she's finally spilled what she's been holding inside too long. "I wasn't angry at you. I never meant to break up. I regret it every single day."

Charlie shakes his head. He remembers that after all those months at the VA hospital in California, he took the train to Chicago, dreaming of her, longing for her, then took a cab directly from Union Station to her house, not even caring what it cost. He thought she'd hold him and weep with joy. They'd kiss. They'd make plans again. It would be fine at last. Against all odds, he'd survived!

Instead when she opened the door and saw him for the first time, she gasped. "Charlie?" He reached out for her and she stepped back. The look on her face was shock, horror, incomprehension. "Can I get something for you?" she asked. "I have cookies."

"Just seeing you is all I need," he said. It seemed she couldn't look at his face, or wouldn't.

And then her eyes fixed on his hand. And when he asked her questions, she had so little to say. Her answers to his questions about her job and friends were monosyllabic.

She didn't ask him anything. She just stared. They'd always felt so at home with each other. Not anymore. Had she found someone else? The tension was painful. He rose.

"I should go home and see my dad," he said. "I should have gone there first."

"Yes. Since your mother . . . The whole neighborhood prayed for you to come home before she died. But you didn't." Did she blame him for that too? For allowing his mother to die without him? He couldn't wait to leave her. How conscious he was that he had to heft his oversize duffel with just one hand. He didn't try to kiss her at the door.

After that, for two weeks, she avoided him. All those loving, longing letters before his capture, more while he was in California at the VA hospital, and with him finally home, she made excuses not to see him. He slept a lot. He drank beer. He talked to his father. He was a man holding his breath. When she called and asked him to come over, he walked to her house, his throat aching with dread. She offered him coconut cake. She still wouldn't look at him as she fussed with the cake and the fork, poured him a glass of Coke.

He couldn't imagine how he'd swallow any of it. She sat down across from him. He left the cake on the table between them.

"See, the thing is," she said. "The thing is . . . I wonder." He could see she'd practiced the words before his arrival. A speech. A question.

"What do you wonder?"

He watched as her cheeks started to redden.

"I look at you and I know you couldn't even hold a baby in your arms or drive a car anymore. Not now. Everything's ruined for us. I think it's important we're honest about it."

It was as though she'd socked him in the stomach. He had no breath in his lungs. It took him a while to answer.

"They have knobs you can put on a steering wheel," he said in a weak, reedy voice. "I'm sure I could hold a baby in either arm . . . I . . . I could. It's not my arm that's the problem. It's my hand."

She licked her satin lips and focused on the wall behind him. "I don't think so. Look at you. You weigh nothing. You're like those photographs of those people they liberated from the German camps. Only you being so tall . . . it seems worse."

"I'm trying to eat. They said not to overdo it. I'll gain weight back. I'll get strong again. I'm getting better." Why did he have to defend himself to the woman he loved, the one who should have been his defender?

"It's more than that," Linda said. "It's that . . . well, forgive me, but I can't look at **it.** I can't bear to look at **it. It's** the most horrifying thing I've ever seen. How could they have done this to you?"

She stood and turned her back and started to weep. And like a dentist's drill hitting a nerve, her meaning became clear to him: His ruined hand repulsed her. Disgusted her. Offended her. Despite the pain, the years in captivity working on the dam with only one hand, the months of scar therapy in California, this was the first time Charlie felt utterly crippled. She said everything was ruined. What she meant was that **he** was ruined.

He got up, walked out of Linda's front door, and slammed it behind him. He felt drugged, dizzy, confused. The sides of his vision closed in. At the same time, the sun's rays were needles. Why was this happening? Why had the woman he thought loved him kicked him? Halfway home, he vomited in the bushes. At his house, he ran past his father in the living room and up the stairs to his bedroom, where he flung himself on the bed. It took him two days before he could bear to let anything pass his lips but water. Her words had poisoned him. He contemplated killing himself again and again after that.

And now she sits here and tells him it was all a mistake?

"You made me feel like a monster," he says.

"It's **me** that was a monster. I can't blame you for never forgiving me." Her cheeks are silvery with tears. Her lips tremble in silence. He's shocked that his first instinct is, indeed, forgiveness. He's overcome with the desire to slide his arms around her, comfort her. How soft and sweet she'd feel. He recalls the yielding swell of her breasts. How he loved to feel her pressed against his heart. But can he absolve her so easily? "God let me down," she says. "And I let you down. I need you to know I'm sorry. More than you know. I've been sorry every single day since . . . the things I said. The things I did."

"You could have come to apologize, or written."

"I called almost every day for weeks after. I realized how cruel I'd been, how wrong. Didn't your father tell you? He said you didn't want to see me ever again."

His father knew he was hurt and angry. He must have been protecting his only son. His father's gone now. As for Peggy, she's never said a nice word about Linda since.

"Why do you still go to church, if you're so angry your faith let you down?" Charlie asks.

"My relationship with Him these days . . . it's not great. I'm disappointed, but I haven't given up."

"No matter what the sisters told us in grade school, I've never thought the Lord has time to fulfill individual requests like tickets at the bakery."

"I know. But He's been screwing up all over. Look at all the Poles and Jews who died in the gas chambers . . . look at all the POWs that the Japanese beat to death or starved—like you. I keep asking myself, have Mary and all the saints and Jesus and God shrugged and said, 'Man's not worth saving. Let them go off and kill each other. Good riddance.' And now this conflict in Korea. They say it's not a war. But more fellows will die. And the Russians have the bomb. One day a city's there. The next day, it's not. People dying again and again for what?"

Charlie has had these very thoughts. They're what's put him off religion. Yet Linda keeps hoping, when he's simply stopped believing.

"Still," she says. "I look at you, and you overcame what happened. You're like you used to be before the war now. Or better. You got your law degree so you could join the FBI. And it's a great job. I know you must be good at it. I didn't stick by you long enough to see you recover. I was young and stupid. Charlie," she whispers. "I love you. You're the only man I've ever loved."

He's felt alone for so long. He feels unspeakably moved and doesn't say anything for a while. The silence pulses. The room seems to breathe.

"Well, don't go telling Stash," he says at last. "He loves you. You've got two kids together and this one." He points to the baby swelling beneath her breasts and then is drawn to reach out and lay his palm flat against it. He's never touched a pregnant belly before. It's incredibly hard. He's startled by the feeling of movement, a life inside.

"Did you feel that?" she asks.

He nods, his eyes wide.

"It's a miracle. Every life is a miracle," she whispers.

"Linda . . ."

"Do you feel nothing for me?" she whispers. "I just can't believe you feel nothing, when I feel so much for you . . ."

He doesn't speak, sorting what he might say. He removes his hand from her belly reluctantly.

"Because if you feel **something,** anything, I could just hold that close. I could think about it and not care that my life's a mess. I could have that little glimmer of happiness and go on." He looks at her, the silken tumble of her blond tresses, creamy throat, soft, pale eyes.

"You should go see to Stash," he says. "You're married to Stash."

"Please tell me you feel something."

He **does** feel something. He just doesn't know if it's pity or sadness or base desire or an inkling of love. And he doesn't think telling her about it would help anyone.

"You broke my heart, Linda. I sometimes think it doesn't work anymore, like a car that's been in a terrible accident. It's the part of me I haven't been able to repair. Look . . ." He gets up. "I do care about you and wish you were happier. I wish Stash was happier. I wish all wars would stop like they said they would when we dropped the bomb . . ." He touches her naked arm, recalls how much he once cherished her skin, the way she tasted, the way she shuddered when he gave her pleasure. But it all feels remote, impossible to claim as his own.

"Bless you, Charlie. I'll never stop loving you. I want you to know I'm sorry I hurt you. I'm sorry I lost you."

"Thank you for that."

She takes his face in her hands and kisses him, chastely, respectfully, but still, he feels her passion. For a brief moment he desperately wants her, relaxes his lips against hers and draws her in, taking in the yielding warmth of her sweet mouth.

Then he flees.

CHAPTER ELEVEN

In the morning, his head throbbing, Charlie takes the CB&Q train to the suburbs. Hemmings was supposed to drive but called at seven A.M. to beg off: He's got the flu. Charlie's been telling himself he's going to ask the Bureau to have a car modified for him so he can learn to drive again. A knob on the steering wheel as he once suggested to Linda. A lever to replace the shift so he can press it in either direction with his wrist. But every time he starts filling out the request, he stops. It sets him apart, shines a spotlight on his injury. Still, this morning he regrets he hasn't followed through.

Charlie glances down at Weaver's wife's address: **Clemence Weaver c/o Adeline Hodges. A friend who's putting her up?** he wonders. As soon as the train starts rocking, Charlie falls asleep and finds it hard to rouse himself to get off at his stop. Christ. He can't go without a good night's sleep much longer. He feels weak and disoriented.

Fortunately, the house he's looking for is only a few blocks from the Hinsdale station. A brick Victorian, set back from the road, sporting one of those crazy turrets with a pointy hat. The lady who owns it must be a gardener. Petunias are tumbling out of every possible crevice. Yellow roses are clutching the chimney wall. He climbs the stone porch steps and knocks. A woman with neat white hair opens the door.

"Yes?" She has one of those sweet Betty Crocker faces that leaves him tongue-tied.

"Ma'am, are you Adeline Hodges?"

"Yes . . ."

"And do you have a Clemence Weaver living here?" he asks.

"Well, yes."

"Is she in?"

"And who are you?"

Charlie displays his badge, introduces himself. He shakes her hand, having always felt that's the right thing to do: to treat people the way he was taught to treat fellow parishioners as a child.

"Well, to be honest," Mrs. Hodges says, "I'm relieved you're here. We've been worried about Mrs. Weaver."

"Have you?"

"She's paid for room and board but she hasn't

been down to dinner in a few days. I didn't want to be nosy or anything, but I checked her room this morning. Thinking, well, you know, she might be ill or need help. Come in, Mr. . . . what did you say your name is?"

"Szydlo."

"Mr. Szydlo. Now, what kind of name is that?"

"I think it may originally be Hungarian, but my family's Polish."

"Oh. I knew it was foreign." He doesn't usually tell that tale—the uncertainty of his family name—wonders why he's told her. To gain her trust? She ushers him into a hallway dizzy with browning wallpaper, a foxhunt pattern on it. The foxes look demented. Their eyes glow red. A dark wooden railing, complex and Gothic, leads upstairs.

"What did you find in her room?" he asks.

"See, that's what struck us as odd. Mrs. Weaver's things are all there. Even her purse. Her wallet too. I didn't mean to pry, but . . . I wanted to know if I should be worried. And her clothes are all just hanging there, like she's coming right back. But no one's seen her."

"May I take a look?"

"Surely."

"How long has she been here?"

"A year, I guess."

"You ever see her husband?"

Mrs. Hodges shakes her head. "No, sir. I guess he works somewhere else and they can't be together. But she told us she's married. She wears a wedding band. She showed me his photo once. A real handsome fellow."

"Has she had any visitors?"

"Not one. And she doesn't speak to the other guests much. Some people think she's snooty."

Mrs. Hodges leads him up the steps. The upstairs hall has the smell that old houses get when their roofs leak, but Clemence Weaver's room smells sweet. It's large and airier than he expects. The woodwork is painted white and the sun pours in on a rug figured with pink roses, on the iron bed, left unmade. Wiggling his hand into the oversize rubber glove he wears to examine a crime site, he throws back the sheets and coverlet. No blood. No unusual marks. Just the wrinkles made by a sleeping person. The closet is hung with little bags of something that smell just short of perfume, the source of the sweet smell. Lavender, that's what it is—the stuff Peggy hangs to keep the moths away. Long, slender dresses dangle from the rack; on the floor, high heels have fallen on their sides. Inside them are the imprints of Mrs. Weaver's feet. The top drawer of the heavy old chest sticks and he has to yank it. Silky lingerie explodes out, and he stuffs it back in. Elegant things that he's sure would feel like cream to his fingers without the glove. Nothing else. He shoves the drawer closed. The rest of the chest is filled with sweaters, scarves.

A dark red square purse sits atop the bedside table. Elegant. Expensive-looking. But no wallet inside. Instead, some folded cash in a silken pocket.

"Does she have other purses?" he asks.

"I'm not certain. A brown one too, I think." Charlie empties the purse entirely. Tucked into a different side pocket, he finds a French passport in a worn green leather case. When he opens it, the name on it isn't Clemence Weaver. It's Victoire Spenard. He takes in the photo, the long face, the darkened lips set in a haughty O, the eyes lined in makeup like an ancient Egyptian. This is the person Weaver married? He glances at her birth year: 1895. She's well over fifty years old. Does he even have the right woman? He turns to Mrs. Hodges, still standing in the doorway.

"Is this Mrs. Weaver?" he asks, displaying the photograph.

She nods. He'll have to show the photo to Rosalind. He thinks she said she saw Clemence Weaver once. Why would this woman have used an alias? Could she be a Soviet agent? Perhaps Weaver's wife is or was his handler? When he gets back to the office he'll look the name up. Victoire Spenard. With his one good hand and some effort, he slides the passport into one of the glassine evidence pouches he always carries and slips it into his jacket.

"Don't touch anything in this room," he warns Mrs. Hodges. "And especially don't clean. Lock it and keep the other guests out. If we don't find Mrs. Weaver, this room will be a crime scene."

"Yes. I was right, wasn't I? It's odd, isn't it?"

"Seems odd," he agrees.

"Do you think she was **murdered**?" she asks him with giddy horror.

"That's rarely the case," he tells her. "She may have left with a small case and a different purse."

He doesn't believe a word he's saying, because why wouldn't she have taken all the cash? And why wouldn't she have grabbed her passport—unless she has others with other names? Still, he needs to tell the landlady something to keep her from speculating with all her guests.

"I'll be back," he says.

"And you'll let me know if they find her, won't you? I won't sleep a wink."

"I'll let you know."

⸙ ⸙ ⸙

The next evening after work, Rosalind takes a piece of paper and a pen and sits at the small desk by the window where she pays her bills.

Dear Sirs,

I would like to inquire about a position at Argonne National Laboratory. As a student of Dr. Enrico Fermi and a scientist on the Manhattan Project, I have long believed in the peacetime potential of nuclear energy. I'm particularly intrigued by your work on light-water reactors.

She stops, stares at the page, notes that her hand is shaking. Should she write to Fermi first and ask him to intervene with Argonne? Would her old mentor welcome her reaching out to him? Or did he lose all faith in her when Weaver penned that report? Fermi never wrote or called after she was dismissed. True, he was at Los Alamos at the time. He had more important things on his mind. And as much as she adored him, he was often more interested in his own thoughts and theories than in people. "People are too volatile," he once said. What must he have thought about the report that most of all stressed her volatility?

She sets down her pen. Later. She'll tackle it later. Pacing, she realizes that she hasn't spoken to Louisa since last Saturday, the day Louisa had her knockdown fight with Henry. The day Roz and Ava and Weaver spent their beautiful after-noon together. Usually, she and Lou speak two, three times a week. Roz knows there's a benefit to this schism: Without the constant trickle of Louisa's carping, Rosalind feels more light-hearted. Still, she picks up the telephone. Her enthusiastic "Hi, Louisa!" meets a wall. "I've been wondering how things are with Henry. You know, after that tiff last weekend . . ."

"So you actually found time to think of us with **his nibs** lurking around."

"What?"

"Ava told me about Weaver."

"Oh."

"How could you see that man after what he did to you?"

"I didn't plan it. It just—"

"And with all hell breaking loose at our house."

"What do you mean?"

"I mean Henry's threatening to move out and get himself a room at the Allerton."

"He's joking, surely?"

"He doesn't think it's a joke. Do you?" Louisa's voice crumples chillingly.

"My God. Let me speak to him. You didn't think to call me?"

"I figured you were too busy with **Tom Weaver** to care."

"Of course I care."

"How can you see that man again? After all he did? Have you forgotten how we all had to pick up the pieces when he threw you away last time?"

Roz feels attacked and yet recognizes, almost immediately, that it's Louisa changing the subject so she doesn't have to talk about what hurts in her own life.

"I'll never forget that," Roz says. It's just like her sister to deflect, to push Roz away when she needs her most.

"And now he's charmed Ava too. I don't want my daughter being exposed to that louse."

"He seems to have changed, Louisa. But I understand why you're cynical. I'm cynical." She can hardly tell Louisa about the FBI. Since the night she made love with Weaver, she's ashamed how much she longs for him. Charlie Szydlo's become Rosalind's excuse for letting Weaver back into her life, and God knows, she needs one. "Tell me about Henry. What's happened?"

"He hates me."

"He doesn't hate you. Maybe he's just angry."

"He says he's had it with me. I know I'm not the easiest . . . I don't know what I'll do if he leaves. I haven't worked since the war. And there are no torpedo plants hiring at present."

"You could do all sorts of things. You're good with numbers. You could be a bookkeeper. Or work in management somewhere. You've got the experience."

"Women don't manage things anymore. Not since '45."

"But you **could.** And it's important to know Henry would give you and Ava money, no matter what. Couldn't you put him on the phone? Let me talk to him?"

"We're not speaking."

"Not even enough to wander in and tell him I want to speak to him?"

"No."

"C'mon, Lou."

"**No.**"

"Okay, I'm coming over there," Roz says.

"What? Now?"

"Yes. Right now. I'll grab the bus, be there in a half hour."

Louisa harrumphs before she hangs up.

All these years, Roz has wondered how Henry put up with Louisa. How he managed to ignore her sister at her most miserable. She recalls how he would sometimes turn to Roz when she was just a teenager and oh so subtly shake his head, his eyes glancing upward as if to say, **Your sister. We'll ignore what she just said, shall we?** Rosalind owes Louisa so much but finds it so hard to breach the trench that's been dug between them. She brushes her teeth, reapplies her lipstick, and grabs her purse. Still, she loves her family, and as small and odd as it is, they're all she has.

⁕ ⁕ ⁕

After getting a full report about school from Ava and a whispered diatribe about how really awful Henry can be from Louisa, Rosalind hugs her sister.

"Please, Lou," she says. "Hand out the olive branch. Let him know you wish to work things out at least. That's all Henry ever asks for."

"He's the one that should be handing out an olive branch, the son of a bitch." Louisa turns back to her dishes. But then Roz sees she's crying. "He's never loved me. Not really. I see that now. When I've loved him all along. When I gave up **everything** to take care of him." She wonders what her sister means.

"Hey." She reaches out to touch her, but Louisa flinches, shoves back an elbow. Rosalind stands for a long time, watching her, her throat sore with worry. "I'm sorry," she says at last. "I'm sorry you're hurt. He **does** love you. I'm certain he does." But Louisa doesn't answer. How many people in the world are so poisoned by sadness, they push love away when it's the one thing they long for most? Even more since the war.

"Please. Please, leave me alone." Roz sees Louisa in a way she's never seen her before: wounded. Sturdy Louisa. Implacable Louisa. Wounded.

"We can talk. Take a walk maybe."

Louisa shakes her head fiercely.

"Later, then, maybe." Shrugging, Roz leaves

her and heads down the hall, knocks softly, then opens the door to Henry's study. Her brother-in-law is leaning over his desk with a chessboard in front of him. She closes the door quietly behind her and asks, "Playing by yourself?"

"Kid. I've missed you." He rises, puts his arms around her. Throughout her childhood, it was most often Henry who was there to clean a cut knee or give her a hug when the world seemed askew.

"I hear that the dam's burst in this household. What's going on?" she asks.

"A guy can only take so much," he says. His mouth presses in at the corners, making him look almost fierce, though Henry is buttered melba toast. He was handsome when he married her sister. A mop of dark hair. Sturdy squared shoulders from his years in the service. He volunteered for World War I and victory was declared soon after, so he never saw battle. He did desk work in Washington during the Second World War and celebrated in the streets on VJ Day. But Louisa is a war that cannot be won. Worn down by the enemy, Henry's skinnier every year. His shoulders roll forward; his scalp shows through the comb marks in his hair. His brush of a mustache now sports white wires among the brown. He's still handsome, but in the threadbare way of a much-loved chair.

"Here, sit." He gestures to the corner where he often reads and turns his office chair to face her. On the walls are all his certificates. Diplomas and CPA licenses. Such a steady guy. Working hard. Never letting anyone down.

"Tell me about what's going on," she says. "Why now? You've put up with her all these years."

"It wears on a fellow. I'm not made of steel. How many years do I have left?" he asks.

"Thirty. Forty."

"If I'm wildly lucky. Do I want to spend them feeling angry?"

"You know she loves you even if she doesn't always show it."

"I've been thinking about this," he says. "How people fall in love and put up with someone who gives them none of what they want. They've chosen badly and then feel stuck. A lifetime of suffering, for what? A glimmer of hope that things will change. Well, it took me years to come to this, but people don't change."

Rosalind can't argue. Weaver withheld so much from her, and yet she clung to the hope that someday he'd marry her, openly love her. The less he gave, the more she craved.

"But you love Louisa. You still wish she'd give you what you want, don't you? Love or patience. What if you give her an ultimatum?" Roz asks. "Tell her you'll stay under certain conditions. Write them out."

He shrugs. "Give **Louisa** an ultimatum? Do you really imagine she'd respond to that?"

"She's scared."

"If I leave, she'll be more scared . . ."

"But you'd leave Ava? Lou could keep you from seeing her."

Henry nods. "It's why I haven't left yet."

"Did something precipitate this?" Rosalind asks.

"A tussle a week ago."

"About what?"

"Her wanting to move to the suburbs. Her prejudice. It's just wrong. She won't give our new neighbors a chance."

"Maybe she just wants a different life? A fresh start? I know you still love her."

He nods almost imperceptibly. "And sometimes hate what she says. I hate her bigotry. Her anger at the world."

"Is saving the marriage in the cards?"

He shrugs.

Rosalind looks at this kind man who came to her rescue when he was very young, and she wavers. Why should he spend his life suffering at someone else's hand? Maybe he could woo some sweet widow, someone who might appreciate him. Maybe he could find real happiness, even if Louisa never will.

She sighs. "If you want to talk to me anytime, you know where I am," she says. Walking over to him, she kisses his receding hairline. "Don't do anything precipitous without warning me, okay?"

"Sure. Hey . . . things going all right with you? I heard Ava talking about Weaver. So he's back?"

"He is."

"You handling that okay?"

"I'm fine," she says.

"And you mentioned wanting to get back to science. Have you done anything about that?"

"I'm working on it. Anyway, it's time to worry about yourself for a change."

"Okay. I don't want to nag."

"I love you," she tells him. "You'll always be family to me, no matter what you decide. You know that, right? And if you do move out, you're invited to come over and share in my lousy cooking anytime. And you can bet I'll visit you at the Allerton."

"Kid," he says. He grabs her wrist and kisses the back of her hand. She feels like he wants to say more but can't put the words together. Men are so bad at declarations of any kind, but she's always felt safe in his love.

⚜ ⚜ ⚜

The phone rings at seven thirty the following Monday morning. Wrapping a towel around her dripping hair, Rosalind runs to answer.

"If you can't speak freely, just say, 'There's no Jane Hart here.'"

She laughs. "There **is** no Jane Hart here. But I'm alone, Agent Szydlo."

"Do you have time to speak to me, then?" He sounds almost shy. Again, he strikes her as a nice man, one she wishes she'd met at a party. Last night, lying in bed, longing for Weaver, she was surprised to find herself thinking about what it would be like to kiss Charlie Szydlo. She imagined he would taste of watermelon. Clean, sweet. She whispered his name out loud. "Charlie." Why is she even thinking these thoughts about the very man who's gotten her involved again with her old lover? It makes her uneasy.

"I promised I wouldn't call and I haven't," he says. "Did you decide to see Mr. Weaver again?"

"Yes."

"Excellent." He sounds relieved. "Have you learned anything you're willing to share?"

She likes that he respects her reluctance. **Willing to share.** "Well, one thing," she's surprised to hear herself saying.

"Yes?"

"It hardly makes sense."

"I know it's hard to talk on the phone. Would you mind coming to see me on your lunch break? My office isn't far from Field's. It's in the Bankers Building, 105 West Adams at the corner of Clark. I'll have sandwiches. There's a photo I want to show you. And you can tell me what Weaver said that doesn't make sense."

"All right. Let me write down the address."

The day is hot and swollen. As Rosalind walks to work, it feels as though her linen dress is growing tighter; her shoes bind. By the time she reaches the Michigan Avenue Bridge, she has to remove her white cotton gloves, picking them off finger by damp finger. She's seeing spots before her eyes as she steps into Field's, which isn't much cooler. The fans spin listlessly over the sales floor. Field's installed Comfort Air back in the thirties but ripped the whole system out for war-effort scrap metal in '41. Now they promise they're going to reinstall it before next summer. Not soon enough.

At the moment, workmen are attaching fluorescent tubes under the counters for cooler lighting. The borers squeal like dentists' drills. The store has so few customers, Janice has time to leave her perfume counter to walk over and tell Rosalind about the medical student she went out with last night.

As they're speaking, Janice whispers, "That man over there. I keep seeing him in the store. I think he's got a pash on you."

"What?"

"**That** man."

Rosalind turns, pretending to straighten her counter. The man looks to be in his fifties, thickly built, with short straw-colored hair—surely it can't be his own; there's nothing about it that looks real. His eyes are so pale they appear empty. He has the face of a bum, but he's surprisingly well dressed: an expensive suit, polished shoes. A pearl stickpin through his tie. There's nothing flashy about the outfit. It's elegant, except it doesn't match his thick, unrefined appearance at all. As soon as he sees Roz sizing him up, he turns his back.

"You've seen him before?"

"He came near the end of the day yesterday and I saw him following you later when we went home. I thought I was making it up, but then to see him again today . . . he must be gaga over you. There, he's gone out the door."

Is the FBI tailing her with a new man now instead of Charlie? **How dare they keep following her!** And why come to her job, where they know she'll be all day?

"Thanks, Jan. I'll watch out for him."

"Yeah. He's kind of creepy, actually. You don't know him, do you?"

"Lord no!"

At noon, she steps out onto the sidewalk, glancing around to see if the pale man is waiting. There are cars parked all along the curb. Cabs to hide in. He could be anywhere among the thousands of people on State Street. There are police officers in view too. This summer she's

seen them, officers walking two by two, thread-
ing through the summer crowds. But no need
for the police. She's pretty sure this fellow is
just one of Charlie's guys, keeping tabs on her.
Then, half a block down, she spots him standing
between two coffee carts, an unrefined man in
refined clothes staring with those awful empty
eyes. She's alongside Wieboldt's department store
so she ducks into its revolving door, and, rushing
past the displays of thin cotton dresses and cheap
men's slacks, she exits two doors south. Hurrying toward Dearborn, she keeps glancing back to
make sure he's gone. She doesn't know why she's
so intent on losing him, except she's disturbed
by the way he looks, and it feels like a game. She
relishes the idea of telling Charlie she shook his
guy. The Bankers Building feels farther away
than she expected. By the time she gets there,
her dress is damp in every place it touches her
skin. She announces herself to the man behind
the desk, and while she waits for Szydlo to come
down, she scans the lobby for her pursuer, expecting him to walk in any minute.

"Miss Porter?" Szydlo says softly. "You okay?"

"Why are you **still** having me followed?" she
whispers.

"Pardon?"

"You know someone's following me."

Charlie's lips part; he looks puzzled.

"Is he here now?"

"No. I shook him."

"Let's get out of the lobby." He sternly grabs her arm. "I shouldn't have had you come here. It didn't occur to me they'd have you followed."

The perspiration on her neck turns icy and goose bumps rise all down her arms. In the elevator she asks, "They? Who?" No one else is in the car, yet she only mouths the words "A Soviet operative?" He nods. She read that word in the paper: "operative." It sounds so threatening somehow. Invasive.

"That man was a Soviet agent . . . ?" She says it to herself more than to him. To help herself understand. To believe it. The man with eyes so pale they seemed utterly empty . . .

They don't say anything else as the elevator rises. It's one of those modern elevators with no elevator man, and they're alone. Charlie is watching the numbers on the indicator. She notes his face. Kind. Sad. Serious. She feels protected in his presence. But out on the street, back at work, will she feel the same?

The FBI offices are blessedly cool. They have air conditioning and she's craved it. But now she's shivering.

"Why would they follow **me**?" she asks.

"To understand who Weaver's spending his time with. Just like I did. You coming here could have compromised him."

"Put Weaver in danger?"

"Hopefully you shook the fellow like you said and he didn't discover you were on your way to the FBI. As for Weaver, I imagine he's been putting himself in danger for quite a while."

Agitated, she follows Charlie past a bullpen of men talking on telephones, discussing things in small clusters, and then into a large wood-paneled room with three circular ceiling vents shooting out more cool air.

"I thought a conference room would be a nicer place to share lunch." Charlie shuts the door. "Without a bunch of wolves howling." He smiles and pulls out a chair for her.

"Should I be worried?" she asks.

"About the wolves?" She can see he's trying to lighten the mood.

"Now I'm kind of scared. You following me scared me. And this guy is even creepier."

"Even creepier than **me,** huh?" he asks. She can see color coming to his cheeks.

"Sorry . . . I didn't mean . . ."

"We'll try and find out who he is," he says. He has a soothing voice. "Don't worry too much. Even if you didn't shake him, it's a big building. There are all sorts of offices here. Not just the FBI. Doctors. Lawyers. And I bet you did get rid of him. You didn't see him in the lobby, did you?"

Roz shakes her head. Settling into the large swivel chair he pulled out for her, she fishes a handkerchief from her purse to catch the perspiration coursing down her forehead. She doesn't know if she's hot or cold.

"I didn't know what kind of lunch you'd like, so I gave you a choice." Out of a brown paper bag, Szydlo pulls various sandwiches and, pointing to them, tells her what's inside. She's having trouble concentrating.

"I think I'll wait a minute. Until I cool off . . ."

She shoves back the hair on her forehead, twists the rest of her mane into a knot, and blots her neck. She must look a mess.

"Want a Royal Crown?" He pushes a dripping bottle toward her. Before he lets her take the bottle, he pops the top with his thumb. The burning-cold froth hits her mouth with a sweet shock. Lifting a folder, he gallantly fans her, watches with concern.

"Describe the man," he says. "If you can."

She recounts the stolid body, his empty eyes, the pale thatch of hair that doesn't look quite real. The expensive clothes. The shining shoes.

He writes down what she tells him.

"You should eat," he says. "We don't have much time until you need to go back."

She reaches for the sandwich marked CHICKEN SALAD in blue ink. He's laid out the lunch nicely, even managed to find plates. Along the rim, the china is stamped with a green circle. The top of the circle reads DEPARTMENT OF JUSTICE; the bottom, FEDERAL BUREAU OF INVESTIGATION. She unwraps the sandwich. It's surprisingly delicious, cold, creamy, and crunchy with fresh celery. She watches Szydlo unwrap his with a single hand. How hard would it be to have only one hand? A challenge to do the simplest things. As he eats, politely, neatly, she feels him watching her, waiting.

"You want to tell me about Weaver?" he asks at last. "Anything."

"I thought you had something to show me."

"You first," he says.

She doesn't want to talk about Weaver. "Weaver's told me only one thing: that breaking up with me wasn't his choice."

Charlie squints at her. "Wasn't his choice?"

"He says someone forced him to be with Clemence, the woman he married."

"He didn't say **who**?"

"No." There's more to tell Charlie. Weaver told her he was a Communist in college. But lots of people were Communists in the thirties. She's not going to share it yet. Besides, Weaver says he's trying to extricate himself. She's surprised to find herself wanting to protect him.

"Did he say anything else about his wife?"

"He said, 'Nothing you think you know about my marriage is true.' Whatever that means."

Charlie looks up from his notes. "Miss Porter, she's missing."

"Who?"

"His wife. That's what I wanted to tell you. She was renting a room in the suburbs. I went out there. She's disappeared. Her clothes, a purse, her passport, are all still there. But no one's seen her."

Every follicle on Rosalind's head tightens. She sets down her sandwich and feels dizzy— like she did this morning in the heat. Clemence Weaver—who stood for all she isn't and will never be—is missing.

"You don't think . . . you're not suggesting Weaver . . . he wouldn't."

"Probably not." She distrusts the smooth tone of his voice and his choice of words: "probably."

"You think he's somehow implicated, though, don't you?"

"We don't know anything yet. That's something you learn in the FBI. Never assume. Look at this photo. Is this Clemence Weaver?"

He hands it to her. It appears to be a blown-up passport photo. The face is unmistakable: the woman who ruined her life. For months after Weaver left her, Rosalind fixated on this woman. He'd chosen Clemence over her and she needed to know why. So she catalogued all she knew: Clemence was older, more sure of herself, more exotic, taller, more slender. She held those superlatives against herself. Seeing the face again brings pain.

"Yes, that's his ex-wife."

The parted hair pulled back to reveal those planes of her face, those sharp cheekbones. Those piercing dark eyes lined in kohl.

"Oh, and . . . as far as we can tell, despite what Weaver may have told you, she's not his ex-wife."

"They weren't married after all?" Rosalind is surprised by how happy that makes her. Sunlight reaching her heart. Maybe that's what Weaver meant when he said nothing she knew about the marriage was true.

"No, we see no evidence they've divorced. As far as we can see, they're still married."

"Oh . . ." Her disappointment is precipitous. But then Weaver never said anything about divorce, did he? She's merely wished it were so. Every time Weaver steps into the picture, she fools herself.

"What name did he call her?" Charlie asks.

"Clemence. Clemence Weaver."

He nods.

"I already told you that."

"You did. He didn't use any other name?"

"Like a nickname?"

"Any name."

She shakes her head at him. "I only found out her name from other people. Once she came along, I was sent packing."

Rosalind can say that now with a sarcastic ring. But why does her heart still ache at the

words? This morning she lifted the little manila envelope Weaver gave her from beneath
the Scandinavian sweater at the bottom of her
sweater drawer and slid it into her purse. The
leather under her fingertips pulses now like a
beating heart. Should she take it out and share
it with Charlie? She absolutely should if she
really **is** doing this for the FBI. But she thinks
of Weaver making love to her, his new tenderness. And that confounding new vulnerability.
Until she knows more, she doesn't feel ready to
tell Charlie any of that. Weaver said his life de-
pended on it. **Life and death,** he said. Why does
he wield such power over her?

"You'll be cautious with Weaver, won't
you?" Charlie says. "You'll call me if you need
help or—"

"He's not dangerous. Weaver's lots of things.
A liar for one. But he's not dangerous."

"I wouldn't be so sure," Charlie says. "Especially when it comes to Weaver, I don't think we
can assume anything."

CHAPTER TWELVE

She's already too late to return to Marshall Field's on time, but instead of rushing, she ducks into the phone booth in the lobby of the Bankers Building and telephones Adele at her counter.

"I'm so sorry," she says, feigning a mix of contriteness and annoyance, "but you may have to stay at my counter a bit longer. I'm at the doctor's and he's taking his sweet time with another patient." She's much better at lying than she ever imagined. "I really hate to put you out. That's why I told them I needed to use their phone. Thank heavens they let me."

"Why are you at the doctor?" Oh, that dry voice. That accusatory tone. Leave it to Adele to pry.

"I have a cyst," she says. "Needs to be lanced. Trust me, you don't want details." She hasn't formulated any. She hopes that if she disgusts Adele enough, the questions will stop.

"All right. But get here as soon as possible, cyst or not."

The only cyst Rosalind needs lancing is the desire to get rid of Weaver's little envelope. Continental Bank, where she's always had her checking account, is just a block from the Bankers Building, on LaSalle. What relief she feels stepping up to Continental's front desk and requesting the smallest possible safe-deposit box. After signing three sheets of paper, she's ushered into a little echoing room lined in rows of brass doors, each opened by two keys at the same time. Turning her key in rhythm with the manager's releases a rectangular coffin far too big for the little manila envelope. Nevertheless, she drops it in with a sigh. That envelope has been a scorching potato. It makes her too curious. And makes her feel guilty for not sharing it with Charlie. At the same time, what might be revealed about Weaver if she opened his safe-deposit box and read the letter inside? Even if it costs her four dollars and fifty cents a month for access to her own box, it's worth having Weaver's key out of her hands. Back at Field's, she slips her own safe-deposit key into the backing fabric of a black velvet cushion that holds big unattractive brooches that few people ever ask to see. **Done,** she thinks. **Good-bye, hot potato.**

〜 〜 〜

Other than when she used it to call Adele this afternoon, it's rare that the telephone rings in the antique jewelry department. What would they ask? **Have you any rings with doves on them?** So late in the afternoon, Roz almost drops the Georgian brooch she's been logging in when the phone shakes itself awake.

"I wondered if you're free tonight," Weaver says, smooth and unruffled. Certainly not a man who does away with his wife, she thinks. "I hope it's okay—me calling you at work."

"Of course. And, yes, I'm free." Her friends have often told her how they played hard to get with their beaux. They ended up married. But somehow, it's never suited her to play games, to strategize. Because then—as she sees it—you're married to someone you've manipulated.

"I wondered, would you be willing to come to my flat tonight?" he asks. "After work, you could go home and pack a bag. Clothes, night-gown, that sort of thing. Then . . ." He clears his throat, as though trying to work up the courage. "Then maybe you'll spend the night with me here? All I want . . . all I want is to wake up to you . . . in my own bed. To feel you near all night."

"Weaver . . ." She wonders if the Field's operator is listening in. Such intimate words for the middle of a sunstruck afternoon. He was tender with her in the past sometimes. But his words were never like this. "Tell me when and I'll be there," she says.

"Thank you, love," he says. He never would have thanked her in the past or sounded grateful. Maybe he was, but he was always too guarded to say so.

⚕ ⚕ ⚕

She hasn't been to Weaver's Hyde Park apartment since the bomb dropped on Hiroshima. After that, she was so depressed, they stopped making love and she stopped visiting his apartment altogether. The way she saw it, how could they revel in pleasure when others who'd died at their hands could seek pleasure no more? Sometimes, in those dark days, he stayed at her place and held her in his arms all night, but she couldn't open up to him even when she tried. Her desire for lovemaking was just reawakening at the time he left her. They'd made love with astonishing passion just two nights before he told her it was over. And later, she recalled there was a desperation to his lovemaking that night. That he whispered again and again, "My Rosalind. My sweet Rosalind. Never forget how much I care for you." It's one of the reasons his departure was so confounding.

From earlier, happier times, she does have joyful memories of the grand old twenties mansion where he rents his rooms on the second floor, his apartment so British and masculine, with dark walls and a drinks cart, horse prints, tweedy furniture, and a rack fitted with five gleaming pipes. She never once saw him smoke them; still, those pipes looked at home there. The apartment's most unique feature was a narrow stone terrace overlooking Drexel Avenue. Nights, they'd spend sweet hours on that porch rocking on a metal glider he'd picked up off the street. How out of place that glider looked on an urban terrace, more suited to a suburban patio. Pressed out of metal, turquoise like an Aegean sky, it's back formed to look like two buttoned pillows. But how happy they were swinging, sipping spiked iced tea, speaking about science and their dreams. Rosalind's dreams were focused on cities, farms, and ocean liners run by nuclear energy. Weaver's wildest fantasies were about nuclear-powered rocket ships to the moon or Mars.

Her most vivid memory is of one scorching night when his apartment was unbearable and they dragged the glider inside so there'd be room to sleep under the stars. Lying on an opened cardboard box and two eiderdown comforters atop each other to shield against the unforgiving stone floor, they made love twice, their bodies slippery with desire and heat, then slept naked and entwined under a perfect half-moon.

Recalling that night makes Rosalind shiver. Weaver. How she once adored him. Now, she can't help thinking that another woman has lived in that apartment, slept in his bed, maybe made love to him on the stone terrace. What has Clemence left behind? Papers, notes? Flowered cushions? Will Rosalind find something worth sharing with Charlie? The desire to see Weaver and the desire to spy on him are less at odds than she might have guessed. All lovers are would-be spies, aren't they? What woman doesn't want to know her lover's most closeted secrets, to search out what he would never tell her? The mixture of excitement and guilt is delicious and disturbing.

She's pondering this as she steps out of Field's and nearly runs into the empty-eyed man. Christ. Though her heart starts to gallop, he passes as though he has no interest in her. As he walks away, she notices that his hands are huge and misshapen. Knuckles raw and thickened. She's certain that as soon as she's not watching, he'll turn around and follow her.

She sets right off down Randolph to Michigan as though she's running a race, weaving around slower walkers. In her rush, she even parts the hands of two lovers, dashing between them. "Sorry," she calls behind her. "Sorry for that." The man's nostrils flare with annoyance. But as far as she can tell, she's lost her pursuer. What is she afraid of? The man has done nothing to her. But she recalls Charlie's worried face when he heard she was being tailed. And it's just the idea that he's a Russian, an enemy, that he's tracking her like a hunter tracks an animal. It all makes her feel watched. The irony that lately she's feared invisibility does not go by unrecognized.

She thinks she's outrun the man, when, as she's about to step into the revolving door of her building, she spots him across the street smoking. Jesus. Her heart starts up again like a motorboat engine with a tug and a jerk and a roar. She runs into the sheltering arms of her lobby. In the elevator, she presses herself to the wall. Once in her apartment, she pours herself a Scotch and drinks it down too quickly. She pulls out the card Charlie gave her. Should she call him? But what would he do? Track her as well. She slips the card back into her purse. She wants to pretend none of it is happening. Later, when she steps out of the building with her overnight case, hoping to catch the bus to Weaver's, her head pounds with worry and that glass of liquor. But she doesn't see the man anywhere.

〰 〰 〰

She's amazed that Weaver's made dinner. They both know how to feed themselves, but neither of them had ever learned the first thing about cooking. He's set the table with chalk-white French damask napkins. Did he buy them just for her? Or did they belong to Clemence? No. They're brand-new: The fabric labels are stiff. He opens a bottle of wine and asks for her to light the white tapers. He's got two steaks laid out on a broiler pan. Green beans in a pot of water. He tells her there are baked potatoes in the oven. "Wrapped in tinfoil," he says proudly. "I can't have them in the oven while I'm using the broiler, apparently. So I hope they stay warm while I make the steaks."

"Potatoes stay hot forever," she says. She thinks of his envelope, which she considered her hot potato.

"No guarantees on the cooking," he warns. "But it's not unlike following a formula in a chem lab, thanks to this." He lifts **The Joy of Cooking.** He didn't own that before.

"Did you cook for her?" she asks. "Clemence?"

He doesn't answer at first, just fusses with the meal to come.

"I guess mostly we ate out," he says. "She couldn't cook."

"It's hard to think of her here," Roz says hoarsely. She can't help herself. He must sense her distress because he stops what he's doing and comes over to her, puts his hands on her shoulders.

"Please put her out of your mind. I swear you don't need to think of her at all."

"But she's here. Between us . . ."

"She'll never be here between us again," he says. "And if you want to know the truth, she never was." **Never was?** The pot of green beans has begun boiling and he turns back to lower it to a simmer. She can't help thinking: Did **Clemence** sit in that chair? Did **Clemence** light that fire? Yet where are the floral curtains that Rosalind thought she'd find, the hooked rug or red canister set? Except for the giant Philips radio having been replaced by a handsome cabinet television, in no other way has the apartment changed. The walls are the same deep green. The furniture overstuffed, covered in wool and leather. Entirely masculine.

"Are you still in touch with her?" Roz asks, watching him gingerly light the broiler. She works hard to make it an offhand comment, complete with a sip of wine. She doesn't look him in the eye or make much of it.

"No," he says. "No reason to be."

He takes a deep swallow of wine, knocking it back the way he drinks Scotch.

"Do you have any idea where she's ended up?" she pushes. "Surely you have some feeling for her. You were married how long?"

"I told you, you can't imagine the truth."

"I **want** to," she says.

He focuses on seasoning the steak: salt, pepper, garlic powder, paprika.

"You like it medium rare, don't you?" he asks.

"Yes."

He looks up. "I don't want to talk about Clemence," he says. "Only you. You and me. That's all that matters now."

Rosalind can't help but notice that on the bar cart, Weaver has set a large machine-turned silver frame displaying a photo of Roz and Weaver as a couple. It was taken five or six years ago at the wedding of Carl Sturgin—a colleague of theirs at the Met Lab. Though the photo is black-and-white, Roz remembers her cream-colored wool suit with the carnation-pink collar, the pink hat with a veil ruched into a flower at the side. It was before the bomb dropped, at a time when everyone was certain that their device would never, ever be used as anything but a deterrent. What a fine couple they made! Weaver, so upright and handsome. She, slender, graceful, and hopeful in her suit. His hand rests on her waist with affection, ownership, pride. He kept this photo somewhere the whole time he was married to Clemence. In a drawer beneath the paper

maybe? In a file cabinet? Did he look at it surreptitiously? Did he think of her, while another
woman sat across the table from him and slept in
his bed?

⁜ ⁜ ⁜

The dinner he cooks is good. Far better than she
could have done.

"Apparently," Weaver says, "all you have to
do is follow instructions. If I'd known earlier, I
would have taken up cooking." She helps him
dry the dishes. He looks tired, though, and eventually sets aside the last few things he needs to
wash to collapse into one of his big tweed chairs.

"Oof," he says. "Work's been hard this week."

"What are they doing to you there? Are you
on a deadline?"

"Rather . . ."

"Can you tell me what you're working on?"

"Quantity."

"Quantity? Of bombs, you mean?"

"I shouldn't have said even that. No more
questions, please." He won't tell her—but he
shares secrets with the Russians?

Later, when he excuses himself to the bathroom, she pokes around his desk, reads the en-
tries on his desk calendar. Next week there's a
scribble on Wednesday. **K—drop, Midway tree,
2:30,** it reads. She lets her memory absorb the

entire page of the calendar. Later, she'll be able to tell Charlie what she saw. She quietly opens his desk drawer and sifts through the bills, papers. There's an envelope with a woman's handwriting on it but no return address. Roz slides the letter out.

There's something about the handwriting that stops her. It's foreign. The same looped **o**'s as the notes in the margins from Madame Rousseau, her French professor in college. The notecard is thick and vanilla colored, with a seashell embossed at the top, iced in shiny clay-green ink. **You can't get away from me,** it says, with two periods after **me.** When she looks up, Weaver is standing over her.

"Aren't you a snoop," he says. It's not a question.

"I . . ." Heat scorches her cheeks. "I was being nosy," she admits.

"Apparently." His eyes are bright, the color of green olives. "Please give it here, if you will." She hands over the letter and he glances at it, slips it back into its envelope, drops it into the wastebasket with something of a flourish. There's a flutter in her stomach. A thrum in her ears.

"That letter was from Clemence, wasn't it? You **do** know where she is."

He turns on her. Suddenly, viciously. "**Stop saying her name!** I don't want that name to come out of your mouth again!" His face is red, and the wolfish quality she's noted in his new leanness seems magnified. Why has she pushed him? Why hasn't she kept her questions, her jealousy, to herself? He turns away, moves toward the kitchen.

"I'm sorry," she calls out.

Nothing.

She comes into the kitchen to see him bent over the sink, leaning on his arms. He looks old.

"I'm just exhausted," he says. "I just can't bear to speak of her." She notes his fingers are gripped and pale. There's a sheen on his brow. What's wrong with him?

"Do you want me to leave?"

He doesn't answer.

"I'll go." She reluctantly goes to the front closet, finds her hat. "I should."

"No."

"I've upset you. Best I go. What did you do with my bag? Is it in the bedroom?"

He straightens up and stops her, his hands on her arms.

"Can you just refrain from asking about her, Roz? You're torturing me. She's not part of this equation. She's not part of **us**." His lips are tight, gray.

Charlie warned her. **Don't ask questions unless they're natural.** She really does wish she could go home.

"Stay," he says. "Go get ready for bed. I'm

awfully tired. You don't know what it means to me to have you here. I'm sorry I lost my temper."

Hesitantly, she steps into the bathroom, washes her face, changes into her nightgown. She's brought this on herself. He tried hard to please her and she's ruined the mood. But it's taught her: She's still angry at him. She's still jealous. She's spying on him because she wants revenge. It's an ugly brew. Wouldn't it be better to extricate herself? She hates that Charlie's the one who's brought her back to Weaver. That she never would be here if he hadn't made her curious about whether her old lover is a traitor. But is she being honest with herself? Wouldn't she have been drawn back by her feelings for Weaver alone? For they still linger, will always be there.

Yet, for some reason, as she slides into bed next to Weaver, she thinks of Charlie's kind, worried eyes as he fanned her, recalls the way he pushed the cold cola toward her with an encouraging smile. He radiated kindness. He wanted to take care of her. Why couldn't she love a man like that?

She and Weaver don't make love. Maybe he's angry. Maybe he's too tired. She doesn't feel she could be vulnerable with him right now. But when she rolls over, he holds her. She feels the kick of his sleep fall, and then the soughing of his dozing breath, even and comforting. He never used to fall asleep so effortlessly. But she lies there in his arms for what feels like hours, Clemence's note etched on her vision: the expensive textured cream paper with the embossed green seashell, the looped **o**'s of the handwriting. The double period after **me. You can't get away from me.** Later, Rosalind will write it out, just as she saw it.

CHAPTER THIRTEEN

Louisa drops Ava off to spend Saturday night. Rosalind notices right away that her niece is chewing on her hangnails, sighing like a man with six children and no paycheck.

"You okay, monkey?" she asks.

"It's **them,**" she says, rolling her eyes.

"Them?"

"My parents. They don't talk to each other now. And they want **me** to talk for them. **Ask your father if he's going to be home in time for dinner tonight. Tell her I may or may not.**"

"That's no fun."

"Even though they're not talking, it's **noisy.** Being angry, that's noisy. You know?"

Rosalind nods. She thinks of the unsaid things that crowd a room. It was sometimes that way with Weaver. **Why don't you love me enough to marry me?**

"Things are complicated for adults," she says.

"They make things complicated," Ava says.

"By not talking. Mommy was crying last night. She wouldn't even talk to **me.**"

"That must have been hard for you," Rosalind says. Ava shrugs.

"She said something terrible."

"What?"

"She said, 'Now nobody will care if I die.'"

"What did you say?"

"I said I'd care. And that she'd better **not** die because I'd never forgive her. She stopped crying at least."

For the first time, Roz worries how hard it must be for Louisa: to be certain of Henry's love for decades. And then to have him suddenly so angry that he turns his back on her, wants to leave. Roz has always taken Henry's side, but now she feels for her sister, understands how it must unbalance her. Nobody supported Roz more when she was spun into oblivion by the loss of Weaver. Shouldn't she do more for her sister? The thought buzzes inside her. Later she'll call; she'll try to break down the wall that Louisa's built. At least right now, she's helping by taking Ava off her hands for the weekend.

"Well, you and I will have a nice weekend and talk all we want. How 'bout it?" She gives Ava a squeeze. "We just have to figure out what we want to do. The world is our oyster."

"See? Another dumb adult thing! Oysters are disgusting. I tasted one. It was a ball of phlegm."

"The world is our Oreo, then? So what do you want to do with it?"

"Can we go to the toy department at Field's?"

"Oh . . . okay."

Ava eyes Roz, perhaps noting her lack of enthusiasm. "I don't mean to buy anything. We can just play a game that we're very, very rich and can have any doll we like and all the clothes and shoes and hats that go with her. My friend Shirley says that there are roller skates for Ginnys now. They must be this big!" She squeezes her thumb and forefinger together. Going to Field's is the opposite of fun for Rosalind. But it would be worth it to make Ava happy.

"Let me grab my things and we'll catch the bus."

Just as she's checking her purse for a handkerchief and keys, the buzzer sounds. When she answers, Wally, the afternoon doorman, announces there's a package from Marshall Field's. They're bringing it up on the elevator.

"What is it?" Ava asks.

"Beats me." Money's been too tight for anything but groceries lately.

She answers the door on the first knock and confronts a carton so unwieldy, two deliverymen have brought it up on a cart. Another smaller box sits on top.

"Are you sure this is for me?" she asks.

The portly one in his green Field's jumpsuit

plucks a piece of paper from his shirt pocket, which is embroidered with the name **Chet.**

"Rosalind Porter?"

"Yes." She wonders with some astonishment if she's won a raffle as a Field's employee.

"Purchased by a Thomas H. Weaver. Where do you want it?"

"It's a gift from Weaver!" Ava says, brightening, clapping her hands.

"If you'll step aside, young lady," Ralph, the other man, says. Rosalind's sat through enough Field's Means Good Manners classes, right beside deliverymen like these two. The men lay a sidewalk of brown grocery paper before they wheel the cart in.

"So where's your pleasure?" Ralph asks.

"I don't know. What is it?"

At her behest, they cut through the edges of the box and pluck away miles of protective packaging—the padded kind with lint between walls of brown paper—to reveal a glowing mahogany cabinet. Weaver went into Marshall Field's to buy it without her knowing. But why would he send her a piece of furniture, as elegant as it is?

"Over there, I guess." Roz points to a space between two chairs.

"No, miss," Chet says. "It's got to be across from the chairs. Or the sofa. And by a plug." Chet points to a spot on the opposite wall. She's bewildered that a deliveryman would involve himself in interior design. And then he grabs both of the elegant pulls—lions biting down on brass rings—and opens the doors with a thwack.

"It's a television!" Ava exclaims. "A really pretty television!"

"A top-of-the-line Philco." Chet slides the doors back to either side of the screen, so the lions' heads just peek out. Louisa has deemed television a ridiculous distraction. But everyone in the break room at Field's has been chatting animatedly about what was on last night, what will be on tonight. Rosalind's been curious. The men move the TV across from the sofa, then plug it in and turn it on. The screen, from a pinpoint of white, opens like an umbrella to a field of sparkling light. A voice speaks.

"And here we have another small fry, Jimmy McHale from Westport, Connecticut, with a wonderful story! Go on and tell us, Jimmy."

"Well, sir, my mother tole me this story and it sure is a doozy . . ."

The TV babbles on, but Rosalind can't see a thing.

"They call that snow," Ava tells her wisely. "It means bad reception."

"How do you know that?"

"I have friends with televisions. I watch at their houses."

"Don't worry," Ralph says, jumping up from where he's been crouched down. "Your fellow purchased some rabbit ears." He cracks open the second box and yanks out a brown Bakelite ball with two silver wands and a curl of wire rising in the middle. As he adjusts the wands, the blizzard coalesces into a little boy in a cowboy outfit speaking earnestly to the camera, an avuncular-looking host by his side. Ava plops herself down on the floor right in front of the set.

"This is the keenest! Our own TV!"

"Okay, then," Chet says. "Just sign here; you're all set. By the way, young lady, **Kukla, Fran and Ollie** comes on channel five at four. Everyone loves that. And tonight's **Beat the Clock** on channel two at eight. My favorite!"

"Never miss it," Ralph says. "My wife's in love with Bud Collyer. I swear she puts perfume behind her ears before it starts." He winks at Rosalind.

When they're gone, Rosalind asks Ava, "You still want to go to Field's?"

"Are you kidding? I'm watching television! Sit down, Rozzie!"

⸙ ⸙ ⸙

Later, as Ava is surprisingly mesmerized by **Howdy Doody**—which seems to be aimed at six-year-olds—Roz pulls a half-written letter out of her desk drawer and rereads what she wrote.

Dr. Ross J. Beckworth
Associate Dean
University of Illinois College of
  Engineering

Dear Doctor Beckworth,
I just read your letter to the editor in the June issue of the American Journal of Physics. **I was intrigued to learn about the new relationship between your department and Argonne National Laboratory. It led me to wonder if your department has plans to pursue a program dedicated to teaching the potential of nuclear energy and the future of its development.**

As a former member of the Manhattan Project, I have long wished to expand upon nuclear energy's possibilities and would be interested in discussing a prospective program with you.

She began writing the note last night after drinking a thimbleful of Scotch. She felt she needed the liquor to push herself to write to this man. The letter she started to Argonne still sits in her desk drawer, mocking her every time she comes across it. Last night, she thought, **Maybe it's easier to begin with a university.** No need to reach out to Professor Fermi. No need to find out how he feels about her. That all feels risky, humiliating. But as she works on this letter, her shame is muted and she begins to believe her time and experience at the Met Lab could truly benefit a new program. It's fulfilling to think her passion for peacetime energy could help set a new course. She finishes, addresses, and stamps the letter. And then she takes the Argonne letter and completes it, too.

⊕ ⊕ ⊕

After dinner, they post both letters, then take a nice long walk along the lakefront, pointing at boats, strolling up to Michigan Avenue. The empty-eyed man is nowhere to be seen. **Do spies take the weekend off?** she wonders. Still, wherever she and her niece walk, Rosalind scopes the street, the shadows, the cross streets. Ava seems to have picked up Rosalind's uneasiness. Later, as she stands in her turquoise pajamas, her face still rosy from washing, she asks, "Rozzie, can I sleep in your bed? If you want to know the truth, I'm kinda nervous."

"About your parents?"

Ava nods. "About everything."

"Okay. But when I come to bed, there'd better be covers for me."

"I'm not responsible for what I do in my sleep."

Rosalind laughs. "Well, you can try, Miss Cover Hog."

"Just don't wait too long to come to bed."

⫷ ⫷ ⫷

Roz goes to bed early but wakes to a catastrophic crash. Horns are blaring on the drive. The clock says only 10:48. She hasn't even been in bed a half hour, and having been explosively awakened during her initial descent into sleep, she's dizzy. Ava is peacefully snoozing, a beatific smile on her lips.

Getting up gingerly, Roz peers out the window. Down on Lake Shore Drive, a sedan lies crumpled against the guardrail, its fender inside out. Another black car lies in the other lane, as misshapen as a tin can crushed beneath a foot. It isn't long until a police cruiser arrives and then an ambulance. She watches, hardly moving, until the emergency workers remove someone from the near car and slide the stretcher into the ambulance. Even from here, she can see black liquid dripping from the victim's hand.

The accident roils inside her. How do we survive a world where death awaits us at all times?

She closes her eyes and tries to absorb the peace that Ava gives off, but she knows she can't sleep now. Stepping out into the living room, she shuts the bedroom door and picks up the phone to call her sister. It's late, but she's sure on a weekend she'll still be up.

Even Lou's "hello" sounds firm and closed off. "Sorry to call at this hour. Just wondering if you're okay."

"Why shouldn't I be?" Was there ever a time her sister didn't deflect? Didn't push her away?

"Ava says you were crying last night."

"My own daughter's tattling on me now?"

"She's worried about you. I'm worried, too . . ."

"Since when have you ever worried about **me**?" Lou's voice is so brittle, it would be easy for Roz to just cut the call short. Everything about her sister's answers says that's what she wants. But Louisa's right: When has Roz **ever** been worried about her sister? When has anyone worried about her?

"Is there anything I can do for you?" Rosalind asks. "Really. Anything."

Lou clearly didn't expect her little sister would be solicitous. She's quiet for a moment. "How's Ava?" she asks.

"She's fast asleep. Fine."

"Then you're doing what I need most."

"Good. Listen, do you remember that

psychiatrist you took me to when I was at my worst?" Roz asks.

"What about him?"

"Maybe **you** should go see him. Maybe he can help."

"He was a charlatan. His only thought: to lock you up in a loony bin. Is that what you and Henry want to happen to me?"

Rosalind sighs. Why are some people so combative when they're hurting most?

"You're right. You deserve someone better."

"You really called just to ask about me?"

"To see if you're okay. I was worried about you." When was the last time she said that to Lou?

"Well. You shouldn't have bothered," she says. "I'm going to bed now."

"I hope you'll sleep well."

"Fat chance," she says. "Night." She hangs up. Rosalind takes a deep breath. She understands why she rarely asks about her sister's happiness. Still, she should do more.

Not ready to get back into bed, even more riled up after talking to her sister, she opens the TV cabinet, then, making sure the volume is at its lowest, switches it on. Down on the Drive, she hears a second ambulance arriving but doesn't want to look. On the channel she last watched, there's an orchestra, a bandleader. It doesn't hold her attention. She flips the dial to what appears to be a film. At the bottom of the screen are the words CIVIL DEFENSE. A man in shirtsleeves is sitting at a desk, smoking and speaking to the camera. She turns the volume up just loud enough to hear.

"Man at last has a weapon that can destroy civilization," he says in an insistent voice. **"Does this mean we are helpless against attack? Note** very **carefully what is to follow."** She shudders. What reckless information might they be peddling?

Stepping over to the couch, she sits, pulls in her feet, leans forward, and watches. It's all a farce: the neatly stocked bomb shelter, the children ducking under their desks with their hands over their heads, the instructions to bury contaminated clothing rather than burn it, to avoid releasing radiation. She's read reports of the Japanese survivors, of their burns and blisters and blindness, the cancer and subsequent diseases. Can it even be called surviving? This film was created to soothe a terrified populace, not to tell the truth. Down on the Drive, the second ambulance leaves with a wail of its siren. Just the right music to punctuate her dark thoughts.

She snaps off the TV, slips back in bed with Ava. She's sick with complicity. What sort of future has she created for her beloved niece? Someday, the entire globe may be ringed in clouds of fire. And all that will remain behind is ash without memory. She only falls asleep after she envisages a safer world, illuminated by clean nuclear energy, and dreams this achievement is partly due to her.

⫿ ⫿ ⫿

On Monday night, she meets Zeke for a drink and dinner. He hugs her close, kisses her cheek. He even holds her hand while describing in detail his latest amour. A married businessman.

"He lives a secret life," Zeke says, shaking his head sadly. "I guess all of us do, in a way," he says. "But he more than most. It must be heartbreaking to live a life entirely based on a lie. I want to rescue him." When Zeke speaks about his homosexuality as a tribe to which he belongs, Roz is happy for him because he feels part of something, but sad because it excludes her. She can only peer in from the outside. "I think I could love this man," he says. "But he'd have to leave his wife for me to even consider it. And then, I suppose, I'd feel bad for his wife, who must be purposely ignoring every obvious signal. It hurts to talk about it, if you want to know the truth."

"Oh, baby." She sets her hand on his. She would do anything to make her best friend happy.

"It's your turn. Tell me about Weaver," he says.

"I don't know, Zekie. How do you trust someone who's betrayed you?"

"You bite the bullet," Zeke says. "And give it a shot."

"Do I?"

"You obviously love the man. If you get hurt again, you've got scar tissue to pad the pain."

"Does it work that way? Or is scar tissue **more** fragile? Doesn't it make one more vulnerable?"

"Give it a shot, Bunny. You and Weaver are meant to be together—even if he once was a total jerk."

Rosalind observes her friend, his spiky red hair so sparse, she can map his scalp through it; his childlike face, small and serious. She would be so happy if Zeke could find love. He wants the same for her. They are two lonely people who adore each other but will never be able to meet each other's needs. Sometimes life is such a tragedy.

After she says good-bye, kissing him on each cheek, she can't help thinking about what he's said: that she and Weaver are meant to be together. Weaver **has** become more vulnerable each time they've met. He so clearly longs to make it up to her, aches to know if she still has feelings for him. The way he looks at her is now so much closer to the love she finds in Zeke's eyes. She'll call him when she gets upstairs, she decides, her feelings for him warming, blooming.

But when the elevator doors part on her floor, she's shocked to see that down the hall, a door is ajar. Hers. Dear God, could she have been so distracted this morning that she left it open? Could one of the janitors have come in, checking for a leak? She steps up to it, taps the door into the apartment and steps back with a gasp. The place is in shambles. Pillows are thrown off the sofa. Drawers are open everywhere. She hesitates. Can she go in? Will someone be there waiting for her? With a gun? A knife? A bludgeon? She thinks of running downstairs, having Frank call the police. Or insisting he come up with her.

But something tells her if the intruder were still there, the door wouldn't be open. So she pushes herself into the apartment, looks behind doors, throws back the shower curtain, opens every closet. In less than a minute, she can see no one is there. Still, the cabinets have been emptied. Plates, vases, glasses, are stacked in a tumble on the countertops in the kitchen. In the bedroom, the contents of her dresser are strewn everywhere. She'd left her mother's diamond ring in a dish atop the dresser. It's her most beloved possession. Feeling certain it's the first thing a robber would take, she frantically pulls aside bras and slips and nightdresses to find the dish sitting right where she left it. She lifts the beloved ring, presses it to her heart, slides it onto her finger. Her earring box also has been dislodged from the drawer and sits atop the dresser. Nervously opening it, she sees that the diamond snowflake earrings Weaver gave her years ago still wait inside. And the little gold knots her father gave her for college graduation. What sort of robber wouldn't take such obvious loot? Nothing seems missing at all.

Her first thought is to call the police. But if it isn't a robber, if it's perhaps the man with the empty eyes looking for something, **should** she call the police? Charlie Szydlo's card is in her wallet with his office number, and written on the back, his home number. She glances at the clock. It's after nine P.M. Taking a deep breath, she picks up the telephone and starts with his office.

CHAPTER FOURTEEN

H ey, Charlie, telephone call," Mack yells down the stairs. Charlie's just had dinner with Peg and her family for the first time in weeks. Pork chops in spiced tomato sauce, scalloped potatoes, chocolate cake. Why doesn't he come home early more often? He loves the laughter around the family table. Mack knows how to crack the kids up with imitations and jokes, which he tells very slowly and with a great deal of fanfare. Charlie loves eating real food that isn't wrapped in white paper. And he's always grateful for the way his sister makes him feel so welcome. After dinner, he helped her with the dishes just to say so. Drying off the big white platter, she told him that she's been thinking of taking a class in stenography, because it might land her an afternoon job at the church during the school year.

"I want to do something other than be a mother," she said.

"I didn't know you were thinking of it."

"Well, the kids are gone all day now. How am I supposed to fill my time? Mangling the sheets twice, ironing Mack's underwear? I think I could contribute to the church, make a difference."

"You could make a big difference, I'm sure."

"They don't like to hire married women. They think it's wrong for the church to give money to a woman when her husband's working. But I could volunteer . . ."

"Seems like they should pay you if you work, Peg. You're a force to be reckoned with. Fact is, I'm sure you could give a lot better homily than Janowski."

"Don't be blasphemous. I could help organize him, though."

"You could do that and more."

Now Charlie's just come downstairs, full, happy, and vowing to come home early more often. He's taken off his shoes. And someone's phoning. He glances at his watch. Who calls after nine P.M.? Besides, when was the last time the telephone was for him?

"Who is it?"

"I don't know," Peggy says. She stands at the top of the stairs, her hand over the receiver, leaning against the doorframe. In a stage whisper she booms, "Mack says it's a woman."

He takes the steps two at a time.

"Hello?"

"Charlie, it's Rosalind Porter."

"Rosalind?" He pauses, tries to get his bearings. "Are you okay? What's wrong?"

"Was I not supposed to call you at home? I tried the office and I got a service."

"No. No. I'm **glad** you called. You sound upset."

"I'm . . . something happened, something . . . frightening . . ."

"What? What's happened?" He hates how the feeling of worry distorts his voice.

As she describes what she came home to, her voice fragile, somewhat desperate, he looks up to see Peggy frozen in front of him, arching one brow. He grabs the back-door handle and steps out onto the stoop with the receiver. The cord forces the door to remain ajar and he feels the damp concrete stoop through his socks, but at least his sister isn't standing in front of him listening.

"And nothing's missing that you can see?"

"Nothing that I've noticed yet. My jewelry's here. Some money still in the drawer. I won't know until I put things back, of course. I didn't know if I should touch anything or call the police or . . ."

"Don't touch anything else. And don't call

the police. I'll come and have an evidence team meet me there. If nothing's missing, the Bureau will be more interested than the police. We'll do the paperwork."

"Thank you."

"Are you scared?" he asks.

"Wouldn't you be?" Her voice is smaller than usual, softer.

"Lock the door. Pour yourself a drink . . . Touch as little as possible. I'll be there as soon as I can. Or if you prefer, you can wait for me downstairs . . . in your lobby with the doorman. Maybe that's better."

"No . . . I'd rather be here."

"I'll come as quickly as I can."

Charlie steps back into the house and hangs the receiver on the wall.

"Who is **Rosalind**?" Peggy asks. She smiles.

"Work," he says.

"Oh, work? And that's why you're lit up like a Christmas tree?"

"It's a case."

"You should have heard the way you said her name. Rozzz-alind."

He shakes his head at her. "It's a **case**!" he snaps, and escapes down the stairs.

"A case you seem to like," Peggy calls after him.

॥ ॥ ॥

Rosalind has a glass of what looks like Scotch in her hand when she opens the door. Although she's still wearing what must have been her work clothes, in the midst of the chaos, she looks relaxed, her glowing dark hair dipping over one eye, her cheeks flushed. It must be the liquor.

"Thank you for coming," she says.

"Are you doing okay? How much have you had?" he asks.

"Three glasses. I was still shaking after the second."

"I'll bet. It's upsetting."

"They had their hands all over my underwear," she says; then color suffuses her cheeks. He can tell she would never say such a thing without a few drinks in her.

"It's an intrusion. I know." The apartment is in disarray. But he notes right away that he's seen worse. The perpetrators didn't break lamps or knock over furniture. Yet, every drawer, every cabinet is emptied. They were clearly searching for something. But what does she have of Weaver's? He walks through, peering into the bedroom, the bathroom, the kitchen.

"Can I offer you a drink?" she asks.

"I'm on duty."

"At this hour? This is duty?"

"A team is coming in a few minutes to help. I wasn't sure I could get hold of them. I got lucky.

With a few men it can be done more quickly. So you can get back to normal."

"That would be good."

He pulls out his notepad. "Can you think of what they might have been looking for? Did Weaver give you something they may have wanted?"

She stares at him, presses her lips together until they're pale.

"What?" he coaxes.

"I haven't a clue what they'd be looking for here." She gives the slightest shrug. Her mouth projects defiance. It stings: that sense that she's hiding something, that she's loyal to Weaver even after all the jerk's done to her in the past. Charlie writes down a few notes in his notebook. When he looks up, she's collapsed into a chair, her eyes closed, tears spilling. He waits for her to compose herself, but after a minute, he walks over, squats down in front of her, not wanting to loom over or intimidate her.

"Here," he says, holding out a clean hand-kerchief.

She opens her eyes and takes it, presses it to her face.

"May I ask why you're crying?" he asks. He feels a bit put out. Still, her defenselessness moves him. "Are you scared?" he asks. "Or shocked or . . ."

"I don't want to believe this is because of Weaver."

"There's a good chance it is. Otherwise things would be missing."

"He says he was a Communist once. But lots of people were Communists . . . He says he's trying to extricate himself from something."

"From the Russians? Did he say that?"

She shakes her head. "He told me it would be dangerous to tell me more."

"Well, that's something. Thank you for sharing what you know. There's nothing more?"

"No."

"I know this is hard for you."

Her lashes are starry with tears. His face is level with hers, but she doesn't look shy or self-conscious. He's surprised by her frankness. It's as though no one ever told her the rules of flirtation. When he looks at her, he sees a beautiful woman who doesn't know it. Creamy skin, soft, dark eyes glistening with intelligence and a surprising innocence. He doesn't know how he finds the courage, but he reaches out and wipes a tear from beneath her eye with his thumb, feels his own lips quiver as he touches her. "I'm sorry you've had to go through this. You don't deserve it. I'm sorry we've exposed you like this." Her lips part. For one moment, while their eyes are locked, while he's touching her, he feels his heart grip—a fist clenching, painful as nails cutting into the flesh of a palm. He has to stand just to breathe again. It will be a long time until the sensation lets go, that utter cramp of feeling he has for her. He can hardly believe he touched her the way he did. Intimacy has been impossible for him since the war. But somehow her brokenness speaks to him, maybe because it echoes his own.

"I better start working or I'll be here all night," he says. "We probably won't find anything. The Russians are trained not to leave a trail. Come on over, Rosalind, if you don't mind. I need to get your prints first." Even the sensation of holding her hand in his as he presses her fingers on the inkpad shoots through him like electricity.

╫ ╫ ╫

Is the sudden attraction Rosalind feels for Charlie the result of the three drinks she's taken? Or was it the way he knelt down to her level, his soft-spoken care? She was inexpressibly moved by his touch, his decency, which washes over her. Once the other men are in the apartment, he moves away, gets down to business directing them, and she longs for him in a way that confuses her.

Calder, the chubby guy whose shirt buttons too tightly over his belly, should have been a comedian.

"You call this housekeeping?" he says to

Rosalind with a wink. She smiles faintly, wondering if he can see that she's been crying. Pace resembles an undertaker. Sober, skinny, with a turned-down mouth and a stick-straight back.

"Ma'am," he says as he enters the apartment.

"Miss," Charlie corrects him, but he doesn't acknowledge it. The men chat with Charlie briefly, each marking off his territory. Calder hums his way through the work. Pace, in the living room, makes small, catlike movements, his face unchanged through everything. By ten forty-five, in perfect concert, they announce they're done.

"See you tomorrow, Szydlo. Miss Porter," Calder says. "I hope tomorrow is a **less** interesting day."

"Ma'am," Pace says, touching his hat. The door closes behind them.

Rosalind's been holing up in the corner of the living room, staring at the window, although with the lamps' lights on the glass she can't see out. She's been thinking that loving Weaver will forever be a dangerous venture, that of course this chaos is because of him and his secrets.

She turns to watch Charlie straightening his items, checking the log where the fingerprints are noted, spinning the dusting jars closed.

When finished, he comes over and kneels down once again.

"Are you going to be okay?" he asks. "I should be going."

"You're done too?" The thought of being alone in the apartment sends a flash of dread through her. She has the urge to reach out and grab his arm.

"It helped to have the other men," he says. "You can start cleaning up, put things away whenever you're up to it."

"Do you think . . . do you imagine I'm in danger, Charlie?"

"I wouldn't leave you alone if I did."

"I feel safer with you here," she whispers.

"Do you?"

For a moment they look into each other's eyes, and the sense of connection is palpable. She feels disappointed when he gets up and finishes packing the case. Snaps it closed.

"When I had asthma as a kid," he says, his back turned, "my mother used to sit up and watch over me. It made me feel safe. I'd wake up and see her stitching in a little beam of light, embroidering those bluebirds I told you about—on handkerchiefs and pillows. Just knowing she was there, maybe it relaxed me, maybe it did stop the asthma in a way."

Rosalind imagines him as a little boy. Though he now seems so sturdy, she doesn't find it hard to conceive of him as a delicate, lanky child. "You were lucky to have someone watching over you," she says.

"You take it for granted when you're a kid. You don't know how lucky you are that someone cares most of all that you're all right."

Rosalind nods silently. "You were lucky to have a mother that loved you so." She thinks of Lou, who may have loved her but often pushed her away.

His eyes are watchful, kind, lit from within. The color of the sea on a fair day.

"I could stay here in your living room tonight," he offers softly.

"Could you?"

"If you want me to."

"You don't know . . . I would be so grateful."

"All right. Consider me your guest."

⚬ ⚬ ⚬

He can hardly believe he's suggested staying. What's he doing? Despite the fact that this operation is a kind of wooing, a seduction even, he's not supposed to actually get involved with her. Yet all he can think about is taking her in his arms, telling her it will be okay. He knows he's responsible for exposing her to this mess. This fear.

"I'll bring you sheets, a blanket, and a pillow too," she says. "And I'll make the sofa up like a bed. When my niece, Ava, sleeps here, that's where she usually sleeps. She says it's comfortable. Of course, you're taller. You saw her at the Berghoff that night, didn't you?"

"She looks like you," he says. **Beautiful,** he wants to tell her.

"People always think she's mine. My daughter." She gets up from the chair, and as she passes, she reaches out and squeezes his arm. It sends a jolt through him. "I'll go get the bedding—if it's where I think it is. They completely emptied the linen closet."

He waits for her, uneasy. He could have called for some uniformed cops to sit outside her door with coffee and their walkie-talkies. But it's Charlie she wants, Charlie who makes her feel safe. He gets up, too nervous to sit.

"I think I'll go down to talk to your doorman. Alert him to keep watch," he calls to her. "Would the overnight doorman be on yet?"

She comes in, her arms piled with bedding, and throws it down on the sofa. "Show me your watch," she says. Charlie turns his watch to her. "He comes on in ten minutes, at eleven, but Frank will tell him. Frank's a good guy."

"Why don't you give me your keys before I go down, then double lock the door. That sort of thumb lock is hard to pick. Go get ready for bed, okay?"

She lifts the keys from where she left them on

the hall table and drops them into his hand. He pockets them. "Thank you," she whispers.

"Listen, in case you're already in bed by the time I come back up," he says. "One more thing."

"Yes?"

"I'm sorry to ask, but I can't help feeling you're holding something back from me. Please tell me what it is—what they were searching for."

At first she looks surprised; then she looks defiant. "I'm not ready to condemn him," she says.

"So you're willing to have his goons ransack your apartment, but you won't tell me?"

"Don't call them **his** goons."

"You asked me to stay here, and I'm staying. I'm going out of my way to make you feel safe . . . so . . ."

"You want something in return? Tit for tat? That's why you've stayed?" She shakes her head and turns her back on him. "Go ahead and leave, then. Fine." She heads toward the bedroom.

Women. He's so bad at this. "No. I know you'll feel better if I stay. I'll feel better if I'm sure you're okay." When he catches up to her, he gently takes her arm in his hand. "Please, Rosalind. I want to keep you safe."

She turns to him. She's so close, he picks up that honeyed scent. She looks up into his eyes and shakes her head. "Charlie, I can't . . . not yet." He should feel angry, yet how he would love to touch her hair, to let his fingers model her face, her white throat. He would kiss her if he had the courage. In the beautiful hollow where her neck meets her shoulder. Instead, all the way down in the elevator, he's a jumble of anger and tenderness. Why does she confound him so? Why is she so loyal to a man who threw her to the dogs?

CHAPTER FIFTEEN

She lies in bed soothed, knowing Charlie is in the next room. And scared because her house has been invaded, every one of her things touched. Should she have told him about the tiny envelope? Should she have taken him to the bank and let him open it? She thinks of Weaver, how when they made love in her apartment that first night, he whispered her name again and again. He was full of emotion, so much more tender, more gentle, than he used to be. And then in the morning when she spent the night at his place, he held her for a long time in his arms, saying, "You have no idea what this means to me." It was easier when she hated him. His new vulnerability mystifies her. And yet the piles of disorder by the window snag the passing lights of cars on Lake Shore Drive. She's been invaded because of him. It's painful to know that there won't be time to clean up in the morning before work, so tomorrow night she'll come home and have to face this chaos, this intrusion, alone.

Maybe it's because Rosalind never knew how Louisa might treat her when she was a child that she craves certainty. Can Weaver ever provide that sort of sureness? He proved once he couldn't. He disrupted her life and now he's disrupting it again. Would he be shocked to discover her place had been ransacked? One thing's certain: She can't tell him she thinks the break-in occurred because of him.

Charlie is a different sort of man. A man one could rely on. She asked him to stay and he stayed. She's left her bedroom door open, wanting the reassurance of his presence, and now, from the next room, she detects his steady breathing. Closing her eyes, she tries to match her breath to his. Like a metronome. Steady. In. Out. In time, she rides the rhythm of Charlie Szydlo's breath to the soft pastures of sleep.

◦◦◦ ◦◦◦ ◦◦◦

Careful sounds in the kitchen wake her. Her door has been closed. The sun is coming through the stripes of the blinds just as the car lights did last night. The clock says seven fifteen. She should be up by now, but she was so overwhelmed last night, she forgot to set the alarm. Tying on a robe and running her fingers through her hair, she encounters Charlie at the kitchen sink with his back to her. He's barefoot, wearing his suit pants with only a white ribbed sleeveless undershirt. Suspenders are buttoned to his trousers but hang around his hips and thighs. For such a slender man, his arms are far more muscled than she expected. Like those ads for he-man equipment in the backs of magazines. And his torso is long and lean, graceful and strong. The sight of him moves her.

He must sense her watching, because he turns. "Morning," he says. "I hope you don't mind. I found a towel. I took a shower." She's surprised that most of the things that had been set down on the counter last night appear to have been put away.

"Did you . . . Have you been cleaning up?"

"I just put a few things away while waiting for the kettle to boil. Probably did it all wrong, but they left a row of things in practically every cupboard. I tried to detect a pattern."

"Thank you. That was nice of you."

"I have to get into the office. No going home for fresh clothes, so I figured at least a shower . . ."

"Of course," she says. "I'd give you ten towels for staying last night. I'm sorry I don't have coffee in the house."

"I rarely drink it," he says. "I found the Lipton's. As soon as the kettle boils. Slowest kettle in the world."

"I know. It's the stove. It looks modern and sleek, but it's not very powerful. I've got some British tea that Wea . . ." She stops.

"That Weaver brought you?"

She nods.

"Sounds good."

"I just need to run to the . . ." She points to the bathroom. "Then I'll take over and make breakfast," she says.

"I need to leave soon."

"It won't take any time to fix you eggs."

"I **am** pretty hungry, actually." He smiles. She can feel that he's taking her in: the lavender seersucker robe, no makeup, the hair uncombed. And yet, his eyes are approving.

"How was the sofa?" she asks.

"Honestly? After the war, the whole world seems pretty comfortable to me."

On the way to the bathroom, she passes a chair where his holster hangs, a gun weighing it down. It confounds her. She's never thought of Charlie wearing a gun. She sees its handle sticking out. What would it be like to carry **that** every day? She also passes the linen closet and realizes the mound of tossed-down towels and sheets is gone from the floor. She was too upset to make sense of it last night. Opening the door, she sees he's put everything back. The sheets are folded with military precision. The towels rolled. What man does that sort of thing? And with only one hand—how?

When she steps out of the bathroom, having brushed her teeth and hair and rubbed on some rouge, he's buttoned his shirt and is standing looking at his tie like it might bite him.

"Everything okay?" she asks.

"I'm no good at ties," he says. "Wasn't even with two hands."

"I can tie a tie. I'd be happy to."

"Really? Would you?"

It's a pretty silk foulard as blue as his eyes. She gently takes it.

"Who normally ties your ties?" she asks. "You wear one every day."

He doesn't answer.

She waits, and nothing.

Why has it never occurred to her before? A lot of men don't wear wedding bands. **Could Charlie Szydlo be married?** For a moment, she has a horrible sinking feeling. No. A man answered the telephone at his place last night. A roommate, she assumed. And he didn't call a wife last night to warn her he wouldn't be coming home. Funny, though, how the idea of him being married upsets her.

"Come here," she says, pointing to one of the two dining chairs. "You're too tall for me to tie it when you're standing." Once he sits, she drapes the tie around his neck and, standing in front of him, biting her lip, she ties the knot Henry showed her when she was a little girl. Left over right, wrap it around, pull it up the back, tuck it in. She wriggles up the knot and makes sure his collar lies smoothly over it. He smells of her soap. His hair is so short, it can't hold much water on the sides, but she spots tiny droplets caught in its thatch. She's tempted to brush her hand over his flattop, to sense the damp on her fingertips and feel the tickling sharp edges of the cut.

"That must have hurt," she says, touching a ghostly scar on his neck. And she notes a comma-shaped one by his mouth. "Something from your wild childhood?"

"Something from the war," he says vaguely.

"Ah." She finishes the knot. "You look dapper."

"Hardly . . . without a shave in twenty-four hours. I borrowed your Pepsodent and brushed my teeth with my finger, though," he says. "I say yes to those eggs, by the way."

"Good."

Rosalind sets about cracking and scrambling. "Cheese in your scrambled eggs?"

"Sure."

Scrambled eggs are one of the few things she's learned to cook well. She keeps the temperature low and whips them continually so the curds are soft and large, just as she'd learned in the **Look Before You Cook** cookbook.

"It's nice, having someone cook for me," Charlie says.

"I'm a terrible cook. But I can make eggs. You don't have a wife to cook for you?" **Why not ask? Why not find out?**

He laughs. "I live in the basement of my sister's house," he says. "I'm not the marrying type, I guess."

"Oh." She feels relief flow from her neck, her arms, the release of a long breath. Why does she care if he's married? This is the person who's injected Weaver back into her life. Something draws her to him, though, and not just his good looks.

"I had dinner with Peggy—that's my sister—and her family last night. She would happily cook for me if I let her. But I'm always in a hurry in the morning and come home late most nights. Since you asked, my sister ties my ties, leaves them half-tied in my closet. I guess I didn't want to say."

"Why not?"

"A man should be able to tie his own ties."

She dismisses him with a shake of the head. Men are so foolishly proud.

"Your sister must be special."

"I came back in rough shape from the war. I

was with my dad for a while. When he got ill, she took us both in."

"My sister took me in when I was a baby," Roz says. "And she took in my father, too, right before he died."

He nods. "Your sister cared for you when you were . . . not doing so well after Weaver, too, didn't she?"

Feeling ashamed, she turns back to fill the plates with eggs. "Is there anything about me you **don't** know?"

"Truthfully, there's a lot about you I'd **like** to know." His voice is so sincere, it stops her for a moment. She's afraid to look up.

"There's not much to tell." She shares the eggs between the dishes, giving him about two thirds. When she sets his plate down, she avoids his eyes, sits across from him.

"For instance, I'm curious what it was about Weaver that attracted you."

Her lips part. How does one explain attraction? A force far less predictable than atomic energy. "Weaver was . . . confident, smart, good-looking. And, he was interested in me."

"I always thought women didn't like men who were interested in them . . ."

"Whoever told you that?"

He shrugs. "Maybe that's why I'm not married. I read the wrong book."

She laughs, then can't help looking at him.

Handsome. Magnetic in his indecipherable aloneness. "Do you want to be married?"

"Do **you**?" he asks. Neither of them answers. They eat their eggs in companionable silence.

"I'm going to have two people assigned to watch out for you, by the way," Charlie says. "One during daylight hours. Another at night. Lots of red tape to have that happen, so you might not get them until tomorrow. Or even the next day."

"Oh . . ."

"I don't think you're in danger. Not really. But after the break-in . . . I want you to have peace of mind."

"Thank you."

"I wish I could do it myself," he says. "But of course, I can't."

"No. Of course not."

"I'll have each of the men introduce himself so you won't be spooked, okay?"

"Yes. That would be best." She finds it hard to imagine having her own bodyguards. Will they count the times Weaver comes? How long he stays? Will they report in to Charlie? And if Weaver spots them, what will he think? She'll have to insist on going to his place. She watches the neat, delicate way Charlie eats, noting once more the odd way he presses his other hand against his ribs.

"What happened to your hand, Charlie?" she

asks softly. She can hardly believe she's asked, bites at the inside of her cheek, regretting it.

"Oh . . . ," he says.

"I'm sorry. Maybe I shouldn't have brought it up."

His blue eyes grow opaque. A flush creeps from his hairline across his brow—like rosy clouds moving in.

"It happened because of a pair of shoes."

"A pair of shoes?"

He nods. "I was a POW. When they moved us from the Philippines to Japan, the first thing they did was burn our clothes and shoes because we were covered in lice. The Japanese didn't make clothes to fit someone like me." He runs his hand over the top of his hair, stares off to a place she cannot see. "I didn't dare complain. One of my fellow prisoners pointed out that there was a tear in the seam of his trousers, and they beat him to death. He had three children, that guy."

"My God."

"I have size fourteen feet. So I ripped open the toes off the canvas shoes they issued and let my feet poke through. Then I wrapped the fronts in burlap from the sacks the shoes had been shipped in." How must this tall, elegant man have looked to the Japanese, his eyes so blue? Foreign. Imposing. Walking in shoes wrapped in burlap.

"There was one kind guard in our camp in the mountains. Gorou. The guards all had medical or mental problems; otherwise they would have been off fighting. And most hated us. The concept of surrender to the Japanese . . . well, they couldn't understand why we wouldn't prefer to die. There were a few decent men who just did their jobs. But some would hit us, kick us, any chance they got. Made us wish we were dead. Gorou was a kind, polite older man who bowed and smiled. He had something wrong with his hip and a limp—that and his age is why he'd been left behind. Maybe it's what made him sensitive to the fact that I was limping. He spoke some English. At the camp in the Philippines, I'd learned basic Japanese. Anyway, Gorou asked me to unwrap my feet and he saw that my toes were bleeding, that I had no soles under the front halves of my feet. We were building a hydroelectric dam for the city of Nagoya. I was outside working on jagged rocks with nothing beneath my toes."

By now, Rosalind has set down her fork.

"So Gorou measured my feet with a piece of string and somehow got hold of two pairs of the black canvas shoes we prisoners wore. I don't know if he bought them or stole them, but he cut both pairs apart and joined the fronts and backs with a sewing machine so I could have real shoes under my toes. He even managed to melt some kind of rubber or wax to join the sole so rain wouldn't pour into the gap between the pairs."

He sets his own fork down, rubs his forehead. She watches the emotions moving through him like a dark tide. "It was autumn, in the mountains, freezing. If he hadn't given them to me, I'd have gotten frostbite and probably died of gangrene. I actually cried the day he gave them to me—cried over a pair of canvas shoes." He shakes his head and she can see his eyes filling now. How she would love to comfort him, tell him she understands.

"Each morning, I put on those shoes and wrapped them in the old burlap so no one would know what he'd done for me."

"Charlie . . . ," Rosalind says.

"You probably wonder what that has to do with my hand."

She nods.

"One night, the head of the camp burst into our barracks in the middle of the night, snapped on the lights. They told us we all had to empty our sleeping slabs and put whatever we had on the floor. Turns out someone had stolen two cans of sardines from the mess.

"When I emptied my bunk, I made sure my shoes were wrapped in the burlap. But that's what caught the officer's eye. A place to hide a can of sardines, I guess he thought. He pulled the burlap off and discovered my secret.

"'Who did this for you?' he asked in Japanese. I understood him. But I pretended I didn't. They would have beheaded Gorou for his act of kindness. The officer hit me with the buckle of his belt. He aimed for my face but I was too tall, so it caught my neck. I already had a wound there from being hit with a bamboo pole. The belt buckle opened the scar. That's what you saw when you tied my tie."

"Oh, Charlie . . ."

"Anyway, the officer said, 'Who made these shoes? Tell us or we kill you.' I decided I preferred to die rather than betray Gorou. His act of kindness was the only thing that made my life worth living anyway. Those shoes said another human being **valued** me.

"When I wouldn't tell them, they dragged me to a cell in another building." Charlie is silent for a moment, staring at his hands—his good hand, his bad hand. She doesn't know if he'll go on, sees that it's hard for him, somehow knows that he's rarely told this story.

"Were you there for long?" she asks.

"A night, then a whole day. There wasn't a single thing in that cell. No blankets, no wood. Just concrete all around, and a trench for a toilet. I've never been so cold sleeping curled up in the corner on concrete. My neck bled and bled. I prayed when they came for me, I'd be dead. Frozen to death or having bled out. No such luck. The next evening, they walked me back to the barracks. There was a fire pit in the floor in the middle of each section of the barracks. The fires burned three hours a night to supposedly heat the room.

"The officer in charge called all the men to gather around the fire pit. Listen, Rosalind, I don't have to go on. You don't need to hear this."

"Tell me," she says, her voice choked. When was the last time she took a breath?

"They asked me again, 'Who gave you the shoes?' When I wouldn't say, three of the guards forced me to my knees. They asked one more time, and I just shook my head. So two of the men grabbed my arm and pushed my hand into the flames all the way until my fingers touched the coals. They held it there . . . for a long time. All my fellow prisoners stood around the fire pit watching. I looked up into their faces, and what I recall is blankness. Utter blankness. Not horror. Not sympathy. Nothing. Then I passed out." Charlie's face is masklike. He shakes his head. "We were broken by then, you see. We were all barely human."

"Dear God." She discovers that she's weeping. How could any human being treat another with so much hate? How could a man survive it?

"Afterward, my hand was infected . . . They brought in the British medic because ours had died. He said he needed to cut it off, but I begged him not to. He told me I'd die. I prayed I would." His voice wavers only slightly. "And then, your bombs saved me."

Your bombs. Two words she never wants to hear together.

"I'm sorry," she says.

"Don't be sorry. **You** saved me. I'm grateful. You saved me even when I didn't want to be saved." She saved him. For a moment, the horror of what she helped bring to the world is lit with a single beam of light. For a moment, her heart lifts. This man wouldn't be here if not for her bombs.

"I'm glad you survived," she says breathlessly. How she yearns to reach out for him, slip her arms around him. She aches with longing to feel his strong chest pressed to her breasts. "You were meant to live, Charlie. I'm so glad."

He looks up at her shyly, then looks away.

"Does it give you much pain?" she whispers.

He shrugs, gathers his thoughts. "Have you ever heard of a phantom limb?" She shakes her head. "When a man loses a hand or foot he often still feels it's there, feels pain where there is nothing. I have no feeling when I touch my hand, as though it's dead or gone, yet it wakes me with its burning. Mostly, I hate for other people to . . . look at it. It mortifies me."

"It's not that noticeable," she says.

"Don't sweet-talk me. It's a prop from a horror movie. I know it. I hate for anyone to see it. Especially you."

Especially her?

"I should go." He stands suddenly, folds his napkin deftly with one hand and sets it by his plate. His movements are like a magician's.

"Charlie. Wait."

Getting up, she comes around the table and carefully reaches for the injured hand. He recoils and looks shocked as she takes it tenderly. She wonders if other women have touched him this way. Cradling his hand in one of hers, she strokes it with the other.

"Don't look at it," he says and starts to withdraw, but she won't let him.

The skin, as she'd imagined, is raised and thickened, ropy with scars, but it isn't repugnant to her. It's still soft. Still warm. Still human.

"I don't find your hand horrifying," she says. "It's part of you. It's been through a lot. I feel sad for it." She lifts it up and presses it to her cheek.

His lips part as though he wants to speak but doesn't quite know what to say. He closes his eyes. Is he blocking out the sight of her holding his injured hand, or is he touched that she's not afraid to caress it?

"Please," he says.

"I refuse to let you think your hand is awful. You seem so capable. You don't let it stop you."

"I've been told it's awful," he says. "Someone I loved once told me it's awful."

His words strike her. "That someone is a fool," she says softly.

In his eyes, she sees complexity and desire. Emotion too deep for her to plumb. And what she feels for him is sharp and full of longing.

"I should go," he says. "I need to go."

She nods. "I know you do."

When she lets go of the hand, her fingers still tingle from having touched it. Like the sizzle off a match, it sets a ripple of fire moving through her whole being, smoldering long, long after he's gone.

CHAPTER SIXTEEN

Around one P.M., Ronnie, the stock man, presents Rosalind with the weekly shipment of new items. Whenever he carries up a delivery from the loading dock, he says the same thing: "For you, Miss Porter. Diamonds for my princess."

"Well, thank you, Ronnie," she tells him. "A girl can always use more diamonds." She watches him walk away, rotund, his hair, once golden, now thinning and translucent. A man with a kind heart. Today, she especially appreciates that kind heart. All day she's been shaky, distracted, moved by Charlie's story and sick at the thought of what men can do to one another. But she's also warmed when she thinks of Charlie Szydlo. She's surprised how intensely she longs to see him again, to feel his warm skin against her fingers. Even his ruined hand felt beautiful to her. Is it only because he played the white knight by staying? She wishes he'd come again tonight. She's dreading going home alone to face the mess, the sense of intrusion that the break-in has left her with. She never knew how bitter fear could taste.

She watches for the man who's been following her, expecting any moment to spot those clear eyes, that mass of pale hair that can't be real. Even when a customer comes at last, a woman interested in some of the oldest and most interesting rings, she finds it hard to pay attention, not to glance around nervously for the intruder.

At about three thirty, she's pinning a garnet brooch in the shape of a soaring bird to the black velvet plaque where she keeps the medium-size brooches, thinking abstractly about Charlie's story of his mother embroidering bluebirds while he slept, when she hears a soft, "Miss Porter," and glances up sharply to see an unfamiliar young woman standing in front of her. Buttoned into a sober blue suit and wearing no hat, the girl looks intimidating, though she's surely younger than Rosalind. Her medium brown hair is tightly wound. Rosalind spots the hairpins: one after another, neat as stitches from a sewing machine.

"Do I know you?" Rosalind asks.

"I'm Special Agent Szydlo's secretary, Donna. He asked me to give you something." Her voice is a whisper. "He didn't think it wise to come here himself if you're being followed." Rosalind nods. "By ten o'clock tonight, you'll have a man watching you. He wanted me to say that first."

"Will I? I'll be glad."

There's something so formal and awkward about the girl that it makes Rosalind feel sorry for her. The woman unsnaps her handbag and pulls something out. "Hold out your hand," she whispers.

Into Rosalind's palm the woman sets a small object so heavy, Rosalind's arm momentarily dips. Positioning it just beneath the counter and turning it toward herself, Rosalind meets the smallest camera she's ever encountered.

"Agent Szydlo says you should put it away, somewhere you can grab it quickly. He wants you to use it if you see the man. Since you need to take the photo in a way that won't be noticed, you can't hold it to your eye. Understand? The round part is the lens. It needs to face the perpetrator as much as possible."

"Yes, I've used a camera."

"And he told me to remind you to keep it steady while you click the shutter—the little round button up top. Or the photograph will blur. Set it on the counter if you can. But tilt it toward the man's face. The film's already been loaded. Thirty-six shots. You may need to take that many to capture him without looking through the lens. Agent Szydlo said not to worry about wasting shots—up to thirty-six, of course. He also asked me to ask you . . ." She frowns slightly. "If you're . . . if you're ummm . . . feeling . . . okay?" The girl clearly thinks the question odd. She's so serious, so nunlike. No lipstick. No jewelry. She wonders if Donna finds Agent Szydlo attractive, or is she put off by his injured hand? And what does Charlie think of her? This is a woman he works with every day.

"Tell him I'm not looking forward to going home."

The secretary nods briskly, as if trying to memorize the words.

"Show me a piece of jewelry," the girl says.

"I'm sorry?"

"Agent Szydlo says I should look like a customer in case anyone's watching."

Rosalind slips a little mourning ring off her finger and hands it to Donna. Donna turns it over and over, frowning.

"It's a baby," she says. Because Rosalind loves the ring, she's been wearing it. On an oval of porcelain, the face of a curly haired, rosy-cheeked baby looks up at her with wide blue eyes. Those eyes were closed and that beautiful child was lying in a coffin by the time the miniature was painted. Two cherub wings etched on the gold bezel below the portrait say so. Inside, the engraving reads: **Affection weeps. Heaven rejoices. Edmund Karl Michael.**

"Yes," Rosalind says. "His mother had this ring painted to memorialize him. That's what people did back then to help them mourn."

"Who would want to wear a reminder of a dead baby?"

"A loving mother would," she says. "I would." She takes the ring and slides it back onto her finger. "Babies died all the time in the eighteenth century. I think it's beautiful, but it's not for everyone. Perhaps you'd prefer this?" She pulls out a regard ring with particularly tiny stones. Rosalind has been thinking of it as the "without much regard" ring, since the stones are so minuscule. Donna tries it on her finger and turns it back and forth under the spotlights.

"They light this counter so the gems shine, don't they?" she says.

"It allows you to see them better."

"It's cheating, though. It won't look that way in the real world, will it?"

"Sunlight will do the same."

"I'm not much for jewelry." Donna hands back the ring as though it's radioactive. "The man outside your door tonight—his name is Gray. He'll knock when he arrives. Another man will join you tomorrow. Agent Lawrence."

"Tonight's man will just sit outside my door?"

"That's the plan."

"But what do I tell my neighbors? Or if Weaver

shows up unexpectedly? What will I say? How will I explain it?"

"I don't know," Donna says. "Call Agent Szydlo if you need instructions."

"Okay." In order to keep Weaver from coming over, she'll have to go to his place often. She takes the camera from behind the counter into her hand where only she can see it. So small, so easy to hide. A camera to catch a Russian. How has she gotten here?

"Is there anything else you want me to tell Agent Szydlo?" Donna asks.

Rosalind slides the gadget back onto the shelf behind the counter. She wishes she could say, **Tell Charlie I want him to spend the night with me again.** Instead, she says, "Tell him thank you for the camera."

⫸ ⫸ ⫸

Just past dark, Charlie stands at the brand-new door of the yellow frame house on Paulina Street, working up the courage to knock. It's red with three windows cut vertically. What on earth made Sondra choose a red door? With the jaundiced siding, the door is ketchup against mustard. He's considering turning tail, telephoning from home to say he's sorry, that he must have picked up the flu. Except he's a terrible liar and

Peggy would never back him up. "Lying isn't a part of the Ten Commandments," he once pointed out to her when he was about ten. "Except for bearing false witness against your neighbor, and I wouldn't even know how to do that."

"What are you, a dope? It's a sin anyway! All lying is a sin."

Christ. Why did he ask his sister's friend to dinner? When he raps sharply, the red door swings back and Sondra stands before him in a fancy dress.

"I thought I saw you out there," she says cheerily. "Come in."

"You got a new door?"

"The old one was rotten. Fell right off one morning. Like it?"

"The door? Oh sure. Who doesn't like red?" He for one. He imagines Peggy shaking her head at him.

She smooths her puffed-up skirt as she lets him by. With her shoulders back, her hair done up, coral lipstick and rouge on her cheeks, coral nail polish—it's far too elaborate for a simple dinner at Kutz's. The dress is black-and-white and flowered, layered up in that see-through fabric that Peggy calls organdy. Sondra looks like a different woman from the one who came to lunch, so natural, so homey.

"So, how are you, Sondra?" he asks.

"Oh, fine. Fine. I just need to gather my

things. A little powder for the nose. I should have packed my purse before you came but I didn't have time." Yes, because she was doing her nails and putting on lipstick and using Spray Net on her hair, he thinks. He tries to tell himself that she's trying too hard because she's a woman still in pain. Hurt by the war like he's been. But he can't help feeling threatened that she's dolled herself up like this just for him.

He glances around. He came to a summer housewarming party at this house with Linda the year Sondra and her husband bought it. Cookies and sandwiches cut into the shape of houses. Relatives, friends, new neighbors, all invited. Still teenagers, Charlie and Linda slipped into the dark narrow gangway between the Beckers' house and their neighbor's and, thinking no one could see them, began to kiss. He remembers pressing himself against his soft, yielding, and very willing girlfriend, sliding his hand up her shirt. Peggy slapped him when they got home. "You're lucky I don't tell Mama," she said. "Do you have any idea how **embarrassing** your behavior was? If I saw, anyone could see. Sondra's **my** friend, Charlie. And it was a nice family-style party. The angels were covering their eyes. What is **wrong** with you?" He flushes now, remembering. Oh, how much desire he had then—like a waterfall: ever flowing, loud, relentless enough to cut a hole in stone.

For the most part, that desire was a victim of the war, of his captivity, of Linda's rejection. Except last night, he'd had a taste of it when he slept on Rosalind's sofa. He'd longed for her in the next room in a way he hasn't longed for anyone in years. Yearned for her in his sleep, dreamt of kissing her, undressing her, woke himself up just in time not to mess up the sheets. It's madness he should feel this way about the woman he's encouraging to sleep with his number one suspect. His responsibility. His asset. And she still has enough feeling for her ex-lover that she's withholding information on his behalf. Yet, this morning, the way she took his hand . . . Nothing has moved him that much since the war. Nothing.

On the flip side, the only thing in his life that has consistently meant anything to him of late is his job. And if he were to start up with Rosalind, he'd be risking what matters most to him. Yet . . . the way she touched his scars, whispered about how his ruined hand was part of him and didn't offend her. Is he only imagining she's drawn to him too? She's clearly still besotted with Weaver. At first, Charlie felt minimal guilt for making her reach out to Weaver. She and Weaver had already been lovers. But now . . . the thought of Rosalind in bed with that man, that traitor, makes him sick with regret.

"Ready, then?" Sondra swirls into the room like

a little girl showing off her new tutu. He takes a deep breath. Her nose is powdered. Her eyelids are colored. She has hopes for this date. Hopes for Charlie. She's utterly forgotten or misinterpreted what he said about wanting to be friends. He's never been willing to disappoint anyone. That's one of the main reasons he's kept so much to himself lately. He has nothing to offer. But it's too late to back out, and she's smiling at him like he's the Christmas package she's always hoped to find under her tree.

⫼ ⫼ ⫼

This morning before work, Rosalind called Zeke to beg him to walk her home and spend the night. She said she'd explain it all when she saw him. He's outside the State Street door when she leaves Field's, shooting photographs of random people. His oversize camera appears to weigh more than he does.

"Stay still and watch that bus go by," he commands, turning it on her.

"What?"

"Just do as I say." She shifts her weight uncomfortably while Zeke clicks off a few shots.

"It's a mystery," he says, "how someone as graceful as you can turn into the Mummy the second you know your photo's being taken."

"Shut up." She kisses him, then has to wipe

lipstick off his freckled cheek. "Thanks for coming."

"What the hell's up?"

"I need to be with my best friend. Isn't that enough?"

"No. We had dinner last night. Wasn't **that** enough?" When she doesn't answer, he hooks his arm in hers. "What's Weaver done now? Spill it."

"It's not Weaver."

"Then what?"

"I was robbed."

"What?"

"I was robbed."

"And this isn't a metaphor?"

She shakes her head.

"When?"

"Last night."

Zeke gasps. "But we were together last night."

"When I got home, the door was open. The apartment was a disaster."

"And you didn't call me?"

"I called the . . . police. But now I'm afraid to go home alone. Also, it's a mess."

"Why would anyone rob you? You don't wear fancy jewelry. Or furs. You're a washout to a robber."

"Thanks. Next time I see them, I'll ask why the hell they bothered."

Knocking her with his elbow, he says, "I don't know if I'd call you droll or sarcastic, but neither is attractive, young lady." He pulls her closer, pats her hand. "I'm glad you're okay, Bunny." Zeke can't do a damn thing to save her, but there's nothing more comforting than his familiarity.

When they reach the apartment, Frank nods and says, "Mr. Adams," then waits until Zeke's halfway to the elevator before whispering, "Miss Porter?" She turns back to him. "That man, that FBI agent last night. Is he your new beau?"

She shakes her head and smiles. "Just a friend. I was lucky he was available to help."

"Nice fellow. It would be good to have a fellow like that for a boyfriend," he says. **Instead of Weaver,** is what he's really saying. "Want to know the truth, I feel bad about it. We haven't had a break-in in this building in ten years or more."

"Frank, it's not your fault."

"I don't get how a thief could slip by me. I try to be aware. I just want to reassure you I'm on the job a thousand percent." He looks stricken.

"I always know you're here to protect me."

"Hurry up, Bunny," Zeke calls from the elevator. "I'm sweating bullets."

"Be right there. Thanks, Frank," she says. "There's nothing to worry about, I'm sure." Still, in the elevator, as warm as it is, a finger of fear slips up her back, causing her to shiver.

〜 〜 〜

When they open the door to her apartment, it's extraordinary how assaultive the chaos feels. Zeke can't stop clicking his tongue at the mess. He's the one who turns around the second they're in the apartment and relocks both locks and hooks the chain too. "Can't be too careful," he says. "But as for **this mayhem,** you need a maid, not me."

"I should have suggested you bring your maid's uniform, duster and all. Me, I'm putting on dungarees."

When she comes out of the bedroom, Zeke grabs a red bandana that's on top of a pile the looters dislodged from the hall table drawer.

"C'mere," he says. "We'll make you into Rosie the Riveter." He ties the bandana around her curls, then turns her to look in the mirror. He's left the requisite two little tails on top. It's soothing to have Zeke here. Still, the panic sifts down on her as she begins to put things away. Someone's touched her possessions. Someone wants something from her. And even Charlie and his team have moved and handled everything: her lingerie, her journal, that box of love letters from Weaver.

Dampening a rag, she picks up the fingerprint grit Charlie and the evidence team left behind, picks up the extra bed pillow Charlie left on the sofa this morning and briefly holds it to her nose to take in his scent—both clean and deeply masculine—before she finds a place for it in the linen closet. Zeke is in charge of putting books back in the bookcases, but every third book he sits down to explore. Around eight, they still have more to tackle but decide they'd better pause for dinner. Pulling out a can of Chef Boyardee, she holds it up to Zeke.

"Gourmet fare?" she asks.

"Who needs filet mignon?"

She keys it open with the can opener and dumps the glop into a little enamel pot. She's turning on the burner when the buzzer startles her.

"Miss Porter, Mr. Weaver's here for you . . . ," Frank says.

Dear God, did Weaver let her know he was coming and she forgot? Frank's tone says, **Send him away.** For a thin moment, she feels panicked, uncertain. She's wearing dungarees and a bandana. She must look a fright. But she has no choice. "Let him up."

"Weaver's here," she calls to Zeke.

"Does that mean I can leave?" he asks.

"And give up a dinner of Chef Boyardee? It's up to you."

"I'll just say hello to the Prodigal Lover and leave you two alone to do **whatever it is** you two do," he says with a lascivious grin.

She sticks the barely heated pan into the fridge and tosses the can in the trash. No need to further prove to Weaver that she's a subpar cook. At the door, she yanks off the bandana. She can't do anything about the dungarees, but she slicks on a layer of lipstick.

When she finally gets everything unlocked, she's astonished by Weaver's appearance. He seems even thinner, and surprisingly more striking. His new sleekness emphasizes his cheekbones, his square chin, and makes his eyes—right now a clear mossy green—more the focus of his face. Has he ever looked so utterly masculine? She wishes she wasn't so drawn to him.

"You didn't say you were coming . . ." At least her FBI escort isn't scheduled to show up until ten, she thinks with relief.

"May I come in anyway?"

"Of course, I— Are you all right?" He looks jangled, distressed.

"I need a drink. Still have some of that grand Scotch? Zeke!"

"I'm just leaving. Don't mind me. You're here to save the day and I can go back to my quiet little life." He kisses Rosalind's cheek, twists one of her curls around his fingers. "See you, Bunny. It will all be okay, I'm sure."

When he's gone, Weaver drops wearily into an armchair.

"What did he mean about it being okay? What's happened here?" Weaver looks around. She and Zeke made some progress, yet there's sheet music thrown under the piano bench, a picture frame crashed and cracked by the radiator, too many books still unshelved because Zeke found them irresistible.

"I was broken into last night."

His eyes grow wide. "Dear God," he says. "And you're just right as rain?"

"It could have been worse. I wasn't here. And, honestly, I can't see that they took anything. Not my jewelry. Not my forty-five bucks in the drawer by the fridge. I'd say they were looking for something and didn't find it. Mistaken identity maybe . . ." She sounds too cheery, but it's the only way she can think to tell him, without letting on she knows it's his fault. She finds the bottle of Scotch and pours him a large glassful, though she realizes this long-hoarded bottle is now only a quarter full.

"You didn't call me?"

"I was out with Zeke when it happened, thank God."

"Did they take that envelope I gave you? Did they take **that**?" His voice bends when he asks. The panic in his face is unquestionable.

"No. It's in a safe-deposit box at my bank."

"Thank God," he says. "Thank God. Did you call the police?"

"Yes. They took fingerprints."

"Oh Jesus."

"What?"

He just shakes his head. "Hopefully, the police don't have **their** fingerprints on record."

"Whose?"

"The people who want that envelope."

"So, in your mind, that's what this is about? **Your envelope?** And you're hoping the police **won't** be able to identify the people who did this? Jesus, Weaver. What have you gotten me into?"

He sets down his drink with a **thunk** and stands swiftly, clearly struck with a horrible thought. Grabbing her hand, he throws open the front door and draws her out into the hall. Shuts it tightly.

"Where are you . . . what are we . . . ?"

He puts his finger to his lips.

Halfway down the hall he whispers, "Christ. Your apartment is bugged."

"Bugged? I don't understand."

"With listening devices. I don't know why I didn't realize. That's the only way they could have known I gave you the envelope. They heard me talk about it when I handed it to you. Goddammit to hell!"

For a moment, she's confused. He's not speaking about the FBI phone tap. This is worse. Is he just paranoid, or is it true? Have they heard her making love to Weaver? Do they know that Charlie spent the night last night even if Weaver doesn't?

"Why would anyone want to listen to **me**?"

"Let's walk down to the lake and I'll tell you," he says. "Grab your purse and I'll take my drink. Just stay quiet, though, until we get outside."

"You don't think anyone will think it odd, you marching down the street with a glass of Scotch?"

"I don't give a damn what they think," he says. "Get whatever you need; then let's get the hell out of the building."

"I've got to change out of these dungarees, for one thing. I can't go out at night like this."

"Then do it and hurry up."

In her bedroom, changing as quickly as she can, she can hear her own heart pounding so loudly she imagines her eavesdroppers could pick it up. If her apartment really **is** bugged, what did she say to Charlie last night or this morning? Won't they realize he's from the FBI? And the other two men who came to dust for prints: the way they discussed sectioning off her apartment for prints. They heard that too. Doesn't it put her at risk? And Weaver too . . .

In the elevator, she finds it hard to breathe. Weaver fixes his eyes on the indicator and doesn't say a word. Frank nods at them as they attempt to walk out nonchalantly, Weaver with a drink in hand. The sky is cloudless, an elegant blue. A Van Gogh sky, magical and starry. The fact it's such a nice evening mocks them. Her breath grows even more constrained, and the street begins to roll before her eyes.

"Weaver, I think I feel faint," she says.

"Oh Christ," he says. "You must be hyperventilating. Take long breaths and be sure to breathe out all the way. You're not actually going to pass out on me, are you?"

"Is my apartment really bugged? Have people been listening to us **making love**?"

"Nothing we can do about it now," he says coolly.

"You always said I was too noisy in bed."

"I was just teasing you. I like the sounds you make. Look, I'm sorry. I'm sorry about this." Transferring his Scotch to his other hand, he slips his arm around her waist. "You're not going to crumple on me here, are you? Breathe slowly."

She breathes. The wooziness lightens but doesn't go away. The bridge of her nose buzzes. But of course, she hasn't eaten since lunch.

"Are you saying it's your fault they're listening in?" she asks.

"It's a good bet."

"And who are **they**?"

He shakes his head weakly. "Breathe," he says.

She takes long breaths, focuses on breathing out. She feels anger to her fingers, senses a narrowing in her throat. Her place being ransacked was awful. But thinking that someone's been listening to every single thing she's done . . . for how long?

"Cup your hands around your mouth and nose and breathe into them. I'd give you a paper bag if I had one."

"You did this to me," she says.

He looks sad, sheepish even.

"I don't know what you're involved in. And yet you've made me a target," she says.

He nods, looking wounded. The color leaves his face. "I don't blame you for being angry. Here, rest for a moment against this wall." She half sits on a brick fence that surrounds a large, attractive house. She remembers that he sat her here once before, to kiss her, long ago, during the war. They walked together all the time then, scouting for windows that were uncurtained and well lit, so they could peep into the houses. What an irony that in those days they enjoyed spying on others, felt it was a fine thing to do! Now Weaver pets her hair, watches her with concern, in a way he never has before. He's worried about her forgiving him. He has no idea the Russians might now know the FBI are involved. And she can't say a word. How has she gotten here? Furious at him, fearful for him. **Breathe,** she tells herself. **Breathe.**

After a long while, he says softly, "What do you think, love? Are you well enough to walk down to our bench?"

"Yes."

"Good," he says. "I came tonight to tell you something."

※ ※ ※

Charlie orders a steak and a beer. He's never been a huge drinker. But he's counting on it to lubricate the conversation. Sondra orders some sort of cocktail with a maraschino cherry stabbed by a fluffy purple toothpick. The last time he ate out was at the Berghoff when he was following Rosalind. He remembers watching her enjoying her niece's company, while he sat awkward and alone. He assumed then that she was unapproachable. He'd give anything to be with her tonight instead of Sondra, who pops the drink's cherry into her mouth first thing.

"I love maraschino cherries," she says. "They're so indulgent."

He smiles, stops himself from saying that he abhors them, that they taste like cough medicine.

"I'm a cheap date," she says enthusiastically. "One drink and I'm in my cups."

"Then maybe you'd better hold off drinking it until the waitress brings bread or something."

"You're no fun." She pokes his arm, and when she does, he thinks of Rosalind tenderly reaching for his hand, stroking it, looking into his eyes. Those dark eyes of hers. The soft scallop of her mouth. He shakes off the memory, needs to get through this evening. And it becomes challenging, for as Sondra continues to drink, she becomes more talkative, until she waves for the waitress to bring another.

"You don't mind, do you?" she asks. She doesn't notice when he doesn't answer. Is this how Sondra acted all the times Peggy set her up with other men? Does she think he wants her a little tipsy? He supposes there are men who would gleefully take advantage of a girl too compromised to know what she's doing.

He's relieved when the salads arrive, heads of iceberg lettuce cut into wedges, buried in thick waves of Thousand Island dressing. She cuts hers into pieces and crunches away, telling him about her job at the church, waving her fork. He cuts his with his knife alone, wondering if he can manage to slice off a piece without launching the wedge, since he doesn't have another hand to stab it with a fork. She talks about her brother, whom he knows. About her parents and how she worries about them growing old. Maybe he should give up on the lettuce? He tries to pry it apart with his fork, then settles on skewering the wedge with the fork and pressing the fork against the plate with his left wrist while he cuts with the knife. He'd be too self-conscious to do this in front of Rosalind. But he recognizes Sondra's too tipsy to care.

"It's always the single daughters that end up moving into their parents' house, tending to them. That's me. The single daughter," she says. "I ought to wear a badge."

After the salad, she waves to the waitress and asks for yet another drink. Charlie imagines crossing his arms and laying his head down on them. It's going to be a long night.

CHAPTER SEVENTEEN

Rosalind and Weaver have reached the beach and **their** bench.

"You okay now? Want to sit?" She claims the same side of the bench where she always sat overlooking the water in the past. How many times did they come here to find solace, to fight, to cry? He leans over and sets his drink on the ground, then straightens and lights a cigarette. He has to cup his hands to protect the flame from the lake breeze, and that's when she sees his hands are unsteady.

"So, tell me," Rosalind says. "Who bugged my apartment and why?"

She waits for the lie, the pivot, the silence. But he stares straight ahead over the water and says, "Some Russians."

She's too staggered to speak for a minute. It's the last thing she expected from him: honesty.

"Oh, **Russians**," she says. If Charlie hadn't clued her in, surely she'd react with sarcasm, wouldn't she? "With **so** much excitement going on at my apartment, of course, how could **Russians** stay away?"

The muscles in his jaw twitch. "I know it sounds absurd."

"You bet."

"For a change, I'm telling you the truth." This shakes her too.

"I got myself into something unknowingly years ago," he says.

"Unknowingly. With Russians?"

"Yes." He sits down beside her.

Looking out over the empty beach, she recalls other nights they sat side by side on this bench in pained silence. He wouldn't talk about marrying her, never spoke about children though she ached for them. Later, when she suffered with pulsing regret over the photographs she'd seen of Japanese buildings reduced to collapsing skeletons, burned bodies, melted faces, "Don't you care what we've done?" she entreated him. "Don't you feel shame for what we created?" While she wept, he just smoked, waiting for her to get over it. He kicked the butts of his cigarettes into the sand after he ground them out on the concrete pad with his shoe. She usually read his refusal to comfort her as his Englishness, his cool intolerance of open emotion. She should have hated him then but didn't. All lovers have their faults, she told herself. All lovers present obstacles. She understood her raw pain was an obstacle to him.

This evening, he hunches over, his eyes peering out at the dark lake, waves lapping in sudsy gulps at the edge of the sand. He sucks on a cigarette, and when he exhales, the wind lifts the smoke, making it dance. As it disperses in a swirl over the water, she lays her hand on his back reassuringly, waiting for his confession. She will always love him. It's her curse. Despite the fact that he's endangered her. By choosing to spy on him for the FBI, she's also endangered him.

He smokes the entire cigarette down in silence, then grinds the butt into the concrete, lights another. All the while, his hands are shaking. She waits. In the loaded silence, she struggles. Whatever he tells her, won't she have to tell Charlie? Won't she be required to betray him? Won't she end up as his judge, perhaps his executioner? She's loved this man. A man who's betrayed his country. **He might have shared information about the atomic bomb. This man may have put the world's fate in the enemy's hands. And now, maybe, the hydrogen bomb. Is it too late to stop him?** She shivers.

"Before I tell you about the Russians," he says, "I need to tell you something else. Something more important."

How could anything be more important?

"Roz, I have cancer." He says it so flatly, the words spin weightless and sharp between them. They send a blade through her throat, cutting off anything she might ask. His new leanness, his surprising exhaustion. Cancer. She immediately hears wind in her ears, sees hospital wards filled with wasting men. Weaver. Cancer. Two more disparate things never existed.

"Do you remember after Hiroshima and Nagasaki . . . how I went to Los Alamos for a while?" he says.

She nods.

"I'd say that's when I was exposed . . ." After a long pause, he says, "At the Trinity Site."

"You went to Trinity?" Trinity was where they first tested the bomb in the Jornada del Muerto desert in New Mexico. The Journey of the Dead Man desert struck her as an uncannily appropriate name, especially after they dropped the bombs on Japan.

"I was brought out there a month after the test, after Nagasaki. They wanted to take readings. You don't remember?"

She shakes her head.

╫ ╫ ╫

He has cancer. It somehow blocks out everything else. She puts her face against his curled-over back, breathes in his distinctive, smoky scent, recalling with horror how she once wondered when it would be **his** turn to suffer for creating the bomb.

He draws on his cigarette. "Right after the explosion they rolled a lead-lined tank out there, and the radiation was much higher than they'd expected. A little over a month later—just after Japan—Kenneth Bainbridge wanted to send a team out to measure it again, to gauge the gamma-ray intensity and see how much decay had occurred. The Japanese were contending that their bomb sites had been left so hot, no one could live in either town for seventy years. They 'volunteered' me to go out to Los Alamos, to oversee a small crew. You were so unhappy after the bombs. You didn't want me around. I was relieved to escape. I know I wasn't very comforting."

She shrugs. "Maybe I couldn't be comforted." She remembers how angry she was. Angry at him, at the world, such an unforgiving lover. She pushed him away. And now she's surprised how the fact that he's ill mutes her present furor. Makes her want to forget what a traitor he is.

"What happened?" she asks.

"We drove out to ground zero with dosimeters. The plan was to prove the Japanese wrong."

"How hot was it?"

"Well, that's the thing. The meters said that the radiation had decayed much more rapidly than expected. The powers that be were delighted. Destruction and hardly any aftereffect. Except, there are plenty of things we didn't know, still don't know about aftereffects. Almost all of us on that little mission have become sick in one way or another. We were tromping all over the site like a day at the beach . . ."

She can't help wondering: Was escaping her misery the **reason** he decided to go?

"How do you feel now?" she asks.

"I'm tired at times. I didn't know I could be so tired. They say I'm beginning to grow tumors in my bones. But I don't feel them yet, thank God. When they start to break the bones they reside in, the doctors have warned they'll become excruciating. I pray I don't live that long . . ."

"Weaver . . ."

"God, whatever you do, don't pity me. I couldn't bear it."

"You should quit the lab."

"And do what? Stare at the wall? I'm not sick enough yet."

"Do things you love."

"I don't love anything but work . . . and you." He looks at her and his eyes are as dark as she's ever seen them. Thoughtful. Devoted. Not his laughing eyes. But the ones that are tired of secrets. "That's why I kept calling. I would have knocked on your door for a century just to get you to give me another chance. Except, of course, I don't have a century." He touches her hair in a tender, focused way that hardly seems like Weaver. All that cool, British bravado gone. At the very moment that she's poised to betray him.

"What kind of cancer is it?" she asks.

"It's called multiple myeloma. My body's producing too many plasma cells. They cling together in the marrow of my bones, will grow, take over. Right now, the only real symptom other than tiredness is that I often run a fever. Maybe you've felt how hot I get . . . Do you appreciate the irony? It's as though our bomb is now inside me. Preparing to explode."

He makes a horrible explosive sound. He's always been so hale. A redwood in a forest of spindly pines.

"I was going to tell you the day we went to Grant Park. But Ava was there. And being with you and Ava—I was so happy that day."

"Me too."

She's astonished to see his eyes glassing with tears.

"And after that, I couldn't seem to get it out. I started to tell you a few times. That time you came for dinner and we had a tiff over Clemence's letter . . . I meant to tell you that night too. Couldn't find the words. But now, time means more to me. And I want to spend all the rest I have with you."

She's so moved, she can hardly speak. When she does, her voice is filled with air and regret.

"Can they do anything for you?"

"I hear they're experimenting with chemical therapy to kill tumors. I've read some of the papers. But half the time the chemicals kill the patients. It's essentially poison. They lose their hair, can't keep food down. Suffer. It doesn't save very many. I can't think of why I'd want to live that badly."

"Don't say that."

"Call me a coward. I don't want to suffer. Mostly, I wake in the night in a panic wondering how you can ever forgive me. I know what happened to you when I left. I want to say it's not my fault, that I didn't choose to do what happened, leaving you like that. Hurting you. They forced me to write that report. But the fact is I didn't have the backbone to fight it. I thought I was made of sterner stuff. We all think that, don't we? Until we're tested . . ."

"But why would they want to hurt my career anyway?"

He shakes his head, looking distant and disturbed.

"It's . . . so damn . . . complicated." She frowns at him, wondering how a young female scientist who had less information about the making of the bomb than Weaver could ever have mattered to a cabal of Russians.

He reaches out and cups her cheek in his hand. His touch still wakens her skin, her heart. "The worst of it is, I'm still dragging you into my mess. People breaking into your apartment, bugging it, for God's sake. It's unspeakable. They'll never leave me alone. They'll always want more." He shakes his head, drops his hand, then looks out over the water. With a sigh, he picks up the Scotch and slugs it back. Until it's gone.

◆ ◆ ◆

Charlie takes Sondra home in a taxi. At the restaurant she'd begun to gesture wildly, mix up her words, snort with laughter. He paid before they'd finished their dinner. People were staring as he steered her out of the restaurant. He had to grab hold of her flouncy skirt to keep her from wandering off when he flagged down a taxi. She was far too unruly to bring home on the L.

Quiet, dignified Sondra. Until tonight, he never would have guessed she so much as lifted an alcoholic beverage to her lips. Peggy will ask for details. Blame him for the failure of the date. On one hand, he hates to betray Sondra to his sister. Peggy can be unforgiving. On the other, it explains all the other dates Peggy arranged that came to naught.

Now in the cab, Sondra is finally silent, dazed, slack-jawed, leaning heavily against him. Her black-and-white dress ripples up between them in a froth of lost hopes. He's terrified she'll get sick in the cab. This is too reminiscent of escorting Stash home. Is this his lot in life? The Boy Scout who ferries ruined people to safety? Liquor doesn't fix anything. It brings a person to the edge and lets them dangle between dignity and shame.

A world of lonely people, scarred by the war, wishing for the security and joy they no longer have. Finding bleak comfort in drink or imposed distance from those they once loved. Or suffering quietly, making others around them suffer too. He thinks of Linda in her nightgown reaching out to say she still loves him while Stash was in the bathroom, vomiting up his fifteen beers. Since the war, the world seems such a mangled place. No one has been left untouched. No one feels entirely safe. Sitting in the taxi beside Sondra, the lights of the city streaking by, he sees a world rebuilding itself higher and mightier every day—to prove what? That America's survived. Every skyscraper a desire to forget and look to the future. All built on scars.

At that moment, Charlie wants to look to the future too. He's tired of feeling unmoored. Unlovable. Irreparable. Didn't he suffer enough in the jungle and at Mitsushima? Doesn't he deserve a future of kindness, maybe even love? He's got to find the courage to reach out for it.

⸱⸱⸱ ⸱⸱⸱ ⸱⸱⸱

"Now that I've got the damn cancer out of the way, it's time to talk about the people who broke into your apartment," Weaver says. "I don't want to tell you too much yet. I don't want to endanger you more. However, I will tell you—"

"No, Weaver."

"No?"

She still needs to know what he's done. But not now. At this moment, the news of his cancer is all she can absorb. Knowing he may only have a few more years left, does she want him to spend them in jail? On the other hand, if he helps the FBI, might he absolve himself before he dies? My God, how is she supposed to handle any of this?

"Roz, I need to tell you, to confess before I can't. It's a poison that needs draining."

She shakes her head. "We're not draining it tonight." All her life, she's been driven by curiosity, asking too many questions. It was part of what made Louisa so impatient with her. But for the first time she can remember, answers feel dangerous, pose too many moral choices. And she is sure that whatever he tells her will make her furious. She needs time to think. To plan. To talk to Charlie too . . .

She reaches for Weaver's face, turns it so she can kiss him. Again, his lips are burning hot. Now she knows why. But those fevered lips are lips she loves, despite herself. She should hate him. She can't. She doesn't. This is the man who first made her feel like a woman, showed her she was worthy of love. "Let's go home and make love. Let's not care that they're listening."

"No. You don't want that," he says. "You'll freeze knowing it."

"Or your place."

"If your place is bugged, surely mine is too."

"Then a hotel. Let's go to a hotel. And let's make love. All night."

"Are you trying to kill me?"

"We'll endeavor to keep you alive for a few more years at least."

His lips curl into a gentle smile. "What a naughty girl I turned you into." He points to the neon sign across the water, the hotel that juts out at East Lake Shore Drive. "How does the Drake sound?" She watches the pink neon sign sizzling against the dark blue sky. It's only a few blocks away. Surely they'll have one room still open?

"Leave the glass," she tells him. "We'd never be able to explain it to the desk clerk. Besides,

I got it at the supermarket in a box of laundry detergent."

"What a classy girl you are," he says. "Naughty and classy."

Laughing in the dark, he links his arm in hers. As they walk toward the neon, she briefly thinks of the FBI agent who is supposed to sit in her hall starting at ten P.M. Hopefully, he won't be too concerned when he knocks on her door and no one answers.

CHAPTER EIGHTEEN

Just before dawn, blue light fills the hotel room like a perfect chord. And with waking comes a pain Rosalind hasn't felt since Weaver left her—grief. Listening hard, she lays her hand on Weaver's back to test the rise and fall of his breath. Someday, sooner than it should, his breathing will stop, like a clock that's run out its winding. How much will he suffer? How much will he change as the cancer explodes inside his body? In the dark, anxious months after he left her in '46, Rosalind learned that the hour before dawn is when she felt the most despair. They say it's the time of day when heart attacks seize seemingly healthy people and ill people succumb to their maladies. The hour when the grim reaper stands in the curtain folds waiting to collect his quota. Not yet. Not yet.

She moves closer to Weaver, nestles into his feverish body. Will she be strong enough to survive losing him yet again? And what on earth will she do about Charlie? These last few days, Charlie's been her savior. And how utterly she's been drawn to him. Honest. Good. Kind. Now Charlie is waiting for her to come to him with information that will convict Weaver. Information that will send him to jail, or even the electric chair.

Weaver breathes out a contented sigh. In his sleep, he's forgotten that something dark waits to claim him far too soon. If the cancer doesn't kill him, she fears, inadvertently, that what she ends up sharing with Charlie might.

⫲ ⫲ ⫲

Charlie opens his eyes to the sound of Peggy calling down the stairs to him, "Telephone." In his baggy T-shirt and pajama pants he trudges up the steps, sighing. After his date last night, he sat up until too late drinking beer on the back stoop. He feels like hell.

"Szydlo."

"Your chicken seems to have flown the coop."

"What? Who is this?"

"Gray. I knocked on Miss Porter's door when I arrived at ten P.M. and she didn't answer. I figured maybe she'd gone to bed early. So I stayed out in the hall. Knocked this morning. Nothing. I just called her from the lobby phone. No luck."

"Did she go off with Weaver? To his place?"

"You didn't tell me she was going to."

"Jesus, Gray. Am I your mother? Who's on as her day man?"

"Lawrence. He's here now."

"Since we don't know where she is, tell him to go to Field's after it opens and make sure she shows up at the antique jewelry counter. Then have him call me." Charlie runs his hand over his face. The dimwit. "All right?"

"Yes, sir."

Now he's worried. While the best outcome is that Rosalind spent the night at Weaver's, the thought of her making love to that traitor chokes him. And by God, he put her there.

"Everything okay?" Peggy asks as he hangs up the phone.

Charlie shakes his head with anger. "All the damn vetting the FBI does doesn't work. Making sure every agent has a law degree or CPA certificate—what a joke. There are idiot lawyers and CPAs too."

"You need coffee? Breakfast? You're looking awfully prickly. How was your date last night?"

He shakes his head. "Don't have time. I've got to get to work."

Peggy presses her lips together and shakes her head as he goes by. He feels her eyes searching him, evaluating. Disappointed again.

⫷ ⫸ ⫷

Later, at his desk, he waits for that call from Lawrence and isn't happy when the phone rings and it's Doug Higgins.

"Szydlo? I was going through a bunch of reports on my desk and we found something in Fullersburg Woods yesterday afternoon that might interest you."

"What's that?"

"Someone reported to the police they found a lot of blood, matted leaves, a bullet casing, and a bullet in a tree. It could be someone shooting rabbits or something else benign. Then they found a handkerchief completely soaked in blood embroidered with initials."

"I'll bite."

"**CW.** Isn't that the alias of the Spenard woman?"

Up until now, he's imagined Victoire Spenard must be in hiding, or that the Soviets have shipped her elsewhere. He hadn't thought of her dead. And he appreciates that Higgins actually read his report and saw that Victoire Spenard has been going by the name Clemence Weaver.

"Anyone see anything?"

"No. Some kids with a dog came upon the scene and their parents called it in."

Charlie shudders at the idea of children out for a walk stumbling upon a scene like that.

"You check the morgues? Unidentifieds?"

"Nothing in the DuPage County Morgue. No one fits her description. Checking hospitals too."

"Is Fullersburg Woods near where she lives in Hinsdale?"

"No more than two miles. We also found a broken necklace. A long gold chain."

"Did you take a picture of it?"

"Yes."

"Share it with me? So I can show her landlady?"

"Yeah, I'll put it in the pouch. You'll have it by morning."

"Thanks."

Hanging up the phone, Charlie sits back with a queasy feeling. If someone attacked or even killed Victoire Spenard, what does that say about Rosalind Porter's safety? Still, it doesn't feel like the Soviets. They wouldn't leave a scene with blood, a handkerchief, a necklace. Could Weaver have seen his wife as some kind of barrier to Rosalind's good graces and needed to get rid of her himself? Would he ever hurt Rosalind? He might. If he found out she's in cahoots with the FBI.

⫶ ⫶ ⫶

Rosalind stands at her counter trying to persuade a customer that a pair of 1930s diamond earrings are a fine investment at a good price.

If the woman only realized the serendipity that went into creating every diamond: the impeccably clean carbon source, the 725,000 pounds per square inch of pressure, temperatures over twenty-two hundred degrees Fahrenheit. And then the hundreds of **millions** of years it took to create a stone like this. It's mad that there's a single diamond available in the world. And here are **two** perfectly matched specimens.

"But the thing is . . . they're used," the woman says. **Ring-ring.**

Damn. It's her phone.

"Loved," Rosalind argues. "Beloved, I imagine."

"So why wouldn't the owner pass them on in a will? How did they end up here?" **Ring-ring.**

"Maybe she only had sons." **Ring-ring.** "Excuse me."

She lifts the receiver.

"Antique Jewelry."

"Where were you last night?"

"Oh . . . Charlie." She's surprised by his proprietary tone. Like a jilted lover.

"The agent assigned to you was worried. He made me worry too."

"I'm sorry. He introduced himself to me here this morning. Mr. Lawrence."

"That's your day guy. Gray will be there tonight. You went to Weaver's?"

"No, we . . ." She hesitates. She doesn't want to tell Charlie they went to a hotel. Why? He's the one who's encouraged her to become intimate with Weaver. And how's she going to handle the news of Weaver's illness? She doesn't want to have this discussion on the phone. "Look. I'm with a customer," she says. "I really can't talk now."

"Sorry. Can you call me back, then?"

"They frown on that here." She hangs up. God, just hearing Charlie's voice, his concern, moves and unsettles her. If Weaver **is** still sharing secrets with the Russians, and she has the power to stop him, mustn't she still do it even if he's dying? Last night, she loved Weaver more than she ever has. It was gorgeous and all encompassing. She let herself feel everything for him. Blocked out her doubts. Charlie's voice has jolted her back to reality.

The woman is rolling one diamond stud between her fingers, staring at it.

"You ought to try them on," Rosalind says. She hears an anxious waver in her words. "I know you'll fall in love when you see the sparkle against your skin. Your dark hair. You've just the right complexion for diamonds. Hold it up to your ear. Here's the mirror." She's talking too fast.

"I . . . no." The woman pushes the tray with the earrings back toward Rosalind. "It bothers me too much that they were worn by someone else. I don't feel good about that. I'm not a secondhand kind of woman."

"But that's what makes them affordable. Otherwise . . ."

The sound of the woman's high heels echoes against the terrazzo as she walks away.

"Well, I'm proud to be a **secondhand kind of woman**!" she shouts too loudly at the woman's back.

Jesus. She needs to get ahold of herself. Even if she is desperate for a commission to pay the rent. She takes a deep breath, recalling the conversation she and Weaver had this morning as they dressed.

"I had a will drawn up last week . . . ," he said. He looked so good this morning, rested, handsome. Impossible that he has cancer. And yet, there he was talking about his will. "I've set money aside and it's all for you."

"But you're married. The money belongs to Clemence."

"I'm leaving it to you, Roz."

"She'll contest it and win."

"She won't." There was an off-putting certainty to his statement that threw her.

"Any wife would contest. You're still married, right?"

"She won't contest it. I can assure you of that."

⫯ ⫯ ⫯

The rest of the afternoon, she feels like she's going to jump out of her skin. And it's slow in the store. Nothing to distract her. Just Ronnie coming up with a new case of jewels that nobody will buy. Late in the afternoon, just when she's counting the minutes to closing up her till, she spots the man with the empty eyes. She's starting to see a pattern: He comes around noon, or like now, near the end of the day, hoping, she supposes, that he can get her alone when she steps outside of Field's. She looks around for Agent Lawrence, who's been walking around the floor for hours. But now, when she needs him, he's nowhere to be found. Her stalker is standing at a counter just down from hers, pretending to peer at wristwatches. Now and then, he glances her way. Again, the expensive clothes. Fabrics like a successful businessman. A dandy with empty eyes and fake hair. She reaches beneath the counter for the miniature camera, looks down to straighten it, and nonchalantly sets it on the glass. She turns it slightly this way and that, tilts it back, hoping to capture him, snapping the shutter again and again. She doesn't have much to give to Charlie, but she would at least like to hand him a full roll of film.

⫯ ⫯ ⫯

Charlie doesn't know how to interpret Rosalind's curt voice on the phone call. If only he could walk over to Field's and see her, speak to her, look into her eyes. Something's wrong. But he can't risk it if she's being followed. He's too identifiable. Not like Lawrence, who's so ordinary he could disappear at his own wedding.

Charlie gets up and walks over to Donna McGavock's desk. On it are three white ceramic cups: one with pencils, one with pens, one with red pencils. All the pencils are sharpened like weapons and sit lead up. The fountain pens are cap down. And except what she's working on at the moment, there's not a single other thing to distract her. If she has mail to tackle, she puts it away until she gets to it. And she's Binder's secretary too. How does she keep it all so buttoned-up, so neat?

Donna, as always, has that flat expression on her face, as though the world doesn't touch her. She seems to have no life except the FBI. He's often wondered why she tries so hard to look so nunlike. Today she wears a gray blouse that washes out any color she might have in her face.

"Yes?" she says.

"Donna, do you have plans this evening?" he asks.

He's unnerved to see her eyes brighten, a half smile change her face.

"No, sir," she says.

"Then, if you're willing, I'd like you to go back over to Field's and intercept Miss Porter before she comes out."

"Oh." She droops visibly. Did she think he was asking her out? He softens his voice, sorry that he's given her the wrong impression.

"Do you think you might be available?"

"Yes. I guess . . . of course, sir." Her face once again is unreadable.

"I'd like you to bring her to this address. I could ask Lawrence. He's watching her. But I don't want him interacting with her too much. Tell Lawrence what's up. Once he sees you're in a taxi on your way to me, he can take an hour and a half off."

Charlie hands her a matchbook with the address of Bellows on it—a small bistro just west of Michigan Avenue on Ontario Street. "As you look for a taxi, you can help watch for the man who's following her. Have the driver drive circuitously if you must. Give Lawrence the address. He can wait in his car outside after his break."

"What if she doesn't want to come?" Donna asks dryly. "She wasn't too thrilled to see me last time."

"She was just surprised. She knows you now. Tell her it's important I see her right away."

"And if she says no?"

"Find a telephone booth and call me at the number on the matchbook."

Donna nods efficiently. "You'll be at the restaurant?"

"As quickly as I can."

"Do you want me to stay with the two of you to take notes?"

Is she trying to find out if this is more than business?

"No need. Just be sure to have her bring the camera if she's managed to take photographs."

CHAPTER NINETEEN

Charlie's been sitting for a half hour at Bellows, drinking a beer, his long legs crossed. At this point, he's exhausted and bored. He ate here a few months ago with his friend Norman Corcoran from law school. Norman told him he was a fool not to join a law firm, as he had. Norman was already a partner, making a load of dough. Sure, the FBI paid well, but being a corporate lawyer paid better and was far less dangerous. Less secretive. What wife wanted her man wearing a holster, carrying a weapon?

Charlie laughed at him. "As though I'm planning to marry."

Norman is engaged to a girl named Shirley Haverstock. "Good society girl," he declared. "I doubt she'd marry an FBI agent."

"Then, it's an excellent thing I'm not in love with Shirley."

Norman shrugged. "Sorry, old man. I guess

I've offended you. I'm saying this because you were top of the class. I'm not sure what the FBI tag is buying you. Look. I'm Irish. You're Polish. Neither has ever bought us a seat at the table. But the war is over now. Things are changing. People like us are making our mark. Look at me. We don't need to be part of a 'troop' anymore to pull it off."

Norman's lecture would have given him heartburn if the veal saltimbocca at Bellows hadn't been so delicious, so tender he could cut it effortlessly with a fork. As they left, Charlie grabbed the matchbook to remind himself of the place. He eats out so rarely, it was the only restaurant he could think of that he'd want to share with Rosalind.

He looks up now to see Donna escorting her into the restaurant, herding her from behind like a border collie. He stands. One glance at Rosalind's face and he feels a sense of heightened awareness. As though all day, the world has been hazy and half-experienced. And now he notes every detail. The thick gloss of her black hair lit from behind, the astonishing creaminess of her skin, then, as she comes closer to him, the soft pink of her cheeks, her lips like an archer's bow. And her eyes so dark, so questioning.

"Here she is," Donna tells Charlie, pushing Rosalind forward. "I'll leave you." She tips her chin upward with the slightest hint of annoyance.

"Thank you, Donna."

Rosalind turns to watch his secretary leave the room before she speaks.

"Well, I didn't expect to be kidnapped this evening," she says. He's relieved when she smiles wryly.

"Sorry. I didn't feel like I could come by Fields. And I needed to talk to you." He pulls out the chair for her. "Would you like a drink? And actually, will you join me for dinner? It's the least I can do." Close to her, he reels at her honey scent. Astonishing, its power, when it's so subtle, so innocent. One step sideways and they'd be touching. He longs to take that step.

"I . . . I'm kind of relieved to see you. I just didn't want to tell you what I have to say on the phone."

"Well, good," he says. "Then . . . good." He hates how tongue-tied she makes him feel. What is it she didn't want to say on the phone?

"I'm not sure what Weaver has in mind for this evening. He said he'd call me when I got home and let me know."

"There's a phone booth in the hall where you came in. If it would put your mind at rest."

"I . . . he wouldn't be home yet."

"Well then, please." He gestures to the chair,

which he holds for her. "Have a drink, and when you think he's home, call. I don't want you worrying." For a moment before she sits, their eyes meet and her look is more accepting than he expects.

"Did you manage to get your apartment back in order?" he asks, taking his seat. He's trying to sound nonchalant, but how, really, to sound casual around her?

She straightens her cutlery, stares at the empty space between her knife and fork.

"It threw me, you know. That someone was in there touching my things."

"It would upset anyone."

"You were great about it, Charlie." He's moved just hearing her speak his name.

"You needed me to stay. I'm glad I did."

For a second her face warms, lights; then she looks down again.

"Listen," he says. "You sounded . . . distant when I called this afternoon. I know you were busy. But I'm curious about what you want to tell me."

"I . . ." She shakes her head. "Here," she says, pulling the tiny camera out of her purse. "I did the best I could. I tried to aim it at the creep. Although he wasn't right in front of me."

"Good," he says. "We can enlarge them. Thank you."

"It can't possibly be his real hair. I think that's what makes him look so scary. And his eyes. Such peculiar eyes."

"He came into Field's?"

"Near the end of the day. Your secretary told me to find a different way out of the store. I'm pretty sure he would have followed if I hadn't. I looked out the State Street door where I usually go out to go home, and I saw him across the street, waiting. I think he wants to get me alone, on the street."

"But he didn't see you leave?"

"I sweet-talked the guys at the loading dock to let me out there."

"I bet you did." He smiles. His heart almost hurts with feeling. The ceiling lights pull rainbows out of her black curls: red, pink, orange, gold. Amazing how shiny black can contain a host of colors.

"And you really don't know what they want from you?"

She shakes her head, but he doesn't believe her. "So far, all he's done is stare."

"And ransack your home, if it's the same gentleman."

"He's no gentleman."

"True enough. How **is** Weaver?" he asks. "Have you seen him?"

"I think I need a drink before I tell you more," she says.

He waves for the waitress, who takes her order for a Scotch. Neat.

"I have something to tell you too. So, while we're waiting for that drink, maybe I'll go first?"

She nods.

He speaks slowly. Purposefully.

"We found—someone came upon—a scene in a forest preserve." He stops, looks up to read her face. But of course, it's blank, waiting.

"A scene?"

"Blood, a handkerchief, a gold chain. And bullet casings. The handkerchief had initials on it."

"Go on . . ."

"CW."

Rosalind's lips part. "CW?"

"I was thinking . . . Clemence Weaver."

"Oh . . ."

"There was no body. Just blood. The handkerchief was soaked in it," he says. "And apparently the leaves on the ground as well. And the broken gold chain lay nearby."

Charlie watches as she visibly shivers.

"When I saw her, she was wearing a gold chain . . ."

The waitress comes with Rosalind's Scotch. It seems she can't get both hands around it fast enough. Taking a swallow, she won't look at Charlie. Does she suspect Weaver?

When she sets the drink down, he reaches out and gently lays his right hand on top of hers. She seems surprised but doesn't pull it away. Reveling in his own courage, he's aware of the satiny warmth of her skin. "What's going on?" he asks. "Please tell me."

She shakes her head.

"C'mon. Maybe I can help."

"Do they . . . do they have any clue who might have . . . shot her, if that's what's happened?"

"It does look like that's what happened. You suspect Weaver?"

When she looks up, there's panic in her eyes.

"You've got to tell me what you know, Rosalind."

How he wishes he could come around the table and hold her. All these years of having so little desire for women. Why the hell does he care about the one woman he should leave alone?

"Tell me. I want to do what I can for you."

"Weaver wouldn't. He can't have . . ."

"But something he said or did is bothering you, isn't it?"

He waits for her to speak, not feeling patient at all. His heart is pounding. But when she opens her mouth, what she says is nothing he expected.

"Weaver's dying."

"I don't understand."

"He has cancer. From radiation. He was exposed when he went out to the Trinity Site a month after the test."

"He's not just manipulating you?"

Her eyes are unfocused. "It's been obvious something's wrong. I just didn't know why he looked so changed. Why he seems more tired than usual. He told me last night. And I feel . . ." She shakes her head, unable to complete the sentence.

What Charlie feels is a gnawing hopelessness in the pit of his stomach. He knows if Weaver's dying, it must have heightened Rosalind's attachment to the man. "I'm sorry."

"You're not, though, are you?" she asks.

"You're sad, and that makes me sorry."

She pulls her hand from his, scrabbles in her purse for a handkerchief. Avoiding his eyes, she says, "So, that's the thing. What if what I find out about him puts him in jail until he dies?"

"Rosalind . . ."

She shakes her head.

"Well, let's start here. You've got to at least tell me what he said about his wife. The woman appears to have been murdered. You're an honest girl."

Looking pained, she raises her chin. "I don't want to tell you," she says.

"If you share it, maybe we'll decide it's nothing. We could talk it out together." He tries to sound gentle. He sees that her hands are balled in fists. He watches as she argues with herself.

"He wrote a will leaving everything to me."

"Okay . . ."

"Leaving me all he has. And he said, 'You don't have to worry about Clemence. She won't contest the will.' I couldn't understand how he could be so sure."

"He sounded sure?"

"Charlie, is it possible the Russians killed her and **told** him about it?" Her eyes are pleading for him to say yes.

"She was an agent of theirs."

"Clemence was?"

"We think she was the one who drew him into the Communist Party years ago."

"Years ago?"

"Did he tell you anything about the Russians, about contacts?"

She freezes, presses her lips together. "After he told me he's dying, I asked him not to say more. Not last night. I couldn't . . . couldn't bear any more . . ."

"Dying or not, he holds secrets, names or descriptions of contacts that could matter to a lot of people. To the world."

She nods, staring down at the tablecloth. "I've been thinking of that, trying to figure out what to do. He seems regretful. I think he would like to make up for the things he's done. But the idea of him dying in jail or being executed because of me . . ."

"Maybe, rather than getting him executed, you can get him to cooperate. Like you said: He has regrets—you could help him make things right. Help him die in peace."

She looks up. "I want that for him . . ." Her voice is a hoarse whisper.

"Maybe you can persuade him to give us names, information. Considering his condition, we can work something out, keep him out of jail."

"You're making this up, aren't you?" she asks. "You have no authority to let him die in peace. You can't have that much authority."

She's not entirely right. The information Weaver has could be invaluable. It's the wolves Charlie fears, the FBI hard-liners who will string up any Commie, dangle him as evidence of a successful fight against an evil empire. How's he going to play this? How will he spare Weaver and Rosalind and still get the information the FBI needs?

"I want to think about it," he tells her. "I want to figure out how to protect him. He's the one who knows what we need to know. The government makes deals. They often do . . . The Brits did with Fuchs."

"Yes, but their law says the maximum Fuchs can get is fourteen years. Doesn't American law kill traitors?"

"I'm not going to lie. Sometimes that's true. But if he were willing to give names . . . it would surely lighten his sentence."

Rosalind shakes her head. "And if he killed Clemence? You'd have the authority to let him off too?"

"I don't know . . . if he murdered Clemence, is that what you would really want?"

Their eyes meet, and very slowly, she shakes her head.

"And as I told you," Charlie says, leaning forward, "Fuchs told us a scientist is in place to pass on information about the H-bomb."

"Weaver?"

"I think there's a good chance he's an important piece of the puzzle. The Soviets aren't beyond exerting who knows what pressure to get what they want. You and only you could make him brave. Make him come to us to confess. We can protect him, and if he hasn't yet passed that information, protect us all."

"Dear God," she says. Her face is pale; her lips are pressed together.

He takes her hand again. How he loves to touch her, **needs** to have that connection. He knows the last thing he's about to tell her will make her angry at Weaver, make her want to push him away. He's been saving it. And yet, he hates to hurt her. "Listen . . . I have something more to tell you about Clemence," he says.

"I don't think I can bear to hear more."

"I think you'll want to hear this."

She nods but closes her eyes, swallows hard.

"Right before I came here tonight, I got a telex from England. I made an inquiry a few days ago and they found an answer for me in the form of a British marriage certificate. Thomas J. Weaver was married in 1938 at the town hall in Cambridge to a woman named Victoire Spenard."

Rosalind nods. "Yes, he told me that. That he was married before he met me. An older woman, he said. From Marseille."

"But what you don't know is that Victoire Spenard's been here in America for four years now, going under an assumed name."

Rosalind frowns, shakes her head with confusion.

"No," she explains gently, slowly. "**You** must be confused. By the time we met, he was widowed. His wife died in a bombing raid in London."

"Victoire Spenard didn't die in London. She didn't die . . . until, well, perhaps two weeks ago."

"I don't understand."

"She came to America under an assumed name."

"I don't understand."

"That name is Clemence. Clemence Weaver."

Rosalind's skin goes entirely white. She stares at him with her mouth agape, pulls her hand away.

"Clemence is Victoire?"

He nods.

"He was . . . wait. He was still **married** to her when I met him?"

Charlie nods.

"He lied to me about being married then?"

"Yes."

She lifts her hands to her face, presses her fingers against her brows. He waits a long while, but she doesn't move.

"Victoire Spenard was on a lot of watch lists as a foreign agent. We think that's why she changed her identity. Are you okay?" he asks.

She doesn't respond.

"Hey, come up for air," he says. "This news isn't all bad. It explains a lot. It's very possible Weaver left you in '46 because Clemence surprised him by arriving unexpectedly. It was after the war; there was passenger traffic across the Atlantic at last. He said it wasn't his choice. She could have threatened to expose him as a married man. And a Communist. The Soviets may have sent her to America to draw him back in or watch over him to make sure he complied. By that time, I imagine he wanted out but felt trapped."

At last she looks up. Her eyes are red, her chin dimpled with bitterness.

"He said there were things I didn't know."

"For once he was telling you the truth. Listen. Let him spill what's going on with the Russians. Let him confess if that's what he needs.

You're the one person who could persuade him not to share what more he knows."

"I don't know . . ."

"Free him in that way, at least. You don't fear he might . . . I mean . . . he wouldn't **hurt** you in any way, do you suppose?"

"Never."

"I don't want you to risk anything. But if you're sure he loves you, that you're safe . . ."

Again, she nods. Weaver's told her he loves her. She believes him.

"Do you think he's home by now? Do you want to phone him?"

"I couldn't control my voice. I couldn't sound normal."

"Okay, wait a while. Stay with me for dinner. What do you think?"

"I couldn't eat."

"Maybe in a little while you can. We'll chat. You'll have another drink. You'll realize this isn't going to be so bad." He's brought her to pain and tears. He wants time to fix it.

She takes a deep breath and then she says, "Is the FBI paying?"

"Absolutely."

"That's good. Because I'm dead broke."

He laughs. "Dinner's on us. Steak, seafood. It's all here on your country's tab." He pushes the menu toward her.

"Not yet," she says. "After another drink."

He notes her Scotch is almost gone. "Do you need bread or anything?" He thinks of Sondra. "I don't want to have to carry you home."

She laughs. "No. If I get woozy, I'll stop. But I am feeling better. I don't know if it's you or the Scotch . . ."

"I hope it's me."

She smiles sweetly, wearily. He waves to the waitress. Is it wrong that he feels giddy with victory? Yet, he knows that at the end of the dinner, she will leave him alone at the table and step out to call the man she really loves.

⫯ ⫯ ⫯

Over dinner, Rosalind's relieved that Charlie does all he can to distract her from the news of Clemence Weaver's possible end and the fact that Weaver has lied to her from the beginning. She can't disregard the anger that roils inside. Still, he's able to charm her with tales about his childhood, his mother, his life in the Polish community, speaking so vividly, so lovingly, about a world she hardly knows. How can she not be moved by a man who has suffered so much, yet so embodies gratefulness?

He draws her out too. When she speaks of her job, the whispers of the past she finds in the jewelry she sells, he rubs his finger over the gold ring she's wearing. "Tell me about this one," he says.

"Read what's inside it," she says. She finds herself reaching out for his good hand, turning it over, and setting the ring into his palm. With the magic dexterity of his fingers, he manages to shake it to their tips so he can hold it up to the light. Squinting, he reads, "For the bravest girl in the world."

"It's the reason I bought it. The ruby is nothing, really. Negligible. But the sentiment . . ."

"It's who you want to be?"

Weaver took so much, left her with so little belief in herself.

"It's who I wish I could be, Charlie. I want to go back to science. I ache for it. But I'm a coward at heart."

"You could be that girl," he says. "Life is giving you a chance to prove you're anything but a coward."

She looks up into his eyes and is bathed in his belief in her. After he slips the ring back on her finger, he reaches out and caresses her cheek. She grabs his hand and holds it for a long, long while. When it's time to call Weaver, she hates to let it go.

CHAPTER TWENTY

Dear girl, I'm so glad to hear from you," Weaver says. His voice is muffled and breathy. He must have been napping. The telephone in his apartment is by the bed, which always struck her as a bit louche. She's never known anyone who didn't keep their telephone in the hall or kitchen. "I tried to call you," he says.

"I went out to dinner with a friend. Would you like me to come by now?"

"God yes. I've been desperate for you all day." She feels a twinge just below her ribs. Why do Weaver's words still hold the power to thrill her? Especially after what she's just discovered. And after the blissful dinner with Charlie.

"I'll take the bus down."

"Take a taxi. I'll pay it back. I need you, Duchess." Loving words, when all this time he's been lying . . .

She hangs up and stands for a moment in the hall with her eyes squeezed shut, her heart pounding. She thinks about what Charlie said: that she could help Weaver find absolution before he dies. That by persuading him to confess . . . she could even protect him. And protect the world by keeping him from sharing more. Could Weaver really be the one in place to share information about the H-bomb? If she's capable of stopping him, how could she walk away from that duty?

"So what's the verdict?" Charlie asks. "Are you going to see Weaver?" She notes reservation in his eyes. Yet, he's the one sending her down there. She nods.

"Well then, let's get you out of here." He sets his napkin on the table, gets up, and gestures back toward the hall.

As they pass, the maître d' says, "So glad you could join us." He no doubt thinks they're a couple in love, that it's just the beginning of their night together. In the dark vestibule between the doors, Charlie says, "Wait here. Let me check the street first."

He steps out the door, and in the late light, she watches his tall figure with a hollow longing. When he returns, he gently sets his hands on her shoulders. "Gray is out there in a navy car halfway down the street." He points. "He'll follow your taxi. Listen, with Weaver, please be careful."

"He won't hurt me. He loves me," she says.

"Even so. It's my nature to worry."

"Really? I wouldn't have guessed that."

"When it comes to you," he says, "I can't seem to help myself."

She finds herself reaching up and touching his face. When he hugs her in return, she feels both safe and deeply thrilled, surprised by how long he presses her close.

"Thank you for dinner," she whispers.

"Rosalind . . . I . . ." He smooths her hair, caresses her lips with his thumb. Oh, how his touch moves her. She waits for him to say more, but he just shakes his head, looking mildly embarrassed. The desire to reach forward and kiss him is almost unbearable. He touched her lips. How she longs to taste his.

They step outside and he hails a taxi, opens the door. "Be safe," he whispers, making sure her skirt is inside before he shuts it. He holds up his hand in farewell, and she watches him grow smaller as the taxi hurtles her toward Weaver.

◆ ◆ ◆

In the cab she wonders how she'll keep from letting on to Weaver all she now knows. She thinks of the engraving inside her ring. **For the bravest girl in the world.**

"You could be that girl, Rosalind," Charlie said. When she looked into his eyes, she saw belief, kindness, truth. Here in the taxi, she tries to muster her courage. She can't help thinking about Clemence, that proud, cold woman with the dark, upswept hair who was the object of Roz's hate for so long. Is it really possible that Weaver's killed her? How could he have lied to Rosalind all these years? And lie to her still? All along, Weaver's the one she should have despised.

As she gets out at his place, she sees Gray driving up nearby, parking his car. That should make her feel safe, but she realizes, with a start, that she forgot to mention to Charlie that Weaver thinks her apartment is bugged. How on earth could it have slipped her mind? It was the first thing on her list. Especially because the Russians surely heard him talking about fingerprinting, might have gleaned that he's FBI. And she still hasn't told Charlie about the envelope. In her life, she's never felt more at sea.

Entering the big house, she climbs the steps. Weaver's bell chirps beneath her index finger. When he comes to the door, she steels herself to hate him, prepares to pretend she doesn't. Yet when his eyes light up at seeing her, his new vulnerability, his mortality, unexpectedly disarm her. How striking he looks in a crisp blue shirt, summer-weight gray slacks, a Scotch in hand. He's always been a shade too handsome: a man from an advertisement. And sometimes he was so distant. But tonight, his pleasure at finding her there momentarily wins her with its gentleness. This man couldn't harm even the most evil wife, she tells herself.

"Come in, my love," he says. "I'm so glad to see you."

The apartment's neat and cozy. Inviting in a way her modern place will never be.

He offers her one of the wing chairs and brings her a Scotch. "You've been standing behind that damn counter all day," he says. "Let me wait on you for a change." As they sip their drinks together, he tells her how his bus never showed up this morning because a woman went into labor at the stop before his.

"She must have been in labor before she got on, because, apparently, she started having the baby right then and there in the last row. Firemen had to climb on board to help. I heard on the radio she had a boy. So who'd you have dinner with?" He tacks this question onto the end of his story so awkwardly, it makes her laugh.

"A friend," she says.

"A man?" His question irks her.

"Yes."

He takes a sip of his Scotch, then sets it down, shakes his head, stares at his hands. "I know you dated others while I was gone. And I can't blame you. Still . . ."

"You weren't **gone,** Weaver," she says pointedly.

"You were with Clemence. What would you have me do?" She watches him wince. The truth is, all these years, Rosalind **hasn't** dated. She said no to every man—the one who asked her out in the produce aisle at the grocery store, the cousin of her floor manager at Field's, the man she met at a lecture. She couldn't risk feeling close to anyone. Not after what Weaver did to her. And now she finds he's been lying all this time. Her rage toward him is caged but decidedly alive, rattling its bars.

"Is this man someone I should know about?" he asks insistently. "This man you had dinner with. Something . . . ongoing?"

"You're the one who has things to confess," she says. "Not me." It feels good to gain the upper hand for a change.

"And I will," he says. "I can't help feeling jealous." He stands up, takes her hand, and makes her stand too, then draws her close, kisses her passionately. "Come to bed. You're what I need to give me courage," he says. "Come to bed, and afterward, I'll tell you everything."

"But," she whispers, "isn't your place bugged?"

"A friend of mine is quite the electronics expert. He helped me get hold of a box this morning that locates devices like that. One was hidden in the light fixture over the toilet, which was rather rude, frankly. No one is listening right now . . .

No one but me. Let's see if we can inspire you to make those gorgeous little sounds you think I don't like."

He draws her into the unlit bedroom. "Damn, I want you so badly," he whispers as he unbuttons her clothes. After what Charlie told her tonight, she was pretty sure she wouldn't be able to even fake desire. But she doesn't have to fake anything. Their lovemaking is fierce and fevered. Maybe her excitement is fueled by anger. Maybe it's his open longing that propels her. She does something she's rarely done: climbs atop of him and rides him, utterly takes control. In the end, he makes her slow down, stretching their climax until she is caught up in a long, blissful eddy. Afterward, she lies beside him with her head on his naked chest. His heartbeat is even and steady, like that of a man who will live thirty more years.

She doesn't understand herself. Lovemaking with Weaver never felt this free. Perhaps Charlie's information has unleashed her, stopped her from loving Weaver too much, weakened the sway he's had over her for too long. Soon he will confess whatever it is he has to confess, and then . . . She's aware she should relish this moment. Innocence, once lost, can never be retrieved. Funny how one aches to know. To be wiser, no matter how painful the truth. After a while, she lifts her head. Any trace of weariness has left his face.

How peaceful he looks: eyes closed, a smile playing at the corners of his lips. His breath is slow, even, certain.

"Weaver," she whispers. "You said you'd confess."

His eyes open. First he stares at the ceiling, and then he fixes them on her with trepidation. "After I do, I know you'll hate me."

She takes in the contours of his face, from his handsome cleft chin to his familiar forehead, more lined now and perhaps taller than before. He will never grow old enough to lose all that beautiful crisp hair.

"I can't really say how I'll feel," she says. "I can't guarantee I won't hate you."

He sits up, rubs his neck. "It matters, you know. It might be the only thing that matters to me." And then he says, "I love you. I'm afraid of dying alone." She doesn't know what to say. Even his loving her might be selfish. She can hear the soft scratch of crickets through the window.

He reaches for the glass of Scotch on his nightstand and takes a long swig. "I drink too much these days. I can't imagine it matters. Not much matters anymore."

"Telling me matters," she says.

"I know."

She reaches for his face. "You're burning up," she says. "Do you want a cool washcloth?"

He shakes his head, takes three or four large gulps of the Scotch in silence, lights a cigarette with trembling fingers. Sitting up, she pulls the sheets around herself, uncomfortably aware of her nakedness in the face of the coming truths.

"It started at King's College," he says. "Have you ever heard of King's?" She shakes her head. "I always considered it the most elite college at Cambridge. It was the beginning of the Depression, people were starving. But our parents had mansions, servants. They gave us whatever we asked for so that we'd leave them alone. Roadsters, horses, holidays abroad. It was an ugly time. International fascism was on the rise. All the things that led to the Nazi madness. But we spoiled scions headed down to the Eagle every night to get drunk and forget who we were. Every morning began with a hangover. And then Victoire told me about the Cambridge Socialist Society."

Hearing the name "Victoire" makes Rosalind move herself away. She can't bear the heat of his flesh against hers. He stares at his glass, oblivious. "I met her at a drinks party at King's. She was smart. Beautiful. Older. Sophisticated. I'd spent my youth in boys' schools chasing the headmaster's daughter and the girls who cleaned our rooms. But Victoire made it her mission to conquer me. She invited me back to her house for a toddy. Liquor was only the first item on her agenda. She was thirty-three and insatiable. You've no idea." Rosalind closes her eyes, feels queasy.

"Lucky you," she says. Men don't need promises of love, she thinks bitterly. Unchecked sexuality is a badge of honor, not a stigma.

"Everything about her was exotic. The fact that she had any interest in a young man like me, the meetings she took me to. Socialism wasn't an ethos about owning things or each man for himself. It was about a greater good. I felt sparked, awakened. I thought I'd found a perfect way of life. Multiple rolls in bed every night with Victoire. Helping poor British workers during the day—when I wasn't doing my schoolwork, which, of course, suffered.

"After that, we both were drawn to Communism. It seemed purer. Better for the greater good. We thought Russia was a Communist state. It's a lie."

"Is it?"

"Russia was totalitarian . . . right from the start. A government with too much power is never about the people."

He smokes quietly for a moment, his eyes distant.

"But for a long time, Russia had my sympathy. I didn't know how bad it was there. And I believed it was wrong for America to have too much power, to have such a fearsome weapon alone."

"Why?"

"It felt lopsided, dangerous. America isn't the land of the brave. It's the land of bravado. We're show-offs. In this country, all we desire is **things.** America is a place that hoards and accumulates and boasts and compares. Meanwhile too many poor people are suffering. I don't admire our way of life. Just as I didn't admire Britain's."

"If you felt that way, why did we never talk about it?"

"Because it was all Victoire and I **ever** talked about. It dulled our feelings, ruined our marriage. I didn't want **our** relationship to be like that. I . . . I loved your innocence, your sweetness."

"Well, that's gone now."

He shakes his head with sorrow. "Look, you need to know I've spent these last years trying to untangle myself. When I came here, and especially after I met you, I wanted to be the man you thought I was. They wouldn't let me go."

"What did they want from you?"

"To share too much."

"Secrets?"

He nods almost imperceptibly.

"From the Project?"

"Yes."

"And part of that information helped them build their bomb, didn't it?" she asks softly.

"Yes."

What she feels is ice. Ice from her heart to the follicles of her hair.

"It wasn't just me. Fuchs was part of it, I now know, and others too."

If he did sell those secrets, he deserves to die.

"Others we know?"

"Why do you care?"

She shrugs. "I want to know if someone influenced you. I want to know who else was involved."

"I suspected two people at Los Alamos, but I couldn't approach them . . ."

"Because they could have turned you in if you were wrong?"

He looks pinched. "They were careful not to let any of us know who else was involved. But since I gave only a portion of the information they needed, others were clearly sharing."

"When was this? After Hiroshima, Nagasaki?"

"No."

"Before?"

"In '44. A year before we dropped it."

She sits back, stunned. "And there I was assuming you and I were so close . . . and I had no idea." Yet she recalls the Saturday afternoons he disappeared, the times he had that abstract look that made her uneasy. The cloud that would block their sun . . .

"What did you give them?"

"Bomb-construction sketches. Dimensions . . ."

The blood is pulsing in her ears. She closes her eyes.

"With all the security at Los Alamos, how could you get anything out?"

"Well, for instance, the construction sketches I copied very small and slipped them under the insole of my shoe. I took the bus to a dentist in Santa Fe. There was a girl. A courier." He shows no emotion, and his eyes don't quite meet hers.

"And?"

"She scheduled an appointment in the same dentist's office, sat beside me in the waiting room. I slipped off my shoe, pretended to shake a stone out of it. I passed her the plans when I got up to see the dentist."

"Did you actually have your teeth cleaned that day?" she asks.

"I assume she did too."

"You passed state secrets and both had your teeth cleaned?" There's venom in her words. "Such good oral hygiene."

"I knew you'd hate me."

"You were a spy and I had no idea."

"I wasn't a spy," he says. "**They** were spies. I was an asset. I just gave them what they needed."

"You've shared a lot more than what you've just told me, haven't you?" Roz hisses.

He blows out smoke, stubs out his cigarette.

"A lot more."

She's overcome by sudden rage. She gets up and begins to gather her clothes hurriedly.

"What are you doing?"

Some man is shouting outside. She slams the window shut. Too quickly. Too loudly. She doesn't answer. Instead, she slips on her underwear, pulls on her blouse, buttoning it as fast as possible. She would like to hit him. Hurt him. Even she is astounded by her rage. Shouldn't she have expected it? Didn't she know he'd say these very things? Why do her feelings seem so outsize, so out of control?

"There's a lot more to confess, if it would keep you here."

She didn't know she was capable of such anger. It fills her chest. Aches. He grabs her wrist. The burn of his skin matches the heat of her fury.

"Roz, I've done things I regret, and in a year or two or three if I'm lucky, I'm going to die. I see it as cause and effect. Crime and punishment . . ."

"**Crime and Punishment.** A Russian novel," she says hoping the irony will sting. She yanks her hand away.

"I hate that that's how you'll remember me when I'm gone: the man who gave America's secrets away."

"That's exactly the way I'll remember you," she hisses, pleased to see her words hurt.

"Please. Stay."

"Tell me one thing," she says. "What did you

mean when you said it wasn't your choice to marry Clemence?"

"I meant they made me leave you to be with her," he says. She notes that his voice doesn't waver. Lying has become second nature to him.

"How could they **make** you?" she persists.

Will he confess? He's already told her his worst sins. This is his chance to reveal that he was already married when they met. That Victoire is Clemence.

He stops to light a new cigarette. "Clemence was a Soviet agent. She was meant to control me."

"Just like Victoire?" she asks.

He doesn't even blink. "I wanted out of the whole thing. They said I had to be with her or I'd be exposed. They also said . . . they told me they might hurt you." He reaches again for her hand but she won't let him have it.

"They threatened to hurt **me**?"

"It was suggested. Nothing is straightforward with these people."

"So let me be clear. The Russians say you're to marry this woman and you did?"

"They didn't parade a line of attractive women in front of me and ask me to choose my favorite." His voice is both weary and annoyed. This is his chance to clear up a lie of many years. Yet, no mention of his wife, Victoire, returning as Clemence. No admitting that he seduced Rosalind while still a married man. That he never intended to marry Rosalind, nor could he. He isn't honest or brave enough to own up to that.

"Turn yourself in," she says, tucking her shirt into her skirt. "Have you ever considered it? If you honestly regret what you've done, talk to the FBI. They'll go easy on you for information."

"Are you joking? They'll string me up by my testicles. Is that what you want for me?"

"Instead, you'll die in your own sort of prison," she says. "A prison of regret." She reaches for the small bag she's brought with her nightgown, her toiletries.

"Please, don't go. You can't leave so late."

"What I can't do is be with you right now."

"Look," Weaver says, his voice rising. "If it makes any difference..." His irises are a bleached green like grass clippings that have dried in the sun. "I've already decided they'll have to kill me because I won't give them the information they're asking me for now. I suspect they will."

She stares at him, wishing she believed a word he says. But how can she when she's seen him tell lie after lie? And so she leaves.

CHAPTER TWENTY-ONE

Once at home, she stays up for hours, pacing her apartment. The voices in her head are loud. Arguing. When she finally climbs into bed, she doesn't sleep. She hates that she could ever have loved someone so misguided. A traitor. A hollow man who's blurred the lines between right and wrong.

Why is she the least bit surprised he's sold secrets? Charlie warned her. Weaver's been hinting at it. Why should hearing it out loud change everything? And yet her anger swells every time she thinks of it: The man she loved handed the bomb they so misbegottenly created to the Soviet Union. And he's been personally betraying her from the very first day they met.

Before dawn, she gets up to sit on the living room sofa, first folded over, her head in her hands, then for a long time staring out at the lake. Her rage at Weaver is a pain beneath her ribs, physical and impossible to ignore. It's because of him that the world is holding its breath. Because of this man who broke her heart yet still owns it, that the world might end tomorrow. And they'd both be responsible.

Just before dawn, she unhooks the necklace he gave her, the little box. She's worn it all these years. Made of fourteen-karat gold and platinum, it's old and probably valuable. She could even get the buyer at Field's to purchase it for her department. But she walks over to the garbage can in the kitchen and drops it in. It clatters against the side, and its top opens before it falls to the bottom of the can. She sees the little curl of parchment with the word "Patience" teeter on a wad of tissues and slip down beneath them, lost forever.

⁂

Charlie's reading through a transcript of an interview with a Russian courier whom the New York office recently arrested. The mug shot reveals a woman with short blond hair, a hard, angular face. She could be a female grease monkey, or a bus driver, a woman with a man's job. But no one would suspect her of shuttling messages to the Russians.

"Who's the tough broad?" A thick hand

reaches down and grabs the folder. Charlie looks up to find Binder. His pug face is particularly agitated, a glowing mottled red.

"She's the courier we picked up in New York, sir."

"What a little sweetheart. She give us anything?"

"I don't know yet. Just reading through it for the first time."

Binder throws the folder back on Charlie's desk and expels a cloud of smoke. Does the man have a waking moment without a coffin nail in his mouth?

"Other than this ballbuster, what do we have?"

"Not much yet, but we're getting there on Weaver. I'm pretty sure he's our guy." Charlie hears the bald uncertainty in his own voice.

"**Pretty sure** won't buy fare for the Michigan Avenue bus."

Binder rarely leaves his office to walk the bullpen. When he does, it never bodes well. What can Charlie tell him? That they've discovered what looks like a murder scene for Weaver's wife? That Rosalind's place has been ransacked for no apparent reason? That Charlie's "perfect asset" has brought them little information so far?

"Miss Porter believes Weaver's about to reveal himself. He's dying, sir. Cancer. Probably from his work with radioactive materials."

"Is that so? Would serve the son of a bitch right."

Charlie blinks. "As long as he doesn't die before he gives us the information we need," he says. But Binder leans over the desk in a threatening, superior way. They're face-to-face, but for once, Binder appears taller. He reeks of tobacco. His teeth are the color of cashews. "She'd better hurry up and get it out of him. I'm getting heat on this, Szydlo."

"From whom, sir?"

"Hoover. Who else? The New York office is busy arresting, the DC Bureau is busy arresting, and it's time I had a little raw meat to feed the beast."

"We're moving as quickly as we can, sir."

"With that McCarthy ass accusing everyone and his sister of being a Communist, the Chicago office is looking pretty namby-pamby. We're about to go down in flames and you're taking your sweet time." Binder straightens up and glowers at him. "Put the screws on the dame to get something out of the bastard now. I mean it. I don't have time for you to jolly her about."

"Yes, sir." Binder walks away, looking taller than the pug he is. His words, his strut, are so extreme, Charlie's sure he's patterned them on Edward G. Robinson in **Little Caesar**. But his boss's admonition has left him uneasy. **Has** he been too kind to Rosalind? Too patient? What would happen if he were harsher? Would she turn away or finally get the information out of Weaver? All he wants is to love this girl. If he were smart, he'd turn the whole damn case over to someone else. He's startled when the phone bleats.

"Szydlo here."

"Charlie . . ."

"Rosalind?"

"Can I see you?" His heart starts drumming. Partly with guilt for thinking he should be crueler. Partly at the sound of her oboe-clear voice. "I need your help."

"What can I do?"

"Weaver said he thinks my apartment is bugged. His was. I wondered if you could find the devices, get rid of them for me? I know I should have told you before."

Why hadn't it occurred to Charlie that they would bug Rosalind's place just to keep tabs on Weaver? But it means something. Bugs are expensive, rare, husbanded. They must be sensing that Weaver's moving away from them. And that he'll spill all to Rosalind. Cold dread moves precipitously up his back and over his scalp. He has no idea how long the bugs might have been there. Have they heard Charlie in her apartment? Did either of them say the word "fingerprinting" out loud? If they knew he was with the FBI, why wouldn't they have warned Weaver by now? Or hidden him? Or even killed him? They can't want him leaking information to the FBI. The only reason to leave him in place is because they're waiting for him to procure some new piece of information. And then they'll simply get rid of him . . .

"Are you still there?" Rosalind asks.

"I'm just thinking things through. I'll come and clear your apartment. You're not calling from there now, surely?"

"I'm in a phone booth at Field's."

"Good. Listen, when I came to fingerprint, did I say anything aloud about being with the FBI? Did I use the word 'fingerprinting'? I must have . . ."

"I've wondered that too. I'm sure you must have said 'fingerprinting.' But maybe not the FBI. They might have assumed I'd called the police."

"Except you knew me . . . You called me to come."

"Yes. There's that. I could have known a policeman, I suppose."

He's sure she's still keeping something from him. Why else would they ransack her place, surveil her? She has something. She knows something. He could ask Gray to sweep her apartment, pick up the devices. But he wants to see her. He needs to see her . . .

"Look," he says. "I don't want them spotting me entering your building. I mean, they probably don't have people watching all the time. But just in case, let's face it, my height makes me identifiable."

"I suppose it would."

"I imagine they knock off for the night after you go silent. But in any case, would you be willing to have me come after they think you've gone to bed?"

"Sure."

"Good."

"Charlie . . . last night . . ."

He waits but she doesn't go on.

"Last night what?" he asks gently.

"He spilled a lot."

"What did he tell you?"

Her breath is staccato, hesitant.

"He told you he's the one who gave them the information?"

"Not the only one. But, yes."

Charlie feels a sharp thrill. It's what they've all waited for. Of course it's Weaver. It had to be Weaver. "Did he give you details?"

"Some. But I almost can't see him anymore. I'm so angry. Angry about everything . . ."

"You can't back out now. Please."

"I know that . . . I know."

"Okay. We're going to get through this to-gether." He's ecstatic that Weaver's finally talk-ing but sad that she seems so pained about it. "If he's opening up to you, I really should put a listening device in his apartment. It needs to be wired in. Did you say he found a Russian device there already?"

"He found and removed them. But I don't want you listening in on him. You'd be listening in on me too."

"Yes. That's true . . ." The thought of hearing her making love to Weaver turns his blood to ice. "There are new listening devices that agents have actually worn on their bodies. They're pretty heavy. But if you were willing, you could wear one."

"I won't do it. I told him to turn himself in, not that he agreed . . ."

"Rosalind, if he knew you had a tape of him confessing, he'd have to turn himself in. It might save him."

"I just . . . I can't."

Charlie closes his eyes, sees a flare of red.

"Okay, let's worry about the bugs in your apartment first, okay? Can you try to be home tonight?"

"Yes. Unless something happens, I'll be home."

"Let's do this: If you know you're going to spend the night at home, call my home number after nine, let it ring once, then hang up. Call again and hang up again. Your eavesdroppers will think you've called two friends whose lines are busy. You get ready for bed as usual—do all your routine things so they hear them—and then I'll come up and silently remove the bugs just in case they're still listening. It would have to be late."

"How late?"

"When do you normally go to bed?"

"Ten thirty. Eleven."

"I could come at eleven fifteen just to be safe."

"All right."

"Rosalind?"

"Yes."

"Is there any other reason you can imagine they're following you? Something Weaver said or something he gave you? Until I know, I can't keep you safe."

"I'll . . . think about it," she says.

He sighs. "Yes. Do that. And, listen, if it's not tonight, the same thing holds for tomorrow night, or the next. A single ring and hang up—twice."

"Okay," she says. "Got it."

⫯ ⫯ ⫯

All day, he's mad with desire to see her, longing to hear what Weaver's revealed. He comes home early and eats with Peggy's family. Again, they're happy to have him there. And the food is so good. **Bigos,** a complicated Polish stew his mother used to make. He helps clean up, then lies on his bed and listens to the Dave Brubeck Octet turned down low, finishes the Hemingway book. Not a great one. Coming home early makes the night crawl. And then the phone rings a single ring. A pause, and then another. Peggy opens the basement door and calls down the steps.

"There it is. Your signal. I hope this isn't some dangerous assignment."

"It's nothing," he tells her. "Besides, I don't have to leave for an hour and a half."

No longer needing to wait for the phone, he climbs the stairs and steps out into the backyard. The trees sway against the last soft light of day. And the stars appear, pricks of pure, piercing light in the thick napped blue, far above the streetlights. Summer nights were magical to him as a kid, how long the sky swelled with daylight, allowing them to play seemingly forever before their mothers called them in. Until the fireflies began to flicker and blink. **Kochanie, come. Come for your bath. Coming, Ma.** How safe he felt, never imagining the world contained abuse and hatred. Never believing that someday he'd be imprisoned, half-starved, beaten, and disgraced. Even the world he lives in now, carpeted in secrets and power and lies, is it a world he could ever bring a child into? Would he dare? Or might it heal him to teach a boy or girl to be kind and peace loving, galvanized by his own hatred of war? Would it change him to have someone of his own to protect and cherish?

He wants to cherish Rosalind, desperately longs to shield her, to be her hero. How dangerous it feels, this need to impress, to protect a woman who matters too much to him. He's learned that life is unpredictable. Can he ever trust it again?

⸜ ⸜ ⸜

Carrying his briefcase packed with the equipment, he waits for the bus. The last thing he told her when they spoke was to leave a message for the night doorman to let him in without buzzing. And she promised to turn out her lights at ten thirty and open her door at exactly eleven fifteen without a word. The doorman nods when he says his name and lets him by. Charlie silently signals to Gray, who's sitting on a folding chair in her hallway. Gray shuts his book, sets it on the chair, and passes Charlie on his way to the elevator. Charlie spoke to him earlier, told him that if Rosalind was at home tonight, Gray could go out for an hour after Charlie arrived to get himself a coffee or take a walk, then get back in his car and wait. The elevator comes and Gray is gone.

Charlie lingers in the hallway alone now, electric with longing. Suddenly the door shifts back and Rosalind's standing in a spill of light from the hall, peignoir and bare feet, a glowing, shimmering apparition. He raises his finger to his lips and she nods, steps back to let him in, and closes the door silently behind him while he removes his shoes. He takes hold of her shoulder, compact and eggshell-like beneath his large hand, and gives it a gentle squeeze. He can't help but touch her, so beautiful before him, so otherworldly. She reaches up and holds his wrist for a moment. They stand there, just breathing, trying to see each other's faces in the dark.

Though he hates to, he's the first to let go. Opening his briefcase quietly, he lifts a solid square instrument out of it: a box that detects radio waves. He's already turned it to silent to keep it from beeping. Instead, it will light when he nears a bug and blink when it's very near. It takes him more than an hour to find the three bugs they've planted. People don't realize that homes are filled with radio waves. He needs to be sure he's located them all. One is hooked into the light socket over her bed, which he finds disturbing. Another is in the kitchen fixture, which dangles down over a small table. It's where he told her about his hand. It sickens him, thinking of Soviet operatives listening to his whole sad tale. The most unreachable bug is wired into the large, flat ceiling fixture over the living room. Anyone else would need a ladder, but he's able to get to it by standing on tiptoe to as silently as possible unscrew the glass shade. He sets it on the carpet, retrieves the bug, and then screws it back on. Nothing in the bathroom.

He told Rosalind on the phone that the technical people at the FBI want to examine the devices and possibly learn from them, so Gray will be waiting in his vehicle to take them directly to headquarters. Of course, in time, the Russians will note the silence. He hopes they'll think it's a failure of their receiver and not realize the devices have been disabled. They're the smallest bugs Charlie's ever seen, each slightly bigger than a pack of cigarettes with two wires attached. The Soviets are masters at covert listening, far ahead of the United States. Why do they think Rosalind warrants the expense of these devices? As he goes out, she places her hand on her heart as though saying **thank you**. In the elevator, he hears the **thunk** and **squeak** of the elevator cords. Do the devices contain some magical battery as a backup to wiring them in?

Are they listening even now? Can they hear the movement?

Outside, he scoops the three bugs from his pockets and hands them silently to Gray, who wraps them in white batting he got from who knows where. Good thinking—just in case.

When Gray's car has driven out of sight, Charlie pauses a moment to breathe, to look across the drive and over to the dark water. The rush of traffic is itself water-like, endless. The ghostly lights of pleasure boats beyond the Drive spark and blink. You can't know Chicago without knowing the lake. Its gravitational pull, the mingled aromas of fish and mud and something metallic and utterly clean. He recalls his mother bringing them to Oak Street Beach when he and Peggy were little. Towels. Sandwiches. Pails and shovels. It was so much cooler by the lake than in his neighborhood. He cried when his mother wanted them to leave. **We go to the beach, then we go home. No tears,** she said. That's when he learned that lake breezes were for rich people.

As he walks back into her building, every nerve in his body sings. He flashes his badge on the way to the elevator, and the night doorman nods. When Charlie knocks, Rosalind opens the door right away and draws him in, closing the door behind him.

"Are you sure they can't hear us?" she whispers.

"I promise. I didn't miss an inch."

She sighs, then speaks in her regular voice. "Can I get you something cold to drink? Or Scotch?"

"No. It's late. But there's something important I need to tell you before I go: We developed your photos. The man who's been following you is Ronald Anson. We've put a team on him."

"Anson. Is he dangerous?"

"He used to be a boxer. Got involved in some sort of crooked dealings, threw a few fights. Made him pretty rich for a while. I'm not sure when the Communists got to him. Other than the fights, he has no criminal record."

"I guess that's a relief . . ."

"Listen, tell me more of what Weaver said; then it's probably best I go. Gray will be coming back as soon as he drops off the bugs." He's afraid of how much he feels for her. The sway she has over him.

"Sit for a while and talk to me," she says.

Her face looks young in the shadows, open. She wants his company. Even in the dark, it's visible.

"Okay," he says. "Just for a while. No sleeping on the sofa tonight . . ."

She smiles. "I wouldn't ask for that again." She gestures for him to step forward into the living room. The windows are cranked wide. Unlike the last time, everything is neat, put away, orderly. Taking a corner of the sofa, he settles in, realizing how tired he is, despite the excitement of being with her. It's late, and as he swept her place, he must have been tensing all his muscles. Now unclenching means exhaustion. She sits near him. The breeze makes him close his eyes for just a moment and luxuriate in the way it tickles his eyelids. And then he peers out at the dark quiet of the lapping black, the Drake at the shoreline, its lights doubled by the water, the Palmolive beacon every now and then brushing her windows, pirouetting across her room. It's the Chicago he's always longed for.

"This is a nice place," he says. "You must love living here."

"I chose it when I was at the lab and making more money. Now I'm just hanging on as long as I can. It reminds me of the girl I used to be—someone with a bright future. I don't feel so shiny anymore."

He takes in the silken sheen of her peignoir, the pale drift of her neck and bosom in the half-light.

"You look shiny enough to me."

She shakes her head. "I was thinking about it the other day, asking myself, 'When was the last time I was truly happy?' I couldn't remember."

"Rosalind."

"Are you happy? I mean, do you think of yourself as a happy person?"

He stares at her for a moment before he answers. He hasn't asked himself that question in years.

"Not since the war."

"Were you once?"

"When I was young, I was ecstatic." Saying it recalls a gleaming moment when he had status in his world, a girl who thought he made the sun rise. "I belonged then," he says. "I was in love."

"What happened to her?"

"After this"—he raises his withered hand—"she left me."

"The girl who said those hurtful things . . ."

He nods.

"She must not have really loved you."

"She apologized recently. She said rejecting me was the worst mistake of her life. It didn't take the sting away." He sits back, crosses his arms, hiding his bad hand.

"After you persuaded me to see Weaver, I thought it might bring back some of the joy I felt with him," she says. "I now believe he actually might love me. But the fact he's been lying all these years sucks all the joy from it."

"We're quite the pair," he says. "I'm sorry I urged you to go back to him. I'm sorry I exposed the lie about his wife."

"I would have mourned him if I'd found out he'd died without my seeing him again. I'm grateful for that."

She's silent for a while and then pulls a handkerchief from her cuff and presses it to her eyes. The lights from Lake Shore Drive pick out a trail of tears on her cheeks.

"You okay?" he asks.

"I always seem to be crying around you. I didn't sleep last night. My emotions are right on my skin. You know?"

"Come here." He opens his arm for her. She looks surprised, then moves closer and leans against him with a sigh. He doesn't know how he found the courage. But nothing ever felt so good as the realness of her in the arc of his arm. "You want to tell me more of what he said?"

"I asked him to tell me if he was the one who gave the Russians information to build the bomb. He said yes."

"You said it wasn't just him."

"There were others—Fuchs, of course, and two scientists he thinks at Los Alamos—but the Russians didn't tell him who. He didn't feel safe to talk to the men he suspected."

"That's their modus operandi. To keep their sources from knowing each other."

"He feels bad about what he did. But . . . how can I ever forgive him?"

"You could help him make up for it."

"Oh, you're talking about . . ."

"If you wore a recording device. If you secretly taped his confession and told him you had it, couldn't you then persuade him to tell us what we need to know? Details could make all the difference . . ."

"You're asking me to trick him. Betray him."

"He betrayed you, didn't he?"

She looks down, shakes her head ruefully. "True."

"You'd be helping him make the right choice."

"I don't know if I have it in me . . ."

"You do. You're the bravest girl in the world."

They're close enough that he can smell the sweetness of her skin. Her nightgown is silky on his fingertips. And so sheer, he can feel the heat of her through it. He draws her closer, hugs her in the embrace of his arm.

"You should know I'm not supposed to do this . . . get involved with you. I could lose my job."

"Do you want to be . . . involved with me?" she whispers, every breath evident in the rise of her bosom.

"More than I can say." He bites his lip. "Am I presuming too much? That you do too?"

"I think I must be mad. I let Weaver back into my life, and now . . . I only find peace thinking about you." Even in the dusky light, he sees her cheeks color, is staggered by the joy her words bring. Kissing the top of her head, he lets his fingers explore the wonder of her hair. Heavy silken threads. Glossy and inviting.

"There's something I should tell you," he says. "I haven't been with a woman in a long time. I haven't so much as kissed a girl since 1941." He says it before he recalls the night Linda stole a kiss. But there's no point in mentioning that.

"When you got back, you never found anyone you thought was attractive? Nine years . . ."

"The war changed me," he says. He has no way to explain how ruined and unlovable he's felt since, viewing the world through a shattered lens. Whenever he met a woman he would like to be with, even casually, his whole body tensed with the knowledge that she would reject him eventually. He didn't think he could bear it. He doesn't understand why Rosalind is different, why he's willing to risk it with her, except that she, too, seems broken. "It was bad," he says. "Worse than I can say. My hand . . . I couldn't allow anyone to hurt me again like she did."

⫿ ⫿ ⫿

Rosalind is moved by the elegance of Charlie's face in the half-light. Noble. Sad. It's grown more beautiful to her each time she's seen him. As though her eyes are just beginning to make sense of the man in front of her. She's inexpressibly touched that while he's been incapable of opening himself to others, he wants her. "I told you: Your hand is just part of you," she whispers. "It only offends me in that it makes your life hard."

When he smiles, his eyes seem to light, even in the dark.

"You know," she whispers, "I hear kissing a girl is like riding a bicycle." Her voice is teasing. Kind. She can only guess how hard this must be for him. She wants to keep it light.

"As I recall, it's nothing like riding a bicycle," he says with a quirky smile. Even so, there's hesitation in his eyes.

She gently takes his face into her hands, runs a finger over his brow, then finds the courage to press her lips to his. His mouth relaxes, invites her in. Satin and slip and honey. My God. It feels like opening the front door after a long time away. Like coming home. Both thrilling and so natural. She's startled and moved when he lets out an animal-like sound, as though the desire she arouses makes him ache. She's never been with anyone but Weaver. This soul-deep longing for Charlie is like nothing she's experienced before. A fierce tide that could push her helplessly toward the rocks. She sees how defended he is.

But if she could get past the barriers, with a man like Charlie there could be such a joyous outcome. A home. A true love. Years of tenderness ahead. And a chance to be a woman she can be proud to be.

"Take me to bed," she whispers.

"Rosalind, you have no idea how much I want to." He lets go of her, sits back.

"But?"

"We've got to think about this. We don't want to just jump in and not think," he says.

"I've thought. **We've** already thought."

"We can't kiss for the first time, then go right to bed."

"Why not? We're not teenagers. We're not virgins." And then a thought burns her. "You're not pushing me away because I've slept with Weaver, are you?"

His gazes at her fondly, shakes his head. "How could you believe that?"

"Then, what?"

"We have to wait until this Weaver thing is over. If we make love, it could compromise everything. You mean too much to me. This is **not** just some infatuation . . ."

"It's not for me either." She feels offended.

"If we're going to play this out, you have to go back and be with Weaver. You'll no doubt sleep with him again. You think you can do that after we make love? If it won't make things harder for you, it will for me. You feel **something** for me, don't you?" he asks. "It's not just . . . loneliness or . . ."

"What I feel for you is like the pull of gravity," she says.

His eyes soften at her words. "Yes, for me too." He presses his face against hers for a moment. "To be practical, we don't have protection," he whispers.

"If I did, would you take me to bed?"

He laughs nervously. "It's hard enough to be honorable."

"Who wants you to be honorable?"

"Hey." He lifts her chin with his forefinger, traces her lips with his thumb. "I'm going to go now," he says. "I'll wait downstairs for Gray."

"Why did I pick such a Good Samaritan?"

"I've waited nine years. I want it to be everything."

"I don't think I can live up to **that,**" she says.

"Oh, I'd put a thousand dollars on it you can. Listen, you asked if I'm happy? I haven't been this happy in years. I'm drippin' happy." She laughs. "What about you?"

"I'd be happier if you made love to me." She smiles devilishly.

"What did they call those women that lured sailors to the rocks to smash their ships? You're dangerous."

"I have no interest in smashing your ship, Charlie."

He laughs and gets up from the sofa, drawing her up too, pressing her body to his.

"This is just a beginning," he says. "Okay?"

"Okay." She looks up at him. How comforted and safe she feels in his embrace. She hates that he's saying no, though she knows to wait will make their first time more precious. A time when Weaver is far behind them.

"Are you going to see him tomorrow night?" he asks.

"I guess . . . I guess I should."

"Would you consider wearing that recording device?" His eyes beseech her.

"I don't know," she says grimly. The thought of stepping into the Hyde Park apartment and back into Weaver's arms terrifies her. This time wearing a heavy, spinning trap?

"Will you think about it?" She nods. "You could come to headquarters before you go to him. We'll help you put it on. If I'm not there, I'll brief Donna. She's reliable. She'll help."

"What if he . . . what if he wants to . . . be intimate with me?"

She notes a momentary flicker in his eyes.

"You excuse yourself and take it off when you undress, alone. You'd have to bring a very large handbag to hide it in. Do you have one? And you should wear a loose jacket if you have such a thing. Okay?"

She nods. He kisses her brow with apparent tenderness. Yet, does he truly feel what he professes? She wishes she felt more confident that a man she so longs for and admires could care for her. Their last kiss is painful, vibrating with repressed longing. "If you decide yes, call me. It's the right thing to do, Rosalind." He turns to the door, to the night. When he's gone, she feels more alone than she's ever felt in her life.

CHAPTER TWENTY-TWO

In the morning, Rosalind is at odds. She's warmed by the unexpected intimacy of the night before. Her bones feel phosphorescent as she reflects on Charlie's touch, his kiss, his presence. Those broad shoulders, that understanding face, his voice. But even as she acknowledges how drawn she is to him, she can't lose the distrust. Could his feelings be true without a hidden agenda? Weaver has made her doubt every man. Will she ever move past it? And then there's Weaver himself. Her new abhorrence for him winds around her love for him—choking it. Choking her. Still, Charlie asked her, begged her, to stay involved.

And so, when her counter is free, she picks up the phone and calls Weaver at his office to tell him she'll see him tonight. He sounds relieved, grateful even. He says he feared she'd never speak to him again.

"Will you answer all my questions?" she asks.

"I'll tell you anything, as long as it doesn't make you hate me more."

Hanging up the phone, she feels a quaking in her chest. Will she have the courage to wear the recorder tonight? A confession could make him turn himself in. Would it save him as Charlie promises? Or would it damn him?

Contending with these conflicting thoughts, Rosalind returns from the ladies' room to discover her brother-in-law standing in front of her counter, chatting with Adele.

"Henry!" Rosalind doesn't think he's ever visited her at Field's before.

"Hey, kid," he says. "This nice lady's been entertaining me while I waited for you." He throws a smile at Adele, who looks utterly charmed. Has Henry been flirting? Rosalind has rarely seen her supervisor smile so openly. "You have time to come out to lunch?" he asks.

"Sure. I always have time for you." She looks over at Adele, who nods encouragingly. "Where are we going?"

"Harvey's. If that's okay."

"You know I love it."

Harvey's Luncheonette on Lake Street is **their** place. When she was a kid, Henry used to be the one to take her downtown for a doctor or dentist appointment "We'll give Louisa a break," Henry would say, and take a morning off from work. As a treat, before he brought her home, they'd stop at Harvey's for matching Coca-Colas and patty melts. Over lunch, he'd ask her thoughtful questions and treat her like an adult. She remembers him explaining the stock market crash to her. Later, as the Depression got worse, he made clear that while money was tight, they were a lucky family. For instance, they could still afford to eat at Harvey's. But there were people who had no jobs, were hungry all the time. He told her she should never look down on their poverty.

"So it's not their fault?" she asked him. "Lou says if they tried harder, they'd find jobs."

"Well, Lou may be off about that," he explained patiently. "Some of those people have tried their best to get jobs and haven't had any luck. There are way too few opportunities out there these days. We should be kind to anyone in need." That lunch changed the way Rosalind has thought about poverty ever since.

During the war, Henry was in his forties, so they stationed him in Washington, DC. She was grown and already working for Fermi, but she missed her brother-in-law. Sometimes, she'd take the bus up from Hyde Park on a Saturday and go to Harvey's, where she'd sit alone at the lunch counter. After ordering a Coke and patty melt, she'd pull out letter paper and write to him. **I just toasted you with my Coke,** she'd write. **Wish you were here with me, Pal.** She signed her letters **Kid.** He always wrote back as soon as he could.

"So," she asks him now. "How are you doing?" As they step into the flow of traffic, she glances back to see Agent Carlisle walking behind them. This morning he introduced himself, saying Lawrence had come down with the flu. He's clearly new at his job, and with his twelve-year-old face and nervous demeanor, he doesn't inspire confidence.

"I came to have lunch with you," Henry says, "because I thought you should know . . . I've moved to the Allerton."

She stops dead on the sidewalk. People pile up behind her, curse, push by with huffs and grunts. He grabs her elbow and pulls her to the side so the crowd can keep moving.

"I guess I should have waited until we got to Harvey's to tell you."

She thinks she might cry, but she swallows down the saltiness and is left with a tingle behind her molars.

"I didn't think it would come to that," she says. "I thought you two would work it out. Poor Ava."

"Ava knows Lou and I both love her."

"Why didn't Louisa call me?" Rosalind asks.

"Who knows? Maybe she's out celebrating."

"More likely she's ashamed. Your pushback

after all these years baffles her. She's used to you ignoring whatever she says."

"I couldn't do it anymore."

"I know. When did you move out?"

"The night before last. I didn't want to tell you on the telephone."

"Thanks for that." She grabs his arm. So steady. So kind. So unselfish. Why didn't she fall in love with a man like Henry in the first place instead of Weaver? She could never take a man like that for granted. Charlie seems a lot like Henry. A thoughtful man. How she wants to believe him, to lose her doubts.

"How will you see Ava?"

"We'll arrange it. Maybe she'll stay with me on weekends. She likes being downtown. She's always loved coming in to see you."

"Do you have room for her?"

"They can bring up a cot. We'll eat room service. She'll love it."

"So it's over? There's nothing you and Lou can do to make things right?"

He shrugs. "Things could be done," he says in a soft voice. "If certain people would be willing to do them."

They reach Harvey's, and Rosalind is relieved there's an open table. She wouldn't want to be talking about this at the lunch counter with a waitress eavesdropping on them while wiping it down. At the table, they chat about other things, but soon she leans forward and whispers, "If things don't happen as you hope, will you get a divorce?"

Henry shrugs, pushes his glasses back in place. "Maybe we'll just live apart." She feels nominally relieved. Divorce seems so ugly, so drastic. Something that selfish, sleazy people partake in. Or movie stars. Not Lou. Not Henry. Not people who have been married for more than twenty years. "I hope you don't . . . unless . . . Henry . . . ?" She stares at him.

"What?" he asks.

"There isn't **someone else,** is there?" She hazily imagines a lady CPA with glasses, a mannish suit, and a wise smile. "Another woman?"

He laughs. "There's no one else, kid. I promise."

"I think you're very brave," she says, "for standing up to Louisa. But I wish she'd change her mind, apologize, learn something."

"Has Louisa ever learned anything?" he asks with a sigh.

That's the way they've talked all these years: as if Louisa were at fault. Rosalind's never thought that much about it. Louisa has always been hard to deal with. And yet . . . why? Does something hurt her? Is she lashing out for a reason?

The waitress comes to deliver their order, and it's a good thing. The uneasiness Rosalind feels is hard to sit with. Later, as they finish their lunches, Henry asks, "You and Weaver . . . how's that going?"

"Oh. He's not well . . ."

"No?"

"He's got cancer."

"Jeez. Really? I'm sorry, kid. That's awful."

Even as she says the word "cancer," she still has a hard time believing Weaver is dying.

"Is that why he came back?"

"Probably." She looks at her brother-in-law, the most stable person in her life, and has the urge to tell him more. "He's not a good guy," she says. "He's done some awful things."

"He hurt you, for one."

"Yes. And that's only the beginning."

"You don't have to stay involved with him, you know. Even if he's sick. Not after what he did to you."

"I know."

She can tell that Henry wants to say something denigrating about Weaver but watches him swallow it down. Instead he says, "If you ever need me—to talk or cry or whatever it is you want to do—you'll let me know, won't you?"

She nods.

"Because you owe him nothing. Absolutely nothing. Look, you don't need a lecture from me. You'll know the right thing to do."

"Do we ever **really** know the right thing to do? Any of us?" she asks.

"You will. I believe in you, kid. I have no doubt that whatever decision you make, whether it comes to Weaver or science or your life, you'll make the right choice. You're the smartest girl I've ever known, and your heart is true. You just follow it."

✳ ✳ ✳

Leaving Henry at the corner of Dearborn and Monroe, wishing her true heart would tell her just what to do about Weaver, she senses someone walking too close. She assumes it's the hapless Carlisle, who sat gaping at them all through lunch. But turning her head, she's chilled to note crisply pressed pants, expensive shoes, swollen hands. **Anson.** For one unnerving second their eyes meet. His so pale, so empty. Where the hell is Carlisle?

She swerves abruptly into the open doors of Carson Pirie Scott, sensing Anson close behind. Carson's is packed with shoppers and a-lilt with music. In the middle of the main floor, a man in a tuxedo is perched on a piano stool before a shining black baby grand, and a girl in a long pink dress is belting "Buttons and Bows" into a microphone. The overly happy tune presses claustrophobically on Rosalind's ears. With Anson on her tail, she veers right, steps up to the perfume counter, and grabs the tester bottle of L'Heure Bleue.

A bored shopgirl with a blond bob glances up from her sales book and declares, "L'Heure Bleue makes a girl irresistible," in a tired voice. Rosalind brings the bottle to her nose, stalling for time, wondering what she's going to do. As long as she's in such a public place, isn't she safe? And then she feels fingers gripping her left arm.

"Rosalind Porter!" Anson says in a jolly, familiar way. Rosalind tries to shake him off, but his hold tightens, so that her fingers begin to tingle.

"You have something I need, dear." He moves close to her and whispers, "And you know just what it is." His breath sliding over her ear makes her shiver in disgust.

"Let go of me." She tries to jerk away. "Let go!" Rather than appearing alarmed, the salesgirl looks up with a sigh as though women get accosted every day at her counter. In a blasé manner, she turns to help a customer on the other side of the perfume island.

"No need to get too noisy, Miss Porter. Neither of us wants to make a scene. If you care about the safety of your friend Tom Weaver, you'll be a good girl." His voice is even, cool, and surprisingly delicate. Like his clothing, it doesn't seem to suit his tough, threatening body. Charlie told her he's assigned a team to follow Anson too. But where are they? It makes sense that they would hesitate to intervene, wouldn't want to reveal themselves, but will they come to her rescue if she's in real trouble?

"What do you want?"

"You happen to have a certain key to a safe-deposit box with you?" His breath smells surprisingly minty, as though he popped a breath mint before accosting her.

"I don't know what you're talking about."

"Oh, you do, dear, you do." He grips her even more tightly. "Mr. Weaver gave you a key and you've put it in your own safe-deposit box."

"I don't have a key," she says. "Let go of me, or I'll . . ."

"You'll what?" he asks. "You'll give me the damn key!" His voice is suddenly terrifying. He's shaking her arm. His nails are cutting half-moons into her flesh. And no agent steps forward. No one is coming to intervene.

In what feels like slow motion, her heart banging, she raises the tester of L'Heure Bleue and sprays him right in the eyes. Anson lets out a high-pitched yelp like a puppy being hit by a car. His hands fly to his face; he doubles over. Rosalind slams down the tester and, weaving between strollers and shoppers, runs past the musicians and the crowd, not daring to look back. She bursts for Madison Street. Her ears pulsate with every clap of her heart. Her breath burns in her throat as she pushes through the noontime crowd. Her only goal: to get up the street to Field's, to find her bodyguard. But even if Carlisle is waiting and there's a counter between herself and everyone else, how will she feel safe?

⊪ ⊪ ⊪

Though her encounter with Anson terrified her, she has no choice but to keep working as though nothing's happened. Spotting Carlisle, she quietly motions for him to come to her counter. Pretending she's showing him jewelry, she tells him what happened at Carson's, noting how shaky her voice sounds. She's exasperated that he seems more interested in excusing how he lost her than showing concern for her terrifying experience.

⊪ ⊪ ⊪

After that, though, Carlisle paces the floor, glancing over at Rosalind too often, too obviously. But she's glad he's there. She can't help wondering, what's in Weaver's safe-deposit box that the Russians need so desperately?

As the afternoon goes on, Field's becomes more crowded. Fridays often are. She sells diamond earrings to a woman who tells her she's visiting from Switzerland. A ruby-and-diamond wedding band to a young woman and her fiancé. A large sapphire brooch in the shape of a flower to a man who came looking for a birthday gift for his wife, whose passion is her beautiful garden. All three sales are larger than usual. She'll get a decent commission. But she barely navigates her way through the light conversations and cajoling, the exchange of money and gift wrapping. Her arm throbs where Anson's fingernails punctured her skin. Surrounding the half-moon lacerations, blue ovals are rising from the pressure of his grip. She feels disembodied and miserable and she can't help scanning the crowd for Anson's face.

At three, she calls Adele over.

"I've got to leave, Adele," she says. "I've **got** to." She makes sure her voice is wavering and weak. "It's food poisoning, I think."

Adele scans her face. "I've got to admit, you don't look so good. Go. Go home. I'll take over."

⫾ ⫾ ⫾

Rosalind, with Carlisle sitting behind her on the bus, does go home, but not to Lake Shore Drive. She knows Ava and Louisa need her right now. And despite all, Louisa's is the one place she feels most safe, most beloved. Even when her sister opens the door and blinks coldly, as though Roz is a vacuum salesman who's interrupted her favorite radio hour.

"You could have called," Louisa says.

"May I come in?"

"Why aren't you at work?"

"I got off early."

Louisa narrows her eyes, steps back to let Rosalind in. She isn't wearing lipstick, looks pale and nervous. Thinner too.

"You don't look quite right," she tells Rosalind, though surely Louisa is the one most altered.

"Hard day," Roz says. She would feel so much better if she could share her terror and confusion about Weaver with her sister. But she knows even bringing up his name would set off a river of vitriol. Rosalind trails her sister into the kitchen, where the dinner dishes are stacked in the sink, a pan sits half-full on the stovetop.

"Henry told me what happened. I wish you'd let me know," Roz says.

"You encouraged him to leave me, didn't you?" Louisa asks, turning to her with a sneer.

"I **never** would."

"The two of you have always conspired against me. You think I didn't know?"

Anson's attack has left Rosalind jangling, but her sister's hurt breaks through, moves her.

She sets a bolstering hand on Louisa's shoulder. "There must be something I can do," she says. Louisa shrugs it away.

"Like what? Introduce me to my next husband?"

"C'mon. I'm worried about you."

"As though that helps."

Rosalind steps in front of her sister.

"Stop stonewalling me," she says. "Are you getting out? Seeing friends? I'm concerned."

"You think I want my friends to know my husband left me? Don't you realize how ashamed I feel? How **ruined**?"

Louisa is often enraged, but today her face is twisted by simple pain.

"Chances are Henry will come back if you just listen to him."

"Listen to **him**?"

"He's asking you to understand he's been unhappy. That he doesn't want to be led around by the nose anymore."

"As if he so much as ever listened to why **I'm** unhappy."

Rosalind wishes she could go to her childhood room and fling herself on the bed. Or head down the hall and find Ava. But she stops. Maybe, she thinks, **she's** the one who needs to listen. She takes a deep breath.

"There's something you'd like to tell Henry?" she asks. "Something he's not hearing?"

"Yes."

"Tell **me** why you're unhappy, then. Start with me."

Louisa looks up, surprised. "You really want to hear it?"

"Of course I do."

"I want to tell him . . ." Louisa's eyes are distant and desperate. "I want . . . I want to tell him I feel stuck," she says. "I want to tell him . . ." Rosalind notes that her lips are quivering. "That I feel taken for granted. That I feel . . ." Tears run along her nose. Tremble at the edge of her lips.

"You feel like Henry doesn't appreciate you?"

"You and Ava don't either. I'm just Louisa who puts the food on the table and does the laundry and vacuums the floor. I'm invisible. Nobody respects me. No one cares what I say or think. I'm nobody."

"You're not nobody."

"What have I accomplished in life? I used to be an A-plus student. Just like you. Did you know that?"

"I . . . I guess not."

"The one time I felt alive was during the war when they took me off the floor at the factory and asked me to join the management. I'd made some suggestions about increasing speed on the line. And my ideas worked, Roz. They worked! They said I was too smart to be just polishing torpedoes. And I made a difference in that office.

I reorganized everything. I created systems that worked better. For the first time in my life, I was respected."

"I knew you liked that job. But then, why did you leave? Why don't I recall?"

"Ava was just four. I only worked because they needed us women during the war. And after a while, you know, it didn't feel right—leaving Ava with Agnes Dodworth and Father. At that point Father was already failing. And Ava was already too smart, too curious, for poor old Agnes. So I gave it up. While, at that same time, you were out changing the world."

"Maybe I was, Lou. But not for the better. Come, sit down," she says, pulling out a chair for Louisa at the table by the window. Roz takes the seat beside her. In the strong summer light, she can see the lines that have mapped her sister's face. They've deepened with time, like streams cutting through stone. When did Rosalind last really look at the woman who raised her? Or think about her needs?

Rosalind has always assumed her sister embraced her narrow, prescribed life, was satisfied in her traditional role. After all, she seemed giddy with joy when Roz's career took its tumble, when her life became **more appropriate for a woman.** But maybe—and how is it that Rosalind never saw this before?—maybe it was because Louisa envied her. Maybe it was because Louisa felt left behind, caught in a web of everyone else's expectations.

"I've taken you for granted, and I'm sorry for that. Deeply sorry," Rosalind says. "But, Lou, you **have** accomplished something."

"What?"

"You've raised me. You're raising Ava."

"It's not enough," Louisa says. "I know you think it should be, but it's not."

"I don't think it should be." It may be the very first time she's really understood her sister. Perhaps they are not so different. Listening to her sister, being there for her, makes Roz feel good for the first time in hours. "You want more. You deserve more. You want to be someone. Not just a wife or even a mother. And you know you're capable of it."

Louisa closes her eyes and nods. "Yes," she whispers. "Yes."

"Maybe this rift between you and Henry, maybe it's not about Henry at all," Roz says.

Her sister looks up with questioning eyes.

"You're unhappy. You take it out on him. But maybe it's not him you're angry at."

Louisa's face is almost childlike.

"Maybe it's not."

Rosalind takes her sister into her arms, relieved that Lou lets her.

"We can change things for you. I know we can. You could go to college. Or you could get a job, find a place to shine."

"Don't be absurd. At my age?"

"I've heard of older people going to college."

"No. I never could."

"You could." Roz hugs her sister tighter, feels her sobbing. "There are answers to this. Now that we understand, we can explain to Henry what's going on. We can—"

"Rozzie's here? What's wrong? What's going on?" Ava wanders in, looking at the two of them with a concerned frown.

"Nothing, Ava," Roz says. "Just adults talking. Give us a minute."

"But I never get to see you."

Louisa sits back. "No. We've talked enough. Go with Ava."

"Ava, give us more time. Okay?"

"Rozzie!"

Roz shoots her niece a stern look.

"It's okay," Louisa says, getting up, lifting the hem of her apron and wiping her tears. "Go with her. Thank you."

"But there's more for us to say."

"Not right now."

"You sure?"

"I'm sure." Rosalind sees that for all Lou's whining and discontent, it's hard for her to expose her vulnerable side, the side Rosalind can love, the side she's always craved to find.

"We'll talk more about this," Rosalind says. "A lot more, okay?"

"Okay." Rosalind smiles at her sister, and Louisa actually smiles back. It's a shy, rusty smile.

Rosalind leans over and kisses her cheek. "I love you," she says. "You're not invisible to me. You're my savior." She says it right to her face. She means it.

⁜ ⁜ ⁜

At that moment, Rosalind's heart tells her what she's going to do. Louisa was there for her when she needed her most: saving her when Rosalind didn't have the fortitude or insight to save herself. When she didn't even **want** to be saved. And now she's helping Louisa when Louisa's first instinct was to push her away. It's time to do the same for Weaver. The FBI already suspects him. How long until he's arrested? Charlie says if Weaver turns himself in, if he puts forward a full confession, they'll protect him the best they can. It's Weaver's only shot at absolution, Rosalind's only chance of finding safety. She shudders at the thought of wearing the secret recording device, at Weaver touching her and discovering it beneath her clothes. She hates that she's trapping him—even if it's to coax him to do the right thing. But she doesn't see that she has a choice.

She goes out Louisa's door to where Carlisle is waiting on the sidewalk, smoking a cigarette, a handful of crushed butts lying all around him on the ground.

"I'm on my way to the FBI office," she says as she passes him. "You'd better keep up."

CHAPTER TWENTY-THREE

Weaver?" Rosalind knocks at his door but there's no answer. "Weaver?" she calls again. She imagines he must be napping and searches for the key he insisted she take a few weeks ago. She stares nervously at the unwieldy men's watch on her left hand as she slips her right one into the dark depths of her purse. The watch contains a microphone. When she reached the FBI office, she discovered that Charlie was spending the day in Hinsdale. But as promised, his secretary had been fully briefed. Donna helped Rosalind snap on the stiff leather harness fitted out to hold the heavy wire recorder. She carefully threaded a wire from the watch up Rosalind's sleeve to the recorder. She showed her how to switch it on. Two and a half hours of recording time. Secrets to be captured. Rosalind has to tell herself, as she's done again and again on the bus ride down, that she's doing the right thing. If only

Charlie had been there. He could have helped her feel so much more certain.

She fears Weaver will ask about the watch. She's decided to say it was her father's, though she's never been a very good liar. The harness bites into her right breast. The Minifon was clearly never meant to be worn by a woman. One hug and Weaver would feel it beneath her jacket. She'll have to stay away from him. She'll insist she's still processing her anger at him, working through it, keeping her distance. At last, her fingers locate Weaver's key at the dusty bottom of her handbag.

She knocks one more time. "Weaver? I'm coming in." She slides the key into the lock and twists it. The door opens to an unlit apartment. It's overcast, sure to rain, and Weaver hasn't turned on the lights. Maybe he isn't home yet, got caught up with work. Or he's resting. He's been so tired lately. Still, he knew she was coming, seemed excited about it. Clicking the wall switch and another lamp by the sofa, she gingerly moves toward the shadowy bedroom. She tries to see through the murk, to make out his form under the covers. She doesn't want to turn on the light and scare him. Still, the bedroom faces a narrow gangway where little light gets in. "Weaver?" she whispers. "Weaver?" She comes to the edge of the bed and reaches out to find cold sheets, sweeps her hand across them and feels something sticky. No one's there. When she switches on the bedside lamp, she gasps.

The wooden headboard is shattered in one spot, as though hit by a bowling ball. And a wide red-brown streak of what surely must be blood runs along the sheets from that spot, all the way to the side of the bed and along its edge. There's blood on her hand, a pool of blood in one spot on the bed. And dark drops on the floor. As though his head might have hit the headboard, shattered it, and then he either dragged himself or someone dragged him off the bed. Terror shoots to the tips of her fingers, to the roots of her hair. Dear God. Backing away from the bed, she runs to the bathroom, its door ajar, the shower curtain open. There's no one in the bathroom, no one in the kitchen either. Where is he?

Panting, close to screaming, the recorder in its harness choking her with every step, she runs down the stairs and cries out for Carlisle.

⫷ ⫷ ⫷

She gives Carlisle the apartment number, tells him that the door is open, but she doesn't follow him back upstairs. She can't face the blood, the tide of violence so evident in the apartment. She knows if it was Charlie, he would have insisted she stay with him. But the young agent doesn't even think of her. And she's glad. She's shaking. **Is this her fault? Because she didn't give the empty-eyed man the key this afternoon?** The thought rolls over her like a dark fog. She pulls a tissue from her purse and tries to wipe the blood from her hands. The tissue sticks and tears. She spits into her hand to wipe it away. Weaver!

She must reach Charlie. She knows there's a broken-down phone booth at the corner in front of a seedy bar. She's passed it many times. Walking there, all she can feel is the deadweight of the recorder, strangling her, reminding her that her last act toward Weaver was a plan to blackmail him into saving himself. Reminding her that she failed. The door to the booth is hanging by one hinge and it reeks of beer and urine, but she finds three dimes in the side pocket of her purse, holds her breath, and slips one into the slot. Standing outside the booth, reaching in, she dials Charlie's office number, praying he's working tonight as he's told her he often does, praying that he went directly to his office when he returned from Hinsdale. The night receptionist sounds half-asleep. "Who?"

"Special Agent Szydlo. Charles Szydlo."

"Hold, please."

The phone rings and rings. "I'm sorry, it seems he's gone for the evening," the receptionist says. "I can take a message."

"No. I'll call him at home."

Rosalind flips the card over to find the number for his sister's house. She slips in another dime. Her heart feels too big for her chest. If only she could slow it down.

"Hello." A housewifey voice answers. It must be his sister, Peggy.

"I'm looking for Agent Szydlo," she says. "It's an emergency."

"He's not here yet. I'm sorry."

"Do you think he's on his way home? Did he say when he's coming tonight?" Rosalind looks at the oversize watch. It's only six thirty.

"Unfortunately, my brother almost never tells me his plans. Did you try his office?"

"They said he's gone. He was out in Hinsdale this afternoon."

"Can I take a message? You sound upset."

"Tell him it's Rosalind," she says. "Tell him . . ." But what can she say?

"I'm ready. I've got a pen."

"Tell him Weaver's gone . . . and there's blood in his apartment. I think something awful's happened. Carlisle's here. But Charlie should come. He's **got** to come."

"Wait, I'm writing this down. Who did you say is missing?"

"Weaver. Tell him I'm not going home. I'm going to my friend Zeke's if he's there. He should try this number to find me." She gives her Zeke's number and hangs up.

Sliding in her last dime and praying he'll be home, she dials Zeke.

⫸ ⫸ ⫸

Zeke is waiting. She sees him watching out his window on the third floor. She climbs the steps to his apartment two at a time and when he opens the door, she flings herself into his arms.

"Dear God, what's happened? You were a madwoman when you called. I couldn't understand a word you said. What the hell are you wearing under this jacket, Bunny? A metal safe?"

"Lock the door," she says.

"What?"

"Lock the damn door!"

"What the hell? Are you in some kind of trouble?"

She nods. "Yes."

"Is this about Weaver?"

"Yes. He's— Something's happened to him."

"Something?" Zeke asks.

She just shakes her head.

"You need a drink," he says. "A martini maybe? I'll make it extra-strong. I'm all out of olives, though."

"Just a Scotch. Can I have Scotch?"

"Bunny, Bunny, Bunny, you've got to clue me in here!" Zeke goes into the kitchen. By the time he returns with a Scotch, she's taken off her jacket and is undoing the last snaps on the harness, unhooking the wire to the watch. She pulls the harness off with distaste and drops it on the sofa between them. For the first time in what feels like hours, Rosalind can breathe.

"What the hell is this?" he asks, lifting a leather strap with two fingers and holding it away from himself as one might the extremity of a dead animal.

While he observes, she unbuckles the watch. "I was wearing a wire recorder. This is the microphone."

"A wire recorder this small?"

With shaking hands, she slips the recorder out of its leather pocket and, just as Donna showed her, sets it into the green leather case she's been carrying in her bag. "It's got three kinds of batteries. It weighs a ton." There's a place in the leather case for the watch too, and she presses it into the white satin shaped to cradle it, wraps the wire carefully on the spool meant to corral it, and snaps the lid shut. When she sits back on the sofa, she's numb, miserable. In too much pain to cry. Zeke lifts the harness between them and drops it on the coffee table, then scoots closer.

"What's going on?" he asks. He plucks at her hair, moving it about with some plan she can't guess. She closes her eyes and enjoys his ministrations for a moment, the comfort of being with her best friend.

"Just hold me, Zekie, okay?"

"Okay, I'm right here. Start at the beginning. What happened to Weaver?"

She is comforted by Zeke's heartbeat through his shirt. "I think he's dead," she says. "There was blood. A lot of blood." She looks down. "God, it's still on my hands."

He gasps, pushes her away to see what she's talking about. But before she leaves to wash, she curls her stained fingers into a fist in her lap and tells him everything. Even about Charlie. Because when Charlie finds out how she's been keeping the information about the key, he'll hate her anyway. And she knows Zeke will always love her, no matter what.

"And who were you recording?"

"Weaver. I was supposed to record Weaver . . . but he was gone . . . he was gone."

When Rosalind finally washes, no matter how she scrubs, no matter how hot the water, the dark red of Weaver's blood clings to the whorls of her fingerprints. She can't help thinking he will mark her forever.

⫼ ⫼ ⫼

It's nearly eight when the phone rings. They've finished dinner—Campbell's Chicken Noodle Soup. She made herself eat it because two Scotches on empty stomachs later, they're both drunk. Zeke rises with a groan, then, clapping his hand over the mouthpiece, holds the phone out to her, whispering, "Bunny, it's Shadowman."

She grabs the receiver. Swallows hard. "Charlie?"

"Are you okay? My sister said . . ."

"I'm so glad you called. I'm so glad to talk to you."

She describes the scene at the apartment, tries to keep her voice from wavering or sounding drunk. But as she goes on, describing the shattered headboard, the blood, the words pour from her.

"Is Gray with you? Or Carlisle?"

"No. Neither."

"Why not?"

"Gray wasn't there yet. I left Carlisle. I couldn't go back up there . . . I . . . Charlie, it's all my fault."

"It's not your fault. What are you talking about?"

"Anson approached me this afternoon. He wanted something. I think he hurt Weaver because I didn't give it to him." She **is** drunk or she wouldn't have spilled it out like that.

"I'm listening," he says.

"I pretended I didn't know what he was talking about."

"And what **was** he talking about?"

"It's a key to a safe-deposit box. Weaver said

keeping it a secret was life or death. He made me swear I wouldn't tell anyone . . ."

"I **told** you I couldn't keep you safe if you didn't clue me in." Charlie sounds furious. "But you felt more loyal to Weaver."

His words plunge a knife into the spot where she's stored her longing for him. An inch or two below the hollow of her throat. A swelling of joy and yearning that hasn't left since he kissed her. Now that very place pulses with pain.

"I'm going to Weaver's," he says. "Do **not** step foot out of that apartment. They must be desperate to find that key. Desperate to find you. And now we know they won't stop at anything. I'll send Gray over." He's brisk, all business.

"Will you come here?" His words have petrified her, and he's the only person who will make her feel safe.

"I need to go to Weaver's. I'll have Gray knock on Zeke's door, then stay outside on watch."

She gives him the address.

"When will I see you?" she asks. "Tonight?"

"Later." The phone goes dead before she can say another word.

⸭ ⸭ ⸭

Charlie hails a cab. All the way to Hyde Park, he's angry in a way he can't quite contain. Furious at Rosalind for withholding information, livid at himself for letting the Russians get to Weaver, upset that he wasn't available when Rosalind called for help. Terrified he can't protect her. If not for his hand, he'd be driving a car equipped with a two-way radio and have gotten her message sooner. He slams his fist into his injured hand. Punishing himself. Punishing the hand that punishes him daily.

The crime scene is just as Rosalind described, but even more shocking. She didn't mention the shattered crystal glass on the floor, one of the pieces edged in thick blood. Did they beat Weaver with his own glass, then cut his throat with a shard of it? Surely his head was smashed against the headboard, vigorously enough to have killed him. And then, as the team bags up evidence and dusts for prints, they call Charlie over.

"Hey, Szydlo, better take a gander at this," Calder says. On the floor by the closet door is a man's finger. The perfectly filed nail. The top joint intact. It's been cut off at the second joint. With wire clippers or something stunningly sharp. There's hardly any blood where it lies.

"Jesus," he and Pace say in unison.

"They must have tortured him."

"Must have." Charlie wonders if he caved. Most men would. Calder lifts the finger with his gloved hand and slips it into a waxed evidence bag. "Happy Halloween," he says.

Charlie's good hand throbs in sympathy.

Thank God Rosalind didn't spot that piece of evidence. If he can help it, he will never, ever tell her. He's suddenly desperate to get to her, to hide her somewhere safe until the FBI's gotten hold of the safe-deposit box the Russians want so badly.

∭ ∭ ∭

It's not quite ten when he gets out of the cab in front of Zeke's building. It's coming down buckets. The cold metal scent of overdue rain lifts from the pavement. He has no raincoat, no umbrella. A rat scurries along the curb and slips into a grate. Even the rat wants to avoid the merciless downpour. He finds the buzzer marked ZEKE ADAMS. APARTMENT 3B. Once buzzed in, he sees Gray huddling in the hall.

"I couldn't stand outside anymore."

"It's okay," Charlie says. "You can head out now." There's no elevator and it's a long climb. Rosalind answers the door, steps back to let him in. At the sight of her, he releases a breath he didn't know he'd been holding. Seeing her safe and whole, he feels his anger and adrenaline slowly ebb. He can tell she's searching for something in his face. Anger. Upset. He can smell liquor on her breath.

"This is Zeke," she says. Her voice is choked and thick. Surely she's told Zeke everything.

It doesn't matter anymore. Zeke comes up and holds out his hand. Charlie shakes it. He remembers following them, jealous of how these two love each other. Zeke slips his arm over Rosalind's shoulders now in a proprietary way.

"Hey, take a breath. He's here," he says. "You need a towel, Agent?"

"Yeah. Guess I could use one. Sorry for getting your floor wet."

"Give me your jacket. I'll hang it over the tub. I'll be right back."

Charlie's shirt is soaked. His hair is dripping. Still, he gently takes Rosalind in his arms, draws her to him.

"I'm sorry I was rough on the phone. I didn't mean to be. I'm so glad you're okay."

He hears her sigh with relief, feels her lean into him.

"I'm getting you wet," he whispers.

"I don't care," she says.

"Listen," he says. "I knew all along you were hiding something. I should have pushed you harder to tell me. I blame myself for putting you in danger."

"I'm the one that's sorry. I made a promise to Weaver I should never have kept."

"Weaver's apartment must have been awful for you."

She nods. A tear runs down her cheek and she wipes it off with the back of her hand.

"Sorry. With you . . . I'm always Blubbering Betty."

"Look, I want to take you to my sister's. You'll be safer there. No one will think to find you in my neighborhood. And she's around most of the day. You can stay with her."

"I can't go home?"

"Weaver's place was pretty rough. And I don't know how to say this gently . . ."

"Say it."

"It doesn't look good for Weaver, Rosalind."

She squeezes her eyes shut. "I didn't think so."

"They'll be looking for you. I don't want you going to work until we resolve things."

"But I can't afford not to work . . ."

Zeke comes back with two fluffy white towels. Charlie blots off his shirt and trousers and hair, hands the other to Rosalind. "Did I get you wet enough for this?"

"What did I miss?" Zeke asks too enthusiastically.

Rosalind's cheeks color.

"You made up with each other. Well, hallelujah! You want a drink, Charlie? Can I call you Charlie? Any friend of Bunny's is a friend of mine!"

"I need to take Rosalind somewhere safer," Charlie says.

"Who would look for her here?"

"I just want her somewhere no one will think

to look. It's raining, so we should call a Yellow Cab. We won't get one in this neighborhood, not in this rain."

"No," Zeke says. "I'll give them a call, let you two have some time."

When he leaves, Charlie takes her hand and walks her to the sofa.

"Are you going to tell me what you couldn't on the phone? What's this key?"

She shakes her head, looks down at her hands. "I didn't tell you because Weaver made me swear I wouldn't tell anyone . . . until . . . after he's gone . . ."

Charlie sighs. "I'd say that applies now."

Rosalind stares at the floor. "I don't want him to be dead. But the thought of them hurting him . . ."

"It looked to me like the hurt is over," Charlie says, shaking his head. "Tell me."

"Weaver gave me an envelope with a key inside." She goes on to explain Weaver's instructions for a safe-deposit box. "They must have heard me tell Weaver I put it in my bank before we knew my apartment was bugged. And now they want it." She shows him her arm. The bruises have turned an angry shade of plum. He winces.

"There must be something awfully damning in that box or they wouldn't be so anxious to get to it."

"It's my fault Weaver's dead."

"You're not to blame. He's been playing with his own safety for years. And by giving you that key, yours."

"I hid it behind my counter at Field's. We have to go there to get it."

"We'll take care of it. An agent can get it, or the bank can drill the lock open."

"I was about to betray him," she says, pointing to the green box that holds the recorder. How fragile she seems. Jangling. Hurt. He lifts a tear-dampened strand of her hair and tucks it behind her ear.

"You were doing it for his own good. You were trying to save him." He's put her in this peril. His longing to protect, love, and even heal her has grown each time they've been together. With Weaver out of the way, whatever's in his safe-deposit box puts Rosalind in more danger than ever, until it's in the FBI's hands.

Zeke comes back into the room. "Twenty minutes," he says. "Fastest they can get here. Have you had dinner, Charlie?"

"Nope."

"You like Campbell's Cream of Mushroom Soup?"

"Sure."

"I'll put a splash of sherry wine in it. It turns Campbell's into haute cuisine!" Zeke expresses the deliciousness with his hands. "I promise you'll never want to eat it any other way. I'm spoiling you for life!"

⁂

Peggy's house is dark when Charlie and Rosalind arrive, except for two lights, one at the front door, one coming from the side of the house. The sidewalks are wet, but at least the rain has stopped. The house reminds Rosalind of a child's drawing: red brick with a perfectly peaked roof and evenly spaced windows. In each window, curtains are drawn back to create a little scallop. White roses bloom behind a short wrought-iron fence, giving off the scent of peaches in the wet night air.

"Come on," Charlie said. "We'll go in through my apartment." He leads her toward the light at the side of the house, along a narrow brick walkway, then down steep concrete steps to a green door.

"Don't judge me," he whispers. "Apartments have been hard to come by since the war."

He's right to warn her. The floor is concrete, with a worn braided rug on top. The furniture looks used and haphazard. No one could even call it a "finished" basement. Hung from a clothesline, a flowered curtain defines a corner of the room.

"What's in there?" she asks.

"I call it my bedroom." He looks chagrinned. "Of course, you'll sleep upstairs on the couch," he tells her. "Peggy's **very** curious to meet you. She promised she'd make up the sofa before she went to bed."

"I have no clothes. Nothing."

"Peg said she'd leave out a nightgown and a toothbrush. She buys toothbrushes by the dozen. She's the five-star general of housewives. Oh, and she promised she'd leave you a clean set of towels in the bathroom on the edge of the tub. Tomorrow, I'll send Donna to your place to gather up a few of your things."

"Thank you."

"You can make a list."

"You sure Peggy doesn't mind having me stay? You call out of the blue and she just springs into action?"

"She knows you're not just any girl." Charlie caresses her cheek. "She's been on to me since that first time you called." Rosalind is surprised and pleased.

"Is everyone asleep now?" she asks.

"They go to bed before the birds stop chirping."

"Can I stay down here with you awhile?"

He smiles gently, looks at his watch. "It's eleven thirty-five now. And we've both been through a lot today."

For a sweet, quiet moment she'd pushed aside thoughts of Weaver. His bloody, battered apartment. She experiences a dropping sensation. As though Charlie senses it, he gently kisses her forehead, presses his face against hers.

"C'mon. Let me get you settled, okay?"

Upstairs they only turn on the lights needed. Whispering, he points out the bathroom, then the sofa, which is indeed perfectly made up with sheets, blankets, a fluffy pillow, and an ironed pillowcase embroidered with bluebirds.

"Your mother?" she asks, touching the shimmering azure threads that make up a bird.

He smiles wistfully and nods.

Standing by the sofa, he kisses her deeply. She's comforted by the sweetness of his soft, cool lips, by how much more peaceful she feels when he holds her close. He whispers, "We'll talk more tomorrow. Get some sleep." As she hears his footsteps retreating down the steps, she feels adrift. Perching nervously on the edge of the sofa, she freezes there. And suddenly, she can't stop thinking of Weaver's apartment. The bed with the smashed headboard, the sticky red swath on the sheets. Is Weaver somewhere suffering? Kidnapped? Or is he relieved of his suffering forever? He was rueful of the life he led. Afraid of the pain to come. She knows one thing she didn't know before he came back: that he truly loved her. Maybe he always loved her, just as she once loved him. But can real love exist in an ocean of deception?

In the dim lamplight, she glances at Peggy's neat living room. The black-and-white school photos in silver frames. The embroidered doilies and antimacassars on the chairs. The crisp curtains with white cotton puffballs hanging from the hems. The wooden cross on the wall.

It must be wonderful to believe that there is order in the world. That there's a higher being watching over whatever you do, whatever might happen to you. Except for the perfect order of physics—a religion in its own right—organized religion is a foreign concept to Roz. Henry believes in God. Louisa never has. And, therefore, at odds over their beliefs, her family didn't go to a church. So Roz, curious, used to tag along with her friends on Sundays. She was fascinated by the spoken Latin and ritual of the Catholic mass, moved by the unscrolling of the Torah and Hebrew incantations at the synagogue she visited, entertained by an Episcopalian Holy Eucharist with a singing, standing, sitting, and kneeling service.

At each sanctuary, she was drawn up into the wonder of a group of people worshipping together, finding strength in numbers. Still, she inevitably felt she was peering out a prison window while others sat in the fresh air. Perhaps one needs to be born into believing. She's never been able to find her way out into that sunlight.

As for Weaver, he didn't believe in God and

may not have fully considered right and wrong, good and evil. She thinks of what he might have suffered if he'd been allowed to succumb to the cancer. And then, the blood, the signs of violence. God didn't rise to protect him. But she supposes that's not the way it works. Since the war, how could one still believe that faith can protect?

Taking a deep breath, she tries to forget, to find comfort in the homey surroundings of Peggy's living room. Everything is clean and orderly, feels lived-in and beloved. She'll never be the woman Charlie's sister must be. But deep inside, she knows that she has something unique to offer. Her grasp of science. Her ability to think the way others don't. Her talent to problem solve. Fermi saw it. Weaver too. Her faith is in science. And though she's discovered science can be a murderer, she also knows it can be the world's most powerful answer. It's time for her to move forward, to be the engine that does the world good.

In the bathroom, she washes her face and brushes her teeth with the toothbrush marked **Rosalind** on a strip of freezer tape pressed to the handle, pulls on Peggy's coral cotton nightdress with the butterfly sleeves. In the mirror, she sees a housewife in a dowdy housecoat. But in her eyes, she sees the woman she can be. She knows she can find the courage. She has to. Climbing under the covers on Peggy's sofa, she sighs. It makes a soft, comforting bed, though she doubts she'll be able to sleep.

She thinks of Charlie downstairs in the basement apartment. The concrete floor. The old furniture. Why does he live like that? FBI agents make decent money. He could find an apartment now if he wanted. They're building them every day. High-rises and sturdy little three-stories made for returning GIs. He could afford an apartment in her building. Two, three years ago it would have been hard for him to find a place. Now, even though she understands his desire to live with family, the basement he lives in tells her he's floundering, suffering still, though the war is long over.

They're both floundering. Yet each time he's kissed her, held her, she's felt an inexplicable alchemy that makes her believe together they can be so much sturdier. So much more.

CHAPTER TWENTY-FOUR

After a few minutes, Rosalind gets up and goes to the basement door. When she opens it, she's happy to see there's still a light shining from behind the flowered curtain. The concrete at the bottom of the steps is cold on her bare feet. "Charlie?" she whispers.

The bedsprings creak and he parts the curtain. He's wearing only pajama bottoms, is holding a book in his hand. She's thrilled by the elegance of his long body.

"Hey," he says. "You shouldn't be down here. The dean will kick us both out of school."

She laughs. "I didn't want to be alone," she says. "Please . . ."

He ducks back into the tent to set down his book, then comes toward her and takes her in his arms. She runs her hand over his bare chest. It's smooth and hard, beautifully modeled, so different from Weaver's. No, she mustn't think of him . . .

"You sleep half-naked," she says.

"In the summer."

"How'd you get these muscles?"

"Push-ups."

How hard it would be with just one hand? she wonders.

"At Quantico, I decided if the other guys could, I could too. I do them twice a day." He looks proud and it touches her.

"I hear being good at push-ups could be useful in lovemaking." Her longing for him is electric, a little dangerous.

"Rosalind . . ." He gently takes her hand from his chest and kisses her wrist. "You know we don't have protection."

"I know, but . . ."

She reaches up to run her fingers down his thick muscled throat, to trace his collarbone. He sighs at her touch, closes his eyes. She longs to know every inch of his skin. To love him in a way he's never been loved. When he draws her up to kiss her, she's newly delighted by the taste of his mouth, soft and cool and unsullied by cigarettes. Their kiss, a long exploration, becomes a surrender. He presses her to him, and his desire is unmistakable. Nine years without love. She would do anything to erase the pain he's experienced.

"My siren," he says as he draws her through the curtain.

In the soft, flowered tent of his "room," with the lamp still burning, Charlie begins to undo the oversize buttons of Peggy's too-large housecoat.

"Even without protection, there's so much more we can do," he whispers.

"Let me," she says. Button by button, she exposes more of her skin, while his eyes glitter blue in the soft light. When she drops the gown to the floor and steps out of it, he lets out a long breath.

"You're beautiful." His words burn into her. And so does his gaze. He stares as though trying to memorize her, then begins to trace the pink lines on her skin with his fingers.

"Your clothes left tattoos," he says softly. Each gentle touch sends sparks. He kisses her shoulders where her bra straps bit down, the V just below her belly button from the waistband of her girdle. She has to remind herself to breathe.

"What left these?" he asks, kneeling down to trace the reddened lines from the bend of her legs to midthigh.

"My garters." When he brings his lips to each of the lines and kisses down them, she lets out a desperate moan. She thought she'd have to seduce him, but he's doing all the work.

Standing, he draws her to his bed, snaps off the lamp. A soft breeze blows from the high window, brushes her shoulders. He slips off his pajama pants, and she can't ignore how ready he is to make love.

"Charlie, I don't care if we don't have protection."

"Don't think of it tonight, **kochanie.** There are so many ways to make each other happy."

"But there's only one way that makes us . . . one."

He smooths her hair. "Don't tempt me."

A watermelon half-moon spills light through the glass, its pure white outer rind and gossamer inner arc bright enough to pick out Charlie's profile. His strong chin, his high cheekbones.

He's right. There are so many beautiful things they can share with each other. But tonight, she knows what she craves.

"I can't give you my virginity, but I've never made love without protection. I want to give that to you," she says.

He looks at her in the shadowy dark, tracing the shape of her face with his fingers. "Nothing between us," he whispers.

"Nothing between us." She's thrilled by the velvet of his naked body against hers. "I know there's no safe time of the month. Still, this is the safest . . ."

"Are you sure you want this?"

"More than anything."

"If something happens . . . I'll marry you. I

want to marry you, Rosalind." Never once did Weaver mention marriage. Never once.

His fingers find the epicenter of her longing. It might have been years, but he hasn't forgotten how to touch. And she touches him, too, with a rush of pleasure. She's never wanted anything more. Just before he brings her to the edge of climax, he raises himself over her and enters. A delicious slip of pure nakedness. She can't help but move wildly at first, but he compels them to go slowly, to make it last. She can hear his wonder with each move they share. Just as the sensation quickens and she's sure to slide over the edge, he stops suddenly. "Open your eyes," he whispers hoarsely. "Look at me. Look at me." Panting, still caught in the powerful rhythm, she's overwhelmed by the tenderness of his expression. "I love you," he whispers. "I love you." Riding the embrace of those words, she bucks against him and is pulled down into the vortex. She has to put her entire soul into staying quiet, even when the aftershocks are insistent and his movement takes her over wave after wave after wave. When Charlie climaxes, he lets out the most soulful sound she's ever heard—nine years of aloneness lifting away.

After a long time, a time in which she both hears and feels the hammering of his heart, they separate and he wraps his arms around her, breathing out a contented sigh. She has never felt so connected to another human being. She would be happy to kiss every inch of him and begin again. To risk everything for this man.

"Do you think they heard us upstairs?" he asks.

"They heard us in St. Louis."

"I meant that about marrying you," he says.

"I loved hearing it."

"You didn't answer."

"Only because we have bridges to cross." How much she already feels for Charlie, and yet what a short time they've known each other. Until these last few days they were strangers.

"My hand," he says.

"What?"

"It's because of my hand you can't imagine marrying me."

"Hey!" She turns and grabs his chin as she might a naughty child, sees his eyes, which are clouding with doubt. "Listen. I'm falling hard for you, and your hand doesn't impede my feelings. I just want to know you better. To have a year of courtship. And flowers. An unexpected engagement ring . . . and a lot more lovemaking like tonight. A **lot** more." She thinks of Weaver. All the years they were lovers and yet she never felt this beloved, never this hopeful.

He shakes his head with wonder. "You sure

aren't like any girl I've ever met. I didn't think I'd ever be this happy again."

"My plan is to keep you that way," she says.

* * *

Once he's walked Rosalind back upstairs and tucked her into the sheets on the sofa, Charlie returns to the basement and climbs back into his own bed with a long exhale. There would be hell to pay if his sister didn't find Rosalind in her assigned bed in the morning. But how much pleasure he would have found holding her in his arms all night. Lying together was almost as satisfying as the lovemaking itself. Because, for the first time since the war, he doesn't feel alone. It's a giddy joy he didn't know he was capable of feeling anymore. To feel entwined, supported, beloved.

He lies there grinning in the dark, remembering how, in the midst of lovemaking, when he asked her to open her eyes—he needed to be sure she knew she was with **him,** that she wasn't dreaming of Weaver—her face lit with delight at seeing him. It moves him that his words of love helped carry her to climax.

Ever since the war, he's tried to figure out why he lived when others all around him died. He thought the FBI would give him answers, but even when he did something that might save a life or catch a criminal, it was just a job. Another man could have done it. He wishes he didn't have to carry a gun or think about what sort of person might do the next bad thing that crosses his desk. But tonight, with Rosalind in his bed, it was as though a door opened and light flowed in. For a moment, he could believe the world was essentially good, that he was worthy of that goodness. Maybe he'll never believe in God again, but he can see God in the touch and love of good people. In her. He could begin to believe again. Surely the word "good" must derive from the word "God"?

Ironic that it was Weaver who brought Charlie together with Rosalind. Did he share the information about the H-bomb with his torturers? He'll probably never know. The lab will be looking at fingerprints from his apartment, fiber samples, all the detailed work and scientific hooey the FBI is so proud of. But Charlie thinks eventually Weaver's body will just show up somewhere. Rising out of its hiding place with the insistence of an angry ghost. A man's life is, in the end, nothing more than what he leaves behind. What Weaver bequeaths will live on to haunt them all. God knows what he suffered at the end. Fear. Terror. Weaver's finger on the floor. It wrenches Charlie's heart. Yet he can't help feeling that the man who sold the secrets that made it necessary for kindergarteners to do drop-and-cover drills got off easy.

∦ ∦ ∦

Rosalind opens her eyes to a little boy standing in front of her frowning. He's wearing red cowboy pajamas and eating a banana.

"Who are you?" he asks.

"Hello. Who are **you**?"

"I live here. What are you doing on my couch?"

She sits up. It's early, but sunlight spills across the living room carpet.

"I'm Rosalind," she says. "Your mom was nice enough to put me up for the night. Where is she?"

"She's sleeping. But Saturday they got **Pow Wow the Indian Boy** on TV and you're where I sit to watch it."

"Well, we'll have to let you do that," she says. She gets up and starts folding up the blankets, the sheets, setting the sofa back to the way it normally must be. She piles the bedding on a chair in the corner.

"What's your name?" Rosalind asks.

"Stevie. Why doesn't a lady like you sleep at your own place?"

"It's a long story. I'll just get out of your

way. I don't want you to miss your show." He shrugs, sits down, and crosses his legs in his favorite spot.

In the bathroom, Rosalind hangs up Peggy's housecoat and, moving the fresh towels to the sink, steps into the bathtub to shower. Washing the stickiness of lovemaking from between her legs, she's rapt with feelings for Charlie. Emotions that are true and deep and might well be love. To think that every night could be like last night, that sensation of not feeling alone for the first time in her life. She never once experienced it with Weaver. Never once felt so cared for or understood or excited or **lucky.** Together they are much more than they are apart. She knows he feels it too. The thought that they could marry, live together, make a life. That she could feel safe in his arms until the day she dies. And he could find solace in her. Charlie, who lost the use of a hand rather than reveal the name of a man who acted kindly. He deserves so much more than he's gotten in life, and she wonders if she deserves him. She, a failed scientist. A misused woman. What does he see when he looks into her eyes?

Then she thinks: **If it weren't for Weaver, we'd never have met.** And within a breath, she's overcome by a vision of a smashed headboard with its shards of wood edged in blood, the streak of dark fluid, the sticky pool of it on his sheets. Weaver. Did he suffer? Did he scream? Did he call out her name? Hanging on to the little ceramic bar at the top of the soap niche, she doubles over in pain, in misery, and mourns. She weeps, hoping the sound of the water keeps others from hearing her heart tear in two. She can't help feeling shame at this nascent love she holds for Charlie. How was she able to find such delight on the very day Weaver died horribly? She wishes she could step out of her own body. She turns the water so hot, it makes her skin sting. She stands as it pelts her, and she weeps. In the end, did he do something noble? In the end, did Weaver keep that one last vital secret even if it cost him his life?

It takes her a while to be able to face the others. Dressed in yesterday's clothes, she returns to the living room, shaky and chastened. There's a little redheaded girl sitting on the couch next to Stevie.

"Are you going to cook breakfast for us?" the little girl asks.

"We'll wait for your mom," Rosalind manages to say.

"If you like **Pow Wow** you can sit down and watch it too," the girl says.

"I think our guest probably has better things to do." A pretty, middle-aged woman with sandy hair and freckles comes into the room tying on a robe.

"You must be Peggy," Rosalind says.

"And you're Rosalind."

She hopes her eyes aren't too bloodshot. "I can't thank you enough. It was so last-minute, and you were so kind." Rosalind tries to sound enthusiastic. Can Peggy hear how her voice wavers?

The show's begun and tom-tom music fills the room.

"Come into the kitchen, why don't you? We can live without **Pow Wow,**" Peggy says. "Besides, I bet you'd like coffee."

Rosalind doesn't say she prefers tea. Or in truth, that she could use a drink. It scares her how much she longs for one. But she's grateful to be here, to be safe and in the presence of Charlie's sister and her family, breathing to the throb of tom-toms.

"Come sit down, dear," Peggy says. "You've been through a lot."

⁘ ⁘ ⁘

At breakfast Rosalind has a chance to meet Mack and discover the source of the family's red hair. Charlie comes up from downstairs looking handsome, relaxed. At the breakfast table, he sits across from her, sharing a secret smile every now and then. At one point, she feels his stockinged foot caress her ankle. After she helps to clear the dishes, Peggy shoos her from the kitchen and Charlie takes her hand and draws her out into the garden to sit on folding chairs. The sun is sweet and not too hot. Bumblebees dance around Peggy's many colored flowers. Rosalind struggles to be present, to pull herself out of her well of upset and mourning. For she has so many reasons to rejoice. And yet: Weaver. Weaver—her lover, her torment.

Charlie touches her wrist. "I'm going to try to get someone to open Continental Bank today so we can get into your safe-deposit box."

"On a Saturday?"

"The FBI has its ways." He smiles craftily. "We need to see what's in there. You won't be safe until we do. I doubt there's much we can do for Weaver . . ." She finds her heart clutching at the sound of his name. "If there's even the smallest chance he's still alive, we want to know all we can. In any case, I suspect there's a treasure trove of information waiting for us."

Rosalind stares at the glistening emerald grass. A world without Weaver. Since he told her he was dying, she often contemplated what it would be like to know he's gone. She never imagined he would go violently, or so soon.

"I need to go get your key to the box, so you'll have to give me some instructions," Charlie says.

An unexpected sound leaks from her throat. A moan of pain.

"Hey." He lifts her chin with his fingers, forcing her to look into his eyes. "What?"

She shakes her head and is only able to say, "Weaver . . . us . . . last night."

She watches his eyes fill with worry.

"You regret it?"

"No. Never. I mean . . ."

A shadow of feeling moves over his face.

"I regret that it made me so happy . . ."

"Ah . . ." His pale lashes draw rays over the aquamarine eyes. "You feel guilty."

"Yes."

He looks into her face, caresses her cheek. "Sometimes, when tragedy strikes, that's when a person most **needs** to celebrate being alive. You know?"

"I know, but . . ." Sick with culpability, she feels like she can't breathe. Slipping on her shoes and standing shakily, she walks to the edge of the yard and stares out over the other houses, her back to him. She feels suddenly bodiless, can no long perceive the felicitous weather, the breeze on her fingers, or the sun on her shoulders. Her only sensation is shimmering misery. It overtakes her, pulsates, demands all her attention.

He gives her time, as though he knows she needs to be apart, but eventually he comes up behind her.

He touches her back and she feels herself flinch. "What can I do?" he asks tenderly.

She turns. "Maybe I just need to be alone for while . . . Maybe if I could just go home . . ."

At a house in the distance, a teenager is bouncing a basketball on a driveway. The sound bruises her ears.

"Rosalind . . . you know you can't. Not now. With Anson trying to get ahold of that key, I can't leave you on your own."

"We could get Lawrence to come with me and I could go home. I can't . . . I shouldn't be with you right now."

"**Shouldn't** be with me?" She can hear his hurt.

"No, don't misunderstand . . . I . . ." Still, she can't shake the feeling she needs to escape. "Please. I'm begging you. Let me go home."

He turns quickly toward the house. She doesn't know if he's headed to the telephone to contact Lawrence or if he's angry.

"Charlie," she calls out, but the door has already closed, leaving her alone in the yard.

⫯ ⫯ ⫯

After the intense sunlight, the dark of the basement is blinding. Charlie feels his way down the steps and folds himself into the threadbare chair that used to be his father's. He just needs a minute, he tells himself. He'll be okay. He just needs to breathe. Since Japan he's found it nearly impossible to deal with his own feelings.

He saw too much hatred at Mitsushima, never wants to be a vessel for that sort of animosity. And since Linda smashed his hopes, his fear of being brokenhearted has hamstrung him. He's swallowed every emotion since he's been back: desire and rage, hurt and pain. His passion for Rosalind is the only true sensation he's allowed. He risked everything. And she says she **can't be with him.** For just today? Or forever? Maybe he's overreacting. Maybe not. One thing he should have known: hurt people are bound to hurt each other.

⫯ ⫯ ⫯

In the taxi on the way to her apartment, out of the corner of her eyes, she sees Charlie sitting straight and stiff, his face pale. She hates that she's hurt him and reaches for his hand. "I just need time," she says. "I promise. I just need time. Okay?" But instead of nodding, he shakes his head. She has no idea how to interpret what he's feeling. As the taxi pulls into the circular drive, Lawrence is waiting, throws his cigarette on the ground and scuffs it out, approaches the cab.

Charlie gets out, walks around and opens her door, offers his hand to help her out—a kind gesture—but she can't ignore the set of his mouth. "Wait for Lawrence just inside," he instructs her. His voice is cool. She goes in but hovers by the door. The plan is for Charlie to continue with the taxi, pick up the key from Field's—she explained just where to find it—and head to the Continental Bank. And then follow the instructions inside the envelope to Weaver's safe-deposit box. She doesn't hear their conversation, but as she sees Charlie leaving, she pushes the door open and catches his words before he ducks into the taxi.

"She's in your hands now."

Rosalind paces her apartment, boils water. Her throat tightens as she drops a bag of Weaver's English breakfast tea into a cup. She feels Weaver with her, the fevered heat of him, his scent, a complex weave of tobacco, wool, and Scotch. She never knew before that when someone is gone, he can suddenly be more present, that loss brings immediacy. She feels sure if she turns, Weaver will be by the open window, watching sails unfurl on the lake, blowing smoke out into the too-blue sky. She can see the tired crinkles around his eyes, that perfect dimple in his chin. She knows he will be a bag of stones—some diamonds, some coal—that she will carry with her for the rest of her life. Just hours ago, she was celebrating her new intimacy with Charlie. How she longs to freely love this tender man who's risked everything to let her into his life. Now thoughts of Weaver have pulled her back to the past. She worries he will never let her go.

The phone bleats. She imagines that even this phone call must be from Weaver. Perhaps she's gone mad.

"Rozzie. Daddy and I've been trying to call you all morning." Ava's voice breaks through the haze. "You said we'd go to **Cinderella** today." When she was at Louisa's house, Ava had begged Rosalind to take her to the movie this weekend, since she was sure Henry wouldn't want to go.

"Oh, Ava. I'm sorry, darling. I know we had a plan."

"You forgot."

"No, I've had to be away," she says. "I just got back."

"So are you ready to go? The movie's at one thirty. Will you pick me up in a taxi? Daddy and I can wait downstairs."

The misery of losing Weaver competes with her desire to please this child. She closes her eyes, envisions Ava's hopeful face. That makes it even harder to say what she must.

"I know you'll be very disappointed, and I can't blame you, but I can't go."

"Why not? You promised. It's the only thing I really wanted to do all weekend!"

"I know. I couldn't be sorrier. Can I speak with your dad? Can you give the phone to him?"

She remembers with a sense of unease that she needs to tell Henry about the discussion she had with Louisa. She will, when the world rights itself. She can't forget.

Ava calls out to Henry and she hears the clatter of the phone being set down. A moment later, her brother-in-law gets on. She discerns a woman's voice in the background talking to Ava and wonders who it can be.

"Roz?"

"Henry. I'm sorry, but something terrible has happened. Can you take Ava to the movie? I know **Cinderella** is hardly your cup of tea, but . . . she wants so much to go."

"What happened? Are you okay?"

Roz can still see the specter of Weaver by the window in his shirtsleeves, smoking, watching her steadily. "Weaver's died," she says softly.

"Roz. Dear God. How?"

She doesn't have the strength to tell him the whole story now.

"I told you he had cancer. Neither of us thought it would . . . end so fast." She finds those words hard to get out. Has it ended? For Weaver's sake she hopes so. "Henry, can you take Ava? I just can't sit through a movie. Not today. And she was so looking forward to it."

"Of course. Don't worry. You just rest."

"I've got to warn you, the **Tribune** says there are singing bluebirds."

Henry laughs. "I'll survive. But are you all right? Do you need Louisa to come be with you?"

"Louisa?" Why would he bring up Louisa? "No. I'm all right. I'm just glad Ava won't be disappointed."

"If you're sure. Maybe we should all come there."

Does he think she'll go to bed and not get up like last time? Part of her would like to.

"I'm okay," she says, though her voice sounds hollow. "I just need time to understand that he's gone. It doesn't feel real."

"When we get back from the show, we'll call. You can tell me what you need and we'll bring it by. Okay?"

"Thank you. I love you."

When Rosalind puts down the phone, her heart is slamming. Her head aches. She stares at the cup of tea she poured, but the thought of drinking it makes her stomach tight. Reaching up into the cupboard, she pulls down the bottle of Scotch and shakes to see what little is left. About a jigger's worth. This big bottle sat abandoned for so many years, dusty and tucked away on the other side of the bar, until Weaver came back into her life. Now it will be gone—like Weaver. She pours the last shot into the hot tea and drinks it down. The tea burns. The liquor burns more.

♦ ♦ ♦

Having fallen asleep after the Scotch, she's sure it's an air-raid siren that's awakened her. She sits up in bed, prickly and confused, then realizes it's the lobby intercom buzzing. Dizzy, she gets up and, holding on to the wall, pads barefoot to answer.

"Yes?"

"It's your sister," Moses, the weekend doorman, announces. "Can I send her up?"

"My sister?"

"Miss, can I send her up?" he asks again.

"Yes, of course."

What's Louisa doing here? Half-asleep, her mind scans for a forgotten plan. Nothing. Running her hands through her hair at the mirror, she imagines Louisa scolding her for looking such a mess. But when she opens the door, her sister steps in and takes her into her arms.

"Jesus, Roz, you could have told me," she says.

"Could have told you what?"

"About Weaver. You didn't say he was dying."

"But how do you know?"

"I was with Henry and Ava when you talked."

"You were?"

"I was going to go with you and Ava to **Cinderella,** but I came here instead—to be sure you're okay."

"You were with Henry and Ava?" she asks again.

"Let's sit down," Louisa says.

Rosalind nods and they find places on the couch. It's been a long time since Louisa actually sat down in her apartment. Years, maybe.

"Tell me how you are," Louisa says.

"I'm okay. Can I get you something to drink? Water? Tea?"

"Oh, for God's sake. No. Tell me everything. Why didn't you say that Weaver was sick?"

"You hated him."

"I know. But only because he hurt you." She frowns. "Have you been drinking?"

"How can you tell?"

"Your breath."

"Oh. Sorry."

"Don't apologize. You're probably in shock."

"I guess so." Rosalind notes an all-encompassing numbness. As though every tear has been wept and she's just a pair of red eyes, an aching heart.

Louisa takes both her hands. She isn't frowning at her, sniping at her, or lecturing. "You loved him, I know," she says. It stuns Rosalind to realize that Louisa knows nothing about Charlie, how deeply she feels for him, how her life has transformed in a matter of days. She softens at the memory of how he stopped their lovemaking to ask her to open her eyes, to tell her he loved her.

Roz looks over toward the window and sees that Weaver isn't there anymore. His image has evaporated. He never did like Louisa. Or maybe thoughts of Charlie have swept him away.

"I loved Weaver and I hated him," she says, surprised to be revealing such a thing to her critical sister.

"After what he did," Louisa says, "how could you not?"

"But what he did is so much worse than you can imagine . . ."

"How is that possible? You know I already think the man was a beast."

"Louisa, why were you at the Allerton?"

"You don't want to hear this now. Tell me more about Weaver."

"I do want to hear it."

"Oh. Well, after you and I talked yesterday, I thought about what you said: that maybe it's not Henry I'm angry at. Maybe I'm just angry at my life and the way it's turned out."

Her sister actually listened to her? Nothing could surprise Rosalind more. Perhaps she was able to listen because Roz listened first. Her sister has been impossible for years. But Rosalind realizes how unfair she's been, never once thinking of Louisa's side of things.

"I came to the Allerton, and Henry and I talked in the bedroom while Ava listened to a radio show in the living room."

"What did he say?"

"I think he actually heard me."

"What did you tell him?"

"I told him why I've been unhappy. And I told him I wanted to understand my part in making him unhappy."

"You did? Louisa!"

"It's not going to get better in a day. He's not going to fly right home . . ."

"No."

"And maybe he really shouldn't. Not yet. What's the point in getting back together if we can't do it better? But we're talking."

Roz breathes with pleasure. "I'm so glad," she says. She leans forward and gives her sister a kiss.

"I'm going through the change, you know. That's part of what's wrong with me. I'm so short-tempered. I told him that too. He didn't know." Rosalind doesn't want to say Louisa's always been short-tempered and malcontent. Still, she feels hopeful. She wants her family to stay together. They **are** her family. As much a mother and father to her as any other adopted child's parents. She's just never thought of them quite that way before.

"I want to hear what Weaver's done. All of it. But, it's way past lunchtime. Have you eaten?"

Rosalind shakes her head.

"I'm starved. Do you think the Wagon Wheel's still open? I'll take you to lunch," Louisa says.

"Sure."

"Are you up to going out?"

Roz nods. "It might feel good."

"Go change and powder your nose and we'll walk over. Eating lunch will help you soak up whatever it is you've been drinking."

"It was only about a jigger. It's just that it was early."

Louisa shrugs. "Go change. I'll read this magazine." She lifts the first one she finds on the coffee table. "The **Journal of Applied Physics.** Sounds riveting. Hurry up."

Roz slips out of yesterday's clothes, which are now twice worn and even slept in, and puts on the linen sheath she wore the day she walked to Charlie's office. Charlie. She tries not to think of how hurt he seemed when they parted, how distant. It leaves her unsettled.

She and Louisa walk west, away from the lakefront, past families heading to Oak Street Beach with pails and towels, past housewives hefting grocery bags and parents pushing strollers. It's a perfect Chicago summer day. Breezy and bright. She looks back a few times to make sure that Lawrence is trailing dutifully behind them. He doesn't acknowledge her.

It's after two, and the Wagon Wheel is nearly empty. A coffee shop with a Wild West theme, it has ceiling light fixtures made to look like wagon wheels, and wall sconces modeled on gas lamps.

Blue wallpaper is chockablock with cowboys on horseback wielding lassos, herds of steer, women in bonnets. A middle-aged man sits at the counter nibbling a grilled cheese sandwich; an older woman is counting out cash for her bill at a table by the front window. A tall woman swathed in a sheer green headscarf glides in through the front door to the tinkle of the bell. Not another soul. Roz and Louisa slip into a booth along the wall. Roz notes Lawrence seating himself at a table in the center of the room. A good place to watch. She takes a deep breath, trying to ground herself, to make herself feel the moment, the setting.

One thing is certain: She's glad to be here with her sister. She wonders if Louisa is only being kind to her because once again, she's needy. Yet, watching Louisa scan the menu, she feels surprisingly soothed by her presence.

"They have good club sandwiches here, don't they?" Louisa says.

"Yeah, they're great."

"I'm just in the mood." How changed she seems. Relaxed. "So tell me about Weaver." She closes the menu. "Tell me everything. Especially why he's so much worse than I imagine."

Rosalind glances over at Lawrence, who's drumming his fingers on the table, waiting for the waitress.

"I'm probably not supposed to say."

"Why aren't you supposed to say?"

Roz bites her lip. What does it matter now? Weaver's gone. Eventually Louisa may actually realize that Lawrence has been following them. Better that she should know.

"Do you see that man over there?"

Louisa glances over and nods.

"He's an FBI agent."

"What?"

"He's here to protect me."

Louisa's face moves through a litany of changes. Surprise. Upset. Skepticism. "You're joking, right?"

Roz shakes her head. And then she tells Louisa everything. Very softly, very slowly. Their lunches come, and Rosalind keeps talking. About Clemence, Victoire, and the FBI, the smashed headboard, the blood. She says nothing about her feelings toward Charlie. She wants to tell Louisa about him in a happy context, not in the shadow of Weaver.

"I told you Weaver's done so much worse than I imagined. Apparently, he's been selling atomic secrets to the Russians for a long, long time," Roz says. "Since '44, before we dropped the bombs on Japan. You wouldn't believe the extent of the information he's shared with them." Louisa's mouth opens in surprise, in horror.

"I knew I hated that man," she says.

"He regretted it at the end. Maybe he's

regretted it for a long time. He wanted some kind of forgiveness. I think that might have had a lot to do with his coming back to me."

"That just makes him more of a rat. He made things dangerous for you. And probably never thought of it." Louisa takes the last bite of her sandwich and pats her lips with her napkin. "He had no right to put you through all he has."

"It's just between us. Don't even tell Henry. Let me be the one, okay?"

"Okay."

Rosalind is glad that her sister is at last speaking to Henry. Just thinking of it makes her smile.

"You finished?" Louisa asks.

"Couldn't eat another bite."

Louisa starts sliding out of the booth. "Sorry. I have to run to the ladies'. Why don't you take that half a sandwich home? For dinner. They'll package it up for you. I'll be back for the bill. Don't you dare try to pay it, okay?"

"As if I could," Roz says. She watches Louisa walk ladylike to the bathroom, purse in hand, then calls over the waitress. The woman takes the sandwich away and a few minutes later brings it back wrapped and bagged. But Louisa still hasn't returned. Rosalind straightens her purse, thinks about Ava and Henry at the movie, frets about Charlie. What on earth is taking so long? Rosalind gets up to check on her. Walking by Lawrence, she surreptitiously points to the hallway where the restrooms are and heads that way. The middle-aged man and the woman with the green scarf are gone. At the counter, two giggling bobby-soxers lean eagerly over a shared milkshake. Rosalind heads down the long hall-way and pushes open the door marked with a frilly bonnet and the word GALS beneath it.

She gasps. Up against the wall, the tall woman with the green headscarf clutches Louisa from be-hind, pressing a knife to her throat. It's when the woman's kohl-lined eyes meet hers that Rosalind knows: She's seen this face in her nightmares.

"Clemence."

She's alive.

There's the faintest nod of acknowledgment.

"Or should I call you Victoire?"

The woman's features harden; her nostrils flare.

"He told you my name?"

The knife pressed against her sister's throat shudders in Clemence's hand. Louisa's eyes are huge and terrified, her lips like chalk. Rosalind forces herself not to stare at the dangerous gleam of metal.

"He told me everything," Rosalind says.

"And you . . . you passed it on . . . to the **FBI.**" Clemence spits out the letters as someone would a mouthful of poison.

Rosalind experiences a dropping sensation.

"It wasn't hard to follow you. We knew you were working with them. Thomas would still be alive, but you compromised him. **You're the one that killed him.**"

Swallowing the idea that Weaver's truly dead, that his death could be her fault, is lye burning all the way down Rosalind's throat.

"But you're the one that **had** him killed, aren't you?" Rosalind chokes out.

The question pierces its mark, for it makes Clemence's mouth tremble.

"What choice did I have? How long until he would have been arrested, until he would have spilled everything. Because of you. For years, he loved me," Clemence says. "He was sent to the US to be our link to secrets, and that's what he did. Then you came along . . ."

Rosalind takes in her nemesis's face. How she once envied this woman. Close up, she sees the furrows of age, the crumbling beauty, anguish written into every line. Never once in all these years did Roz imagine that while she was jealous of Clemence, Clemence was equally jealous of her.

"He didn't tell me about you. He kept us both in the dark," Rosalind says.

"Yes, he was good at that."

"He said you were dead."

"Of course he did." Clemence's voice is a soft, broken whisper.

As they've been speaking, Rosalind's been watching Clemence's green chiffon scarf drop imperceptibly backward, and now, in its shadow, she can make out a shocking gash above her left ear: the hair shaven away in a wide swath, a thickly scabbed line running across the center like the median on a highway. Roz can't help but wince. All that blood Charlie said they found in the forest preserve . . . was it a scalp wound, a bullet graze?

"Weaver tried to kill you, didn't he?" Rosalind asks. "He tried to shoot you."

"**Tais-toi!**" Clemence draws the scarf back up. Her movement with her left hand presses the knife in the other hand even tighter to Louisa's throat. Rosalind sees it's actually nicking her sister's skin, leaving a thin, red, seeping line. She swallows hard. "I gave him years of my life. And you turned him against me. I wouldn't have had to kill him but for you." Tears begin to spill over the lines of kohl, drawing dark rivers down Clemence's cheeks. "Now it is right that I kill **her.** To punish you." Rosalind sees her sister's eyes squeeze shut, her face go utterly gray.

"You hurt her, and you'll **never** get that key!" Rosalind shouts.

"Or maybe I'll torture her the way we tortured Thomas. He wept and wet his pants when they snipped off his finger." As Clemence says it, Roz sees her visibly shiver. **They snipped off**

Weaver's finger and Clemence watched? Roz's stomach clenches. An icy sensation runs up the sides of her neck, over her ears. Lou looks so scared. She loves her sister, has never loved her more than in this moment. If she faints, the knife will surely cut her on the way down.

"You want the key," she tells Clemence. "If you let her go, I'll lead you there. You **need** me with you. Not her. Let her go!"

When will Lawrence realize that things are taking too long? When will he come to the door with his gun drawn? And even if he does, can he stop Clemence from hurting Louisa? Rosalind needs to be what her ring says: **the bravest girl in the world.** But how? She can see the rise and fall of Louisa's chest with each panicked breath. She doesn't have much time, but what can she do with the knife pressed to Louisa's throat?

Suddenly, the bathroom door is thrown open and one of the bobby-soxers walks in, arms in front of her, head down, paying no attention. Clemence swings the knife away from her sister and holds it toward the girl.

"Get the hell out of here," she hisses. The girl's eyes snap open in terror. "Don't even think of screaming or telling anyone or I promise I'll slit your little face in two." All the color drains from the girl's face. As she backs away and the door begins to close, Roz knows this is her only chance. Rushing Clemence and cutting rightward with as much velocity as she can muster, she spikes the hand holding the knife as she once did a volleyball. Clemence lets out a quack of surprise and the knife clatters under a stall. Roz shoves with all her weight so Clemence's head and shoulders slam into the wall-mounted towel holder. Then she grabs Louisa's arm. Running past the teenage girl, dragging her sister behind her, she bounds down the hall toward Lawrence, screaming the entire way.

⏽ ⏽ ⏽

It's past eight P.M. when Rosalind, Louisa, and now Agent Gray head toward the Allerton in Gray's car. After Lawrence managed to handcuff Clemence, statements had to be taken, the knife had to be recovered. The place was soon swarming with agents—though not Charlie—and the owner of the Wagon Wheel was practically crying, insisting that Saturday night was his big family night and the FBI was going to bankrupt him.

Eventually, Agent Lawrence insisted that Louisa needed to be taken to the emergency room to be checked. The thin, oozing cut on her throat was minimal, but Lawrence thought she might be in shock. She kept gulping air.

Somewhere in the middle of the hospital wait, Rosalind managed to find a pay phone and called Henry. He kept saying, "Is she okay? Are you okay? How could something like this possibly happen?"

Now in Gray's car, Louisa touches her bandaged throat.

"Does it hurt?" Roz asks.

"It stings."

"You can use it as an excuse. To be coddled by everyone. I'm so sorry you had to go through that," Roz says.

"Weaver haunts us even though he's gone. Do you think that was true—what that woman said about torturing him?"

Rosalind whispers, "Yes."

"So he didn't die of cancer. He was murdered. Did you know?"

Rosalind nods, reeling with the awfulness of how Clemence described Weaver's demise. "Sorry. I didn't want to lie . . . I just wasn't ready to tell you."

"At least now I know why you were drinking Scotch before lunch."

Louisa squeezes Roz's arm. Roz is pretty sure she never wants to drink Scotch again.

⊹ ⊹ ⊹

Later, at home, Roz feels an overwhelming lassitude—the letdown that floods the body after adrenaline. It was good leaving Lou at the

Allerton with Henry and Ava. They kissed and hugged her sister.

"We're going to baby you," Henry promised Lou.

"And I'm going to do all the housework for a week. You'll be amazed!" Ava said.

"If that's true, I **will** be amazed," Louisa agreed.

Now Rosalind is relieved to be alone in her apartment, looking out over the lake. She imagines Weaver somewhere out there, deep beneath the water, his body caressed by the soft underside of waves. How odd that one minute a man can be alive, prickly, confounding, loving, and the next, an element of a lakebed, a copse of trees, or the soil beneath an engraved stone.

When Weaver came to Chicago, she's sure he had no idea he'd die here. We walk through life with no script or certainty, she thinks. Even if someone else murders us or holds our hands at the last moment, even if we have dozens adoring us or an entire world hating us, we end utterly, pristinely alone.

⸎ ⸎ ⸎

Just after ten P.M., as Rosalind is about to step into her bath, the buzzer sounds. She reties her robe, asks Frank who it is.

"It's your friend the agent," Frank says.

Rosalind is flooded with relief. She expected Charlie to come to the Wagon Wheel, to worry over her and Lou. Other agents did. When he didn't arrive, she believed he must still be angry at her for wanting to go home.

Now when she opens the door, he shakes his head softly and draws her into his arms. For the first time in hours, she feels her jaw unclench.

"I'm so sorry about what happened." She can hear his heartbeat, smell the fresh scent of his laundry soap. "Lawrence **should** have watched out for Victoire Spenard. We weren't sure she was dead. So I should have briefed him, shared her picture . . ." Charlie's talking too fast. She gets the sense that he's gone over these words again and again on the way over. He looks miserable, guilty even, as he takes her chin, scans her face. "Are you okay?"

She nods. She doesn't know how to explain that the experience has wrapped her in numbness. The world seems oddly remote, as though she's peering at everything through the back end of a telescope.

"I wanted to come as soon as I heard, but . . ."

"You had to interview Clemence?"

He's silent for a moment, then says, "I would have. I was supposed to . . ." Rosalind watches him, trying to discern why he's broken off mid-sentence. Rubbing his forehead, he doesn't meet her eyes. "She died . . . in the car on the way to headquarters."

"She died?"

"Russian agents carry cyanide. She was searched. They didn't find it."

Rosalind's throat aches. "My God."

"The agents should have been so much more careful. Sometimes the capsules are sewn into hems, cuffs. There's so much she could have told us."

"She's dead. Clemence is dead?" She suddenly feels incredibly unsteady, has to grab Charlie's arm.

"Come on, sit down." He guides her to the sofa. Weaver is gone. Clemence is gone. It's as though the whole world has shifted. She feels him watching her carefully.

"Why didn't you come to the Wagon Wheel?" she asks. "I hoped you might."

"My boss insisted I go through what Weaver left in his box."

"Was that really why?"

He straightens the journals on the coffee table. She sees his good hand tremble slightly.

"If I hurt you by asking to go home, I'm sorry," she says.

He shrugs. "You loved Weaver."

"You knew I did. He was my past," she says. "You're my future. I just needed time."

He nods, then shakes his head, as though arguing with himself. "The thing is . . ." His voice is pinched. And then he's silent. He's a beautiful man. She's astonished at how much she feels for him. A deep, binding connection right down to her atoms. "When you pushed me away, I had a realization."

"Tell me."

"I used up my lifetime quota of pain at Mitsushima. I don't think I can take any more."

His face is a mask she cannot read.

"Are you saying you want to walk away from this? From us?" She aches at the thought. "You can't run from pain or jealousy. Or anger or loneliness. They come with life. They'll find you."

"But . . . you . . . you have the power to stir them up in me. The way Linda did. I hate you for that."

She cringes. "You have that power over me too. That's what love is, isn't it? The power to both enchant and wound."

He doesn't look at her.

"Do you want to be alone all your life?" she asks.

"I'm used to it now."

"But you don't have to be," she says. She takes his damaged hand and presses it to her face. "Not when someone loves you the way I already do. I love you, Charlie. I love you."

Her words make his breath catch. And as if he can't help himself, he reaches for her, nestles his face into her neck, says nothing for a long while.

"I'm scared," he says at last. "And I hate that."

"Who isn't scared?" she whispers.

After a while, he straightens his arms, and she's not sure at first if he's trying to put distance between them or to truly see her. As he stares, she wonders what he's searching for. Or whether she can supply it. All she knows is she wants to give him whatever he needs. And she expects nothing in return except his willingness to accept her as she is.

"We're all scared," she says. "And that will never change. Isn't it better that we should be scared together?"

⫿ ⫿ ⫿

In the morning, she wakes to Charlie standing by the window, dressed in his white shirt and trousers, drinking a cup of tea. Again, their lovemaking was gorgeous. And all night he held her in his arms. She never felt so safe or beloved.

"I meant to give this to you last night," he says, setting the teacup down. He reaches into his trouser pocket and pulls out a folded sheet of paper. "But I'm kind of glad I didn't. It's just a copy. They insisted on filing the original." Like all mimeographs, the ink is purple and gives off its cucumber-soaked-in-gin scent. "He wrote it to you."

She unfolds it and recognizes Weaver's hand-writing, which appears more careful and pur-poseful than usual.

Dearest Rosalind,

If you are reading this, I am gone. I hope you are not too pleased about this. I would not blame you if you were. I encourage you to throw a party if that suits your mood. You are the one thing I regret most in my life, and trust me, I regret a lot. Because of my "entanglements" (what other word can I use? Intrigues? Imbroglios?), I didn't treat you as you deserve. I want you to know I love you. And I'm happy to die for all I did to hurt you. It pleases the physicist in me to create this symmetry at the end of my own counterproductive life.

In any case, I'm grateful that you've allowed me to give you access to this package. Within, you will find a group of papers marked "FBI." Please find a way to give this to them immediately. It's important and they will be glad to have it.

Once in a while, please try to remember days when we were happy. Enclosed is my lawyer's phone number. Call him

regarding my will. If you can ever forgive me for being the selfish, weak, and unworthy bastard that I am, I would be so grateful.

Yours,
Weaver

Rosalind looks up at Charlie, who is watching her read.

"The contents of the box were for the FBI?"

"Yes."

"My God. What was inside?"

"A confession. Fourteen pages—every detail about the Russians that he could think to jot down. Descriptions, code names, methods. He said he wasn't sure if what he left would be helpful. But when you add it to what we already know, it's a gold mine. Hoover's feeling pretty jolly. There's one more thing I think you should know, though," he says.

"Yes?"

"On the last page of the confession, he wrote about Clemence."

"Oh." Rosalind feels a catch in her throat, has to force her breath through her lips.

"He said that she was his handler, tried to control him, even made him write that letter that got you fired because she was jealous of you. In the end, she wouldn't let him out of what she considered a contract. He lured her out to the forest preserve for a nice day together . . . and he shot her in cold blood. Those were the words he used: 'in cold blood.'"

"But of course, she didn't die."

"No. But when he wrote this, he thought he'd taken her life. He also said he wasn't a 'jot' sorry."

CHAPTER TWENTY-FIVE

Autumn comes early and the little trees planted along Lake Shore Drive lose their leaves in a shower of color. Winter edges in. Without sailboats, the lake waits silent and icy. Then, spring balks. The evenings elongate but the temperatures still dip into the low forties. Rosalind is glad she wore her heavy coat to work this morning. She steps into her building's lobby and unwinds her scarf. Chicago: too cold on the outside, too warm on the inside. After saying hello to Frank, she heads for the bank of mailboxes. Each day for weeks, she's turned the key in the box with longing and trepidation. Today, at last, the letter she's waited for has come. An elegant envelope with the words "Argonne National Laboratory" embossed on the corner. The thought that it might contain bad news makes her slip it into her handbag and head upstairs. She pours herself a glass of red wine before she opens it. Last night, Charlie asked her to marry him. In just a month, they will have known each other for a year. How surprisingly happy they are together. His sister has embraced her. Louisa and Henry and Ava already love him. ("Almost as much as I loved Weaver," Ava confided.) When Charlie proposed, Rosalind said yes. She told him she had just one thing to figure out before they could set a date.

And now she holds the answer in her hand. She settles into the sofa with the wine and the envelope, taking a sip before she slips her finger under the flap. She tells herself that if the letter doesn't contain good news, her life won't alter. Yet, recently, the reminder that once she was someone special has been a stone in her shoe. It's time, she thinks, to shake it out, to move forward.

Charlie arrives at six thirty, whistling. He's been in such good spirits lately, he can't contain it. He wakes happy. He sleeps well with fewer nightmares. And he has hopes for the first time in years. Even when evil memories overtake him, thoughts of Rosalind serve to steady him, the way a seasick man seeks the horizon to settle the misery of the waves. Even work feels renewed. Binder's respect for Charlie has grown exponentially since Weaver's pages yielded oceans of information. Binder even agreed (after some arguing) that since Rosalind was no longer an asset, Charlie could continue to see her.

The peace he finds in Rosalind's arms, in her bed, in her mere presence, has healed him in ways he never imagined. When he asked her to marry him, she looked up into his eyes and caressed his face. She whispered, "Yes," with a sense of wonder. How happy she seemed.

To add to his bliss, his team at headquarters experienced a breakthrough today. One of the most definitive leads emerging from Weaver's papers was a flower shop on Damen Avenue—Weaver's designated place to pick up and leave messages. The owner is a mother of four grown children—the most unlikely Communist operative. The FBI immediately set a tap on her phone, bugged her walls, and listened. But months have passed with nothing. Then, today, a man came into her store and they discussed in hushed voices another scientist they've persuaded to help them. The woman said they're all hoping he'll supply the information that "Weaver wouldn't." Gray is tailing the scientist. Another agent has been sent to watch the man who shared the information in the flower store.

"Did Weaver bring you flowers often?" Charlie asks now, hanging his coat in her hall closet.

"He must have gone into this lady's shop numerous times for instruction. I imagine he came out with flowers as a cover?"

"Weaver liked flowers," she says. But he realizes her voice seems distracted, distant.

He turns to her. "What is it?" he asks. "Are you all right?"

"Do you want some wine?" she asks.

"You know me: beer. Any in the fridge?"

"I bought it just for you."

He scans her face. "Looks like I might need some." Grabbing a cold bottle, he sits down beside her on the sofa. "Did something happen?"

"I've gotten a letter," she says.

"What sort of letter?"

She takes a gulp of air like a swimmer about to do a lap, then lets it out slowly before she says, "Do you know Argonne Labs in Lemont? I used to go out there near the end of the war, to work on Pile-3, our heavy-water reactor."

"I don't think I know it," he says, hesitant because her face is so solemn.

"Two weeks ago, I took the train out there to interview. It was actually a second interview."

He frowns. "You didn't tell me you went . . . not the first time, not this time."

"I know. Maybe I should have. But the process has drawn on with no answer and I'd pretty much figured I didn't have a chance. Then last week, they asked me to come in again. I didn't want to get my hopes up. The University of Illinois seemed ready to hire me for a while. And they eventually turned me down."

"I didn't know about that either."

"I didn't tell you any of this because I didn't want you to see me fail."

He blinks at her. "You're allowed to fail in front of me," he says.

"Not today." She holds the letter out to him.

He unfolds it, smooths it. **I'm happy to inform you** . . .

"They offered me a job. A good job."

"This is wonderful! It never made sense for you to be stuck at Field's."

"I'd convinced myself any atomic lab would reject me after Weaver's report. But I found the nerve to write to Fermi. I owed it to him to tell him what happened with Weaver—to counteract any gossip he may have heard. And since I was writing, I explained what happened to me before I was fired. He'd only heard Weaver's side of the story and said it always troubled him. Anyway, he's still on the board at Argonne."

"And?"

"And I called him long-distance after I got the offer tonight. Apparently, he told them if they didn't hire me, he would. I've wasted so much time thinking I didn't have a chance. This is everything I want. Argonne is dedicated to utilizing atomic energy in peacetime—for power."

Charlie picks up the bottle to pour her more wine. "We should make a toast!"

"The thing is . . ."

He notes that she isn't looking at him and it gives him an uneasy feeling.

"Argonne is building a gigantic nuclear reactor out in the high desert of Idaho. The letter says that's where they want to train me. The job they offered is extraordinary. The salary is so much more than I made at U of C. And the job title . . . well. Then maybe I can come back and work in Lemont."

"Maybe?" Charlie runs his hand over his face.

"I . . ."

"You plan to leave Chicago?" he asks. "You plan to leave me?"

"I've just found out. I didn't say yes yet."

"You **want** to leave me." It's not a question but a statement. His voice is flat. And that's precisely how his heart feels, run over like that coyote in the Road Runner cartoon.

"It's the last thing I want . . ." She moves closer, smooths her hand over his back. But he stands and walks to the other side of the room.

"I can hear in your voice you've decided."

"I wanted to talk to you first. The training is only for a few months. Unless . . . I mean, any chance the FBI would reassign you out there?"

"It doesn't work that way," he says. "They tell

us what to do, not the other way around. In the FBI's point of view, men don't follow their wives."

"No, I guess not."

"Besides, how much crime do you suppose takes place in the high desert of Idaho?"

"Fence smearing? Cow tipping?"

He doesn't smile. How can she leave him? She's cured him of so much bitterness. And it seems she's healing from the scars Weaver left behind. He vowed that she was safe with him. But is he safe with her?

"You're upset," she says.

"You said maybe."

"I wouldn't be entirely in charge of what happens, just as you aren't, but if things go right . . ."

He stands. "I think I should go home," he says.

"What?"

"I can't take this . . ." He stands, heads for the closet, for his coat, his hat.

"Wait. Don't walk away."

⊕ ⊕ ⊕

Rosalind sees the heartbreak in Charlie's expression. Even as she coaxes him to sit down again, she has the sense that he's not fully in the room anymore. His eyes have gone dull. His face is closed off to her. Both of them have struggled to believe happiness is possible since the war, and yet in these last months, they've mended each other. She knows to lose this man now would be a travesty.

Women are expected to give up their dreams for men. But the thought weighs on her like an anchor. She was raised to say, **I'll turn down the job. Marrying you is enough for me.** These words, however, go silent before they reach her lips.

"It's not about you, Charlie. I need to do this for myself."

He's quiet for a long time. She listens to herself breathe, terrified.

"But does it mean you need to leave me?"

"I want to make a difference in the world . . . I know it sounds foolish. I need to believe in myself not just as a woman but as a scientist."

He shakes his head. "It doesn't sound foolish."

"So do you see? It's my one chance . . . a chance I wasn't sure would ever come again."

"It's not because of me?"

"Not at all. We're happy together, but it's hard to feel fulfilled when I'm not proud of who I am. And since Weaver, since the war, I've walked away from my own aspirations. This is my chance to reclaim them."

"I understand," he says, his voice tight. "But you said you wanted to marry me. When you go off to Idaho, what happens to us? What if they don't send you back?"

"Of course I want to marry you. But I don't want to become just another housewife who adores her husband but lost her dreams." A siren runs by on Lake Shore Drive, then trails off into the night. "Is there any way you can understand this? You mean everything to me . . ."

"Not everything, it seems."

She can hear the clock on the table by the sofa, the heat rising through the pipes. She can't think of another word to say. She is astonished by how heavy she feels, how exhausted.

Then Charlie gets up and walks to the window. He crosses his arms, stares out at the night for a long while. She's afraid she's lost him. She wonders if any man could ever understand. Even a man as decent and kind as Charlie. What she's asking breaks all the norms. And yet she had no choice but to ask it.

"Talk to me, please," she whispers when the silence has gone on too long.

He turns. The look on his face is so complex, she can't begin to read it. "I wouldn't make much of a husband if I didn't want you to be proud of yourself," he says finally. "I **do** understand that. And I don't expect to be the only thing in your life. You wouldn't ask that of me . . ."

"No." She waits for him to go on.

"Chicago's your home. And wherever I am—I want to be that too—your home."

"Charlie . . . you are."

"So go to Idaho." He takes a deep breath. "We'll marry when you're ready."

"I **will** come back," she says. "I'll find a way." She goes to him and slips her arms around him. He smells of mint and herbs. Of comfort. Of home. "Did you know the word 'atom' comes from ancient Greek?" she asks.

He looks up, surprised, shakes his head.

"In Greek, the word 'atomos' means indivisible. They thought an atom was the smallest particle on earth and could never be divided. I've spent my life's work proving that untrue. But it's what I want our love to be. No matter how far apart we are. No matter what happens in our lives."

"Indivisible," he says. He draws her to him with the sort of desperation that comes from impending loss. Holds her close. Love is so unfair. Two people rarely need the same thing, seek the same answers. And yet, what becomes possible when two discrete dreams spin into one?

With his arms still around her, they stare out at the city together. Below, the cars on Lake Shore Drive paint the highway red and white. The Drake's pink neon clicks on as they watch.

The Palmolive Building's spinning beacon illuminates the room for a blink on its way around its cycle. And a crescent moon rises over the lake, spilling phosphorescence in a single, widening band, a clear pathway through dark water.

COMBUSTION

Sara Eliza Johnson

If a human body has two-hundred-and-
  six bones
and thirty trillion cells, and each cell
has one hundred trillion atoms, if the spine
has thirty-three vertebrae—
               if each atom
has a shadow—then the lilacs across the yard
are nebulae beginning to star.
If the fruit flies that settle on the orange
on the table rise
like the photons
               from a bomb fire miles away,
my thoughts at the moment of explosion
are nails suspended
in a jar of honey.
                  I peel the orange
for you, spread the honey on your toast.
When our skin touches
our atoms touch, their shadows
merging into a shadow galaxy.
And if echoes are shadows
of sounds, if each hexagonal cell in the body

is a dark pool of jelly,
if within each cell
drones another cell—
                    The moment the bomb
                        explodes
the man's spine bends like its shadow
across the road.
The moment he loses his hearing
I think you are calling me
from across the house
because my ears start to ring.
From the kitchen window
                        I see the lilacs crackling like
                            static
as if erasing, teleporting,
thousands of bees rising from the blossoms:
tiny flames in the sun.
I lick the knife
and the honey pierces my tongue:
                    a nail made of light.
My body is wrapped in honey. When I step
    outside
                    I become fire.

AUTHOR'S NOTE

I've always longed to write about a female scientist. My mother was one of them. Trained as a biochemist at the University of Chicago during World War II, she remained at the University working on important cancer research. But as was typical in that era, when she married, she was told that no decent man "forced" his wife to work, especially in a field as male-centric as science. So she gave up her career to be "a wife." She desperately missed science. As a result, science flowed into her cooking, cleaning, our health care. She measured, she weighed, she considered, she hypothesized. And, eventually, she volunteered at our local hospital doing cancer testing for free.

My mother's best friend was her cousin Jean. They walked to campus together each day, discussing everything: the family, romance, their hopes. But no matter how many times my mother asked, Jean refused to tell her a single detail about what was going on at the Metallurgical Laboratory where she worked. As it turns out, Jean was a clerical worker for the Manhattan Project, and she stayed true to her oath of secrecy until long after the atom bomb was dropped.

That story of silence stuck with me. When I matched it with my desire to write about a female scientist, I was happy to find there was indeed just one female physicist involved in those early Chicago years of the Manhattan Project: Leona Woods. Under the guidance of her mentor, Enrico Fermi, Woods was the youngest member of the team, but also an important one. She's credited with designing the boron trifluoride counter that gauged that first man-made nuclear reaction, and was the only woman present among forty-nine scientists that cold day when Chicago Pile-1 went critical. This book is in no way based on Woods's life. Unlike Rosalind Porter, Woods always maintained that the atomic bomb was essential to ending the war. Still, her presence at that momentous time and place in history allowed me to create Rosalind.

And there was one physicist who obliquely inspired Thomas Weaver. Theodore Hall shared crucial atomic secrets with the Russians while at Los Alamos, and continued to do so postwar while doing research at the University of Chicago. But because the FBI obtained their knowledge about Hall by decrypting Russian messages, the information was thought to be inadmissible in court. Also, unless the case against Hall could be backed up through independent investigation, the FBI feared the Russians would realize their code had been compromised. Thus, despite their efforts, Hall was never convicted and lived out his life in England.

Another personal note is that my mother came by her love of science naturally. Her father, Dr. Joseph Springer, was Coroner Physician for Cook County right about the time gangsters took over Chicago. A curious and persistent seeker, my grandfather was key in developing the nascent science of forensics. Testifying as an expert witness in many sensational trials, he became a well-known figure in the Al Capone era. My mother told of being awakened in the middle of the night, bundled into the open "rumble seat" of the family car, and motored off to their house in Michigan when some bad actor warned my grandfather that if he testified in court the next day, the safety of his five daughters couldn't be assured. My mother and her sisters stayed in Michigan for a while, my grandfather testified, and, happily, no one was harmed. When Dr. Joseph Springer died, more than fifteen hundred newspapers from coast to coast printed his obituary; he'd become that much of a national celebrity. He was the man on whom I based Rosalind Porter's father, Dr. Joe.

One more note about Chicago: I grew up in a suburb north of the city and spent ten years of my adult life living Near North, walking distance from Michigan Avenue. My apartment—just like Rosalind's—overlooked Lake Michigan. Though it's been many years, my love for Chicago, it's beauty, architecture, and people lives on. Chicago will always feel like home to me.

ACKNOWLEDGMENTS

For someone who rarely shares her work until it's finished, I'm astonished by how many people helped me write this book in so many ways. I want to thank Annie Solomon for her helpful tips on writing suspense. Yona Zeldis McDonough, as always, gave me invaluable direction, as did Ann Patchett who accomplished the amazing feat of reading the manuscript in a single day from six A.M. to nightfall. Thanks to Kory Wells, James Hayman, Sally Schloss, Rachel Gladstone, and L. B. Gschwandtner who read and advised superbly. And to Xan Holt for helping me with the Polish translation. Thank you to the late William Bailey who worked as a special agent in the Chicago office of the FBI during the 1950s and so kindly described the office environment and answered my endless questions.

The Fine Arts Work Center in Province-town, Rivendell Writers' Colony, and Rockvale Writers' Colony all provided me with lovely, uninterrupted writing time without which this book could not have been written.

My new agent, Susanna Einstein, gets a huge thanks. She's done miracles representing me, and I feel so lucky to have her on my side.

One of the people who deserves the most credit is Tara Singh Carlson, my brilliant Putnam editor, whose ideas were so fabulous they made me smack my forehead and lament that I didn't think of them first. And thanks to her entire team, especially Helen O'Hare. I am so grateful, too, to my UK editor, Jillian Taylor, for her many thoughtful comments. I can't thank her enough for her incredibly generous encouragement.

Finally, a big hug goes to my best supporters: my husband, Russ, my dear friend Lindy DeKoven, and my ever-walking dog, Violet Jane, all of whom were always there to lift my spirits when I needed it most.

ABOUT THE AUTHOR

JENNIE FIELDS received an MFA from the Iowa Writers' Workshop and is the author of the novels **Lily Beach**, **Crossing Brooklyn Ferry**, **The Middle Ages**, and **The Age of Desire**. The daughter of a female scientist, Jennie is a Chicago native and, after many years of living in New York City, now lives with her husband in Nashville, Tennessee.